SAVAGE SISTERS

HEATHER ATKINSON

Boldwood

First published in Great Britain in 2023 by Boldwood Books Ltd.

Copyright © Heather Atkinson, 2023

Cover Photography: Depositphotos and iStock

The moral right of Heather Atkinson to be identified as the author of this work has been asserted in accordance with the Copyright, Designs and Patents Act 1988.

Every effort has been made to obtain the necessary permissions with reference to copyright material, both illustrative and quoted. We apologise for any omissions in this respect and will be pleased to make the appropriate acknowledgements in any future edition.

A CIP catalogue record for this book is available from the British Library.

Paperback ISBN 978-1-80415-192-1

Large Print ISBN 978-1-80415-191-4

Harback ISBN 978-1-80415-190-7

Ebook ISBN 978-1-80415-194-5

Kindle ISBN 978-1-80415-193-8

Audio CD ISBN 978-1-80415-185-3

MP3 CD ISBN 978-1-80415-186-0

Digital audio download ISBN 978-1-80415-187-7

Boldwood Books Ltd
23 Bowerdean Street
London SW6 3TN
www.boldwoodbooks.com

1

The rain had soaked Carly Savage through to the skin. Her long, light brown hair was plastered to her face and her thin green jacket was completely unsuited to the dreich October weather. In each hand she carried a heavy carrier bag, the plastic handles digging into her palms, her trainers squelching with each step. She'd been born and raised in Haghill and had never thought much of it before. It had merely been a backdrop to her difficult life but today it just looked depressing. It was autumn and the rain had been relentless lately. It always seemed to wait until she'd set foot outside the door to start pouring down. One of the drains had overflowed and a stream of water rushed down the road, clogged with a heap of dead leaves and crisp packets.

As she crossed the road onto the next block that was lined with dark red sandstone tenements, a car sped by, purposefully driving through the large puddle that had formed at the kerb, drenching her with cold, dirty water. Anger vied with envy. How she would love a nice, warm car... but her family couldn't afford one. They could barely afford the few groceries she carried.

With a sigh of relief, she turned the corner onto her street to see the beige three-storey block of flats where she lived. The building overlooked a cemetery, which had never really bothered her but she had to admit that it looked rather eerie in the rain.

Carly was glad she lived on the ground floor. As her hands were full, she kicked the front door with her foot rather than bothering to knock. One more scuff mark wouldn't make any difference. It was opened by her younger sister, Rose, who was a lanky girl of sixteen with the same long straight hair, delicate bone structure and large hazel eyes as her older sister. Whereas Carly's lips were thin, Rose had a pretty little heart-shaped mouth and eyelashes that were the envy of every female in the area.

'You look wet.' Rose grinned at her.

'Really? I hadn't noticed,' said Carly sarcastically as she stepped inside and gratefully dumped the bags on the floor. The palms of her hands were bright red, thick lines cutting across them.

Rose picked up the bags and carried them down the hall into the kitchen while Carly stripped off her shoes and socks with a grimace, leaving the shoes to dry in the hall and carrying the socks through to the kitchen where she tossed them straight into the empty washing machine. The coat she hung over the back of one of the chairs at the kitchen table. The far end of the room looked more like a living room than a kitchen with its television on a stand, small bookcase, purple couch and dark brown armchair. As the flat only had three bedrooms, they'd had to turn the living room into a bedroom for their father, so the kitchen had become the heart of the home and was where the family congregated. Due to how quickly their father's condition had deteriorated, he spent the majority of the time in his room, so it was only the sisters who gathered here.

'Oh, look,' said Rose, glancing out of the kitchen window as she put away the shopping. 'The rain's easing off.' She plucked a clean towel from the top of the laundry pile on the table and tossed it to her sister.

'Bloody typical,' muttered Carly, catching it with one hand and using it to dry her hair. She shivered again. It didn't feel much warmer in the flat than it had outside.

Their mother had died six years ago of cancer, leaving their father Alec to raise three daughters alone. Jane, the oldest of the sisters, had been fifteen at the time. Alec had carried on valiantly, attempting to balance work with his home life but with his other two daughters aged just ten and thirteen, it had been difficult, especially as all three had been traumatised by their mother's death. Eventually he'd had to give up work to be there for them and life had been an endless struggle ever since.

'I got Da' the curry he likes,' Carly told Rose.

'I'll warm it up for him,' she replied, producing it from one of the bags.

Carly patted her sister's arm when her sunny smile faltered. Rose was the one who cheered them all up when they were feeling low, who distracted them from their lack of money and got them to dance around the room and laugh when things started to get on top of them. But sometimes even her pain overcame her natural optimism.

Rose warmed the Thai green curry in the oven but it was Carly who dished it up onto a plate and carried it down the hall to the room at the front of the flat. Gently she tapped on the door and a voice called, 'Come in.'

Carly pushed open the door and walked in to find her father sitting up in bed, supported by pillows, reading a book that was propped up on a tray before him. His hands shook too much to hold it steady.

'Hello, sweetheart,' he mumbled, his voice lacking tone and emotion. 'You look damp. Did you get caught in the rain?'

'Just a bit.' She smiled. 'I got you your favourite curry.'

'You didn't need to do that, it's not cheap.' It took him a while to get the words out; talking was difficult for him and he had to pause to swallow.

'It's fine. I got some good tips at work this week,' she replied, placing the plate on the tray beside the book. It was a wheeled tray, the sort that was used in hospitals and that went right across the bed.

'I hope you treated yourself too?'

'I got myself a fruit and nut bar, my weakness.'

'You're such a good girl, Carly,' he said, picking up his fork and digging into the food. He sighed with frustration when his hand shook and some of the rice fell off.

'Let me help you.' She took the fork and scooped up some of the curry.

'I hate being fed like a baby,' he muttered before taking the food into his mouth. He paused to chew and swallow a few times. Carly anxiously watched him. His swallowing had got worse lately and she was always afraid he'd choke. It was why he could only eat soft things. Inwardly she sighed with relief when he managed to get it down without choking.

'I know you do, Da',' she said. 'But you have to eat and stay strong. We need you.'

Alec gave her a gentle smile and nodded. It broke Carly's heart to see her dad reduced to this. He stood at six foot three, and had been a builder for years and an avid rugby player, so he'd always been physically strong. But a year after they'd lost their mother, their father had started experiencing muscle stiffness, tremors in his hands and impaired balance. He'd gone to his doctor and, after several tests and visits to various specialists, he'd been diagnosed with early onset Parkinson's disease. He'd deteriorated faster than anyone had expected. Even though he was only forty-seven years old, he could barely walk and the simplest of tasks was now beyond him. A couple of nurses visited twice a day to give him his medication and bathe him and assist in any way they could but everything else was on the girls, with some help from the neighbours. Jane worked full time in a call centre to support them all and Rose had to go to school, so the majority of his care was on Carly's shoulders. Carly worked part time at the local pub, planning her shifts around her father's needs and Jane's hours. They all hated seeing him suffer but Carly kept all this pain hidden as she fed him and chatted with him.

When he'd finished, she took the empty plate back into the kitchen. Rose was watching television, her back turned to her, so Carly felt safe to bury her face in her hands and quietly shed a few tears.

'Carly,' said a voice. 'Are you all right?'

She raised her head and forced a smile for the sake of her younger sister, who had turned in her seat to regard her, looking concerned. 'Fine. Have you done all your homework?'

'Don't I always?' Pain filled her lovely eyes. 'He's getting worse every day.'

Carly didn't know what to say as she could hardly deny it was true. 'What do you fancy for tea?' she replied instead, attempting to inject some cheerfulness into her tone.

Rose ignored the question. 'Soon they'll say we can't look after him any more and he'll have to go into a home. I don't want that to happen.'

'Don't worry, this is his home. We're his family, so it's only right we take care of him.'

Carly panicked a little when it looked like Rose was going to cry. She wasn't any good at comforting people, that was Jane's territory. Carly didn't know what they would do without their older sister, who had risen to the occasion magnificently when their mother had died and their father had become ill. They'd been forced to move into this flat three years ago when they could no longer afford the home the family had occupied for twenty years. Plus they'd needed something on one level for their father. Jane had found this flat and arranged everything, taking all the burden upon herself, as well as comforting her sisters about the massive upheaval in their lives.

It was an enormous relief when Carly heard the slam of the front door, indicating Jane was home.

'Carly,' she said breathlessly as she dashed into the kitchen. Jane, like her sister, was also tall and lithe but her light brown hair was cut short with a thick fringe that had the tendency to flop into her eyes. 'Thank God you're here.'

'What's wrong?' she replied.

'I've just heard that Cole's been released from prison.'

Rose gasped and looked to Carly, who stared back at Jane in shock.

'But he has another six months to serve,' breathed Carly.

'He's been let out early for good behaviour, although from what I've heard he wasn't very well behaved. He was released yesterday. Mrs Carson down the road saw him. She was waiting to pounce on me when I got off the bus; she couldn't wait to tell me all about it.'

'The old bat was winding you up.'

'Her husband confirmed it. They'd just come back from the corner shop and he was in there, buying a magazine.'

'If Cole has been released early, surely he would have come here?' said Rose.

'He told me not to visit him in prison any more, so he probably wants nothing to do with me,' muttered Carly.

'That's crap. He's mad about you.'

'You mean he was,' she replied, looking down at her hands so her sisters wouldn't see the pain in her eyes. She took a deep breath and raised her head. 'Would you mind doing tea, Rose?'

'No, course not.'

'Don't bother with anything for me, I'm not hungry.'

With that, Carly slunk into her room to digest the shocking news.

Her room was small, containing just a single bed, wardrobe and a dressing table. The wall beside her bed was covered in photographs that had been stuck to the fading cream-coloured paint with tape and all contained her happiest memories. There were photos of herself and her siblings growing up, their beautiful mother and their father when he was healthy and strong, as well as images of her friends. There were also many photographs of her and Cole together, smiling and laughing and looking like their love would last forever. Cole was the youngest son of the Alexander family, who were almost as infamous in Haghill as the Savages. Everyone had warned her not to get involved with that family, including her own father, but she'd fallen for Cole immediately when they'd met at the party of a mutual friend three years ago. He'd homed in on her the moment she'd walked through the door and they'd spent the entire evening together. She'd only been sixteen and Cole eighteen and, despite their youth, their relationship had been very intense. Carly had never much bothered with boys before, but she'd found Cole irresistible. It was the mischief that twinkled in his green eyes, which, along with the sharpness of his cheekbones, made him look like a particularly mischievous cat. He was tall, standing at six foot one but slender and lanky-looking but that was an illusion because he was very strong, every muscle in his body taut and defined. He wasn't one for going to the gym and working out but he was full of restless energy and was constantly on the move. He had a very high metabolism, meaning he ate a lot but never seemed to gain weight. His chestnut-coloured hair was thick and perpetually messy, his lips lean and usually curved into a wicked smile. He was a beautiful-looking man.

Their relationship had been passionate, intense but tumul-tuous, mainly due to the interference of his family. Carly had wanted Cole to get onto the straight and narrow but he was constantly being pulled into criminal activities by his older brothers who were determined to drag him down to their level. Cole was close to his brothers, so Carly had quite a battle trying to steer him onto a better path.

Then had come the day she'd dreaded. Cole's oldest brother, Ross, had planned to rob a grand house in the west end of the city and had managed to convince Cole to be the getaway driver. Cole was a genius with cars. Not only was he a brilliant driver but he could fix any vehicle. A silent alarm must have been triggered in the house because the police showed up unexpectedly. Ross and his best friend had escaped empty-handed but an oblivious Cole had been left behind and the police had arrested him waiting outside the house in the getaway car.

The case against him would have been very tenuous without anyone to give evidence against him – Cole had refused to give up the names of his accomplices – but CCTV had caught him on camera parking the car just down the street from the house and the would-be robbers climbing out of the back. They hadn't been iden-tified because they'd worn balaclavas. It had been so stupid, espe-cially when Ross had sworn to Cole that he'd thoroughly researched the job first and knew the position of every camera and alarm when clearly he hadn't. So, while Ross, the ringleader, had got off scot-free, Cole had been given eighteen months in Barlinnie, the toughest prison in Scotland, with time added because he'd headbutted one of the arresting officers. Carly had been in court when he'd been sentenced, watching with tears streaming down her face. His gaze had connected with hers and she'd seen only sorrow and regret in his eyes. Carly had been so furious that her boyfriend was taking all the punishment that she'd threatened to kill Ross outside the court, which was completely out of character for her, and she'd never forgotten the dangerous look in his eyes that had said if she tried he would happily crush her windpipe.

Ross had friends in the prison who looked out for Cole. Carly had visited him three times before he'd told her not to bother again, that he hated her seeing him in that place. When she'd protested, he'd yelled in her face in the middle of the visits room in front of everyone that they were finished and he didn't want to see her ever again, compounding her humiliation. After that, he'd shunned all her letters and emails and had refused to allow her a visit order. He'd cut off contact with her completely which had broken her heart. So desperate had she been to see him that she'd even gone to his family and begged them to intercede on her behalf but they'd refused, telling her Cole was a grown-up and had the right to decide who visited him. There had been a look of triumph in their faces, particularly Ross's and his father's, both of whom had resented her trying to steer Cole onto the straight and narrow.

Now he'd been released and hadn't bothered to contact her, telling her she still meant nothing to him. Perhaps it was for the best. The Alexander family were nothing but trouble and her dad had never liked Cole. The last thing she wanted was to upset him when his health was so fragile.

After an hour's moping in her room, Carly shoved her feelings deep down inside herself and returned to the kitchen to find Jane and Rose clearing up after tea.

'You okay?' Jane asked her.

'Fine,' she replied, forcing a smile.

'Are you going to see Cole?' said Rose.

'No way. He made it very clear that he didn't want me, so he can get stuffed.'

'Are you sure? I mean, he was in prison when he said that and was probably depressed. Maybe he's changed his mind.' Rose had always liked Cole. He was sweet to her and made her laugh.

'I think you're making a wise decision,' said Jane, throwing Rose a warning look. 'We have enough on our plates without him coming back and causing his usual chaos.'

'Don't mention Cole to Da', will you?' said Carly anxiously. 'It'll only upset him.'

'Course we won't, will we Rose?'

'Nope, not at all,' she replied.

Although none of them said it, all three feared what Cole's return would mean for their family.

2

Carly changed and headed to the local pub to begin her shift. The shock of Cole's release had left her feeling disconnected from the world, as though the surprise had jolted her out of her body slightly. It was an uncomfortable feeling and she hoped some hard work would help her get back to normal. She walked the streets, oblivious to everything around her. Haghill was a residential area in the larger ward of Dennistoun in the east end of Glasgow. It was mainly composed of ex-council houses and post-war tenements, although some of these had been pulled down and replaced with new houses. Carly's flat was in one of the tenements.

The pub she worked at was called The Horseshoe Bar. She'd been employed there for a year and enjoyed her job, and because she spent so much of her time caring for her father, work was her only social outlet. The Horseshoe had recently had a makeover, to the disgust of some of the regulars, and was now quite trendy with its lacquered wooden floor and wooden panels, craft beer and comfy chairs, but it was as popular a local haunt as ever and still proudly exhibited its Rangers FC memorabilia. The landlord, a widower called Derek, had been a good friend of her father's for many years and had given Carly a job when Alec had no longer been able to work. He was a big man, as broad as he was tall, with a thick black beard and a heart of gold. He always made sure Carly's shifts fitted in with her father's care roster. He did not tolerate troublemakers, who soon found themselves slung out on their arses by the burly landlord and were never welcomed back, forced to go to The Wheatsheaf a few streets away, which was The Horseshoe's nearest rival and nowhere near as pleasant.

'Hi John,' said Carly to the old man propping up the end of the bar.

'All right, sweetheart,' he croaked back. 'How's that da' of yours?'

'Oh, no' so bad. His appetite was good today and he ate all his curry.'

'That's great, doll. Gi'e him my best.'

'I will,' she replied before heading into the office behind the bar to lock up her handbag and hang up her coat. She returned to the bar to find Derek emerging from the cellar hatch in the floor, carrying a box of salt and vinegar crisps.

'Good timing, Carly,' he said. 'I really need a pish.'

'I'm shocked.' She smiled, taking the box from him. Derek might have been a big man but he had a bladder the size of a teabag and often needed to nip to the bathroom. 'Away you go, I've got this.'

'Cheers, doll,' he replied before closing the hatch and rushing out from behind the bar, through the main room and down the passage that led to the toilets with a speed that belied his size.

Carly got to work. It was a Tuesday evening, which was one of their quieter nights, the clientele mainly comprised of the older generation piling in after bingo from the hall down the road. But everyone was friendly and chatty, telling her about their various ailments and gossiping about who was having an affair or who was in trouble with the police.

The routine of the work and the friendly chatter of the clients soothed Carly's nerves and she began to relax. She even managed to put Cole to the back of her mind as she laughed, chatted, served drinks and cleared tables.

As she was serving two sweet old ladies who were favourites of hers, a deep voice said, 'Pint of lager, please.'

Carly froze, her hand outstretched to one of the ladies as she was handing her her change. Turning, she saw Cole standing at the bar regarding her with that mischievous smile of his, green cat's eyes as brilliant as ever and full of naughtiness.

'Oh my gosh,' whispered one of the ladies to her friend, catching her change when Carly dropped it in her shock.

'Hello beautiful,' Cole added, leaning on the bar. 'Well,' he continued when she failed to reply. 'Aren't you going to say hello?'

It was the sudden silence that drew Carly's attention and she looked around the room to see everyone was staring at her expectantly.

'I'll get his pint,' said Derek who had returned to the bar and was as usual trying to be helpful.

'No, it's okay,' she replied, recovering her voice. 'I'll do it.'

With that she calmly poured Cole's drink, intensely aware of the fact that everyone was still watching her.

When she'd finished, she placed the lager in front of Cole and took his money. Once that was safely stowed in the till, she snatched up the glass before he could even pick it up and threw the contents in his face. As he wiped the liquid from his eyes, she turned on her heel and stalked into the office, slamming the door shut behind her, the pub erupting into applause.

'You deserved that,' Derek told Cole, tossing him a bar towel to clean his face with.

Cole caught it with one hand and nodded. 'Aye, I know,' he

replied, wiping his face. 'Could I have another pint, please? This one's a wee bit tepid.'

Derek poured him his drink and placed it before him, making sure he paid. Just because the last one went in his face didn't mean he was going to get a freebie in his establishment.

'Can I go through and talk to her?' Cole asked him.

'Gi'e her a bit of time to calm down. She might throw something a lot more painful than lager at you if you try now.'

'Wise advice.'

'I hope you're no' here to upset her. She's going through enough without you adding to it.'

'I don't want to upset her. I want her back.'

'You've changed your tune after you told her to get lost.'

'I was ashamed of what I'd done. Has she been with anyone else since?'

'That's none of your bloody business.'

'I suppose you're right. Splitting up with her was the biggest mistake of my life. I missed her so much when I was inside. I only hope she'll take me back.'

'I wouldnae hold my breath if I were you,' Derek told him dourly before moving to serve another customer.

While Derek was distracted, Cole snuck around the bar and into the office where he found Carly sitting on a chair, her face buried in her hands. She looked up when he entered, the pain in her eyes quickly morphing into anger when she saw who the intruder was.

'Piss off,' she told him, leaping to her feet.

'Just hear me out,' he replied, holding up his hands, fearing something else would be launched his way.

'Why should I? You made your feelings very clear when I visited you in prison.'

'I was messed up back then and I was so ashamed. You tried to warn me but I wouldn't listen. And I didn't want you to see me looking like a caged animal.'

Carly folded her arms across her chest. 'You brought it on yourself.'

'I know and I'm sorry for not listening to you. If I had, I wouldn't have lost a year of my life. But prison made me realise how much I love you and I want you back.'

'You seriously think you can swan back into my life and pick up where we left off? Well, you can't. You've no idea how much you hurt me, especially after I stood by you and defended you.'

'I've changed, Carly. I've finally realised what's important to me.'

She snorted with derision. 'Shite. You'll soon be back to running errands for Ross and I am not going through all that heartbreak again. Just piss off. I'm done with you,' she yelled.

'Please don't shout,' he said, glancing over his shoulder, expecting Derek to come storming in.

'Don't you dare tell me not to shout. I'll bloody well shout if I want to.'

At this, Derek did rush in and he scowled at Cole. 'I told you no' to come back here.'

'Sorry but I really wanted to talk to Carly.'

'Well, she doesnae want to talk to you so you can bugger off out of it.'

'Carly, please,' said Cole desperately, turning his attention back to her.

'Just go,' she told him in an exhausted voice.

'You heard the lady,' growled Derek, who was very protective of Carly. He felt someone should be looking out for her and her sisters now Alec couldn't. 'Sod off before I sling you through the window.'

'All right, I'm going.' He looked back at Carly. 'I'm staying at my maw's if you change your mind.'

'I won't.' She glowered, folding her arms across her chest.

A dejected Cole left and she breathed a sigh of relief.

'Thanks, Derek,' she said.

'Nae bother, sweetheart. Are you okay?'

'Aye. He just gave me a shock. I heard he'd been released but I wasn't expecting him to turn up here.'

'You're better off without him. His family's nothing but trouble and you have enough on your plate. Take some time to get yourself together before coming back through. I'll gi'e you a shout if I need another pish.'

'No worries,' she replied with a fond smile.

Carly wasn't sure how she got through the rest of her shift but she managed it somehow. Every time the door opened she looked round, half hoping it wasn't Cole, half hoping it was, but he didn't return.

Derek told her he'd close up and that she should get herself home because she looked done in after the shock she'd had.

Carly left the pub and looked up and down the darkened street, which was quiet, for once. Often there were wee weans hanging about, some of whom would mug you if they got the chance. Once she'd even walked out to find a bunch of teenagers battling with golf clubs they'd nicked from the local golf course but tonight there was a light drizzle in the air which was keeping all those sods indoors. Luckily Carly and her sisters were never targeted because Alec had been a feared and respected figure in Haghill. When he'd been fit and strong, he'd been more than happy to give any trouble-making bastard a battering. His enormous frame had been a deterrent and he'd cultivated a reputation for being firm but fair, so the Savage family had never endured any of the violence and anti-social behaviour that had plagued the area. Alec's daughters had forged reputations of their own, especially Jane, who had been the leader of a vicious all-female gang, until she'd given up that way of life when their father had become ill. Carly felt confident walking these darkened streets alone even here where there were no houses, just businesses, which were closed for the night, except for the Chinese takeaway a few doors down. The smell emanating from within made her stomach rumble; she loved Chinese food but she didn't have enough money to take something home for the rest of the family and she would feel guilty about enjoying a treat alone. She would have toast and jam when she got home instead.

As she passed the takeaway, a figure darted out of the doorway clutching a white polythene bag.

'Carly,' said Cole, smiling.

She sighed. 'What do you want?'

He hurried to catch her up as she strode on at her usual brisk pace.

'I bought you your favourite – chicken chow mein,' he said, holding the bag out to her.

'I don't want it.'

'Course you do, you love chow mein.'

'People change. I'm not the woman you remember.'

'Aye ya are. You'll always be my Carly.'

'I am not your Carly any more and that is your fault. I would have happily waited for you to be released but my loyalty wasn't enough, was it? You humiliated me in that prison. You couldn't even dump me quietly, you had to shout it out. I was laughed at by criminals.'

'So that's why you're so mad at me – because a couple of morons laughed at you?'

Carly stopped and rounded on him. 'I'm mad at you because you wouldn't listen to me about Ross. Not only were you stupid enough to go out on that job with him, you malkied a polis.'

'Well, the bastard deserved it. He was trying to put the cuffs on me.'

'He was only doing his job. If you hadn't been such a bloody idiot you might have got a shorter sentence. I was willing to forgive your breath-taking stupidity but that was the last straw. You were sent down when my da's condition got a lot worse.' Tears filled her eyes. 'I needed you and you weren't there.'

The pain in her voice shocked him and it finally made him understand just how much he'd hurt her.

'So you can stick your chow mein right up your arse,' she added. Carly was astonished when he smiled. 'It's not funny,' she yelled.

'I'm not laughing, I'm just happy because I've realised something – you do still love me.'

'I do not.'

'Aye ya dae,' he said, stepping closer, their faces just inches apart. 'If you really didnae gi'e a shite, you wouldn't be so angry.'

'Course I would.'

'For a year I've wondered if you'd forgotten about me and moved on but now I know you haven't, so there's still a chance for us.'

'Why do you still want to be with me? Am I just a habit to you?'

'No. You're my future wife.'

Carly was thrown. Despite the intensity of their relationship, neither of them had mentioned marriage before. The prospect of being tied down like that had always scared Cole.

'Was there anyone else while I was inside?' he asked her.

'That's absolutely none of your business. You're no' my boyfriend any more.'

His eyes flashed. 'Is that a yes?'

'Wouldn't you like to know? Now it's late and I'm tired, so I'm going home.'

'I'll walk with you.'

'No. I just want to be alone.'

'It's late and these streets can be dangerous.'

'Not since you were sent to prison,' she said stonily before continuing on her way.

Part of Carly longed for him to pursue her and continue trying to win her over but he didn't. He just stood there watching her go and that hurt too.

3

Carly was woken the next morning at six thirty by the sound of Rose singing in the kitchen. She smiled. Her sister had the sweetest voice, unlike herself and Jane, who were practically tone deaf.

She got out of bed, showered and dressed before heading into the kitchen, yawning.

'Sorry,' said Rose. 'Did I wake you?'

'Yeah but not to worry, I have to give Da' his breakfast soon anyway. Why are you so chirpy?'

'No particular reason.' She smiled. 'I'm just happy.'

Carly smiled back at her. 'That's nice. So there's no boy on the horizon making you sing like that?'

'No. They're all idiots. So immature.'

'You're not wrong.'

'Do you want a brew?' Rose said, switching on the kettle.

'Yes please.'

Carly and Jane were very aware of how lucky they were to have Rose, who always did everything she could to help and never complained.

'I'll see if Da's awake,' said Carly.

She walked down the hall and gently tapped on his bedroom door. When there was no response, she opened it and peered inside. He was lying so still on the bed that her heart lurched, until she saw the rise and fall of his chest. Every day she feared walking in and finding he'd passed away in his sleep.

Not wanting to disturb him, she closed the door quietly and returned to the kitchen. She and Rose enjoyed breakfast together and half an hour later Jane walked in ready for work, wearing a smart blouse and black trousers, her short hair neat. Her tall, athletic frame carried clothes so well that her cheap, fast fashion outfits always made her look like a powerful businesswoman. Carly had no doubt that one day she would be.

Jane made herself a cup of tea and some toast and joined them at the table.

'I heard Cole turned up at the pub last night,' Jane told Carly.

'What?' said Rose. 'Why didn't you tell me?' she demanded of Carly.

'I wasn't ready to discuss it. How do you know?' she asked Jane.

'I woke up to a text from Georgia Johnson. Her gran was in The Horseshoe last night.'

'So word will already be all over Haghill by now?'

'Yep. Sorry,' said Jane with sympathy in her eyes.

'Great,' she muttered.

'What happened?' said Rose excitedly.

'He said he wanted me back,' replied Carly. 'So I threw a pint of lager in his face and told him to sod off.'

'Oh, that's a shame.'

'Why? He deserved it.'

'I know but I always liked Cole. Yeah, he behaved like an idiot but he really did love you, I've no doubt about that.'

'Even when he told me to piss off,' she said, eyes flashing with hurt.

'He did that for you. He didn't want you dating someone stuck in prison.'

'And now he's out he thinks we can pick up where we left off. Well, we can't. I'm done with him.'

'If you're sure?' said Rose uncertainly.

'I am.'

'That's a very wise decision,' said Jane. 'At heart he's a nice man but he attracts trouble, especially being an Alexander. He'll never be able to escape his family.'

'That's true. That lot are a nightmare.'

'Hopefully he's got the message and will leave you alone.'

Carly just nodded. If that was what she wanted, then why did the prospect hurt so much?

* * *

After Rose had headed to school and Jane had left for work, Carly watched some television with her father in his room. He loved cookery shows. Cooking had been a big passion of his and they enjoyed discussing recipes together that they knew neither of them would ever make. His eyes used to light up with animation during these discussions but now his face was expressionless, having developed the mask-like appearance so common to Parkinson's disease sufferers.

Alec's room was the largest in the flat and he needed it with all the equipment he required. His bed was an electric profile one, which could be raised up and down at the touch of a button to help him sit up or lie down and there was a grab rail on the left side to assist him to get in and out. The sheets were satin, which made it easier for him to turn over and to get out of bed. He could still manage that on his own and he could get to the toilet himself with the aid of the walker, which always stood close by. There was also a large pill box to organise his medications, of which he had to take several every day, and a little bell for him to ring when he needed something. Because the illness had affected his speech, it was difficult for him to shout.

Alec loathed the sight of the commode in the corner of his room, which he had so far refused to use. He dreaded the day he needed help going to the toilet but it was inevitable that it would come and take away what little dignity he had left.

The armchair was raised to make it easier for him to get in and out and sometimes he would sit in it, but Carly had noticed that lately he preferred to remain in bed. She didn't think this was entirely due to his condition. Depression seemed to be slowly settling over him and she knew it wasn't just sadness about his illness. He was worried about what would become of his girls when they'd lost both parents. Parkinson's disease itself wasn't fatal, it was the associated problems such as pneumonia, falling or choking that they all feared.

Alec had unknowingly lived with Parkinson's disease for years before he was even diagnosed because the symptoms had crept up on him so gradually and Alec himself wasn't even sure when they'd begun. He recalled feeling a little out of sorts nine years ago when his wife had first been diagnosed with ovarian cancer but he'd put that down to the stress of the situation. He'd only realised something serious was going on a year after she'd died. Alec hadn't mentioned it to his children as they'd been through enough and he'd attended all his medical appointments without them realising anything was wrong. Because he was still quite young, the doctors had investigated other possible causes first. It had taken a specialist in the condition to finally pinpoint what was going on, which meant he went for years without any treatment and was why his condition had seemed to deteriorate so suddenly when it had in fact been a long progression. Alec had been so proud of his girls when, rather than collapse under the weight of this fresh shock, they'd rallied round him. He couldn't have asked for more from them and it was a never-ending source of pain that they had to look after him when it should have been the other way around.

His carers arrived at eight thirty and began the business of assisting him into the bathroom for a shower, which had a flip-down seat so he could sit while washing.

While Carly waited for them to finish, she wandered into the kitchen and picked up her phone. Before looking at the screen, she was distracted by the framed photos on the fireplace. Her mother Margaret was in every single one. She'd been a very pretty woman, slender and willowy, just like her and her sisters. Their dad stood beside them all, looking large and hulking with his kindly smile. One of the photos had been taken on holiday in Inverness a year before their mother had fallen ill, when life had been easy and full of laughter. A lump formed in Carly's throat at the sight of all those happy faces. They'd not had a clue that very soon their world would be torn apart and everything would change. Carly and her sisters had been forced to grow up very fast.

Both she and Jane would have liked to have gone onto further education but instead they'd abandoned their plans and got jobs. They'd sworn however that Rose would have no such hardship. She was a bright girl and was already talking about going to university and they would make sure she got there. She was in her final year of high school, and as university tuition in Scotland was free, thank God, they at least didn't have to worry about funding. They would ensure Rose could devote herself to her studies and forging a career and Carly and Jane could always follow the paths they wanted to take later in life. Right now, all Carly could think about was getting through each day, making sure the bills were paid, food was put on the table and her dad was well cared for.

It was already October and every time she thought about winter she felt a little sick. They were already in debt to the greedy bastard energy company to the tune of £2,000. Her father's condition meant they could never be cut off but that huge debt would only keep increasing because they didn't have a hope of paying it off and she constantly feared another price hike. Neither did she know how a bad cold spell would affect her dad's health. On top of all that, they were behind with the rent, the washing machine was on its last legs and the landline had been cut off because they couldn't pay the bill. It was only thanks to Jane working at a call centre for a mobile phone company that they still had their mobile phones as she got a good staff discount that they could just about afford.

Carly was so fed up of worrying about everything. Each night she struggled to get to sleep because of the weight of anxiety bearing down on her. It was a horrible feeling that she constantly carried around with her, like a nasty little creature had burrowed under her skin and was gnawing at her insides. So to take her mind off it she sat on the couch and went through her phone. There were a couple of messages from friends telling her about Cole's release and asking if she'd seen him, which she didn't have the energy to reply to right then.

She went onto social media and hesitated before going onto his profile, which had of course remained stagnant since his stint inside. Anger shot through her when she saw photos had been posted at two o'clock that morning from a local nightclub of an obviously drunk Cole with his arm slung around some tart, both of them smiling stupidly at the camera. It was accompanied by the caption: It's good to be free again.

'Ya wee bastard,' she hissed, shooting to her feet.

His protestations of love couldn't have meant very much if he was already shagging some orange-faced tart squeezed into an ugly silver dress two sizes too small for her. Hot, angry tears filled Carly's eyes. Cole had been locked up for a year, so she could guess what his most urgent needs would have been – lager and sex. But what right did she have to complain? She'd told him to get lost. He was a free agent, so he could sleep with whoever he liked. She could have been with him last night if she hadn't been so proud. Despite her protests, she did still love him and she'd had to fight the impulse to launch herself at him and beg him never to leave her again. But her dignity had come first.

After the initial hurt, the reality of the situation struck her. Being in a relationship with Cole was like being carried away by a hurricane. He was wild and reckless and had brought that out in her too, which had been fine when she was younger but now she had heavy responsibilities on her shoulders and she couldn't afford to get carried away in the moment. Plus, when you got Cole you got his entire family and the last thing she wanted was to get wrapped up with the Alexanders again. The matriarch, Jessica, wasn't so bad. She'd seemed to approve of Carly's efforts to get her son onto the straight and narrow but his father and two older brothers had other ideas and they'd resented her for trying to reform him. They'd left her alone since Cole had broken up with her but before that they'd sent plenty of veiled threats her way, especially Ross, the oldest. He was a scary man and she didn't want him back in her life, hassling her.

No, she'd done the right thing. Cole was on a path she couldn't follow. It was finally time to put him out of her mind and move on. Besides she didn't have the time for a relationship between working at the pub and looking after her dad. She wanted to give him all her time and attention because she didn't know how much longer he would be around. Cole was like a child, he'd always needed to be her centre of attention and had got jealous when she'd shown affection to other people, even her close friends and family. She couldn't have that with her father the way he was. No, the best thing she could do for her family and herself was to stay away from Cole Alexander.

She froze when the doorbell rang. Could it be Cole? The excited flip of her stomach annoyed her.

Carly went to answer the door and was greeted by a pair of sly green eyes and thick chestnut-coloured hair but it wasn't Cole, it was his older brother, Ross. Whereas Cole was slender, Ross was a thick knot of muscle. He was obsessed with pumping iron and had the physique of a bodybuilder. Carly found it odd that someone who was a career burglar had bulked up so much when his natural slender frame would have been ideally suited to his chosen profession. She kept hoping he'd get wedged in a window on a job, arrested and flung into prison for the rest of his natural life.

'What do you want?' she demanded, hand on the door, ready to slam it shut should it become necessary. His expression was not friendly but then again, it never was, even if he was in a good mood.

'I want to know what you and Cole talked about in the pub yesterday.'

'That's none of your business.'

'Aye it is. I hope you don't think you can try and turn him against his own family again, because I won't have it. We've only just got him back and we don't want you trying to drive him away again with your poison.'

'First of all,' she replied indignantly, 'it was not poison. I was trying to protect him. If he'd listened to me, he wouldn't have spent the last year in prison.'

Ross's eyes hardened, telling her she'd hit a nerve. 'The family's pure happy to have him home and we don't want you trying to steal him from us.'

'I wasn't trying to steal him from you,' she sighed.

'My maw's so happy, so keep your fucking nose out, okay?'

'Who do you think you are speaking to me like this on my own doorstep?'

He took an aggressive step towards her and, even though Ross had always intimidated her, Carly stood her ground.

'I know Cole went to your pub last night and you talked. I want to know what was said.'

'Why don't you ask him?' she retorted. 'Oh, I see,' she continued when his brow creased. 'He won't tell you and why's that? Because it's none of your bloody business.'

When she tried to close the door, he slammed his hand against it. Even though she put all her weight against it, he easily managed to keep it open.

'I'm not going until I know,' he said. 'Are you back together?'

'That's nothing to do with you,' she retorted.

'Then you'll have to get used to a draught because I'm no' moving until I get an answer. Who are you gonnae get to throw me out?' His smile was sadistic. 'Your da'?'

'You bastard,' she spat.

Ross shook his head. 'No, you're no' back with Cole. If you were, you'd be with him now. Hopefully he's finally realised that you're no good for him.'

'Actually, he begged me to take him back but I said no because I knew he'd continue to let you drag him down and I can't watch that happen to him.'

'You mean he didnae want you,' he hissed. 'Prison obviously screwed his head on the right way. Just know that if you do consider trying to get him back it will be very dangerous for you.' He peered inside the flat and she moved her body to prevent him from seeing anything. 'This place is more shite than the house you were in but at least you have a roof over your head. It would be a shame if anything happened to it, like a fire. It would be difficult for your da' to get out.'

Carly's temper spiked and she flung the door wide open and thrust her face into his. 'You threaten him again, you piece of shit, and I'll slit your fucking throat.' She was infuriated when he chuckled.

'You know what, Carly? I'm finally starting to realise what Cole saw in you. Maybe you're no' such a fucking goody-goody after all.'

4

Carly's encounter with Ross had left her feeling edgy. Since Cole had dumped her, she felt like she'd finally been set free from that family. They hadn't bothered her for nearly a year. Despite what she'd told Ross, she had the feeling he would give her another warning to ensure she stayed away from his brother. He was a vindictive man and would enjoy coming up with ways to inflict further misery on her.

'What's the matter, doll?' Derek asked her sympathetically as she worked her shift that evening. 'I hope your da's no' taken a turn for the worse? Or is it that wee fanny, Cole?'

'My da's okay and I've no' seen Cole since,' she replied. 'It's his brother, Ross.'

Derek's eyebrows knitted together. 'No' that nasty piece of work.'

'He came to the flat demanding to know if me and Cole were back together. It was a relief that I could tell him no. I shudder to think what he would have done if I'd said yes.'

'That is one vicious sod, I can tell you. He lives for causing trouble. It's any excuse with him.'

'Just when I thought I was free of the Alexanders,' she said, raking her fingers through her hair.

'Don't you worry, hen. Something else will happen and he'll find another person to pick on. Honestly, he's like a wee wean but if he does gi'e you any bother, you just let me know and I'll have a word. I've always got on with his da'. Brian's the only one capable of stopping Ross when he's on a mission.'

'I really appreciate that, Derek. Thanks.' She smiled. It felt good knowing someone had her back. The only other people she could rely on were her sisters but she didn't want them anywhere near Ross Alexander.

The door opened and once more Carly's heart skipped a beat but it was just three middle-aged women who were regulars on a Thursday evening because it was karaoke night. Anxiety had gripped her every time the door had opened that evening, expecting it to be Ross.

'All right, sexy.' One of the women beamed at Derek.

'Hello, Pauline, doll.' He smiled, leaning on the bar. Derek was a bit of a local heartthrob with the middle-aged women in the area, especially since his divorce three years ago. The fact that he ran a prosperous business also went heavily in his favour, as did the fact that he was quite good-looking, as well as big and burly.

'You all set up for the karaoke tonight?' purred Pauline, flashing her large white teeth at him.

'You know me, always ready for action.' He grinned back, making the three friends howl with laughter.

Carly cringed with embarrassment. She could never take old person flirting. This time it was a relief when the door opened again. It wasn't Ross but it was just as bad. In strutted Emma Wilkinson, leader of a local girl gang called the Unbeatable Bitches, the gang Jane used to run but had left when their dad became ill. Some of the Bitches, as they were known for short, hadn't taken very kindly to being abandoned. They'd stalked Jane and her sisters for a bit afterwards and threatened retribution that had never come, mainly because they were all intimidated by Jane, who hadn't always been the responsible, sensible woman she was now.

Emma was flanked by three women from her gang, which had nearly twenty members in total, although this figure constantly fluctuated. Carly didn't understand why they were here as The Wheatsheaf was their local and they'd not set foot in The Horseshoe for years.

Derek straightened up, expression grim. 'What are you lot wantin'?' he demanded.

'Just a drink, Derek,' replied Emma. 'And to enjoy some karaoke. No need to burst a blood vessel.'

Emma was a lovely-looking, elegant woman and the last thing she looked like was the leader of a violent gang responsible for vandalism, muggings and attacks in the area. She wore her knee-length cream dress and cropped leather jacket well, her thick blonde hair pulled back into an elegant top knot, looking as though she were going out for a night at some posh west end club rather than to sing karaoke in a second-rate pub. The Unbeatable Bitches had been around for about five years but their activities had really gone into overdrive with lockdown. There had been a surge in gang activity all over the country during this time thanks to bored teenagers with nothing better to do. In Haghill, the Bitches had been the dominant force and had recently gathered more followers which had given Emma a very exaggerated opinion of herself, seeing herself as some all-powerful figure in the criminal under-world rather than the head of a group of thugs and vandals.

'Why aren't you at The Wheatsheaf?' continued Derek, still very suspicious. 'That's where you normally go.'

'Because they don't have karaoke,' replied Emma.

He frowned. 'They used to.'

'So they did, until there was a fight and the machine got smashed up. Lonny said he refuses to get a replacement if that's how everyone's gonnae treat it.'

'Cannae say I blame him,' retorted Derek, narrowing his eyes. Normally he wouldn't dream of taking the side of Lonny Donovan, who had been his main rival for over a decade, but in this case, he could sympathise with the bad-tempered sod.

'Then we remembered you had karaoke, Derek, and we just had to come,' she added, fluttering her eyelashes at him.

'Well, if that's all you came for then you can stay,' he replied, the thought of taking customers from his rival appealing to him more than her attempts at flirting. 'But one ounce of trouble and you're barred. I'll have none of your shite in my pub.' He jabbed a digit at the girl standing on Emma's left. At eighteen, Karen Donohue was two years younger than her illustrious leader and couldn't have looked more different with her dark blue baseball cap, long straggly brown hair and lumberjack shirt with a cropped top underneath revealing her smooth belly. Tight blue jeans completed the outfit. 'And none of your crap either, Karen, you got it?' She was known for her fondness for breaking anything made of glass – windows, bottles, glasses and even bus shelters.

'She'll be on her best behaviour,' said Emma. 'We all will.' She looked to Carly. 'A glass of dry white wine and soda, please.'

Carly nodded and set about pouring her drink, conscious of Emma watching her. This turn of events made her very uneasy. Was it a coincidence that they'd come in here the same day Ross Alexander turned up on her doorstep? The Bitches had been known to support the Alexander family when they needed it, for instance causing a distraction so Ross could commit a robbery, so it wouldn't surprise her if he'd sent Emma here to intimidate her. But Carly wasn't easily intimidated.

She finished pouring the drink for Emma, who coolly picked up the glass, took a sip and smiled. 'This wine is so much better than Lonny's.'

Carly wondered if she was going to get the whole drink thrown in her face, or perhaps the glass but Emma stood back so her friends could place their orders, which they did politely, and after Carly had poured a gin and tonic, a Bacardi and coke and a pint of lager for Karen, Emma handed Carly a twenty-pound note and politely told her to keep the change. Carly thanked her with equal politeness and put the money in the till, sticking the tip in the glass jar beside it. The Bitches then took a table in the corner of the room and began to chat. Perhaps Emma had been telling the truth and they really were just here for the karaoke?

'What do you think?' Carly quietly asked Derek, both their eyes locked on Emma and her cronies as they talked and laughed.

'I think they're no' just here to sing,' he replied. 'But I could be wrong. At least, I hope I am. The last thing I want is that lot causing a rammy in my pub.'

'I suppose we'll see when the singing starts.'

'Speaking of which, I'd better get set up.'

Carly wondered if the Bitches would choose now to start trouble, while Derek was distracted, but they remained at their table, drinking and talking and behaving themselves.

Ten minutes later Derek was back behind the bar with Carly, both of them grimacing as Pauline belted out Whitney Houston's 'I Will Always Love You' extremely badly, her wail reaching ear-splitting levels. Pauline was oblivious to the discomfort she was causing, the look in her eyes saying she thought she was just as good as, if not better than, the great Whitney herself.

'Christ, it really makes you appreciate the professionals, doesn't it?' Derek accidentally yelled out across the room when the music ended sooner than he'd expected. 'Pauline, doll, I'm sorry, I didnae mean you,' he added hastily when she glared at him in outrage.

She threw down the microphone, the whine of the feedback making them wince again.

'That sounded better than she did,' commented one woman, her friends laughing while Pauline snatched up her jacket and stormed to the door, Derek hurrying after her while attempting to apologise.

'Carly, take over will you?' Derek called to her before following Pauline outside.

She nodded, retrieved the microphone from the floor and walked over to the machine to see who had their name down to go next. To her dismay, it was Emma Wilkinson.

As Carly set up the requested song, Emma approached her.

'Thank you so much,' she told Carly, accepting the microphone from her.

'You're welcome,' she slowly replied, not trusting all this bonhomie. This act was far too polite and civilised for Emma. Despite how elegant she looked, she was violent and cruel.

Carly wondered if now would be the time the trouble started but Emma's friends settled down to watch, drinks in hand, as their friend took the spotlight.

Emma's voice was soft and rather haunting as she sang Adele's 'Set Fire to the Rain'. Everyone stopped what they were doing to listen, including the gossiping crows at the back of the room. Even Carly found herself entranced and she wondered what Emma was doing running around with a group of thugs when she could have had a bright future as a singer. She was good at the showmanship too, her presence demanding everyone's attention, which she revelled in.

Glancing around, Carly saw Derek had managed to coax Pauline back into the pub and she sat on a stool at the bar, her lower lip stuck out like a child, although she did accept the brandy he offered her.

As Emma reached the climax of the song, it was then Carly recalled something – Emma Wilkinson was the queen of distraction.

There was a loud smash and the large window to the right of the front door erupted inwards, screams bursting from those sat closest to it. A large black lump landed in the middle of the floor.

'Jesus, is everyone all right?' exclaimed Derek, abandoning Pauline to attend to the customers sitting by the window.

Carly rushed over to help too, after snatching up the first aid kit from behind the bar. Thankfully there were no serious injuries, although one man and his wife had small cuts to the backs of their necks. Fortunately no one had been sitting right in front of the window.

'What's that on the floor?' said Brenda, one of Pauline's friends, her dark brown hair curled into a tight perm. 'It looks like a bit of slag.'

'Naw,' replied a man. 'It's just a big stone.'

'But it's jet black, look at it.'

Brenda paused to chew her lip before replying, 'Obsidian?'

'Why would anyone throw obsidian through a pub window? They'd have to be aff their nut.'

'You're both wrong,' said Derek grimly. 'It's a lump of coal.'

'Coal?' Brenda frowned. 'I don't get it.'

'I do,' said Carly, looking across the room to Emma, who had re-joined her friends. All four women were on their feet and staring back at her. 'It's a message.'

'About what? Don't tell me it's one of those environmentalists making a protest?'

'It's a symbol for Cole, my ex,' she replied, gaze locked on Emma, the corner of whose mouth had curved into a malicious smile. 'It's a warning for me to stay away from him.'

'But you have stayed away from him,' replied Brenda. 'He came to you.'

'Try telling that to the idiot who threw that lump of coal,' sighed Carly.

'It's funny how this happens for the first time in the ten years I've run this pub,' Derek told Emma. 'And you lot are here.'

'I think you'll find none of us could have possibly thrown that ugly lump,' retorted Emma.

'No, you couldn't, but you were making damn sure we were all looking the other way when it happened. There's still a bit of daylight outside, someone could have seen the person responsible, but we didn't because we were all looking at you.'

'Can I help it if my voice is hypnotic?' She smiled.

'Go on, piss off out of it. I know you lot are something to do with this and I want none of you here again. You and your entire gang are barred. Do you hear me? Barred,' he yelled.

Emma's smile broadened. 'Let's go girls, we've got what we came for. Let's go back to The Wheatsheaf, which is far superior to this dump.'

'Dump?' exclaimed Derek. 'Get out before I sling you oot the window, you cheeky cow.'

'No, Karen,' Emma said when her friend grunted and picked up her pint glass. 'We're not savages.'

Karen dumped the glass back on the table and the punters all remained silent as they watched the four women leave. Once the door had closed behind them, the room erupted into excited chatter.

While Carly attended to the minor injuries, Derek swept up the broken glass and called his brother-in-law, who was a glazier, who promised to come round first thing in the morning. He then called a couple of friends to come and board up the hole.

'At least it's no' raining,' he muttered. 'Oh, that's just typical, isn't it?' he exclaimed when the sky suddenly darkened and the heavens opened.

'At least it's not windy too,' said Carly.

'Don't tempt fate, hen.'

* * *

When all the customers had cleared out of the pub and Derek's friends had finished hammering sheets of wood across the broken window, he insisted on driving Carly home, just in case any of the Bitches were hanging around. His car was parked at the rear of the building and he walked out to find his windscreen had been battered by lumps of coal, the cracks in it looking like a spider's web. The missiles had landed on the bonnet too and dented it.

'What the actual fuck?' he exclaimed.

'I'm so sorry, Derek,' said Carly, her stomach dropping. 'This is because of me. I don't know if it's Ross or Emma and her Bitches but they're telling you to sack me.'

'I don't gi'e a shite what they're trying to tell me. I decide who I employ, no one else.'

'Maybe I should quit before anything else happens?'

'Don't you dare gi'e them the satisfaction. You gi'e into them once and they'll keep coming after you. You'd better stand firm on this,' he told her sternly.

'In one night you've lost one of your windows and your windscreen.'

'So what? I've got good insurance and I've been paying it for years without making a claim. Well, it's time I got some of my money back. I'll easily get a police report.'

'And next time what if a firebomb comes through the window?'

'It won't. Like I said, I'll go and talk to Brian Alexander tomorrow. He'll make it stop.'

'What if he doesn't?'

'He will, trust me. I know what I'm doing.'

'Okay, Derek. Thanks.'

'You're welcome, doll. Now, I cannae drive you so I'll walk you home.'

'If you're sure?'

'Aye I am, it's no' far and the rain's stopped. Alec would never forgive me if he knew I'd let you walk home alone in the dark after all this.'

Carly smiled as they set off together. They turned the corner and sure enough, Emma and her three friends were there, hanging around outside the takeaway.

'Just keep walking,' Derek quietly told Carly.

'What if they attack us?'

'Then we'll batter the shite out of them.'

Carly smiled. 'Fine by me.' Jane had a ferocious reputation but Carly had her own reputation too, although admittedly she hadn't had a fight in quite a while. Hopefully it would all come back to her if she was forced into a corner.

Derek and Carly locked eyes with the Bitches as they passed them by but the four women didn't speak or even move. Carly released the breath she was holding once they were past the group of women. She glanced back over her shoulder to see they were watching them but they made no move to follow.

'This is getting really weird,' she said.

'It'll settle down after I've spoken to Brian,' replied Derek. 'Hopefully he can get it through Ross's head that you and Cole are really over.' He frowned when Carly didn't reply. 'Please don't tell me that you're thinking of getting back with that wee fanny?'

'God no, but I won't deny that I still feel a little sad that we're over.'

'I suppose that's natural. Cole's no' bad. It's just a shame you get the rest of his family too.'

'If it hadn't been for them, we'd be together now and he wouldn't have gone to prison.'

'Probably, but you cannae save him. If he's dead set on self-destruction, that's his business.'

Derek glanced over his shoulder and saw the four women were following them at a distance but decided not to mention that to Carly, who seemed to be lost in her own thoughts, her large eyes sad. He could kill Cole for disrupting her life like this. She and her family had finally settled into a routine that suited them all and they were just managing to keep their heads above water. They had enough to worry about without idiots like those vicious cows or the Alexander family. Carly's family never interfered with anyone, they just got on with their lives and it was infuriating that other people couldn't give them the same courtesy.

The Bitches followed them all the way to the end of Carly's street but they didn't come any closer. Derek wondered if that was due to the intensely creepy graveyard, which hadn't taken a new burial in years after a second and much more picturesque cemetery had opened on the other side of the estate. The most recent grave dated to the late 1950s and the only people who visited it now were teenagers seeking a thrill and a couple of ghost hunting groups. Derek didn't know how Carly coped with living right across from it. Although he would never admit it out loud, if he was Carly, he wouldn't be able to get a wink of sleep.

'Well, here we are,' he said.

Carly smiled at the way he glanced nervously at the graveyard. 'I appreciate you walking me home. You'd better get yourself off too before the dead rise from their graves.'

'What?' he exclaimed, looking alarmed. 'That's not funny,' he added when she grinned.

Derek looked down the street and was relieved when he saw no one. The Bitches had gone, although he was more worried about ghouls than them. 'Right, well, you're back safely, so I'd better get home.' Derek lived in the flat above the pub.

'Do you want to call a taxi?'

'Nae thanks, doll. The last taxi I got was driven by a robbing bastard who took me the long way round. The night's quite mild, so I'll walk.'

'Okay. Thanks and be careful, won't you?'

'Those pricks don't worry me. Tell Alec I'll visit him soon.'

'I will. He'll appreciate that.'

Derek nodded, once again glancing nervously at the graveyard. 'Well, goodnight, hen.'

'Night Derek.'

He waited until she'd unlocked the front door and stepped inside before leaving, heading in the opposite direction to which they'd come, intending to circle back down the next street to avoid Emma and her gang. But all the violent nutters in Glasgow weren't as scary as that cemetery.

5

It took Carly a while to drift off that night, as she was half-expecting a lump of coal to come crashing through the window. She woke feeling wrung out, the previous night's events making her feel down. Most of all, she felt guilty about poor Derek and all the trouble he'd been put to. Hopefully he was right about Brian being able to stop his son.

She wandered into the kitchen in her pyjamas, yawning. Jane and Rose were sitting at the table eating breakfast, both looking smart and beautiful, making her feel even worse.

'You all right?' said Jane when she slumped into a chair.

'Fine, just tired. Work was busy last night.'

Jane's gaze said she knew more was going on than her sister was saying but she didn't press the issue in front of Rose. 'I've given Da' his breakfast, so you don't need to.'

'Thanks,' she yawned.

When Rose went into the bathroom to brush her teeth, Jane said, 'I heard about what happened at the pub last night.'

'Is there anything you don't know?'

'Not in Haghill.' Jane might have been out of the gang life but she still had contacts who were always quick to let her know when something was happening. 'I'll talk to Emma.'

'Please don't do that. She'll only use it as an excuse to target you too.'

'She's started dating Ross Alexander.'

'Then she's an idiot with terrible taste. Anyway, Derek said he'll have a word with Brian Alexander and he'll make it all stop.'

'Maybe,' said Jane.

'What do you mean, maybe?'

'From what I've heard, Ross has been getting out of control recently. Brian's getting older and his hold over his sons is slipping. Ross might listen to him, or he might not.'

'Great,' she sighed.

'Ross isn't just targeting you because he's worried about you getting back with Cole, he's doing it because he enjoys it. I wouldn't be surprised if he gets a sexual thrill from it.'

Carly grimaced. 'Urgh.'

'The same applies to Emma. She gets off on throwing her weight about and intimidating other people.'

'They make a good couple then,' sighed Carly.

'Yep, and their relationship won't be good for anyone. They'll only encourage each other to do more dangerous and violent things.'

'Hopefully Cole will get another girlfriend and Ross will lose his reason for harassing me. He's only doing it to get his own back because he thinks I looked down on him when I was going out with Cole.'

Jane studied her sister carefully. 'I don't think you mean that. You'd be distraught if you saw Cole with another woman.'

'I won't deny it would hurt but it's for the best. My main concern is for you, Rose and Da'. No one else matters, except Derek. He's been so good to me and I feel terrible that he was targeted last night.'

Jane got to her feet and placed her bowl in the sink. 'I still have people who owe me favours. I'll call some of them in.'

'You don't need to do that,' said Carly, knowing her sister was referring to people who would be willing to attack Emma and Ross for her. 'Leave it be. It'll all settle down.'

'No, it won't.'

Jane's cool assessment made Carly feel nervous. 'At least let Derek talk to Brian first. It will be much better if he can make it stop. We don't want to bring war to Haghill.'

'It's inevitable. The Alexanders and the Bitches have to have their rule challenged one day.'

'Let someone else do it then. We can't get involved in anything like that.'

'Okay, if you think that's the right thing to do but one day soon, we may have no choice.'

Carly watched her sister leave the room with a distinct sense of unease. A lot of people thought Jane rather cold but Carly knew that wasn't true. It was just a front to hide her emotions. Jane in fact felt things very deeply, it was what made her such a ferocious fighter. Carly hoped her sister didn't get dragged back into the old life she'd fought so hard to escape.

* * *

Carly was watching the morning cookery shows with her father, her sisters having left for work and school, when there was a knock at the front door. Alec caught the way his daughter's head snapped round to the window, which looked out onto the main road and faced the cemetery.

'What's wrong?' he murmured before swallowing hard.

She forced a smile. 'Nothing. The knock just made me jump; I wasn't expecting it.' She was careful not to exhale with relief when she saw who their visitor was. 'It's Derek. He said he'd come and visit you.'

Alec didn't respond at first. Carly had got used to interpreting her father's emotions, despite the mask-like expression he permanently wore. The illness hadn't affected his eyes and in them she read his every thought. He enjoyed having company, especially Derek's, who was one of his oldest friends; they'd even gone to school together. But at the same time, he didn't like anyone seeing him this way. He'd been known for his stature and physical strength and he felt ashamed that he was now so weak.

'I'll let him in,' said Carly, leaving the room before he could object. Her father needed the company of people his own age and she didn't want him losing out because of his pride.

She hurried to the door and pulled it open, smiling when she saw Derek glancing nervously over his shoulder at the cemetery. 'Why does that place freak you out so much?' she asked him. 'They're all dead; they can't hurt you.'

'Aye but... it's just creepy, even in broad daylight. I don't know how you stand it.'

'Like my da' said when we moved here, it's the living you have to watch out for, no' the dead.'

'Hmm, I'm no' so sure.'

'Come on in, you're letting in the cold.'

'Sorry,' he said, stepping inside, relieved when she closed the door, blocking out the sight of the cemetery. 'Is Alec awake?'

'Aye and he's waiting for you.' She lowered her voice. 'He doesn't know about Cole being released or Ross and Emma. I don't want to worry him.'

'I won't say a word, although I've just come from Brian Alexander's. He said he'll make Ross stop.'

'Thanks, but do you think he can?'

'Aye, I reckon so. There have been whispers that he's been losing his touch but that's no' true.

If you ask me, Ross is responsible for putting about that rumour.'

'I wouldn't put it past him. Would you like a brew?'

'No thanks, I'll just go and see Alec.'

Carly showed him through to her dad and left the two men to it. Some male company would do her father good. He'd used to have regular visitors but that had trailed off as Alec's condition had progressed and friends couldn't handle seeing him like that. It felt so unfair that their dad's condition had deteriorated so rapidly, especially after watching their mother die of cancer. Why couldn't they have been left with one parent? At least she still had sisters. They kept her fighting every day.

Carly's phone pinged and she picked it up to see her friend Sylvia had sent her a message. It told her to look at Cole's social media profile immediately. She was tempted to ignore it but if she did she'd only endlessly fret over it, so she went onto Cole's profile. Tears filled her eyes when she saw he'd updated his status to 'in a relationship' and his profile picture had been changed from a dog on a skateboard to the photo she'd seen of him with the orange tart.

Anger rose inside Carly and she swallowed down her tears. 'Well, you can deal with Ross bloody Alexander instead,' she hissed at the woman's image before placing her phone down on the kitchen table. Of course she still loved Cole but this was for the best. Now she could put him and his sodding family behind her and look to the future. Desolation swept over Carly. And what was her future? Her father was slowly dying and she had no job prospects. Great.

She was cheered by the sound of laughter from her father's bedroom. It wasn't often she heard that sound and she didn't know for how much longer she would get to hear it. Bugger the Alexander family. She had her own and they were her priority.

After his visit, Carly escorted Derek to the door, the smile he'd been wearing when he'd exited her father's room slowly falling.

'Thanks for coming,' she told him. 'I know how much he appreciates your visits, especially as you have a pub to run.'

'I'll always make time for Alec.' He sighed heavily. 'I won't deny it's so hard seeing him like that, especially when he was so active working as a builder and playing rugby. It's a crying shame.'

'You're not wrong,' Carly said sadly.

'He's still got his sense of humour though, that's important. Anyway, let me know if you have any more trouble with the Alexanders, all right?'

'I will. Thanks so much, Derek.'

'You're welcome, love. I'll see you later at work.'

'Bye,' said Carly, smiling as she watched him head down the road while nervously glancing back at the cemetery, as though he expected a legion of the undead to rise from their graves and chase him.

Later that morning, Carly left the house to purchase a few bits and pieces from the shop on the next street. The day was sunny, albeit chilly. She was just relieved it wasn't raining.

She entered the shop, picked up a basket and began browsing. As she was studying a tin of broth, considering whether her dad could swallow it or not, a voice spoke behind her, making her jump. She turned to see an attractive woman in her mid-forties with dyed curly reddish-brown hair. Her make-up was immaculate and her clothes designer. Over one shoulder dangled a Versace handbag. What caused Carly a pang in her chest was the fact that her green eyes were just like Cole's.

'Hello Carly,' said the woman, smiling.

'Hi Jessica. Fancy bumping into you here.'

'It's lovely to see you again,' she replied, voice warm and friendly. 'You're looking great.'

'Thanks,' said Carly. 'So are you, as always.'

'How's your da' keeping?'

'Not too bad. He has his good days and bad days.'

'Give him my love, won't you?'

'Of course.' Carly had always liked Cole's mother but she hoped that was the end of the conversation. They'd barely exchanged two words since her son had dumped her and she felt awkward.

'I believe Ross has been giving you some bother?' said Jessica.

Carly nodded, hoping she wasn't about to get another warning off.

'For that I apologise,' she continued, to Carly's surprise. 'He's always been volatile and when he gets a stupid idea in his head there's no shifting it. Derek came to the house to have a word with Brian. I was out at the time but my husband told me what was said. I can promise that he'll leave you alone from now on.'

'He seemed pretty set on continuing his persecution of not only me but Derek too.'

'I blame that awful Emma Wilkinson. They bring out the worst in each other but he seems pretty smitten and refuses to dump her. Anyway, they'll stop giving you any bother, I personally guarantee it.'

'Good because me and Cole aren't getting back together.'

'I'm sorry to hear that. I always thought you were good for him and that you might get him onto the straight and narrow. Seeing my youngest child put in prison was the worst day of my life.'

'It was Ross's fault,' said Carly, eyes flashing, her anger still evident.

'He was partly to blame, I grant you, but Cole has to take some responsibility. Anyway, what's done is done and can't be changed.'

'Exactly. I just want to put it all behind me and move on with my life. What Ross doesn't understand is that my only concern right now is my da'.'

'And I'll make sure he realises that. Just leave it with me.'

'Thanks, I really appreciate your help.'

'You're welcome.'

'Does Dominic share Ross's concerns about me and Cole?' she added, referring to the middle Alexander brother.

'No, but unfortunately he is easily led by his older brother.' Jessica's smile was gentle. 'At one point, I really did think you would be my daughter-in-law and that would have made me so happy.'

Carly just nodded, doubting being part of the Alexander family would have made her happy.

'Well, I'll see you later,' said Jessica before leaving.

Carly noted she left without buying anything. Had their meeting been accidental or had Jessica followed her? The notion was a disturbing one.

* * *

At the pub that night, Brenda couldn't wait to tell Carly that Cole had got himself another girlfriend. Apparently, the orange-faced tart was called Kimberly. She was a twenty-year-old trainee hairdresser from Riddrie and they'd met in a nightclub.

Although Carly acted disinterested, she was hurt. So much for Cole being desperate to get her back. She forced a smile, told Brenda she was pleased for him and hoped he found happiness before turning to serve the next customer while inwardly seething.

The pub door burst open and Rose rushed in with two of her friends.

'What are you doing here?' Carly demanded.

'Someone threw a brick through da's bedroom window,' she cried, eyes wide and full of tears.

'Oh my God, is he all right?'

'He got a little cut on his face but he's fine. Just shaken up.'

'You go on, doll,' Derek told Carly. 'I've got it covered here.'

'Thanks,' she said before grabbing her coat from the office.

'Let me know if you need anything,' he called after the sisters as they tore out of the pub followed by Rose's friends.

Carly was relieved her sister had the good sense not to wander the dark streets alone, even if her friends were only sixteen-year-old girls.

'Did anyone see who did it?' said Carly as they ran down the street.

'Mr Thomson was walking his wee dug at the time,' replied Rose. 'He said it was Ross Alexander. Emma Wilkinson was with him.'

'Bastards,' hissed Carly. 'Get home, girls,' she told Rose's friends. 'You don't want to get tangled up in this.'

They immediately started to protest but Carly snarled at them to do one and they obeyed without question. Rose remained quiet the rest of the journey home. It was rare to see her sister so furious but when Carly was in that kind of mood it was best to leave her be.

Carly stormed into the flat, followed by Rose, and rushed into her father's room to find him being tended to by Mary McCulloch from the flat next door, as well as Jane. Mary was a gentle, kind woman in her early sixties who used to be a nurse. As there was glass on the floor and the bed, Alec had been moved to the armchair at the other side of the room. The curtains had been torn and one of the window panes smashed, allowing in a gentle breeze.

'There you are,' an angry Jane told Rose. 'I told you not to go outside; I could have called the pub to let Carly know.'

'I know but... this was quicker,' she replied.

'How is walking there quicker than making a phone call?'

'It doesn't matter, it's done now and Carly's here,' retorted Rose.

The truth was, she couldn't bear to see her father so distressed and had needed an excuse to leave the flat. At least he seemed to have calmed down now.

'Are you okay, da'?' said Carly, rushing to his side and taking his hand.

He sighed with relief and grasped her hand in his own. He paused to swallow before answering. 'Fine,' he sighed. 'Gave me a fright, that's all.'

Carly's heart ached at the sight of the cut to his right cheek. It was only small and the damage could have been so much worse but that cut broke her heart. 'That's good,' she said. 'You're a tough bastard, Da'.'

He had to pause to swallow again. 'No swearing... in front of Rose.'

It took him longer than usual to get out his words, which was indicative of how shaken up he was, even though he was doing his best to hide it. In his prime he would have gone after Ross Alexander and ripped his head off; Carly hadn't been lying when she'd said he was a tough bastard, but now he was as helpless as a lamb and it enraged her that he'd been put through this. Ross and Emma would have known that was his bedroom window.

'Sorry, Da,' replied Carly with a gentle smile. 'We need to do something about that window.'

'It's all in hand,' said Jane. 'Ronny from the flat upstairs has gone to get some wood to cover it up until we can get it repaired.'

'Let's hope the council pays to have it fixed because we can't afford it.'

'There,' Mary told Alec when she'd finished tending to his cut. 'All better now. You'll be as right as rain. Now we need to get this room cleaned up.'

'I'll go and get the brush and dustpan,' said Jane while giving Carly a meaningful look.

Carly nodded and followed her sister into the kitchen, closing the door behind her.

'Rose said Ross and Emma did this,' said Carly.

'They did. It wasn't just Mr Thomson who saw them. Jimmy Taggert and his wife were coming back from the bingo and saw them too.'

'The utter twats,' Carly hissed. 'I spoke to Jessica Alexander in the shop today and she said she'd make Ross stop. Derek spoke to Brian too and he said the same thing.'

'Ross doesn't listen to his parents any more, he does what the hell he likes. You know how a couple of the Bitches are still my spies?'

Carly nodded.

'They told me there's trouble in the Alexander family. Ross and Dominic are going rogue, disobeying their parents. That family's always been into petty crime. Brian and Jessica are pretty good at it too, they're subtle and choose their targets carefully, which is why they've never been caught, but the two older brothers are wanting to branch into more serious business.'

'You're saying there's a family rift?'

'Aye, and a big one.'

'If Ross wants to become a more serious criminal then why is he throwing bricks through people's windows like a fucking wean?'

'I don't know but whatever's going on goes deeper than your relationship with Cole.'

'But that's all it can be. Our family doesn't have any other links to the Alexander family.'

Jane shrugged. 'Then there's something we're missing and we need to find out what that is and fast.'

'I could speak to Jessica again. We always got along pretty well.'

'She might not want to discuss family business with outsiders.'

'From what you've said, we both have the same problem – Ross.'

Jane nodded. 'All right, go for it. I'll see what else I can find out.'

'We might both be dragged into something we don't want to be a part of.'

Jane's expression turned dark. 'I'll burn the fucking world if it keeps you all safe.'

Carly had seen this darkness in her sister's eyes many times when she was younger but not since their father had become ill. Jane had turned into a very responsible, upright woman, holding down a job while supporting her family financially and emotionally. Now her family was being threatened, the old Jane was returning.

6

The Savage sisters' priority was ensuring their father's safety. With the assistance of the nurses when they arrived the following day, they swapped Alec's room with Jane's which looked over the rear of the flat into gardens that could only be accessed by the residents. Alec was pale and down, feeling awful for being unable to defend his daughters. He sat silently in the armchair in his old room, head bowed while his daughters and the nurses swapped bedroom furniture around. He hated that they were doing all the work while he sat there, useless.

Once everything was in place, they assisted him into bed in his new room and tucked him in. Alec sank back into the pillows while they all fussed around him, ensuring he was comfortable.

When the nurses had gone after cleaning and feeding him, he summoned his daughters. It was a Saturday, so Jane and Rose were off work and school, although Carly had to work her shift at the pub that night.

'You need to call your uncle,' he told them weakly.

The sisters regarded each other in surprise.

'Da,' said Carly, 'you can't be serious.'

'I cannae take care of you but he can.'

'But Uncle Eddie's unpredictable to say the least.'

'He can do this.'

'Why would he even come?' said Jane. 'We haven't seen him or his sons in years.'

'He'll come,' rasped Alec. 'He owes me and we've been talking lately.' As he was tired and upset, his words ran into each other but his daughters could still follow him. He paused to swallow again, frustrated when it became increasingly difficult to express himself. 'He'll want to help. He was always fond of you three.'

'If you think it's the right thing to do then we'll call him,' said Rose.

'Good girl,' he said, resting easier. 'His number's on my phone.'

'I'll make the call,' said Jane, a little perturbed by this turn of events.

She picked up her father's phone and left the room with Carly, leaving Alec under Rose's watchful eye.

'Do you really think this is wise?' Carly asked her sister, following her into the kitchen. 'Uncle Eddie might make everything worse.'

'We don't know who he is any more; we haven't seen him or our cousins in years. If Da' thinks it's the right thing to do then so do I and it'll be worth it if it gets Ross and Emma off our backs.'

'Say Da's plan works and they do back off. What if Eddie won't leave? He might turn out to be worse than the Alexanders.'

'I trust Da's instincts. Maybe Uncle Eddie's changed and Da' knows it but we don't? He did say they've started talking again.'

'Or he could be even worse.'

Jane looked down at the phone in her hands. 'This is what Da' wants and we said we'd do everything we could to keep him happy.'

Carly sighed and nodded. 'All right. Make the call.'

She anxiously listened to her sister talk. After introducing herself and relaying news about her father's condition, Jane told Eddie about their recent troubles.

'Well?' said Carly when she'd hung up.

'He said he's coming straight over.'

'Alone?'

'He didn't say.'

'Is he still living in Clydebank?'

'Aye.'

Carly glanced at the clock. 'Then he should be here in about half an hour.'

'I don't know that he was setting off immediately. He'll have to pack and make arrangements. If he's working, he might have to book time off. We might not see him for a few days.'

Personally, Carly hoped they never saw him but she seemed to be in the minority.

'Have you called Uncle Eddie?' said Rose, bounding into the kitchen with her usual energy.

'I have,' said Jane. 'And he's coming.'

'Great. I like Uncle Eddie; he's funny.'

'I think you're confusing funny with psychotic,' frowned Carly.

'He's not that bad,' said Jane. 'And I'm sure age has mellowed him.' She pretended not to notice Carly's sceptically-raised eyebrow.

'Is he bringing Dean and Harry with him?' said Rose, referring to Eddie's sons and the sisters' cousins.

'He didn't say,' replied Jane. 'We'll just have to wait and see.'

'It's a shame we can't put them up here but we don't have the room.'

'I made that clear to him and he said it won't be a problem,' replied Jane.

'Do you think he really can help?' Rose asked her sisters.

Carly wiped the doubt from her face, wanting to reassure Rose. 'I'm sure he can.'

'Oh, good because I don't want another brick coming through the window. It was so scary. Poor Da'.'

She broke off and turned her back when tears filled her eyes, wanting to be as strong as her sisters.

Carly prayed Eddie would help and didn't make the situation worse because she had the feeling Rose and Alec would be the ones to pay the price.

* * *

From her experience of the Alexander family, Carly knew Jessica visited a local café every morning for a croissant and a latte. She hoped Cole's mother hadn't changed her routine but sure enough, Carly entered the café and saw her sitting at a table in the far corner, gazing thoughtfully into her coffee. It seemed she was a creature of habit.

'Carly.' Jessica smiled as she saw her approach her table. 'What a pleasant surprise.'

'Can I have a word?'

'Of course.' She gestured to the empty chair across from her. 'Do you fancy a coffee? It's on me,' she added, knowing the Savage family needed every penny.

'Thanks, that would be nice.'

Once Carly was settled with her coffee, Jessica said, 'So what do you want to discuss with me?'

'Have you heard about the brick that came through my da's window last night?'

'I have and it's terrible. Is he okay?'

'Thankfully he just got a little cut on his face but it really shook him up and that's the last thing he needs. Three people saw it happen and they all said Ross and Emma were responsible.'

Jessica sighed and replaced her cup on the table. 'Oh God, I'm so sorry, Carly.'

'Did you and Brian have the chance to speak to Ross?'

'Aye, we both did.'

'And?' she pressed when Jessica went silent.

'I admit, it didn't go very well. He snarled at us in his usual way but in the end, we got him to promise to leave you and your family alone.'

'Then he went straight out and broke that promise.'

'So it seems.'

'What I don't understand is why he's targeting us? There's got to be more to it than not wanting me and Cole to get back together. Do you know something?' she said when Jessica's eyes flickered.

'Me? No,' she replied.

'Please Jessica, if you know something you have to tell me. What if next time my da' isn't so lucky?'

'All right, but you won't like what I have to say.'

'Maybe but I still need to know.'

Jessica nodded. 'This isn't to do with you and Cole. Actually, that's a lie. It is a little bit but it's primarily to do with Jane. Emma knows she still has spies in her ridiculous little gang. In fact, most of the girls are still all for Jane and want her back running things. Emma's trying to make her look weak.'

'So this is really about Jane and not me?'

'Aye, although Ross is taking the opportunity to make sure you and Cole don't get back together. My youngest son's been moping about looking sodding miserable without you.'

'Never mind; he has Kimberly to console him now,' said Carly acidly.

'Who's Kimberly?' Jessica frowned.

'Some slag he met in a nightclub. They're in a relationship.'

'You've got that wrong, hen. Cole's no' in a relationship with anyone.'

'But he updated his status on social media to say he was in a relationship. He even posted a photo of himself with the tart.'

'Oh, now it's making sense. Ross hacked into his profile, probably to fool you. Cole isn't seeing anyone. That girl was someone Ross set his brother up with but he wasn't interested. Cannae say I blame him, by the looks of her she has absolutely no class.'

'And I do?' said Carly wryly.

'Aye, you just don't realise it. Does that make you feel better knowing Cole's still single?'

'I don't feel anything about it.'

Jessica's look was knowing. 'Course not.'

'I hope Ross isn't trying to drag Cole back into his world. He's still on probation and will go straight back to prison if he's caught doing anything.'

'Thankfully his brothers are pretty much leaving him be, except for trying to set him up with wee slappers.'

'He's been in prison for a year. I thought he'd be straight in there.'

'Cole's experience in prison changed him. He's got more maturity about him now, he's not as impulsive, although he's still a cheeky wee bastard,' she added with a fond smile. 'And I've told my other two sons that if they get their brother in trouble with the polis again, I'll cut aff their baws. I won't have it. It's too late for Ross and Dominic, they've chosen their paths, but I'm sure my youngest can be saved, just as long as he keeps his nose clean. It helps that his older brothers have moved out of the family home but they don't live far away, so he can't escape their influence altogether. That's why I have so much respect for you, Carly – you cared about what was best for Cole, not yourself, and you saw his potential. I do wish you'd reconsider taking him back; you could be just what he needs.'

'I couldn't keep him out of prison before and Ross would disrupt my life even more if we did get back together.'

Jessica's eyes shone with hope. Carly hadn't entirely ruled out the possibility.

'Could you tell Ross and Emma that Jane has no intention of re-joining the Bitches? She's got enough on her plate working full time and helping look after our da'. Being part of a gang is the last thing she needs.'

'I'll do my best but I don't think either of them will listen. The problem is, they enjoy causing trouble. It's any excuse with them.'

'Where did they get that idea from in the first place?'

'I've no idea but I think someone's been stirring up trouble. Some people aren't happy unless there's some drama going on somewhere.'

'You're no' wrong there. What does Dominic think about all this?'

'He doesn't care if Jane wants to take over the Bitches or not but he doesn't want you getting back with his younger brother, unlike me and Brian.'

'Brian wants us to get back together too?' said a surprised Carly.

Jessica nodded as she sipped her coffee.

'But I thought he didn't like me?'

'I won't lie, he wasnae keen at first but after Cole got sent to prison, he realised what a good influence you were on him.'

'I see.'

Jessica tilted her head as she studied Carly. 'You look tired, sweetheart.'

'All this business has been keeping me awake at nights.'

'You've got enough going on what with looking after your da' and keeping your head above water. Is there no other family who can help? Doesn't Alec have a brother?'

'Aye, Uncle Eddie, but they haven't spoken in years. They fell out because my uncle kept scrounging off my da'. He has two sons; they'll be in their early twenties by now but I haven't seen them since I was a wee girl.'

'That's such a shame. The only family you have and you're estranged from them.'

Carly shrugged. 'I don't think of them much; I've got enough on my mind.'

'I'll bet. So you haven't seen your uncle or cousins for a while?'

'Not in years.'

'It's so sad when family members become estranged. Do you remember anything about them?'

'Yeah, I think I was twelve when we last saw them. I remember two annoying little boys and my Uncle Eddie. He was pretty funny, he made us laugh.'

'What does he do for a living?'

'I've no idea. From what I could gather, he was a bit of a Jack the Lad and did some ducking and diving but that's all I know.'

'I expect he's big, strong and handsome, like your da'?' said Jessica gently.

'He's big and strong but I don't remember him being very handsome. My da' got all the looks,' replied Carly with a sad smile.

'Does he know about Alec's illness?'

'Aye but he hasn't been in touch. My da' made it very clear he didn't want him around the last time they spoke, so that's probably why.'

'It's a shame because I think you could really use his help. It's important to have family around you when times are hard. Perhaps you should call him? I have a brother and I'd want to help if he was ill.'

'I don't even have a number for him.'

'You da' will.'

'I don't want to mention Uncle Eddie and stress him out, his health's so fragile.'

'Or he might be glad to know his daughters have some help.'

'Maybe. I'll think about it.'

They chatted a little more about more mundane things. Carly had decided before she'd even met Jessica that she wouldn't tell her about Uncle Eddie's imminent arrival in Haghill. She couldn't even be sure he'd turn up; he was rather unpredictable and she didn't want to rock the boat.

Carly was touched when Jessica hugged her and the two women went their separate ways. She felt a little more upbeat as she headed home, hoping Jessica could get through to her son and his vicious cow of a girlfriend. Otherwise that unholy alliance meant the whole of Haghill was doomed.

* * *

'Just me,' she called as she entered the flat.

'In here,' called back Jane.

Carly followed her sister's voice into her father's new bedroom. She came to a startled halt in the doorway when she saw that not only was her Uncle Eddie present, his enormous bulk occupying her father's armchair, but so were his sons Dean and Harry, who stood either side of him as though on guard duty. Her father was sitting up in bed and Jane and Rose sat either side of him.

'Uncle Eddie,' said Carly, recovering from her shock. 'We didn't expect you so soon.'

'Why would I hang about when my family's in trouble?' he boomed in his loud, deep voice.

'I don't know,' she slowly replied. 'Well, thanks for coming. We appreciate it.'

Eddie and his sons certainly made a strong first impression. Eddie himself was very tall and broad like his younger brother, although he had a huge, pendulous belly, something Alec had never developed because of his very physical job and the sports he'd enjoyed playing. Eddie was an idler who did everything he could to avoid work which was one of the reasons the brothers had never really got on, especially because Eddie had continually borrowed off Alec and never paid him back. Eddie too had the thick light brown hair of his brother but he chose to keep it closely cropped to his large head. He wasn't as handsome as Alec but his hazel eyes possessed an intensity that many women found fascinating, a fact he took full advantage of. His sons had both inherited those eyes and when Carly's gaze met theirs she felt herself become slightly flustered. Why was she surrounded by men with incredible eyes? Both men were handsome, tall and strapping, their hair thick and dark blond. Harry was the oldest at twenty-four and Dean was twenty-two. They appeared to be serious and intelligent and were a long way from the little boys who had endlessly irritated her when she was younger.

'All right?' she asked them.

They both nodded in response.

Jane was her usual cool self but Carly noticed Rose kept glancing at the cousins coyly from beneath her eyelashes.

'Jane was just telling us about the problems you've had recently with those shite bags the Alexanders,' said Eddie.

'Language in front of Rose,' murmured Alec.

'What's that?' said Eddie. 'You know I cannae hear very well in my left ear, so speak up.'

'He can't speak up,' Carly told him, the irritation clear in her voice. 'It's part of the illness. And he said no' to swear in front of Rose.'

'Oh aye, sorry pal,' Eddie told his brother.

Alec nodded.

'I'll try and cut out the swearing but it won't be easy,' continued Eddie. 'You know it's just how I speak. Anyway, we're here to help, so what do you want us to do?'

'That's very kind but I've just been speaking to Jessica Alexander, that's Ross's mum,' said Carly. 'She says she's going to talk to her son. Hopefully that should sort it out.'

'I was told she'd already spoken to him and it had done bugger all,' countered Eddie.

'Aye, she did but she's going to try again.'

'And will this second talk be any more successful?'

Carly steadily met her uncle's piercing gaze. He might be a lazy sod but he was very intelligent and knew there was more going on than she was saying. But she'd already decided not to mention what Jessica had told her about Emma thinking Jane wanted to take over the Bitches because her dad would only worry. 'I don't know but it's worth a try.'

'Pricks like this Ross don't gi'e up because their maw tells them to. The only way to stop him from coming at our family is to take direct action. Me and the boys will break his legs, that should do it,' said Eddie, nodding at his sons.

Dean and Harry looked like they were more than capable of snapping a limb but this wasn't what Carly wanted. 'I don't think that will help. I was thinking you could give him a wee scare instead.'

Eddie chuckled. 'That won't do anything. We need to go in hard and fast, hit him before he knows me and the lads are even in Haghill. That's the best way.'

'When Da' said to invite you here I didn't imagine you'd want to start breaking people's legs.'

'Aye, well, this fanny Ross Alexander deserves it. Throwing a brick through the window of a sick man is pathetic and cowardly and he needs to be punished for it.'

There was something very dark that ran in the Savage family's blood and that was the ability to take pleasure in violence. Eddie had it, as did his sons it seemed. Alec used to have it in his younger days, and Carly as well as Jane had inherited it. Even sweet Rose could be very ferocious when provoked. That was why Eddie's words sent a thrill of excitement through Carly. He caught the gleam of pleasure in her eyes and smiled approvingly.

'Then it's settled,' he announced, slapping the arm of the chair. 'We'll solve this with leg snapping.'

'What? No,' she exclaimed. 'And it's not just the Alexander family we need to consider but the Bitches too.'

'Oh aye, I've heard all about them,' he chuckled. 'Wee girls running around vandalising bus shelters and robbing old biddies.'

'Actually, they're a very violent gang who've caused lots of mayhem. Jane kept them on a tight leash but since Emma took charge, they've gone really bad. Dismissing them as silly little girls would be a huge mistake because they're dangerous.'

Eddie's look was sceptical. 'Aye, right.'

'It's true,' said Alec, a look of annoyance crossing his face when he had to pause to swallow.

'Don't you worry about them, pal,' Eddie told his brother. 'We'll deal with them too.'

Alec's sigh indicated he wished his brother would take the threat of the Bitches more seriously but he was unable to express it.

'Anyway,' said Eddie. 'First off, me and the lads plan to scout about a bit. It's been a while since we were last in the area.'

'I thought you said you wanted to keep your presence here a secret?' said Carly.

'I did but then I thought it would be better if our enemies knew we were here. It might make them think twice about chucking another brick through the window. Now, is anyone gonnae get me a drink? I'm parched.'

'Aye,' sighed Carly, already wishing they hadn't called Eddie in. 'I'll do it. What do you want?'

'I don't know. I'll come through and see what you've got.' He looked to his brother. 'Don't you want a drink, Alec?' he said loudly.

'There's no need to shout,' Carly told him. 'His hearing's fine.'

'Was I shouting? Sorry.'

Alec managed to communicate that he didn't want a drink, so Eddie followed Carly through to the kitchen.

Once in the kitchen, Eddie closed the door. 'I'd no idea he'd got so bad so quickly,' he said.

Carly was surprised by the pain in his eyes. 'Aye, the illness progressed quicker than anyone thought it would.'

She was a little startled to find that not only had Eddie followed her into the kitchen, but his sons too. She noted Dean was staring at her a lot more intently than his brother and father and it made her stomach flutter with excitement. She pushed the disturbing notion aside. He was her cousin, for God's sake.

'It makes me wish I hadnae been such a stupid, stubborn bastard and that I'd visited more,' said Eddie. 'But me and your da' have never got on that well, so I thought I was best staying out of his way rather than stressing him out.'

'He missed you.'

'I missed him too. He's the younger brother but it was always him looking out for me. He always was the responsible one. It's a shock seeing him so weak.'

'Only in his body,' she retorted. 'Mentally he's stronger than ever; he has to be to get through each day.'

Eddie's smile was gentle. 'It's really nice how much you and your sisters obviously love him. He's going through a really bad time but in other ways he's really lucky.'

Carly felt some of her anger towards her uncle drain away. 'That's nice of you to say.'

'Don't sound so surprised.' He smiled. 'It does happen occasionally.'

Carly nodded and turned to the kettle. 'We've only got tea, I'm afraid.'

'That'll do nicely.'

As she filled the kettle, Jane entered the room. 'I thought I'd give you a hand with the drinks,' she told Carly, not wanting to leave her sister alone with family who were relative strangers to them.

'It's no' tea we came in here for,' said Eddie. 'It's the information you held back in there,' he added, nodding in the direction of Alec's room.

'Me?' said Carly.

'Aye, you.'

Carly sighed. 'I didn't want to worry Da'.'

'What is it?' Jane asked her.

'Jessica said Emma thinks you want to take over the Bitches. That's another reason why they've been targeting us.'

'That's rubbish,' replied Jane. 'I don't want to get involved with that lot again. It took me long enough to get myself out. Where did she get that bloody stupid idea from?'

'No idea, although Emma does know you have your own supporters who would prefer to have you running things again.'

'It's because Emma's really pushing the boundaries and getting the Bitches into heavier stuff and I've heard she won't let anyone leave. Now she's teamed up with Ross, it'll get even worse for everyone.'

'That makes sense,' said Eddie. 'This Emma tart is feeling threatened and she's trying to take out the competition. You were right Carly, hen, when you said this will get worse.'

'I'll talk to Emma face to face,' said Jane. 'Convince her I'm not interested in leading again.'

'People like that don't want to talk, they only want trouble,' Eddie told her. 'If you speak to her, she'll only twist your words and gi'e herself another excuse to cause more mayhem.'

'He's right,' Carly told her sister.

'I know,' sighed Jane. 'But it's worth a shot. I might take some time off work to deal with this crap; I am owed some holidays.'

'You don't need to worry about cash,' announced Eddie with a satisfied smile before pulling a thick roll of notes out of his jacket pocket and dumping it on the worktop. 'Four grand,' he told his astonished nieces. 'I worked out how much I'd borrowed off Alec over the years and I reckon that covers it as well as the interest.'

'Where did you get four grand from?' Jane asked him.

'I made ten grand betting on the horses. It's about time I paid my debts.'

'That's really good of you Uncle Eddie,' said Carly. 'Thanks.' Relief washed over her. At least they'd be able to put the heating on this winter, as long as the ridiculous fuel prices didn't rise any further.

'You can get a new washing machine,' he said. 'It looks to be on its last legs.'

'It is. Every time we switch it on, we pray it works.'

'We're here to help now. I should have come sooner to help out with Alec but the truth is I was ashamed knowing I owed him so much money and was unable to pay it back. Then I won on the gee-gees and I knew now was my chance. Me and the lads are renting a house a couple of streets away, so you lassies don't need to shoulder the burden alone any more.'

'That's good to know,' said Jane. 'And we appreciate it. The last few years have been so hard.'

'What do you two think about moving to Haghill?' Carly asked her cousins, who had remained silent throughout this exchange.

Harry shrugged. 'We don't mind.'

'Don't you have lives back in Clydebank?'

'Aye, but we can make new lives here.'

She was impressed by how casual they sounded but she wondered if inwardly they were really as blasé about it as they were making out. Dean's eyes met Carly's and once again a thrill ran through her. It was such a shame he was her cousin. The way he stared back at her indicated he didn't care.

Carly turned her back on him to make the tea. Life was complicated enough without adding to it.

7

Eddie bought them all fish and chips for tea and Alec managed to eat the fish with the batter removed. It had been a while since they'd had food from the chippy and they all enjoyed it, their moods lightening. Carly noted the way Rose kept glancing flirtatiously at both Dean and Harry and she feared one of them would respond. After all, Rose was a beautiful girl, but thankfully the way they spoke to her indicated they thought of her as nothing more than a sweet kid. Dean's attention seemed to be more taken up with Carly and when Rose realised this she pouted and transferred all of her attention onto Harry, who seemed a little nonplussed by it.

'Don't forget they're your cousins,' Carly told her little sister when she managed to get her alone while they were tidying up the kitchen together.

'So what? It's legal,' she retorted.

'It's also a bit weird.'

'Course it's not. First cousins get together all the time.' Rose's eyes filled with mischief. 'Dean can't stop looking at you.'

'I know,' she sighed. 'And I wish he'd stop.'

'Oh, come on, why don't you let yourself live a little? There's nothing wrong with having a bit of fun.'

'You're too young to be talking like this,' said Carly disapprovingly.

'I'm sixteen, I've had boyfriends.'

'I don't want to get into all that but I have enough going on and I won't complicate matters.'

'It doesn't matter what you want,' twinkled Rose. 'He won't stop looking at you because he fancies you.'

'He can look all he likes, as long as he doesn't act on it.'

'We'll see.' Rose smiled as she dried a plate and placed it in the cupboard.

Eddie and his sons left the flat at seven o'clock that evening to go to the house they'd rented. The sisters were delighted to see their father looking a lot more cheerful.

'I knew Eddie wouldn't let me down when I really needed him.' He beamed at his daughters. 'And I can't believe he paid me back all that money.'

'I'll put it in the bank first thing tomorrow,' said Carly. 'I don't want to risk it getting nicked.'

'It was great seeing him and my nephews again,' continued Alec.

'His sons are very quiet, aren't they?' commented Carly, ignoring the smile Rose gave her.

'They always were,' replied Alec. 'Right from being wee.'

'I don't remember them being quiet when we were weans. In fact, they were bloody annoying calling me Carly Barley, as though that was funny.'

'Wee boys are daft,' said Rose. 'I should know, I go to school with enough of them.'

'They got silly around you girls...' began Alec, his daughters patiently waiting while he swallowed and dabbed at his lips with a tissue, 'because you were pretty. Dean always had a crush on you, Carly.'

'I knew it,' exclaimed Rose. 'He couldn't stop staring at her.'

'We all noticed,' said Jane.

'Never mind that,' mumbled Carly, embarrassed. 'We need to concentrate on getting Ross and Emma to back off.'

'And we will,' said Jane. 'Don't worry about it.'

'It was great spending time with my brother today,' murmured Alec. His eyes misted over. 'So many years lost because we fell out over money. Promise me you three will never let anything come between you.'

'Of course we won't, Da',' said Rose.

'Good, because family is so important...' Alec's words trailed off. The day had really taken it out of him.

'Get some sleep,' Carly told him. 'Eddie will be round in the morning.'

After ensuring he was comfortable and settled, the sisters returned to the kitchen to talk.

'I'll call work on Monday,' said Jane as they sat around the table. 'I'm owed some time off.'

'Won't they complain about it being such short notice?' Carly asked her. One of her worst fears was Jane losing her job. They couldn't cope without her wages.

'Naw, they'll be fine if I tell them it's a family emergency.'

'Can I stay off school?' said Rose.

'No,' Carly and Jane replied in unison.

'That's not fair. I'm under stress too.'

'You've got exams coming up,' Jane told her. 'So it's important that you go in.'

'Fine,' she sighed. 'Only a few months to go then my slavery will be over.'

'Until you start college,' Carly told her.

'Maybe I should get a job instead? We could use the money.'

'No,' said Jane firmly. 'We can manage. You're going to get a proper education.'

'But we need the money more.'

'We're fine as we are. Besides, there's no jobs about. You're much better off getting an education so you can have a good career.'

'I feel so bad when you two had to give up your own educations.'

'We can always go back to them in a few years,' said Jane. 'And we gave it up for you. Please don't let our sacrifice be in vain.'

Rose nodded and bit her lip.

'What's wrong?' said Carly when her eyes filled with tears.

'I don't want you to make sacrifices for me. It makes me feel really bad.'

'Please don't. We're happy to do it.'

'But you shouldn't have to put your lives on hold for me. It's not fair.'

'It is fair,' Jane told her. 'Because you're the best of the three of us with the brightest future.'

'That's a load of shite.'

Jane's expression became severe. 'Don't swear. It upsets Da'.'

'He can't hear me and I'm old enough to say shite. Besides, you're only trying to change the subject. You two are so clever and you deserve real careers, not working in a pub or a call centre.'

'I love my job actually,' said Carly. 'Only last week Derek was on about promoting me to manager. I'd be happy running a pub; it's fun.'

'Serving auld biddies and drunk jakeys.'

'Don't let Derek hear you say he lets jakeys into his pub. Anyway, never mind about us. We're talking about you. Once you've gone through your education, we can finish ours, so you'd better get on with it.'

'And you don't hate me for it?'

'Of course not,' said Carly, taking her hand. 'We love you so much. All we have is each other and Da'. You're the one who cheers us all up when things get us down and you help us get through each day. You've no idea how much me and Jane treasure that.'

'You're not just patronising me, are you?' said Rose suspiciously.

'Of course not. Jane knows what I mean, don't you?'

'I do,' she said, taking Rose's other hand. 'So let us support you like you support us,' she told her younger sister.

Rose's smile returned. 'Deal. Besides, we're not alone any more. Now we have Uncle Eddie and our cousins.'

Carly forced a smile. 'True.' She wasn't convinced yet that the three men would help their situation. There was the strong possibility they could make it a hell of a lot worse.

* * *

Carly had promised to help Derek with the stock take before the pub opened that day, so she was going in early. It was the least she could do after all he'd done for her. Just as she was pulling on her coat and shoes to leave the house, her uncle and cousins arrived at the flat.

'Looks like you're just in time, Dean,' said Eddie.

'What do you mean?' Carly frowned.

'He's going to escort you to work.'

'Why? I know the way.'

'Because Ross and Emma may choose to attack you when you're

alone and vulnerable. From now on, no one goes about by themselves. Rose will get a lift into school.'

'Will Harry be taking me?' Rose said, trying to sound casual and failing.

'No,' said Eddie. 'I'll be driving you in.'

Jane smiled when Rose pouted and folded her arms across her chest.

'I really don't need an escort,' protested Carly, glancing at Dean, who was still staring at her.

'Listen, hen,' said Eddie reasonably. 'You called me in to help and this is me helping, so let Dean take you to work, okay?'

Carly glanced at Jane, who nodded. She looked back at her uncle. 'Okay, fine.'

'Good. Off you go then, you don't want to be late.'

Carly left the house with Dean, the pair of them walking in silence.

'Don't you ever speak?' Carly asked him when she could take the silence no more.

'What do you want me to say?' he replied.

'We haven't seen each other in years, so there must be something.'

He shrugged. 'You still into Barbies?'

'What a bloody stupid question.'

'You wanted me to say something, so I did.'

'What do you do?' she said, unable to think of anything else.

'For a job?'

'Aye.'

'This and that.'

'What does that mean?'

'Sometimes I have work, sometimes I don't.'

Carly huffed, getting the feeling he was playing with her. 'How old are you now, twenty-two?'

'Aye.'

'And Harry's twenty-four?'

'Aye.'

'You're not big on conversation, are you?'

'Should I be?'

'People who rabbit on are annoying but you should at least say something.'

'Why?'

'I don't know, just… because it's polite.'

His smile was amused. 'I only speak when I have something to say.'

'Surely meeting up with a family member involves a little chit-chat?'

'Only if that family member has something interesting to say.'

'Are you calling me boring?' she demanded, becoming increasingly irritated.

'I don't know if you're boring because we haven't seen each other for ages.'

Carly grunted with annoyance. 'You might find out if you spoke to me.'

'But I have been speaking to you.'

Carly had to bite her lip to prevent herself from snapping at him in irritation. 'Let's start again. So,' she said, attempting to come up with a question he might consider interesting. Her mind drew a blank.

Dean didn't fill the silence as they continued to walk down the street together, Carly frantically trying to think of something to say.

'Do you have a boyfriend?' he asked her before she could think of something witty and scintillating.

'That's a bit personal, isn't it?' she replied.

'You're the one who wanted to chat and find out about each other's lives.'

Carly had to admit that he had a point. 'No, I don't. Do you have a girlfriend?'

'I did but we broke up six months ago.'

'Why, did she find you annoying too?'

Dean smiled. 'Naw. She annoyed me actually. She wouldn't stop talking.'

Carly raised an eyebrow. 'Seriously?'

'Aye.'

'You probably confused the hell out of the poor lassie. She wouldn't know whether to talk or keep her mouth shut. I should know because I'm experiencing the same thing myself.'

'Give over, Carly. You're the type of woman who always knows exactly what to do and how to act.'

'No, I don't. Like everyone else, I stumble through life just trying to do my best.'

'You have good instincts, better than most. They'll see you right.'

'How can you know that about me when we've only just met after years apart?'

'Because I can tell these things. I have strong instincts myself and we are a lot alike.'

'Okay,' she said slowly.

Dean lapsed into silence, to Carly's relief, although she couldn't help but keep glancing sideways at him. This man was an enigma. With Cole what you saw was what you got but Dean definitely had hidden depths.

'The pub's just there,' she told him when they turned onto the street, gesturing to the signage.

'I've to come in with you.'

'You don't have to.'

'It's my da's orders.'

'Do you always obey your da'?'

'Do you?'

Carly was annoyed that she couldn't deny it. 'Fine, you can see me inside.'

'I've to wait while you work your shift.'

'But I'm on an eight-hour shift today. I'm doing a stock take.'

'That's fine. I can entertain myself.'

'Not by drinking, I hope? Because I'm no' carrying you home.'

'I rarely drink alcohol, just the odd pint now and then.'

'Really? Then you're a novelty in this family.'

'Alcohol makes you lose control and I don't like losing control.'

Carly thought his statement a very admirable one. 'Do Harry and Uncle Eddie drink?'

'My da' likes a bevvy but Harry's like me, although he does go clubbing more than I do. What about you? Do you get much chance to blow off steam?'

'No, not really. When I'm no' working I'm at home, looking after Da'. Rose goes to school and Jane works full time.'

'So most of his care lands on you?'

'A couple of nurses visit twice a day. They help him shower and take his medication.'

'So the answer's yes?'

Carly sighed. 'Aye.'

'That must be hard.'

'Sometimes.' She was about to confide in him more until she recalled that she was supposed to be starting work. Dean was once again staring at her intently and excitement as well as unease swelled inside her.

It was a relief when she entered the pub and was greeted with Derek's cheerful smile.

'Thank Christ you're here, Carly,' he told her. 'I really need a pish.'

'What's new?' She smiled. 'Away you go then.'

Derek's eyes flicked to Dean. 'Who's this?'

'My cousin, Dean. He's come to stay for a bit.'

'Oh, I see.' He extended his hand across the bar. 'Nice to meet you.'

'You too,' replied Dean politely, shaking his hand.

'Go to the loo before you pee yourself,' Carly told her boss when he stood there, jiggling.

'Aye, I'm off,' he said before tearing out from behind the bar in the direction of the toilets.

Carly put her bag and coat in the office and took up position behind the bar. 'Do you want a drink?' she asked Dean. 'On the house, seeing how you're my designated bodyguard for the day.'

'I'll have an orange juice, please. That's all I drink when I'm working.'

'Working? Wait, is this actually your job?'

'Sometimes.'

'You're a professional bodyguard?'

'I wouldn't say professional but it's no' the first time I've done it.'

'For who?'

He shrugged. 'Anyone who needs my help.'

'You get paid for it?'

'Aye.'

'Does Harry do the same thing?'

'Aye.'

'Dammit, you're gonnae make me ask every individual question, aren't you, rather than just tell me the whole story?'

'Aye because that's who I am.'

Carly stared back at him as she formulated her next question. She was finding Dean Savage increasingly fascinating.

'I think a person could know you for fifty years and never really find out who you are,' she said.

His response was a smile that she found very seductive.

Carly realised she was staring at him and snapped herself out of it. She had work to do and life was complicated enough without getting involved with her own cousin. 'I've got to start the stock take.'

Carly poured Dean his drink and placed it before him on the bar while avoiding his gaze, not wanting to get caught up in it. His eyes were like nets. Once you looked into them, they captured you.

Derek went down into the cellar to count the stock they had there, leaving Carly alone upstairs with Dean. The doors were kept locked as the pub wasn't officially open yet, so they didn't need to worry about anyone walking in.

As she worked, counting the lager bottles behind the bar and making a note of each total, Carly could feel Dean's gaze boring into her. Twice she made the mistake of glancing in the mirror behind the bar and their eyes met. The third time she looked, she was disappointed to see he had his head down, reading a book. She straightened up and turned to look at him.

'What are you reading?' she said. 'And if you say "a book" I'll spray you in the face with the post mix.'

He looked up and smiled. '*War and Peace*.'

'Tolstoy?' she said sceptically, thinking he was having her on. 'Seriously?'

'Aye. How no?'

'Because...' She trailed off, embarrassed by her own thoughts.

'Because you think I'm too thick to read a book like this?'

'No, course not.'

'That's exactly what you were thinking.'

'I wasn't, honestly. I've no idea if you're clever or thick.'

'Well, I'm not thick,' he replied. 'I like classic literature, classical music and art.'

'Really?'

'Aye, or is a son of Eddie Savage not allowed to enjoy the finer things in life? Would you prefer it if I got into fights at football matches and crushed beer cans against my forehead?'

'Like your da'?'

He nodded hard. 'I grew up watching him do things like that and swore I would never be the same.'

Carly smiled when anger flashed in his eyes. 'Wow, I touched a nerve there.'

'That's because I'm sick of people thinking I'm stupid just because I'm a Savage.'

'Hey, people don't say that about us.'

'Because Alec's your da'. If you had mine it would be different.'

Carly decided a change of tack would be a good idea. Still, it was nice knowing which buttons to push. 'Is it a good book?'

'Hard to say. I've only just started it. Do you like to read?'

'Aye, sometimes.'

'What do you read?'

His eyes had lit up with eagerness. Clearly this was a subject that was close to his heart but she didn't think he'd like her answer. 'I like factual stuff, biographies mainly.'

'Whose biographies?'

'Famous actors and actresses.'

The pain the disappointment in his eyes caused Carly rather surprised her.

'We can't all be intellectuals,' she added with an impish smile.

She was glad when he returned her smile.

There came the sound of Derek hauling himself up the cellar steps and the spell was broken. Dean returned his attention to his book while Carly got back to her counting.

8

The stock take was completed in time for the pub doors to open at eleven o'clock that morning. Brenda and her two friends were the first customers, in for their usual Sunday bender. They walked in and came to a startled halt when they saw Dean sitting at the bar. Recovering themselves, they immediately strode up to him. As his head was buried in his book, he failed to notice them until they were standing right beside him.

'And who is this?' purred Brenda.

'My cousin Dean,' replied Carly.

'Oh.' Brenda smiled, her two friends standing either side of her cooing over him like pigeons. 'Are you a Savage too, Dean?'

'I am,' he replied. 'Our da's are brothers.'

'I can see the resemblance,' said Brenda, her eyes running up and down him appreciatively. 'Alec Savage always was a fine-looking man, so I'm assuming your da' is the same?'

'Not really,' commented Carly.

'How long are you in the area for, Dean?' said Brenda.

He gave her another of his shrugs. 'Dunno. We're playing it by ear.'

'We? Are there more of you?'

'My brother Harry and our da.'

'There's three of you?' said Brenda, her eyes lighting up.

'Aye.'

'You hear that, girls?' Brenda grinned.

'I think they do,' said Carly flatly when the women – who were all old enough to be Dean's mother – began to squawk excitedly.

Derek returned to the bar after another trip to the toilet. 'Brenda.' He smiled. 'Lovely to see you, as always.'

'Aye, all right, Derek,' she muttered, waving a hand in his general direction while keeping her gaze on Dean, who was pretending not to notice the attention.

'I think you have some competition,' Carly told her boss.

'How the bloody hell am I supposed to compete with that?' he replied, nodding at Dean.

'Just be yourself, you're fine as you are.'

'Tell them that,' he muttered, gesturing to Brenda and her friends, who were still cooing over Dean.

'So,' said Derek. 'Who wants a drink on the house?' He beamed with satisfaction when the three women finally turned their attention on him.

Dean breathed a sigh of relief and buried himself deeper into his book.

'Do you want another orange juice?' Carly asked him.

'Aye, go on then.'

Just as she placed Dean's drink before him, the door opened and in walked Cole, who didn't look very pleased to see Carly serving a very handsome man. He hesitated in the doorway, glaring at Dean. Sensing he was being watched, Dean turned in his seat to regard him and the two men stared at each other.

'Hello, Cole?' called Carly.

This snapped him out of it and he stormed up to the bar. 'Who the hell's that?' he demanded.

'My cousin,' Carly told him. 'And there's no need to be so rude.'

Dean merely regarded the other man disinterestedly before looking back down at his book.

Carly nodded Cole over to the far side of the bar, away from everyone.

'What are you doing here?' she hissed at him. 'If Ross finds out you came anywhere near me...'

'That's why I'm here. Maw told me about what he's been doing. We've both had a word and told him to stop bothering you and he's promised he will.'

'Aye, right. He never listens to anyone; he just does what he wants.'

'No, he really will. He even said he wouldnae mind if we got back together.'

'That's absolute bollocks. He's a spiteful bastard who enjoys tormenting people and he'll use any excuse. Besides, we're not getting back together.'

Cole's eyes slipped to Dean. 'Why, is that your new boyfriend?'

'Don't be ridiculous. Like I said, he's my cousin.'

'So?'

'He's here to keep an eye on me because of your brother and that cow Emma Wilkinson.'

'There's really nothing between you and Dean?'

'No. Don't be gross; I've known him since I was wee.'

'You've never mentioned him before.'

'Because we haven't seen each other in years. My da' asked us to call my uncle Eddie when your brother chucked a brick through his bedroom window.'

'I heard about that and I'm so sorry,' Cole said, looking genuinely upset. 'Is Alec okay?'

'Aye, thankfully, although he was really shaken up.'

'That was fucking cowardly. Ross knew that was Alec's window.'

'What do you expect? Your brother's a bully and like all bullies he's a coward at heart.'

'You're probably right. Anyway, I came to ask if you'll come out with me.'

'You mean like a date?'

'Aye. We need to talk properly.'

Carly sighed. 'I don't want anything else to happen to my family because of our relationship.'

'It won't, I promise. I've already run it past Ross and he's promised to back off and leave you all alone.'

'And you believed him?'

'I did. I know what you think about him but he's really not all bad.'

'I'm no' so sure about that,' she muttered.

'Please, Carly. We have things to sort out.'

She chewed her lip as she considered her options. She really did want to go out with him; he was right, there was unfinished business between them but she was so afraid of Ross going back on his word. There was her father to consider too but with Jane taking a few days off work, he would be looked after. When she gazed into Cole's beautiful green eyes, she was decided. 'All right then.'

'Great,' he said, smiling.

'But on the understanding that it's nothing romantic. We're just going out as friends.'

'Got it.'

'And we go somewhere away from Haghill. I don't want to risk bumping into Ross or Emma.'

'No problem. My maw said I can borrow her car, so can I pick you up tonight?'

'Aye, all right. My shift ends at four and I'll need to shower and change first.'

'I can pick you up here and drive you home.'

'No,' she replied, not wanting her father to see him because he'd only worry that they were getting back together. 'Pick me up at six at the end of the street by the post box.'

'Why, are you ashamed of me?' he said, eyes narrowing.

'I don't want to do anything to worry my da'. His health's so precarious right now.'

Cole's gaze softened. 'All right, I can understand that. I'll see you at six then.'

As he left, he glanced at Dean and was reassured when he saw he was paying them no attention.

When Cole had gone, Carly got lost in her own thoughts, wondering if she was doing the right thing.

'You should stay well away from him,' said a voice.

Carly looked to Dean and frowned. 'What did you say?'

Dean raised his head from his book to look at her. 'I said, you should stay well away from him. He's nothing but trouble.'

'You don't even know him.'

'I know enough. You're making a mistake.'

'We're only going out as friends.'

'There are some people that trouble follows everywhere and he is one of them.'

'How can you say that about a man you've not even spoken to?'

'Remember what I said about my strong instincts? Well, I wasn't lying.'

'You know nothing about it,' she snapped.

'Oh dear.'

'Oh dear what?' She scowled.

'You have got it bad.'

'No, I don't. He's my ex; we broke up ages ago.'

'That doesn't always mean you stop loving someone.'

Carly glanced at Derek but he was too busy chatting up Brenda and her friends to notice. She leaned on the bar to hiss at her cousin.

'That is absolutely none of your business.'

'Actually, it is,' replied Dean. 'I've been brought here to protect you and if that creep...'

'His name's Cole.'

'If Cole is going to put you in danger then I wouldn't be doing my job if I didn't warn you.'

'He won't put me in danger. He said he's already spoken to his brother and Ross has said he'll leave me and my family alone, so you don't need to hang around any more.'

'Ross might have told him that but I doubt he meant it. People like that never do.'

'So you know all about Ross too, do you?'

'Oh aye. A petty bully boy who wants to get into the criminal big leagues but is too wild and impulsive to make it. Loose cannons like him always end up dead or in prison. He won't care what his wee brother says.'

'You have done your research, haven't you?'

'Course I have. We never take on a job without looking into a situation first. It's only sensible to understand what you're getting into.'

'Not that it's any of your business but me and Cole have things to discuss. We need to put our relationship to rest properly so we can both move on.'

'He's no intention of moving on. He's gonnae try and win you back. Don't give in.'

'Just keep your nose out of my life.'

'I'm here to help, Carly. When you're ready to accept that help, I'll be waiting.'

To her intense irritation, he returned his attention to his book. He smiled when she grunted with frustration, yanked open the glass washer door and pulled out the tray full of hot, steaming glasses, making them clatter together.

* * *

Carly's shift passed uneventfully, and Dean walked her home in silence. She refused to speak to him as she was still pissed off about what he'd said and she couldn't decide whether that was because she thought he was unfairly judging Cole or if it was because she knew he was speaking sense.

She only deigned to speak to him when they turned onto her street.

'Don't say anything to my da' about me meeting Cole this evening, will you?'

'How no?' replied Dean.

'Because it'll upset him and that will impact on his health.'

'If you don't want to upset your da' then don't go out with Cole.'

'It'll just be this once.'

'Aye, right.'

'God you're annoying.'

'You find me annoying because you know I'm right.'

'Just promise not to tell my da', okay?'

'Fine, I promise but stay safe tonight. Don't go anywhere isolated with him.'

'Cole would never hurt me.'

'Probably not but you can't trust that his family won't.'

'It's only Ross who's dangerous.'

'I looked into the Alexander family. They're thieves and muggers who'll do anything for a few quid.'

'The two older brothers and Brian maybe, but not Cole and Jessica.'

'Yes, them too, Carly. They're all as bad as each other.'

'What do you know about it? You've never even met them.'

He gave one of his annoying shrugs. 'I know enough.'

She sighed with exasperation and shook her head.

'Where will you tell your da' you're going tonight?' said Dean.

'I'll say I'm working an extra shift. Jane will cover for me.'

'You're going to tell her the truth?'

'Yes.'

'All right but don't say I didn't warn you.'

'I won't,' she muttered, eyes flashing as she stalked into the flat.

Rose was already back from school and was doing her homework in her bedroom. As she was constantly aware of the sacrifice her sisters had made so she could get a good education, she was very conscientious about her schoolwork. This gave Carly the opportunity to speak to Jane in private. Eddie and Harry were watching television in the kitchen, so they went into Carly's bedroom to talk.

'I need you to do me a favour,' began Carly, her voice a whisper.

'What favour and why are you whispering? Da's asleep.'

'I don't want anyone else hearing this. I'm meeting Cole at six o'clock.'

'Oh no, you've not given in to him, have you?'

'There are things we need to sort out. It will never be over between us until we have this talk.'

'It's been over for months. Don't do this, he'll only draw you back in.'

'I need to do this.'

Jane looked into her sister's eyes and saw the anguish there. If this conversation finally helped Carly lay her relationship with Cole to rest then that could only be for the best but Jane had the horrible feeling it wouldn't work out that way. 'Okay, fine, you're an adult and can do what you like. I'll make sure Da' doesn't hear about it, but please be careful.'

Jane's eyes were filled with disapproval but Carly had no choice. She had to do this.

* * *

Carly was tempted to put on make-up and her best clothes for her date with Cole, but instead she stuck to jumper, jeans and just a dab of eyeshadow. No lipstick. She knew she'd made the right decision when Jane gave her an approving nod on her way out the door.

'What are you doing?' said Carly when Dean followed her outside.

'Protecting you. It's my job, remember.'

'You are not coming out with me and Cole. I'm not having you sitting there like a big gooseberry reading a book.'

'As if I would,' he said, amused by the idea. 'I'll just wait with you until Cole arrives.'

'He'll already be waiting for me. He won't leave me hanging around on the pavement.'

'What if he's not?'

'He will be,' she said confidently as they headed down the street together.

'Don't you find it weird living across the road from a graveyard?' he said, nodding at it as they passed it by.

'Not really. I barely notice it any more. Why, are you scared?' she said with a mischievous smile.

'No, although I do find it interesting. I'd like to take a walk through it sometime.'

Carly thought that he may be really hot but he was a little odd. 'Whatever floats your boat,' she commented.

As they reached the end of the street, Carly smiled to see a white BMW sitting at the kerb with Cole in the driver's seat.

'See, there he is,' Carly smugly told Dean.

'Be careful, won't you?'

'I'm only going out for a drink with my ex, not hiking up Everest.'

'There are different types of danger,' he said, regarding the BMW mistrustfully.

'I'll be fine.'

'What time will you be back?' he asked as she walked up to the car.

'No idea,' she replied before opening the door and getting in.

She glanced at Cole, who was staring back at her with a smile. He wore a black leather jacket, smart black shirt underneath and black trousers. His green eyes had never seemed brighter. He looked sexy and dangerous and excitement ran through her.

'What the hell is he doing?' he said, nodding at Dean, who was regarding Carly disapprovingly through the window.

'He's still on bodyguard duty.'

'You're on your own street.'

'Let's just get out of here. It's weird the way he keeps staring at us.'

Cole put the car into gear, indicated, checked his mirrors and pulled out into the road. Carly glanced in the passenger wing mirror and saw Dean standing on the pavement, still staring at them. Was there something wrong with the man?

'Ross said he'll leave you alone,' said Cole, eyes flashing. 'So there's no need for your cousin to follow you about any more.'

'You're jealous, aren't you?' She smiled.

'No,' Cole retorted, then sighed. 'All right, I am. If he had a face like a bulldog, it wouldn't be a problem.'

'Yes, he is good-looking, isn't he?' she said, enjoying winding Cole up.

'A bit I suppose,' he muttered, wrenching the gearstick. 'Anyway,' he said, forcing the smile back on his face. 'I thought we could go into the west end, grab something to eat and then go on to a couple of clubs.'

'This is supposed to be a quiet chat, no' a night out.'

'But we've been apart for a year. I want to spend time with you.'

'I am not going clubbing. You can take me for a meal but that's it.'

'How long is it since you went to a club?'

'That's beside the point,' she said, thinking how nice it would be to drink and dance and let herself go. It had been so long but she knew Cole. He was hoping to suck her back into his world and the thought of her dad and sisters was enough to give her the strength to resist. 'A meal and that's it or you can take me straight home.'

'Fine, I'll take you somewhere really nice. I want to spoil you.'

'A greasy spoon will do. I'm not dressed for anywhere fancy.'

'I bet it's been a while since you ate out?'

'Don't start all that again. A simple, quiet restaurant or the deal's off.'

Carly didn't ask where he'd got the money from to spoil her. He was still on probation, so she hoped his parents had given it to him and that he hadn't obtained it illegally.

'Have it your own way,' he muttered.

Carly knew he was pissed off that things weren't going as he'd planned but she was determined to stick to her guns. Cole was very charming and knew how to get his own way, so she would have to stay on her guard.

9

Cole drove to the Glasgow Fort shopping centre ten minutes away from Haghill.

'Is this boring enough for you?' he said as he switched off the engine. All the shops had closed but the restaurants and cinema were still open.

'This will do fine,' replied Carly.

They got out of the car and walked into a large chain restaurant that was already busy. Cole requested a quiet table in a corner, away from the other diners. The waitress led them to their table, handed them menus, took their drinks order and left them to it.

Cole dumped his menu on the table and placed his hand over Carly's, which rested on the tabletop. 'Thanks for coming out with me tonight. I really appreciate it.'

'You're welcome.' She wondered if it would be rude to remove her hand from his. After all, she wanted to keep things civil. She would much prefer it if they could remain friends, so she decided to leave her hand where it was.

'It's much more than I deserve. When I was inside, I kept

thinking about all the warnings you gave me. You tried to save me so many times but I was too stupid and stubborn to listen.'

'You mean you let your brothers lead you astray?' she said with a disapproving frown.

'Aye, I wasn't strong enough to tell them no, but things have changed. Prison made me grow up and I'm my own man now. I won't let them drag me back into that life. I mean it,' he added when she raised a sceptical eyebrow.

'We'll see. Ross can be very persuasive.'

'I'm stronger now and I won't let him bully me into things any more.'

'He didn't bully you; you were more than happy to go along with all his stupid suggestions.'

Cole sighed and nodded. 'You're right, I won't deny it but this time things will be different. I don't want to go back to prison.'

'Was it really bad inside?'

'I wouldn't say that. My brothers have friends in Bar-L and they looked out for me. Having my freedom taken from me was the hardest thing. The nights were difficult too. Knowing I was locked in and unable to get out drove me demented. I'd rather die than go back there.'

'Don't say things like that.' She shivered.

'I have to, so you know I'm serious about changing my ways. I'm well out of my old life.'

'How can you be when you hang around with your brothers? And I know your maw and da' get up to their old tricks sometimes. It's how they can afford that BMW. Ross has one too.'

'My brothers have moved out and got their own places.'

'But they're still in Haghill, close by.'

'Aye, it's their home and that will never change.'

'And they'll always be a bad influence on you, especially Ross.

He's incapable of changing so he wants to drag everyone down to his level.'

'He's no' all bad you know. He can be a good laugh and he's really generous with his cash, when he has some spare. He's looked out for me all my life.'

'Looked out for you? He was the reason why you were sent to prison.'

It was then they realised the waitress had returned to take their order.

'I can come back,' she told them awkwardly.

'No, it's all right,' said Carly before ordering a burger and fries.

Cole ordered fish and chips. The waitress gave them their drinks and then left them alone again.

'Ross didn't mean for that to happen,' Cole told Carly. 'Anyway, that's all water under the bridge. I want to put it all behind me and get on with my life.'

Carly didn't want to get into an argument about Ross Alexander in the middle of a restaurant, so she decided to let that particular subject drop. 'That sounds like a good idea. Have you got a job?'

'Aye. Ross has got me one at a garage as a mechanic.'

'Really? That's great news. You love cars and you're so good at fixing them.'

'Yeah, it's pretty perfect for me and they get in some nice motors too. It's no' all old bangers.'

'Do they treat you well?'

'Aye. I work with two other blokes. They're friendly and we have a good laugh. The pay's no' bad too. My probation officer's pleased.'

'That's good. I'm so happy for you.'

'I have to stay with my parents until my probation's finished, so I'm saving up to get my own flat. Maw's only charging me a wee bit of rent so I can save.'

'That's kind of her,' she said, smiling.

'She's the best.'

'You're very lucky to have her.'

'I know. She's been really supportive.'

'How's your da' been with you?'

'Okay. He was pissed off with me at first for getting caught but he's come round now. He slips me a few quid when he has some spare cash to add to my savings and he's pleased I'm working as a mechanic.'

'Well, I think that's great. I just hope you manage to stay on the straight and narrow.'

'I really mean to this time.'

The conversation turned to Carly's life, Cole asking how things had been for her while he'd been inside. He was kind and sympathetic, gently taking her hand when tears filled her eyes as she discussed her father's condition. They then discussed more pleasant topics and talked and laughed like they used to. Carly found she was really enjoying herself for the first time in months. Cole had always been able to make her laugh.

When they'd finished their main courses, he ordered salted caramel chocolate cake for them both, knowing how much she loved salted caramel. Carly even let herself go and had a couple of glasses of wine but refused a third when he tried to press it on her. She was pleased that he didn't have any alcohol as he was driving. He had been known to drink and drive before. Perhaps this really was a new, sensible Cole after all?

He paid the bill and they left and Carly was in such a good mood she even let him take her hand as they walked back to the car.

'Do you want me to take you home now?' he asked her.

Carly longed to say no and ask him to take her on to a club. She was having such a nice time and she didn't want it to end but she'd made herself and her sister a promise and she would keep it. 'Yes,' she told him.

Cole's eyes flickered with disappointment but he didn't press the issue. 'Okay, whatever the lady wants.'

They got back into the car and left the Fort. As they took the road that would lead them back to Haghill, Cole said, 'I want you back, Carly.'

'I had a feeling you were going to say that.'

'I want you to move in with me when I get the flat I'm saving up for.'

'You dumped me, remember?'

'Only because I was ashamed of who I was, but I've changed. I'm not the man you deserve yet, but I will be one day. I've got a steady job, I'm keeping my nose clean and I've matured. I'm not the stupid, headstrong boy I used to be. Please give me another chance.'

'I can't. If my da' found out...'

'Don't tell him. Not until I can prove myself anyway.'

'I thought this evening was about finally laying our relationship to rest,' she said, gazing at him sadly.

'No' to me it wasn't.'

'And what if you decide to dump me again?'

'I would never do that. My plan is after a couple of years of living together we get married.'

Carly's eyebrows shot up. 'The word marriage always used to terrify you.'

'Aye, I found it intimidating but when I was in Bar-L I had a lot of time to think and what I missed most when I was inside was you. I imagined us together in our own place, waking up in the same bed every morning, curling up on the couch together in the evenings.'

'You'd soon get bored and want to go out clubbing every night. You could never settle down.'

'No, really I can and I want to spend the rest of my life with you.'

Carly sighed heavily and turned her gaze to the window. Cole glanced sideways at her when she didn't reply, being careful to keep one eye on the road.

'What are you thinking?' he asked her.

'I don't know,' she murmured.

He took this as a sign that she was actually considering his proposal and hope rose inside him. 'We can have a great life together, I know it.'

'We're both so young,' she replied. She turned to face him, forehead creased with anger. 'And who was that orange tart in your photos on social media?'

'She was nothing to do with me; she's a friend of Ross's. He thought I'd want to err...'

'He thought the first thing you'd want to do when you were released from prison was have sex with someone who looked like they'd spent too long on a sunbed?'

'Aye,' he sighed. 'But I didnae touch her. You're the only woman I want.'

'So you really haven't been with anyone since you were released?'

'No. I'm no' lying,' he added when she studied him suspiciously. 'Have you...?'

'No.'

Cole breathed a sigh of relief.

'I would have waited for you,' she said. 'You didn't need to dump me but you did.'

'What are you saying?'

Carly took a deep breath. She had to be strong for her family if not for herself. 'That we're over. I don't want to get back with you.'

He stared straight ahead but didn't speak.

'Did you hear what I said?' she asked him. 'Cole?' she repeated when he failed to reply.

Carly gasped and grabbed onto the door when he suddenly swung the car to the left and pulled up at the side of the road.

'Jesus,' she exclaimed. 'What are you doing?'

He switched off the engine and turned to face her. 'We can't be over.'

'Well we are. The problem is I won't just get you, I'll get your whole family too and they'll never stop trying to cause trouble between us. It'll be a nightmare.'

'Ross has already promised...'

'Ross is a fucking liar,' she yelled in his face. 'Everyone seems to understand that except you. He'll make our lives a misery and we'll break up again and I can't go through all that. My da's illness is taking all my spare time and energy. I don't have room for anything else in my life right now and that includes a relationship with you.'

'Then maybe there's hope for us when your da'...' He went abruptly silent.

'Were you going to say when he dies?' she exclaimed.

'No,' he mumbled.

'You haven't changed at all; you're still selfish and self-absorbed.'

'I am not self-absorbed,' he retorted. 'I just love you. Why is that so bad?'

'It's not but you don't seem to understand that I can't deal with a relationship right now, especially one that will bring me no end of hassle. Every morning I get up terrified that my da's condition will have got worse or that he might die. I worry about Rose going off the rails or Jane breaking under the weight that's been placed on her shoulders. I worry about how we're going to put food on the table and pay the bills. I can't deal with worrying about your brother throwing bricks through our windows or you going back to prison on top of all that.' Tears shone in her eyes. 'It will break me and if you care for me at all you'll back off.'

'I'm sorry,' he said, stricken by the pain in her eyes. 'I'd no idea it was that bad for you.'

When he enveloped her in his arms she collapsed into his chest and sobbed. Cole didn't speak, he just held her and kissed her hair.

When her sobs began to ease before trailing off altogether, they remained with their arms locked around each other, Carly resting her head on his shoulder.

'Thanks for letting me get that out,' she murmured.

'You're welcome. You needed to vent.'

'I did. I keep it all in and, before you say it, I know that's no' healthy.'

She gazed up at him and he stroked her face with his thumb. Carly felt too exhausted to object when he pressed his lips to hers. She responded to the kiss, which was gentle and tender and filled her with longing. There was no doubt she still loved this man and part of her was tempted to throw caution to the wind and rekindle their relationship but just the memory of her father, scared and trembling after that brick had come through his window, was enough to stop her. If anything happened to him because of her she wasn't sure she'd be able to go on living. This time in her life was about sacrifice – of her education, career and her love life. All she could do was hope she earned some grace and got repaid for this sacrifice later in life.

When the kiss grew more passionate and Carly felt that familiar desire gripping her, she pulled away.

'Think of that as a goodbye kiss,' she told him, pressing her hand to his cheek.

Cole sighed and released her, eyes flashing.

'I'm sorry,' she said softly. 'Really I am and I hope we can be friends.'

'Friends,' he grunted. 'I don't want to be friends, I want more.'

'Sorry, that can't happen. I really hope you understand why there's no room in my life for you.'

He turned to her, green eyes bright with anger. 'I bet you've got room for your cousin, haven't you?'

She frowned. 'Dean?'

'You don't want me because you've got him now.'

'Don't be ridiculous.'

'He fancies you. Any idiot can see that.'

'You're wrong and my da' only called in him and my other cousin and uncle because of what your brother did,' she retorted. 'Anyway, this isn't about anyone else, it's about us.'

'I thought you said there is no us,' he muttered sulkily.

'Not romantically but please be my friend, Cole. I could really use one right now.'

'You've got friends.'

'Not as many as I used to. They abandoned me when I stopped going out. I'm still in contact with a couple but that's it.'

Cole looked out of the window, unable to face her. 'I can't be around you if we're not together. It'll hurt too much.'

A tear spilled down her cheek. 'I'm sorry for that.'

'Me too,' he said, starting the engine.

They completed the rest of the journey in silence, Cole staring angrily ahead, Carly crying silent tears, keeping her head turned so he wouldn't see. She hastily wiped them away when he pulled up at the end of her street.

'Well, thanks for the meal,' she rasped. 'It was nice.'

Cole just nodded, his beautiful eyes full of pain.

She pressed a kiss to his cheek. 'Goodbye, Cole.'

When she moved to open the door, he grabbed her hand. 'Don't leave me. Please.'

'We can still see each other as friends.'

He shook his head. 'No, it's not enough.'

'I'm sorry,' she said, fresh tears spilling down her cheeks.

She pulled her hand free, pushed open the door and hastily climbed out. Carly didn't look back as she closed the door and rushed down the street, frantically wiping away the tears and attempting to compose herself before returning home. She was glad it was dark so no one would see the state she was in.

The BMW roared past her and Carly just managed to glimpse Cole glaring at her through the driver's window before he sped up and the car disappeared down the street, the red tail lights vanishing into the darkness.

As Carly reached her front door, something drew her attention to the cemetery. She hesitated, attempting to peer through the iron bars of the gate from where she stood but the orange glow from the street-light outside it was too weak to illuminate the interior. The strong sense that someone was in there watching her grew by the second.

'What are you doing?' said a voice.

Carly jumped and whirled round to see Dean standing in the doorway to her flat. 'Jesus Christ, you scared the crap out of me,' she exclaimed.

'Sorry, but I saw you through the window and wondered why you were staring at a graveyard.'

'I got the weird feeling someone was watching me.'

'Really?' Dean turned to call his brother's name over his shoulder.

'What are you doing?' said Carly when the two brothers marched purposefully out of the house wearing only T-shirts and jeans, seemingly immune to the cold.

'Checking it out,' replied Dean as they walked past her.

'There's no need, I'm probably imagining things.'

'I don't think so.'

She watched as they strode across the street and nimbly vaulted the cemetery wall, vanishing from view as they dropped down on the other side.

Jane and Rose emerged from the flat.

'What are they doing?' the latter asked her.

'Wasting their time,' replied Carly.

'What do you mean?'

'I got a weird vibe from the cemetery and they've gone to check it out.'

'They're so brave,' she said, adoration in her eyes. 'How many people would wander about a graveyard in the dark?'

Jane and Carly smiled at each other, finding their younger sister's crush entertaining.

'I think they'll be fine,' Jane told her. 'Everyone in there's dead. They don't tend to cause much trouble.'

'Course they do. They haunt people and drive them mad and kill them.'

'I knew it was a mistake to let you watch *The Ring*.'

'I don't know what the fuss was about. It wasn't scary at all.'

'Really? So why did you insist on sleeping in my bed for three nights after watching it?'

Rose gave her a haughty look and folded her arms across her chest.

The brothers returned, agilely vaulting back over the wall.

'They're so athletic,' a starry-eyed Rose told her sisters. 'I bet they play loads of sports.'

'Well?' Carly asked her cousins as they strode back across the road.

'Nothing,' replied Harry. 'Although I think I saw a shadow going over the far wall but I can't be certain. It's almost pitch black in there.'

'Maybe it was a ghost?' said a wide-eyed Rose, immediately

regretting her outburst when the brothers regarded her with raised eyebrows.

'Well, it could have been,' said Jane, smiling.

'Aye, right,' said Harry. 'You'd better get back inside.'

The five of them filed back into the flat, Carly and Jane heading straight into the latter's bedroom for a whispered conversation.

'How did it go?' opened Jane.

'We had a nice time,' replied Carly. 'We had a meal at a restaurant at the Fort.'

'Please don't tell me you're back together.'

The panic in her sister's eyes convinced Carly that she'd done the right thing. 'Course not. I told him we were definitely over. He said he's turned over a new leaf. He's got a job as a mechanic and he's saving for his own flat. He said he wants to marry me when he's got his own place.'

'But Cole was always terrified of marriage.'

'Not any more apparently. He said he's a new man and his criminal past is behind him.'

'Was he telling the truth?'

'I think so but the problem is his family, particularly his brothers. Jessica's already told me she'd like nothing better than for me and Cole to get back together but it's not what I want. I do still love him but I can't be with him. I said I'd like us to be friends but he told me that wasn't enough for him. He looked really hurt. I feel horrible.'

'Don't. He was the one who went to prison because he wouldn't listen to all the warnings you gave him and he was the one who dumped you. Then he expects you to go running back when he clicks his fingers.'

'I hadn't thought of it like that.'

'Because you're blind where Cole's concerned, you always have been,' Jane said gently.

'You're no' wrong there,' sighed Carly.

'It's better this way. If you stayed friends, you would end up getting back together, it's inevitable. He'll come crawling back in a few days when his pride's recovered, begging to be friends because he'll realise it's the only chance he'll have of getting you back.'

'Maybe. Anyway, how's Da' been?'

'Pretty good. Since Uncle Eddie came, he's been a lot more cheerful. Eddie was in with Da' earlier, talking about old times.'

'That's great.' Carly smiled.

'Eddie's even helped out with some of his care and he bought us all a takeaway for tea. I had my doubts about calling him in, but I must say, I'm glad he's here. How was it having Dean at work?'

'A bit weird actually. He sat there reading *War and Peace*.'

'What's wrong with that?'

'I don't know, I just didn't expect him to read a book like that.'

'And what should he read?' said Jane with another of her amused smiles.

'I don't know. I just found it weird.'

'You find it strange that a member of our family is an intellectual?'

'To be honest, yes. He told me he and his brother regularly act as bodyguards.'

'Harry told me the same thing.'

'I wonder if they're any good?'

'I get the feeling we'll soon find out.'

'Why, has something happened?'

'I haven't shown this to anyone yet,' said Jane, producing a piece of paper from the pocket of her jeans and handing it to her sister.

Carly opened it. '*You're dead*,' she read aloud. 'Not very imaginative. We don't even know who it's supposed to be for. Whichever moron wrote it hasn't put a name on it.'

'It's for me from Emma. You see the way the top right corner's been folded?'

Carly nodded.

'That's a secret signal that it's from the Bitches. Only I would know that.'

'I'd chuck it in the bin and not think about it again. It's stupid and childish.'

'I agree but it does indicate that Emma's not about to give up soon. I need to have a parley with her. It's the only way.'

'Perhaps you're right but if you do, me, Dean and Harry will come with you.'

'Okay. Now let's get back in there before Rose comes in to find out what we're doing.'

'She won't bother with us, she'll be too busy drooling over our cousins.'

While Jane went into the kitchen, Carly popped in to see her dad. She didn't stay long as he was tired. After asking if he wanted anything, she kissed him and left the room, quietly closing the door behind her.

She entered the kitchen to find Rose sitting on the opposite end of the couch to Harry. He was watching television while she kept giving him sideways glances. Dean sat in the armchair reading his book and Jane was busy with some paperwork at the kitchen table.

'Where's Uncle Eddie?' she asked the room.

'He said he had some business to attend to,' replied Jane.

'What business?'

'No idea,' she replied, casting a suspicious glance at his sons. If they heard her they didn't show it.

'What's this?' said Carly, indicating the paperwork.

'Just household stuff. Thanks to Uncle Eddie we're out of arrears with the rent and I've paid off the bill to the energy company.'

'So we've cleared our debts?'

'Aye.'

Carly breathed a sigh of relief as the awful, gnawing anxiety that had dogged her for weeks finally left her. 'That's a weight off. I'll sleep better tonight.'

'I've also ordered a new washing machine. It'll be delivered in three days and I want to get Da' some new clothes too. He's not had any for a while.'

'Good idea. Let's treat him. Rose as well.' Their younger sister failed to hear them from across the room as she was continuing her adoration of Harry.

Jane smiled and nodded. 'We'll take her shopping. Her prom's coming up soon, so we can get her a really nice dress. We'll have lunch out; let's really treat ourselves.'

'Sounds great,' said Carly. Just being back home with her family was making her feel a lot better after the awkward conversation with Cole.

Carly glanced at Dean and was once again startled to see him looking back at her. Not at all abashed about being caught out, he held her gaze for another few seconds before returning his attention to his book.

Carly looked to Jane to see if she'd noticed but she was too busy with her paperwork and Rose was more concerned with Harry. When Carly looked back at Dean, she was sure he was smiling down at his book.

10

The following morning, Carly got to enjoy a very rare lie in. She didn't have to be at work until two o'clock that afternoon and Jane had told her she would take care of their father to give her a break. She didn't rise until ten o'clock. To her consternation, only Dean was in the kitchen, sitting at the table with his nose buried in a book, as usual.

'Where is everyone?' she yawned as she padded into the room wrapped in her dressing gown.

'Jane's in with Uncle Alec,' he replied. 'Rose is at school and Harry and my da' are out on business.'

'What business?'

'No idea,' he replied.

Carly got the impression he was lying but knew pressing him would be useless. 'Do you want a brew?' she asked as she shuffled over to the kettle, still yawning. It always took her a good hour to wake up properly.

'No thanks.' His eyes slipped down to her pink fluffy bunny slippers and he smiled.

'Problem?' she said.

'Not at all,' he replied with another of his annoying amused smiles.

'You still on *War and Peace*?' she asked him.

'No, I finished that last night.'

'Already? Doesn't it have loads of pages?'

'Aye, loads.' He smiled again, giving her the urge to slap him.

'So what are you reading now?' she said, switching on the kettle.

'*The Woman in White*,' he replied. 'Wilkie Collins. I like the gothic authors.'

'Was that inspired by your jaunt through the cemetery last night?'

'No' really.'

His withering look made her feel ridiculous, which annoyed her. She wished he had said yes to a brew so she could put something nasty in it.

'How was your date with Cole last night?' he asked her.

'It wasn't a date, it was just two friends having a meal together.'

'And how was it?'

'It was all right.'

'You didn't get back with him, did you?'

'That's none of your business.'

'So you did then?'

'Not that it's anything to do with you but no, I didn't.'

'Actually, it's everything to do with me because if you had got back with him his family would have kicked off and made my job a lot harder.'

'What job? So far all you've done is sit about reading.'

'Is it my fault that no one's attacked you yet?'

'You don't need to hang around me all the time. I can take care of myself.'

'So I've heard.' He gave her another of his amused smiles.

'Why is that funny?' she said through gritted teeth.

'It's not funny because I know it's true. I was just thinking about all the stories I've heard about the fights you've had.'

'And no doubt you found them hilarious.'

'No. I found them impressive.'

His expression became so serious, his words loaded with so much meaning that Carly was stuck for a reply. She could not work this man out at all. Just when she thought she was starting to understand him, he threw her again.

'Well,' she mumbled. 'That's all right then.'

Thankfully at that moment the kettle boiled so she could turn her attention to that.

'What business have your da' and brother gone out on?' she asked him as casually as she could.

'Just business,' he replied.

After pouring out her cup of tea, she replaced the kettle on its stand and turned to face him. 'Is your family into criminal activity?'

'Criminal activity?' he replied. 'You sound like a polis.'

'Insulting me won't get you out of having to answer my question. Uncle Eddie didn't win that money on the horses, did he?'

'He bets a lot.'

'That's not answering my question.'

'I've no idea what they've gone out to do, they didn't tell me and that's the God's honest truth.'

'All right, I'll take you at your word on that but tell me honestly – how does your family earn their living?'

'Well, I've already told you about the bodyguarding me and Harry do.'

'And what else? What does Uncle Eddie do?'

'This and that.'

Carly sighed with frustration. 'Fine, don't tell me but I promise you this – if you are up to anything dodgy and it comes back on my sisters and da', I'll make all three of you suffer.'

'If you like,' he said before looking back down at his book.

Carly gritted her jaw, hands curling into fists with rage. Did nothing bother the man?

Irritated, she took her tea and cereal into her bedroom. After she'd finished her breakfast, she took a shower and was annoyed to find Dean still sitting in the kitchen, reading.

'You'll end up needing glasses the way you go on,' she told him.

'I would go to the gym,' he replied without looking up. 'But Da' told me to wait here and I never watch television.'

'Really, never?'

'Never. It kills your brain cells.'

'How did Eddie ever have a son like you? I don't remember Aunty Judith being an intellectual.'

'She's no',' he replied. 'But her da' was. He was an art historian and an author.'

'So that's where you get it from?'

'I suppose so,' he replied without looking up. He turned a page of the book. 'What are your plans for today?'

'None of your business.'

'Aye they are because I've got to come with you.'

'You're sodding not.'

'I am.'

He looked up and smiled. Carly took that smile to be a smirk. 'Fine. I don't start work until two this afternoon, so I'm going to the supermarket. Happy?'

'Which supermarket?'

She told him and he nodded.

'Let me know when you're going and I'll drive you there.'

'You have a car?'

'Aye. All three of us brought our cars.'

'I didn't know, I thought you came in Uncle Eddie's.' The fact that all three of them could afford a car made her even more suspicious about where they got their money from.

Carly headed into her father's room to say good morning. He was sitting up watching one of his beloved cookery programmes on the television with Jane.

'Morning,' she told them both.

'Morning, sweetheart,' replied Alec. 'I heard you chatting with Dean; you sound like you're getting on quite well.'

Carly forced a smile. Obviously he hadn't been able to overhear the details of their conversation. 'Aye, no' bad.'

'That's great,' he said, beaming.

It had been a while since Carly had seen her father so alert and happy. 'You look really good this morning, Da'.'

'Rather than the pile of shite I normally look like,' he replied with a twinkle.

'I didn't mean that.'

'I know, sweetheart, I'm only joking.' He had to pause before continuing, dabbing the excess saliva from his lips with a tissue, just a slight tremor in his hands. 'I'm happy because I've got my brother back. I was worried we were permanently estranged but that's no' the case.' Once again, he had to take a break before continuing, his daughters patiently waiting. 'We've enjoyed catching up on old times and it's such a relief knowing there's someone looking out for my girls. It's given me a new lease of life.'

'That's brilliant,' she said. 'I'm really happy for you.'

'It's even better that you get on with your cousins. Family is so important.'

Carly just smiled and nodded, praying her suspicions about her uncle and cousins were wrong. She wondered what Eddie had told her father about where he got all his money. Had he told him he'd won it on the horses too? Carly decided not to ask; she didn't want to worry her father, not when he was looking so much better.

* * *

'I half-expected you to read while you were driving,' commented Carly as Dean drove her to the supermarket.

'I would if I could,' he replied.

'Don't you like spending much time in the real world?'

'It's not as interesting as fiction.'

'Then you're no' doing it right,' she told him with a mischievous smile.

He caught that smile and couldn't help returning it. 'So, are you here to do the big shop?' he said as he pulled into the car park.

'No, just a top up shop,' she replied. 'Uncle Eddie has eaten us out of bread and nearly polished off all our teabags.'

'Sorry about that.'

'Don't be. He's made my da' really happy, so I'm grateful to him. Da's so glad the rift between them is healed.'

Dean drove into a space close to the supermarket doors, pulled on the handbrake and switched off the engine. 'What did your da' tell you about the reason for the rift in the first place?' he asked her.

'He said it was because he got fed up with Uncle Eddie scrounging off him all the time when he had his own family to support.'

Dean just nodded and gazed out of the window thoughtfully.

'Why, what did your da' tell you?' she replied.

'The same thing.'

Her eyes narrowed. 'You're lying.'

'No, I'm not. Well, come on then,' he said, opening the door and getting out of the car.

She hastened to follow, rushing after him as he strode towards the supermarket doors. 'What did your da' really tell you?'

'I've already told you,' he replied without looking at her. 'Just his version though. He said why shouldn't Alec lend him money? He was his brother after all and brothers should look out for each other.'

'There's something else, isn't there?'

'Naw.'

'Aye there is. Why won't you tell me?'

'Because there's nothing to tell,' he replied, grabbing a trolley before walking through the automatic doors, which opened for them.

Carly knew when to press an issue and when to back off and she realised this was the time to retreat, for now. If she kept pushing, he'd never tell her.

They wandered around the supermarket in silence, Carly absently picking up the items she needed and dumping them in the trolley.

'Is there anything you want?' she asked him.

'Sorry?' he said distractedly.

'Is there anything you want?' she repeated, gesturing to the shelves around them.

'I'll get mine. Don't worry about me.'

Carly could see he was troubled, it was clear in his eyes, but she knew asking would be futile. She would have to get it out of him with subterfuge.

They paid and Dean wheeled the trolley outside.

'Oh no,' sighed Carly when she saw Cole strolling towards the doors with Ross. Clearly their presence here was just a coincidence because neither of them had spotted her and they casually chatted as they walked.

'Oh God, that's Cole and his brother, Ross,' Carly told Dean. 'Maybe we can leave without them noticing us?'

'Too late,' said Dean when the brothers' gazes settled on them and their faces creased with anger.

Rage filled Cole's green eyes, turning them bright and piercing and he charged up to them, Ross hurrying after him.

'What the fuck are you doing with my bird?' demanded Cole, thrusting his face into Dean's.

'Oy, I am not your bird,' Carly told him. 'We broke up and he's only helping me with the shopping.'

'Oh aye?' said Cole, rounding on her, bristling with fury. 'You've only got two bags of shopping. Like you need help with those.'

'Who is this walloper, Cole?' said Ross, nodding at Dean.

'He's my cousin and he's only here because you keep threatening my family,' Carly told him before looking back at Cole. 'If you want to blame someone for Dean's presence then blame your brother because it's his fault he's here. I don't enjoy going around with a babysitter you know.'

'There she goes again trying to turn you against me,' Ross told Cole. 'Like she's always done.'

'You're still a pathetic child,' Carly told Ross with disgust. 'Jealous when anyone goes near your little brother.'

'And you're still a fucking witch,' he snarled, thrusting his face into hers.

Dean placed himself before her and pressed a hand to Ross' chest. 'Back off.'

'Piss off Captain America before I ram my fist down your throat.'

'Try it.'

Dean's voice was low and quiet but dripped menace. Carly actually felt the hairs rise on the back of her neck. She hadn't thought it possible to look and sound so threatening without shouting or any physical aggression. Dean just stood there, arms down by his sides but she could see every muscle in his body had tensed and the veins stood out in his neck. Even Ross appeared wary.

Now that Ross had simmered down, Dean felt it safe to turn his attention to Cole. 'You don't need to be jealous, there's nothing going on between me and Carly. We're family and that's all there is to it.'

The way Dean spoke was so straightforward and honest even Cole recognised it. 'All right. I get it.'

'Good.' Dean looked back at Ross. 'And I suggest you leave my cousins and uncle alone. They're just trying to get on with their lives.'

'Oh aye,' said Ross, recovering his lairiness. 'And what are you gonnae dae about it, big man? Beat me up?'

'No. I'll kill you.'

He spoke so matter-of-factly that all three of them were shocked into silence.

'Come on Carly,' said Dean without taking his eyes off Ross. 'Let's get this lot back before the freezer stuff melts.'

'Aye, all right,' she murmured.

Dean marched off with the trolley and Ross let him go unhindered, although he did glare at his back.

When Carly moved to follow, Cole gently took her arm. 'Be careful around him,' he told her. 'You don't know who he is, you havenae seen him in years.'

She nodded, knowing that was good advice. 'I will.'

'I'm still using my old phone number. Call me if you need me.'

Her heart swelled with love as she gazed into his beautiful green eyes. 'Thanks. See you around,' she said gently.

'Aye, you will,' he replied equally gently.

Dean and Carly returned to the car with the Alexander brothers watching them.

Carly got into the passenger seat and pulled on her seat belt, feeling a little uneasy. 'What you said back there,' she began. 'Did you really mean it?'

'Which bit?' he said, starting the engine.

'About killing Ross.'

He gave her another of his amused smiles. 'I was only trying to intimidate him and get him to back off.'

'So you don't really plan to kill him?'

'No. What do you think I am, some sort of psycho?'

That's the problem, Carly thought to herself. *I don't know who you are.* 'You were very convincing.'

'Good. Hopefully I've convinced him to stay away.'

'Have you…?' she began before trailing off.

'Have I what?'

Carly steeled herself to ask the burning question. 'Have you ever killed anyone?'

'No. I was only having him on. Don't take it to heart.'

'In that case, you should be an actor,' she added, forcing a smile.

He realised she looked genuinely edgy. 'Listen, I don't know you and you don't know me but I'm only here to help you and your family. You don't need to be nervous around me.'

'It's hard not to be after that little display. I mean, I've seen a lot of fights and I've heard people threaten to kill each other loads of times but I've never seen anyone who really meant it.'

'I'd do anything for my family and that includes you.'

'I appreciate that but I don't want Ross to get badly hurt or worse. I just want him to leave me alone.'

'He will,' said Dean confidently. 'I'll make sure of it but not by killing him, okay?'

Carly nodded, not knowing what else to say.

'Good,' he said, putting the car into gear and setting off.

She glanced sideways at him as he drove. His expression was calm but there was steel in his eyes.

11

Jane noticed her sister was a little quieter than usual after returning home. When Dean headed into the bathroom, she decided to quiz her about it.

'So, how did your shopping trip go?' Jane asked her.

'Oh, fine,' replied Carly, stacking tins in a cupboard.

'Something happened, didn't it?'

'We bumped into Cole and Ross, but Dean made them back off.'

'How did he achieve that miracle?'

Carly sighed and turned to face her sister. 'He told Ross he'd kill him. Ross believed him and so did I.'

'Why does that bother you? Because it seems like it really does.'

'Because he meant it, I'm sure of it. Dean was actually pretty scary.'

'Good. We need scary right now.'

'It was the way he said it, like he could happily snap Ross's neck and not think twice about it. You had to be there to know what I mean but it was really intimidating. I asked Dean if he'd ever killed anyone and he said no but I'm no' so sure.'

'You really think he could be a murderer?'

'I don't know. Maybe. I also asked him where his family got their money from and he was really cagey about it.'

'Is that a surprise? Uncle Eddie's been into dodgy business for years. It was one of the reasons why Da' stopped contact between our families.'

'Aye, but I got the impression there's something he really doesn't want us to know. I'm afraid of it landing on us and that we'll be tainted by association.'

'You don't think you're being a wee bit paranoid?'

'Probably. I think it's Dean; he drives me mad.'

'Oh yes?' said Jane, smiling.

'I don't mean like that. It's just the way he is. He barely talks and when he does, he never gives a real answer to my questions.'

'Maybe that's why you're suspicious of him. He might not have anything to hide.'

'Possibly,' Carly sighed. 'He's keeping watch over me during my shift at work today, so I hope to get more out of him. I would try and get him drunk but he doesn't drink. The only thing that man enjoys is his books. Are we sure he's really related to us?'

'Hey, I like to read too.'

'Light and fluffy books, no' the heavy, classical stuff he always has his nose buried in. If anyone did attack me, he probably wouldn't even notice.'

'I think I would,' said a voice.

They both jumped and turned to see Dean standing in the doorway leading into the kitchen from the hall.

'How long have you been there?' Carly demanded of him.

'Not long,' he replied enigmatically.

As he returned to his seat at the table to continue reading his book, Carly glanced questioningly at her sister, who shrugged. They were both thinking the same thing – how much of that conversation had Dean overheard?

* * *

The pub didn't get busy until seven o'clock that evening. Carly had carefully watched Dean all afternoon; he had set himself up at a table close to the bar with his books and a laptop, taking the opportunity to study while he was waiting for her to finish her shift. Apparently, he was taking an online course in English literature.

As the pub became busier, Dean found himself the subject of many curious looks and word soon spread that he was Carly's cousin. They all found it even stranger that he was only drinking water.

'Why bother coming into a pub if you're gonnae sit there without a real drink?' demanded Jim, one of the regulars. 'He's taking up a valuable table there.'

'He's here to keep an eye on things since the brick through the window incident,' Derek told him.

'Oh, I see. So he's a bouncer then?'

'Aye.'

'You sure he's up to the job? He's only a young pup.'

'That remains to be seen,' muttered Derek, glancing at Carly. He'd noticed she'd been giving her cousin strange looks all day, as though something about the man concerned her. Derek had quizzed her about it but she'd brushed off his questions with a cheerful smile.

Despite his odd ways, Dean's good looks drew a few people to his table, including a gaggle of attractive young women on a night out. They had the temerity to sit at his table, penning him in. Dean looked up and regarded them all one by one with disinterest before turning his attention back to his laptop. When he responded to their twittering questions with monosyllabic replies, they soon gave up and left him to it.

'Maybe he's gay?' Derek commented to Carly.

'Doubtful,' she replied. 'He told me he broke up with his girl-friend a few months ago.'

'Ah, then maybe he's still getting over her after she broke his heart?'

'He said he dumped her.'

'He could have said that to protect his feelings.'

'I don't think so, he didn't seem bothered when he was telling me about it. He did say he dumped her because she talked too much and those women did nothing but gab away at him.'

'I've never seen a lad that age ignore girls for learning.'

'He's certainly one of a kind,' she said thoughtfully while studying Dean.

'Oh aye?' Derek grinned. 'You getting a thing for him, doll?'

'No, I am not. He's my cousin.'

'That doesn't matter, it's legal.'

'So everyone keeps saying,' she sighed.

'He's a good-looking boy.'

'That's true but there's something odd about him.'

The door opened and in strode three men Carly knew were closely affiliated with Ross Alexander. They were accompanied by two Bitches.

'Oh no,' she murmured as they homed in on her immediately and strode up to the bar.

'I'll deal with them,' Derek told her.

Carly nodded and went to serve Brenda and her pals.

'What are you lot wantin'?' Derek demanded of the newcomers.

'This is a pub, isn't it?' retorted Stuart, a tall, broad man in his early twenties with a pointed goatee beard that made him look like Satan. He was one of Ross's closest friends.

'Aye,' replied Derek.

'Then we want a fucking drink.'

'Don't talk to me like that, ya wee bastard,' retorted Derek, jabbing an index finger at him.

'Or what?'

'Or I'll boot your arse right oot that door,' he snarled back.

'Don't talk to Derek like that,' one of the Bitches told Stuart. She was a squat, round girl called Meg. 'He's no' bad.'

'Aye, thanks, doll,' Derek told her.

'You're welcome. We'll have three pints of lager, a Bacardi and coke and half a cider please.'

'All right then, as long as you all promise to behave yourselves.'

'We will,' Meg replied sweetly.

Silence hung heavy in the pub as Derek poured their requested drinks. Carly caught his eye, wondering if he wanted help preparing their order but he shook his head, telling her to stay at the other end of the bar. She looked to Dean, who glanced up at the group before turning his attention back to his laptop.

The group paid for their drinks, picked up their glasses and looked around for a table. Carly felt decidedly nervous when she realised they were headed Dean's way.

'Oy, you,' said Stuart.

Dean looked up and regarded him coolly. 'What?'

'You're taking up a table there all on your own. Fuck off, we want to sit down.'

'There are other empty tables. Sit at one of those,' Dean calmly told him before returning his attention to his laptop.

Stuart looked to his friends, who nodded at him encouragingly. He turned back to Dean.

'I don't think you fucking heard me,' he growled.

'I heard,' replied Dean while continuing to type. 'I'm just not interested in anything you have to say.'

Stuart hadn't expected this response and once again looked to his friends for guidance.

'Do something,' Meg hissed at him.

'Aye, right.'

The whole pub watched as Stuart poured his entire pint over Dean's laptop. Fortunately it wasn't plugged in but its immediate reaction was to switch itself off.

Dean's head snapped up, rage shining in his eyes. He slammed the lid shut while Stuart and his cronies brayed with laughter.

'Oy, you lot,' yelled Derek.

He never got to finish his sentence as Dean got to his feet, snatched up the laptop and smashed it into Stuart's face. Stuart was spun sideways before collapsing to the floor, blood pouring from his nose.

His friends' laughter abruptly stopped and they stared at Stuart in astonishment before rounding on Dean.

'You're gonnae pay for that, you fucking twat,' Meg yelled at him.

The two men lunged at Dean simultaneously. Everyone watched in amazement as Dean grabbed one of the men and hurled him across the room, sending him crashing into a table, which was fortunately vacant. He punched the second man in the face, grabbed his right arm and twisted it so hard the man sank to his knees, crying out in pain.

Carly's eyes widened when she saw Meg slyly pull a knife from inside her jacket. She rushed out from behind the bar, grabbed one of the brass drip trays and clobbered her in the back with it. Meg fell forward with a cry, the weapon falling from her hand; Carly kicked it out of reach of Meg's friend, Fay, when she tried to grab it. Fay rounded on Carly and tried to punch her but she raised the drip tray, which met Fay's fist. Fay screamed with pain, clutching her hand to her chest.

'Right, you lot,' said Derek, who had shaken himself out of his surprise. 'You're barred.'

He stalked out from behind the bar, grabbed the man Dean had thrown by the back of his coat and dragged him to the door, kicking him up the arse before hurling him outside.

Dean released the man he was holding, who rushed out of the door, cradling his aching arm. He knelt by Stuart's side and began rummaging in his pockets. He produced a couple of twenty-pound notes and waved them before Stuart's face.

'I'm keeping these,' he told him. 'They can go towards a new laptop.'

'Bastard,' mumbled Stuart through his broken nose, from which blood still dripped.

'Piss off before I batter your fucking head in with my busted computer.'

Stuart tried to haul himself to his feet and failed, so Derek dragged him upright and hurled him out the door.

'You're going to pay for this, you bitch,' Meg told Carly as she and Fay stumbled towards the door. 'You and your cousin are fucking dead.'

'Aye, good luck with that.' Carly smirked at her.

With one last glare, Meg and Fay left too.

The entire pub erupted into applause.

'That was bloody brilliant.' Derek beamed at Dean, shaking his hand.

'Aye, thanks,' he muttered, regarding his laptop with a forlorn look.

'Don't worry, you can get yourself a new one.'

'Aye but all my work's on this one. God, I hope it can be retrieved. I'd nearly finished my essay too; it took me days.'

'I'm sure you'll be able to save it,' said Derek, patting him sympathetically on the shoulder.

'Thanks for what you did,' Dean told Carly. 'I mean with the drip tray.'

'Nae bother,' she replied. 'But they will come back at us harder.'

'Aye, I know,' he muttered, still looking depressed about his computer.

'You did the right thing,' said Jim. 'It's about time someone brought those twats down a peg or two. The Alexanders and their cronies, as well as the Bitches, have thrown their weight about Haghill for too long.'

'That's true,' said Derek.

'Who are you calling?' Carly asked her cousin when he took out his phone.

'My brother,' he replied. 'They might come back mob-handed.'

Derek appeared a little alarmed at this prospect and considered closing for the night but his customers congratulated Dean and bought more drinks, so he decided against it.

12

Carly was worried when neither the Alexander family, the Bitches nor anyone associated with them turned up at the pub that night. She would have preferred to get the inevitable confrontation over with but when it didn't happen, she knew that meant they were preparing something extra nasty.

Dean drove himself and Carly back to the flat in silence when her shift had ended, Harry following in his own car. On their return, Dean walked inside clutching his ruined laptop, still miserable about its destruction.

'I feel really bad about what happened to his computer,' Carly told Harry once they were inside the flat. Dean had headed straight into the kitchen to see if anything could be done for it.

'It's no' your fault,' replied Harry. 'But he's gonnae go fucking mental about this. He'll make them pay.'

'I think he made them pay enough tonight.'

'He won't think so. He never loses it that much but he'll tear them to pieces. I'm hard but Dean's on another level.'

'Really?'

'Aye. The Alexanders don't know what's about to hit them.'

With this he walked into the kitchen, leaving Carly to frown after him. That was it, she had to do some digging on her cousins.

She went into her bedroom to do a little research on her phone. Nothing popped up, so she decided to go to Clydebank to find out what she could about them. The question was, how did she get there without her ever-present bodyguard? She could sneak out but she didn't want her dad to worry. There was no choice, she had to confide in Jane and get her to cover for her.

Carly popped into her dad's room but he was asleep, so she quietly crept out. Rose was already in bed as it was after eleven o'clock. Jane was in the kitchen with the brothers.

'Thanks for seeing me home safely,' Carly told them. 'But you can go now.'

'We don't think that's a good idea after what happened in the pub,' said Harry, replying because his brother was too busy taking his laptop apart with the help of a screwdriver. 'Me and Dean are staying the night.'

'But... there's no room.'

'I'll take the couch and Dean has an airbed in his car. He can put it on the floor in here.'

'It won't be very comfortable.'

'We'll be fine, we've slept in rougher places.'

'Like where?' said Carly, seizing on the opportunity to learn a bit more about them.

'Camping with the scouts,' he replied.

'Oh aye,' she said, smiling. 'Did you have wee woggles too?'

'Yes,' he replied, deadpan.

'Oh.' Carly glanced at Jane, who appeared amused that her sister's joke had fallen flat. How would she talk to her sister in private now? Then inspiration struck. 'I need some fresh air, to get rid of the stench of beer.'

'If you're going for a walk one of us will come with you,' said Harry.

'I'm just going into the back garden. You don't need to come; I'll be safe enough.'

'I'm no' sure about that.'

'Jane can come with me, can't you Jane?' she said, throwing her sister a meaningful look.

'Course I can,' she replied, catching the look.

'Okay, but leave the door ajar so we can hear if you scream,' said Harry.

'You really are an optimist, aren't you?' said Carly wryly before exiting the kitchen via the back door.

Jane pulled on her trainers and jacket and followed.

'What's wrong?' Jane whispered to her sister the moment they were outside. 'Is it about what happened at the pub tonight?'

'In a way,' replied Carly. 'Dean was pretty impressive by the way.'

'I knew it, you do fancy him.'

'I do not.'

'Course you do and there's nothing wrong with that, he's really good-looking.'

'It sounds like you're the one who fancies him.'

'Naw, I prefer older men.'

'He's strange, I can't work him out. Anyway, that's not what I want to talk to you about. I want to go to Clydebank and ask around about our uncle and cousins. There's a lot they're not telling us and I want to know what that is.'

'Have you thought that there may be a good reason why they're not telling us?'

'Aye, and it makes me suspicious.'

'I don't think this is a good idea.'

'We have to know what they're involved in. What if it bounces back on us?'

'They might not be up to anything.'

'Has Harry told you anything about how they earn their money?'

'No, but I haven't asked.'

'Why not?'

'Because it's none of my business.'

'It is if they're up to something criminal and we get dragged into it.'

'Even if they are, why should we get dragged into it? And what if by poking around you're the one who drags us into it?'

'I'll be subtle.'

'I think you should leave it be; no good will come of it.'

'Forewarned is forearmed.'

'By running away from what we fear we end up running right into it.'

Carly frowned. 'What?'

'You're going to make everything worse. Please don't go.'

Carly sighed. 'I was hoping you'd cover for me so I could go to Clydebank, otherwise my plan won't work.'

'Good. I don't want it to work. Please drop it, Carly. It'll make everything worse.'

'All right,' she mumbled. 'If you insist.'

'Thank you,' Jane breathed with relief. 'I'll tell you what – I'll see what I can find out but I won't do it by poking around in Clydebank.'

'What will you do then?'

'I still have contacts from my days in the Bitches. I'll see if they know anything.'

'That would be great, thanks. I really think we should do something.'

'Perhaps you're right but no wandering off on your own, okay?'

'I won't.'

'You promise?'

'Promise.'

'Good. Now let's get back inside, it's freezing out here.'

They were distracted by a strange noise from the rear wall of the garden.

'What was that?' said Jane.

'Carly,' whispered a voice.

A face peered over the wall and a hand waved at them.

'I think it's Cole,' said Carly, peering into the darkness, which was lit by a single streetlight.

'You're right, it is,' said Jane.

'Don't let Dean know he's here,' Carly told her sister. 'He might take what happened at the pub out on him.'

'I'm sure Cole can hold his own.'

'Actually, I don't think he could against Dean.'

Jane's eyebrows shot up in astonishment.

'I'd better see what he wants before our cousins realise he's here,' said Carly.

Jane was surprised by the anxiety in her sister's eyes for Cole's safety. Dean really must have put on a hell of a show at the pub. 'I'll come with you in case there are more of them on the other side of that wall.'

The sisters hurried to the rear of the garden. Because of the height of the wall, Cole was only visible from the chin up.

'I heard about what happened at the pub,' he told Carly. 'I wanted to check that you're okay.'

'You could have sent her a text,' Jane told him coldly.

'I wanted to see her,' he retorted before looking back at Carly. 'So, you weren't hurt?'

'No,' she replied. 'But I can't say the same for Meg and Fay.'

'They're really pissed off. They've been riling up the rest of the Bitches to get you back. Stuart and his pals are furious at Dean. Stuart had to go to hospital, his nose was broken and Mike's arm was badly sprained by Dean twisting it.'

'They all deserved what they got,' said Carly passionately. 'They behaved like morons and they poured beer all over Dean's laptop.'

'Why did he have a laptop with him?'

'He was writing an essay.'

'In a pub?'

'It doesn't matter why; the point is, Stuart and his friends acted like pricks. If they got hurt, they've only themselves to blame.'

'Ross sent them in to test Dean and see what he could do. He's raging about what happened.'

'He should have taken on Dean himself instead of sending his minions.'

'He's planning an attack but he won't tell me the details. I think he's worried about me warning you. All I know is that he won't hit you here in the flat. A lot of people were really pissed off about that brick being thrown through Alec's window and he doesn't want to look like a cowardly twat by going after a man who can't defend himself. But the rest of you are fair game, even Rose.'

'Bastard,' hissed Jane, hands curling into fists.

Carly was dismayed by the violence that filled her sister's eyes. Jane used to be an absolute terror and was capable of a lot of carnage when enraged. Since their dad had fallen ill, she'd kept it in check but Carly was afraid this turn of events would bring out her bad side again. 'So Ross thinks attacking a sixteen-year-old girl won't make him look like a coward?'

'You need to be really careful,' said Cole. 'I'll let you know if I find out what Ross is up to.'

'Thanks,' said Carly tenderly. 'We really appreciate that, don't we Jane. Jane?' she repeated when her sister stared straight ahead, rage still sparking in her eyes.

'If your brother's stupid enough to take on our family,' Jane hissed at Cole, 'then I swear to God he'll end up with all his fucking limbs snapped, if he's lucky.'

'All right,' said Cole slowly. He had never seen Jane this way before. This was the ferocious gang leader and not the responsible, caring older sister. The contrast was a shock.

'Can you give me a minute?' Carly asked her sister.

Jane gave Cole a hard, scrutinising look that made him distinctly uncomfortable before nodding and retreating back towards the flat, although she remained outside to watch over her sister.

'Thanks for the warning,' Carly told Cole. 'I really appreciate it.'

'Nae problem. I was so worried about you when I heard what had happened at the pub. Listen, I did a little digging on your cousins. Please don't be angry but I only did it because I care about you. I've a couple of pals in Clydebank. They told me Dean and Harry are the terrors of the town; everyone there is shit scared of them.'

'Why?' she said, wide-eyed.

'Their da's a known robber with a fierce reputation. He trod on the toes of a local family who are known for being pretty savage themselves. He sent his sons after them and they twatted all the men in that family. They put three of them in hospital; it took months for them to get over their injuries. After that, Eddie was left well alone. Those boys batter anyone who gets in their way.'

'I knew Uncle Eddie didn't win that money on the horses.'

'He's no' just a robber, he's a drug dealer too and Eddie and his sons will beat up anyone, as long as they're paid enough cash.'

'I knew it,' said Carly, eyes narrowing.

'They're dangerous, babe. You need to be careful.'

'Have you told anyone else about this?'

'No. I came straight here as soon as I found out.'

'Please keep it to yourself. Don't even tell Ross.'

'I have to. He needs to know what he's up against.'

'I don't want my da' hearing about this. It'll upset him so much. He and Uncle Eddie are talking again after being estranged for years and if he finds out what his brother's into, he'll disown him and that will make him so unhappy.'

Cole's smile was tender. 'Still putting everyone else first. It's one of the things I love about you the most.'

His hand reached over the wall and Carly extended her arm to take it.

'Hey,' yelled a voice.

Carly turned to see Harry and Dean burst out of the back door of the flat. Jane made no move to intervene as they tore across the garden towards them.

'Go,' Carly told Cole. 'I'll stall them.'

'I love you, babe,' he told her before running down the back street.

Carly turned and held out her hands to her cousins. 'Stop,' she said.

'Was that Cole?' demanded Dean, looking furious.

'Aye, it was. He was making sure I was okay after what happened at the pub, that's all.'

'More like he was scouting for his bastard brother.'

'No, he wasn't,' she snapped back at him.

'You should have told us he was here,' Harry practically snarled.

'I didn't tell you because I knew you'd react like this.' Carly didn't want to admit that she was a little intimidated by the brothers. They were pumped up with aggression, which made them look even bigger and the rage glittered in their eyes. If they got hold of

Cole, she was positive they would tear him limb from limb. 'You'll leave him alone; he meant no harm.'

'You must be joking,' said Dean. 'He's an Alexander and they always mean harm.'

'What do you know about it? You don't even know the family.'

'Let's continue this conversation inside,' said Jane when she spotted some of the residents of the surrounding flats peering out of their windows.

The four of them returned to the kitchen, Harry closing the door behind them.

'You're being way over the top about this,' Carly told her cousins. 'One pint of lager over a laptop and you lose your minds.'

'It's no' just that,' said Harry. 'It's the brick through Uncle Alec's window and you being threatened and terrorised. I don't get why you're sticking up for the Alexanders.'

'Because she's still in love with that wee rat, Cole,' said Dean, regarding Carly disapprovingly.

'Yes, fine, I do still love him but that is absolutely nothing to do with you.'

'Keep your voices down,' hissed Jane. 'You'll wake Da' and Rose.'

Dean took a deep breath. 'Sorry.'

'Look,' said Carly in a gentler tone. 'I know you're upset about your laptop, which seems to mean a lot to you.'

'I knew you'd say it like that,' retorted Dean, eyes flashing angrily.

'Now what have I done?'

'You said it like I was an idiot for liking my laptop.'

'After the books I've seen you read the last thing you are is an idiot but I do think you need some perspective. You're talking about starting a war between two families over a computer.'

'As Harry said, it's no' just about the bloody computer. It's about you lot. But fine, if you like, we'll go home and leave you two to sort it all out.'

'You cannae go, it would devastate my da'.'

'Make up your mind.' He glowered at her.

'What Carly is trying to say,' said Jane, who had recovered her equilibrium and was once again being the diplomat. 'Is that we really appreciate your help, especially now it seems the Alexander family and the Bitches aren't going to back off, but we do need to be careful and not do anything rash. Yes, Ross will want revenge for what happened today. He has to do something to save face. Cole said he sent his friends into the pub today to test you, Dean. He didn't know what he was dealing with but now he does and he will learn from it. We need to be ready when he comes back at us and arguing amongst ourselves won't help. So, if we could put aside the squabbling, put our heads together and figure out how we're gonnae handle the situation, that would be great.'

'Well said,' Harry told her with growing respect in his eyes. Now he could see why Jane was such a good leader.

'Thank you.' She looked to Dean, who sighed and nodded. Her gaze then turned on her sister.

'Aye, you're right,' mumbled Carly.

'Good. Now, Cole did tell us something useful – he said Ross will leave our da' alone. A lot of people were pissed off about him targeting Da' and thought him a coward but Rose is a different matter. He might use her to get at us, so from now on she's your priority,' she told the brothers.

'Cole could have told you that to distract you from Ross's real plan,' replied Dean.

'I agree,' said Harry.

'No he didn't,' said Carly. 'He wouldn't do that to us.'

'Maybe not intentionally. Ross could have fed him some misinformation knowing he'd run straight to you with it. While we're looking after Rose, they go after you or Jane.'

'That is a possibility,' Jane told her sister reasonably.

'Aye, maybe, but Cole was only trying to do his best for us.'

Dean's look was sceptical but he didn't comment.

'It might be best if you took a break from working at the pub,' Harry told Carly.

'I can't,' she replied. 'If I don't work, I don't get paid and we need the money.'

'Surely you're given paid holidays?'

'Aye but I've already used them all up. There were a lot of days I couldn't go in because Da' wasn't well and Derek let me take them as holidays, so I'd still get paid. He's been really good to me and I won't leave him in the lurch.'

'Fine, but we drop you off and pick you up every shift and one of us stays with you at all times.'

'Okay.'

'We'll put up cameras outside the flat too, so we can see anyone coming.'

'We can't afford that,' said Jane.

'Don't worry, we'll cover it.'

'Thank you, we appreciate that, don't we Carly?'

Carly gave Dean a sulky look, which he returned. 'Aye we do,' she said.

'Our da' will be around more too,' continued Harry. 'We haven't told him yet about what happened tonight and when he hears he'll be raging.'

'Where is he anyway?' said Carly.

'He's busy,' replied Harry dismissively, making her sigh with frustration. 'He'll be here in the morning. In the meantime, I suggest we all get some sleep. We'll discuss it again with Da' when he arrives tomorrow.'

13

Carly was woken the following morning by the sound of voices quietly murmuring in the kitchen. Glancing at her clock, she saw it was half past seven.

She got up, pulled on her dressing gown over her pyjamas and wandered into the kitchen. A fully dressed Jane was sitting at the kitchen table with her cousins and uncle.

Carly sank into a chair and yawned, dragging her hands through her hair.

'You look knackered,' Jane told her.

'I feel it. I didn't get much sleep last night worrying about everything.'

'Don't you fret, hen,' said Eddie. 'We'll sort out those bastards.'

'We were just discussing how we're going to do that,' said Jane. 'I'll get you a coffee. Uncle Eddie brought some really nice stuff.'

'Cheers,' replied Carly.

'Anyone else want a top up?' said Jane.

The three men all nodded.

While Jane prepared the coffees, the conversation resumed.

'I've got some pals I can bring in to help on this,' said Eddie.

'But I would prefer to handle it ourselves if we can. They can step in if it gets too heavy for us.'

'Oh aye, what pals?' said Carly curiously.

'You won't know them,' he replied.

Carly narrowed her eyes at Jane when her sister's lips twitched with amusement that another of her attempts to get information out of them had failed.

'From now on, me and the boys stick to you and your sisters like glue,' Eddie told her.

'Great,' she said with a distinct lack of enthusiasm.

'Now I don't want you to be scared, doll,' her uncle told her, patting her hand.

'I'm not.'

'We'll sort out these bad men for you,' he added as though she were five years old.

'Thanks,' she said flatly.

'You're very welcome. Now, is there any grub? I've no' had my breakfast yet. The boys will need something too; it's important they keep their strength up.'

'I'll rustle something up,' said Jane.

'You're an angel, hen, a pure angel,' said Eddie, reclining back in his chair with satisfaction and clasping his hands behind his head.

Carly got the feeling he was enjoying having a woman cook for him. He was the type who liked being looked after.

Jane cooked the three men a fry-up while Carly opted for a bowl of cereal, unable to face fried food so early in the morning. Rose joined them ready for school, once again casting coy looks towards her cousins, who remained oblivious to her crush.

'So, who's taking me to school today?' she asked.

'I am,' replied Harry.

She grinned. 'Great.'

When Harry regarded her with a raised eyebrow, Rose cleared her throat and attempted to look cool and calm. 'I mean, whatever.'

When everyone stared at her, she blushed and looked down at the table.

'Oh aye?' Eddie grinned. 'Have you got a wee crush on my boy?'

Rose's head snapped up and she looked mortified. 'No, course not. He's way too old for me.'

'Aye, right.' Eddie winked at her knowingly.

Rose's cheeks turned positively scarlet and she lowered her head again.

'Don't tease her, Uncle Eddie,' said Jane.

'Sorry, doll.' He smiled at Rose, who gave him a small smile in return, telling him he was forgiven.

When Carly had finished her breakfast, she popped into her father's room to wish him good morning. Once again, he seemed livelier and happier, enjoying having all his family about him. She left him watching another of his cookery programmes and went to get dressed.

'I've to look after you today,' Dean told her. 'But I need to go and buy a new laptop.'

'I'm not stopping you.'

'It would be best if you came with me.'

'Why can't I stay here?'

He shrugged. 'You can but I thought you'd like a wee trip into the city.'

'Why? I don't need anything.'

'You should go, Carly,' Jane told her. 'It'll do you good to get out of Haghill for a bit.'

'Aren't I best hanging around here if we're expecting trouble?'

'We'll be fine. Eddie and Harry will be here.'

'Aye, we've got it covered,' said Eddie. 'You go and enjoy yourself.' He delved into his jeans pocket, produced a wad of notes and placed it on the table before her. 'Take that, buy yourself something nice.'

'I can't take this; there must be four hundred quid there.'

'Actually, it's five hundred.'

'Did you have another win on the horses?' she said cynically.

'Aye, I did. They're doing me proud right now.'

'You should sell your secret; you'd make a fortune,' she said with a raised eyebrow.

'That's a good idea. Perhaps I will,' he said with a jovial smile.

'What about Da'?' she asked her sister.

'I'll look after him,' replied Jane. 'Work's given me a couple of weeks off, so it's my turn. You deserve a break, so go and have fun. It's not often you get the chance to have a splurge.'

Carly regarded them all suspiciously, getting the sense she was being got out of the way, but for what reason?

'For God's sake, Carly, take the money and spend every last penny,' Rose told her. 'If you don't, then I will.'

Whatever was going on, Carly was certain her younger sister wasn't part of it. 'I'll get you those trainers you've been after.'

Rose's eyes filled with delight. 'Brilliant,' she exclaimed excitedly. The eagerness faded. 'But that money's for you.'

'It's for all of us and I'm getting you the trainers.' Poor Rose had to make do with her older sisters' hand-me-downs, something she'd been teased about quite a bit by her peers. It was time she had something brand new and designer.

Rose leapt to her feet to hug her sister. She then looked to her uncle. 'Thank you, Uncle Eddie.'

'You're very welcome, doll,' he replied magnanimously. 'Are you ready? You need to be at school soon.'

'I just need to brush my teeth,' she replied before rushing from the room like a gazelle.

Harry left with Rose and half an hour later Dean was ushering

Carly out to his car. She kept looking back over her shoulder at the flat, Jane standing in the doorway with Eddie to wave her off. Something strange was going on and she was determined to find out what it was.

* * *

Dean was his usual quiet self as he drove them into the city centre. After visiting a couple of electrical stores, he selected a new laptop. Carly then bought Rose her trainers and Jane a warm winter coat she knew she'd like as her old one had a tear in the sleeve.

'Are you going to get something for yourself?' Dean asked her.

Carly had been rather impressed by how patient he'd been wandering around with her in a woman's clothes shop. 'I don't like buying stuff for myself,' she replied. 'I always feel guilty.'

'Why?'

'Because I think the money could be better spent on someone else or something for the flat.'

'That's a load of shite. Why shouldn't you have nice things?'

Carly shrugged. 'I don't need them.'

'You could use a new coat of your own. That one you're wearing is crap.'

She scowled at him. 'Whenever I think you're being nice you go and ruin it.'

'Why, what have I said?'

'You insulted my coat.'

'Well, you've got to admit that it's past it. Get a new one.'

All of Dean's clothes were designer, as were his trainers. Clearly he had no problem with treating himself. 'Fine, I'll get this one,' she muttered, snatching up a grey coat from a rail simply because it was the nearest one to her.

He took it from her and replaced it on the rail. 'This one would be much nicer on you,' he said, picking up a deep plum-coloured knee-length coat. 'It'll compliment your eyes perfectly.'

She was annoyed that he was right. 'So you're my personal shopper now as well as my bodyguard?'

'If you like,' he said with a shrug and a smile.

Carly didn't know whether to be annoyed or smile back. She glanced at the price tag. 'It's eighty quid.'

'So?'

'It's too much.'

'It's a good quality coat that will last you a few years but fine, get the cheap shite at twenty quid so by the time next winter comes around you'll need another one, only by then you might not have the cash.'

Carly knew he was right but she was being gripped by guilt she'd had since money had become scarce for her family and they'd had to prioritise the most vital things like food and rent. Now she found herself incapable of spending that precious money on anything else.

'Where are you going?' she said when he marched up to the till.

'I'll buy it for you.'

'You really don't have to.'

'No, but I want to, so don't argue, okay?'

Carly knew she wouldn't be able to stop him, so she let him buy it for her. He asked the woman on the checkout to cut off the tags and then turned to Carly. 'Take that old thing off and put this on. You'll be much warmer.'

When the woman on the till beamed at them, Carly blushed and shrugged off her old coat and took the new one from him. Dean shoved the old one into the carrier bag he held.

'There, much better,' he said when she'd zipped it up.

Carly had to admit that it felt lovely on and would be much

warmer than the old one. 'Thanks,' she told him. 'That was really nice of you.'

'You have such a lovely boyfriend,' the woman on the till told her.

'Oh, he's no' my boyfriend, he's my cousin.'

'Well, you have a very nice cousin then.'

'Yes, I suppose so,' she murmured. 'Thanks, Dean.'

'You're welcome. I'm starving, let's go get some dinner. My treat.'

'No, I'll get it as a thank you for the coat.'

He shrugged. 'If you like.'

They went to a pizza place, Carly gratefully sinking into one of the booths by the window. Dean sat opposite her, both of them placing their purchases on the bench beside them. After ordering, he gazed thoughtfully out of the window at the world passing them by. Carly opened her mouth to speak then closed it again, getting the feeling he found being in a busy place a little fatiguing. He might be a big tough man who threw people across pubs but she was starting to realise that he was sensitive too and he needed a bit of peace and quiet.

Only when their food was placed before them did she feel it was safe to talk.

'Did you manage to get any data off your old laptop?' she asked him.

'A pal of mine has got it,' replied Dean. 'He's working on it.' He picked up a slice of pepperoni pizza and bit into it.

'Good. So, what are your da' and brother up to today?'

His eyes narrowed slightly with suspicion. 'Watching over your sisters, like they said earlier.'

'Oh, right. I thought they might be doing something else too.'

'Why would you think that?'

'It's just the impression I got.'

He studied her for a moment before continuing to eat his slice of pizza.

There was a moment of silence as Carly bit into hers too. The cheese was gooey and delicious. It dripped down her chin and she hastily wiped it away before Dean noticed but he was gazing out of the window again. She found his silence rather restful. Everyone these days was so intent on talking, even if what they were saying was rubbish. With anyone else it would have been awkward but with Dean the silence was companionable and comfortable. She found herself unwinding a little, allowing herself to drift into her own thoughts as she ate.

When he'd finished his pizza, Dean looked to Carly. 'Thank you,' he said.

'For what?' she replied.

'For not chattering away like an idiot. I can't stand small talk. It bores and drains me.'

'You're welcome,' she replied, glad her instincts had been right because she'd formed a new plan. She intended to make a friend of him and hopefully he would confide in her about his family. 'Do you want anything else? Another drink or a dessert?'

'No thanks, I'm stuffed.'

'Me too. That was a great pizza. Do you want to go anywhere else?'

'Aye, Waterstones.'

'Okay. I'll pay and we can go.'

They left the pizzeria and headed into the bookshop. While Dean went straight to the classics section, Carly wandered around general fiction. Not finding anything of interest, she headed back upstairs to find Dean. His back was turned to the room as he studied the shelves, but his phone was pressed to his ear. She ducked into the travel section, which was divided from the classics by a single shelf, to eavesdrop.

'No, I can't,' she heard him say. 'Because I'm busy.' He sighed with frustration. 'I said no, are you deaf?'

The way he growled into the phone indicated that he wasn't speaking to a love interest. He sounded threatening and pissed off.

'If you do,' he hissed into the phone, 'you'll regret it; I promise you that.'

When she didn't hear him speak again, Carly assumed he'd hung up, so she stepped out from her hiding place, smiling at him breezily as though she'd just happened upon him. 'You nearly done?' she asked him.

'What?' he said, surprised to see her. 'Oh, aye. Nearly.'

He turned back to the shelf, eyes still glittering with residual anger. After studying the books for another couple of minutes, he selected two and took them down. 'I need these for my course,' he mumbled.

She followed him to the till and they waited in the queue in silence. He was definitely distracted, barely seeming to notice the man who served him.

Together they left the shop and wandered down the pavement in silence.

'Where to next?' she asked him.

'Do you mind if we go back to Haghill?' he replied, still seeming upset by that call.

'No, not at all,' she replied, glad because she still had over half her money left. She'd use it to stock up the food cupboards at home and get in some treats for her dad and sisters.

'Good.'

He didn't speak again the entire journey home. Although Carly knew full well his mood had nothing to do with her, she decided to take the opportunity to do some gentle probing.

'Have I done something to offend you?' she said.

Finally, Dean dragged his mind off his brooding and looked at her. 'No, why?'

'You've been really quiet since we left the bookshop, even more so than usual.'

'Oh, right. Sorry, I've just got something on my mind.'

'Want to share? I might be able to help.'

'No one can help.'

The desolation in his voice surprised her. Dean sounded as though he had the weight of the world on his shoulders. 'I'm sure that's not true. Problems are never as bad as they seem.'

'This one is.'

'Why, what's wrong?'

'Nothing, it doesn't matter.'

'I want to help you like you're helping me.'

'I can handle it,' he said, changing gear aggressively.

He had that look in his eyes again that said he wouldn't be moved on this, so she decided to back off. She was learning when to attack and when to retreat. A direct assault never worked with Dean. She needed to be more subtle to wheedle the required information out of him.

He parked outside the flat back in Haghill, grabbed all the bags out of the boot, including Carly's, locked the car and strode inside, leaving her to hurry after him.

Carly followed him in suspiciously, wondering if she would see something to tell her what the others had got up to in her absence, but Jane was cleaning the oven, Eddie was chatting with Alec in his room and Harry was watching television in the kitchen.

Jane straightened up, clutching a grimy sponge, yellow gloves on her hands. 'Did you have a nice time?' She smiled at her sister.

'Aye, it was good,' Carly replied.

'I like the new coat.'

'Thanks,' she said. 'I got you a new one too.'

'You didn't need to spend any money on me.'

'I know but I wanted to,' replied Carly, producing the gift from a carrier bag.

Jane smiled with delight. 'It's lovely, thanks.'

'You're welcome. I got Rose's trainers too.'

'Nice one. She'll be over the moon.'

'So, what have you been up to?' Carly asked Jane while glancing at the brothers, who were whispering together at the opposite side of the room.

'What do you think?' she said, indicating the oven.

'That can't have taken you all day.'

'It was really dirty.'

Carly studied her sister. She was lying. 'I get the feeling I've missed something,' she said, glancing again at the brothers, who were still whispering.

'I'm afraid not. It's been a really dull day.'

Carly felt sad. Jane had never lied to her before, not that she was aware of anyway, but she had to trust that she must have a good reason. Jane probably thought she was protecting her but if her older sister was involved in something dangerous, Carly wanted to help.

Jane returned to cleaning the oven before she could be quizzed any further and the brothers had ceased their furtive conversation.

'Something wrong?' Carly asked the men.

'Nope,' replied Harry. 'Everything's fine.'

She narrowed her eyes. Why was everyone lying to her?

14

Derek noticed that Carly seemed miserable at the start of her shift that evening. She wasn't her usual chirpy, smiley self. Not surprising he supposed, considering recent events.

'You all right, hen?' he asked her when there was a lull in customers at the bar.

'Aye, no' bad,' she replied.

'You look really down.'

'I'm not, I've just got a lot on my mind.'

'Don't let those bastards grind you down.'

'It's not them, it's my own family.'

'You mean your cousins and uncle?' he said, casting a glance Dean's way, who was sat at his usual table reading a book.

'Aye. I'm worried about Jane too,' she said quietly, not wanting anyone to overhear. Derek was the only person she could confide in because she could rely on him to not only be sympathetic but to keep it to himself. 'I think Uncle Eddie and his sons are into something dodgy and they've dragged her into it.'

Derek's eyes filled with concern. 'What makes you think that?'

'Nothing definite, just a feeling. Dean took me into the toon earlier; Uncle Eddie even gave me some money to spend.'

'That was nice of them.'

'I reckon they only did it to get me out of the way. They were being really weird.'

'So, you've no definite proof?'

'No, but I know I'm right.'

'Talk to Jane. You could be barking up the wrong tree. There's a lot of pressure on you at the moment, so you could be reading the situation wrong.'

'Maybe, but I know if I ask her, she'll just say everything's fine.'

'It might well be.'

Carly nodded, still troubled. She had hoped he'd soothe her worries but he hadn't in the slightest.

'How did you get on with Dean?' he asked her.

'Okay. He was kind to me, he bought me a new coat. He doesn't talk much but I actually like that. It's quite relaxing once you get used to it. With him, there's no pressure to keep talking.'

'Oh dear, it sounds like Cole's got some competition.' Derek smiled at her before turning to serve a customer at the bar.

Carly was a little startled to realise that she hadn't thought about Cole all day for the first time since they'd met, but it definitely wasn't because she was falling for Dean, it was just because she was so scared her older sister was being dragged into a dangerous situation. She glanced at Dean, who appeared to be engrossed in his book. As she watched, he slyly took his phone out of his pocket, glanced at the screen, frowned and replaced it again. Maybe he was checking the time but she doubted it.

'I'm just nipping to the loo, Derek,' she said.

'Nae bother, doll,' he replied, in the middle of pouring a pint.

She headed into the women's toilets, making sure all the stalls were empty before taking out her phone and calling Cole.

'All right, beautiful?' he said when he answered, making her smile.

'Are you free to talk?'

'I am. I'm at home alone.'

'Good. Can we meet up? I really need to speak to you.'

'Fine by me but can you lose your babysitter?' he replied, bitterness in his tone.

'I'll sneak out when everyone's asleep.'

'I'll meet you outside the flat. I don't want you wandering around alone at night with everything that's going on.'

'Thanks but wait down the street, just in case.' She didn't want to tell him about the cameras Eddie was putting up outside the flat in case he told Ross.

'Will do. What time?'

'Is one o'clock okay?'

'Fine. See you then.'

'Thanks, Cole. I really appreciate it.'

'Anything for you,' he said tenderly.

At the sound of someone entering the toilet, she said, 'Got to go,' before hanging up and shoving the phone into her pocket.

She returned to the bar and glanced at Dean, who was staring back at her with his usual solemn look. Carly had the disturbing notion that he knew what she'd just done.

* * *

Tiredness claimed Carly after her shift at work that night, even though the evening had been mercifully quiet. Feeling on edge, she made her excuses and went to bed early. She listened to the flat around her grow silent as the family settled down to sleep. She remained fully clothed and sat up in bed, not daring to lie down in case she drifted off and missed her meeting with Cole.

When one o'clock came around, she pulled on her trainers, as well as her new coat, opened her bedroom window and jumped out, silently landing on the paving slabs outside. After quietly pushing the window closed, she paused to listen, but when she heard nothing she rushed across the garden to the wall at the bottom. She stood on the storage box that held the lawn mower and used it to scale the wall, dropping down on the other side. Without pause, she raced down the street and turned the corner where she saw Cole waiting for her a few doors down from her flat. It took him a moment to notice her in the darkness, only realising she was there when she stood under the glow of a streetlight. Carly beckoned him and he rushed down the street towards her.

'Hey gorgeous,' he said, beaming.

'Let's go.' She took his hand and practically pulled him away, afraid her cousins would realise what was going on and take it out on Cole.

They didn't stop until they were two streets away from Carly's flat. They headed into a small park to talk. The darkness was almost absolute but she didn't feel nervous with Cole by her side.

'Thanks for meeting me,' she told him breathlessly.

'I'm glad you called,' he said. 'I've missed you so much. I know I said I didn't want to be friends, that it's no' enough, but I've realised I'd rather have that than nothing at all.'

'I'm glad,' she said, smiling. They were still holding hands and she squeezed his hand gratefully. 'I need to talk to you. I don't know what else to do.'

'What's wrong?' he said, coming to a halt and turning her to face him.

'It's my cousins and uncle. I'm afraid they've dragged Jane into a bad situation.'

'Like what?'

'That's the problem, I've no idea. It's just a feeling and she has been acting strange lately. I know my sister and something is going on. I wondered if you'd learnt anything else about my cousins and uncle?'

'Actually, I have. They've spent time in prison.'

'All three of them?

'Aye. Harry got six months for common assault, Eddie got eighteen months for burglary and Dean two years for assault but he only served fourteen months.'

'I'd no idea, although it doesn't surprise me. I'm amazed anyone gave evidence against them if everyone's so feart of them.'

'They got sent down before they'd really cemented their reputations. Prison made them all harder and they came out determined never to go back, so they scared everyone so much no one would dream of grassing on them.'

'I bet my da' doesn't know they've all been inside,' Carly said sadly.

'Probably not. I wish my brother and Emma had left you alone so your da' hadn't felt it necessary to call them in. I get the feeling they're a lot more dangerous than anyone in Haghill.'

'I reckon you're right, which is why it terrifies me that they might have dragged Jane into their world.' She sighed and raked a hand through her hair. 'What do I do, Cole?'

'You need to send them packing.'

'Easier said than done.'

'You need to figure out a way and fast. My theory is they're after taking over Haghill. They've milked Clydebank for all they can get out of it, so they want some new territory.'

'And they're using the excuse of helping us to do it.'

'Aye. Sorry, babe,' he said, looking stricken for her.

'Haven't me and my sisters got enough on our plates without these bastards making everything worse?'

'What can I do to help?'

'Nae idea. I don't even know what to do myself.'

'When you figure it out, let me know, won't you?'

'Aye, I will and you'll let me know if you find out anything else?'

'Of course.'

'Thank you.'

They smiled shyly at each other.

'If they hurt you in any way,' he said, 'I'll kill them.'

He leaned in to kiss her and Carly didn't pull away, even though she knew she should. Life was scary and uncertain and Cole's presence was familiar and comforting. When he kissed her, she allowed herself to fall into the moment, sliding her hands through his hair, remembering how things had been before he'd been sent to prison and when her father hadn't been so ill.

To her surprise, Cole was the first to break the kiss.

'What is it?' she said when he glanced around.

'I thought I heard something.'

Carly frantically scanned the area, afraid her cousins had realised what had happened and were at that point creeping up on them, but she could see no one.

'Let's get out of here,' she said, taking Cole's hand.

'Aye, good idea,' he replied.

They left the darkened park, both grateful to return to the lit streets.

'I'll walk you home,' he told her.

'Thank you for being there for me.'

'It's the least I can do after everything I put you through. I'll always love you, Carly.'

'I'll always love you too,' she replied, voice cracking.

'Hey, it's okay,' he said, stopping to enfold her in his arms.

'I'm scared,' she breathed.

'I won't let anything happen to you, I promise.'

She smiled into his chest, enjoying the feel of his body against her own.

Carly gasped with surprise when Cole was suddenly torn from her arms. She was astonished to see a furious Harry dragging him backwards by the scruff of his jacket.

'Let him go,' she cried, chasing after them. 'Get off me,' she added when strong arms encircled her.

'This is for your own good,' said Dean, refusing to release her.

'No,' she screamed when Harry slammed his fist into Cole's stomach, folding him in half. 'Leave him alone; he hasn't done anything wrong.' She fought harder against Dean but his grip was like iron and she was unable to free herself.

'Hasn't he?' Dean murmured in her ear.

Carly was astonished when Ross, his older brother Dominic and three more men tore around the corner and charged towards them.

'What the hell is going on?' she exclaimed.

Dean released her. 'I'll explain later,' he said, readying himself to fight.

Harry shoved Cole to his knees, produced a knife from inside his jacket and pressed it to the side of his neck.

'Don't hurt him,' cried Carly.

'Stop,' Harry told Ross and his friends.

'Let him go, you fucking twat,' snarled Ross.

'Take one step closer and I'll cut him.'

He spoke so icily a shiver ran down Carly's spine.

Dominic grabbed Ross by the back of the jacket when he took a step towards them and held him fast. 'Stop, all of you,' he told the others. 'He's no' fucking about.'

The group of men came to a halt.

'Will someone please tell me what's going on?' yelled Carly.

'This prick here,' said Harry, nudging Cole in the back with his knee. 'Came here to lure you out so his brothers could abduct you.'

'What? That's ridiculous. Cole would never do that to me.' She looked to her ex-boyfriend, who appeared to be thoroughly pissed off. 'Would you Cole?' she added when he failed to respond.

His narrow green eyes slid her way but he didn't respond.

'It's true?' she croaked.

'He's not the man he was before he went inside,' continued Harry, whose gaze was locked on Ross and the others.

'I don't understand,' she said, bewildered.

'The Alexanders targeted your family to draw us to Haghill,' Dean told her gently. 'This was never about you.'

'But why?' she said, turning to him with wide, sad eyes.

'I'll explain later, promise,' he replied.

Carly nodded and turned to look back at Cole, whose gaze was still locked on her. He didn't dare move his head because of the knife pressed against his throat. She couldn't read the look in his eyes because it was one she'd never seen before.

'Go home,' Harry told the Alexanders and their friends. 'And if this wee shite ever goes near Carly again, I'll cut his throat wide open.'

The five men started to back off, melding into the darkness one by one. Only when they were a safe distance did Harry kick Cole in the back, knocking him onto his front.

'Run,' Harry told Dean and Carly.

Dean grabbed Carly's hand and the three of them broke into a run, the Alexanders making chase.

As they turned onto the street where Carly lived and pelted towards the flat, Eddie stepped out from behind a transit van parked at the kerb, brandishing a shotgun. Carly gasped but Dean pulled her on past his father.

'Stop, you bunch of fannies,' Eddie told their pursuers, cocking the weapon aggressively.

The Alexanders skidded to a halt before turning on their heel and speeding off into the night.

Carly's eyes remained locked on Cole as he vanished into the darkness. He didn't even glance back at her.

She looked so anguished Eddie wrapped an arm around her. 'Let's get you inside, hen.'

Carly just nodded and allowed the three men to escort her back into the flat.

15

Jane greeted them at the door in her pyjamas.

'Thank God,' she said, embracing her sister.

This kindness almost undid Carly but she managed to keep in her tears as she hung onto Jane.

When the three men entered and closed the door behind them, Harry ensuring it was locked, Carly released her sister. 'Will someone please tell me what's going on?' she whispered, conscious of Rose and her father asleep in their rooms.

Jane nodded and indicated the kitchen. The five of them entered, Eddie still carrying the shotgun.

'I'll get you a hot drink,' said Jane, steering Carly into a chair at the table.

Dean sat beside her, Harry on her other side. Eddie lay the shotgun on the worktop before taking the chair opposite his niece, who sat there shivering in her new coat.

'Why did Cole do that to me?' Carly's voice was hoarse as she was desperately fighting against the threatening tears but she refused to shed them in front of everyone.

'It all started a year ago, in Barlinnie,' began Eddie in the gentlest tone Carly had ever heard him use. 'He was in there at the same time as my boys.'

She nodded. 'Cole told me all three of you have been in prison but he never mentioned it was at the same time as him.'

'When did he tell you that?'

'Just now. How did you find me anyway?'

'Jane's bedroom is opposite yours. When she felt a cold draught blowing through the flat, she realised it was coming from your room. She got up to find you gone and your bedroom window standing open, so she woke us up and sent us out to find you.'

Carly thought it a blessing that the window had popped open again. 'Why didn't they snatch me when I was in the park? That would have been more sensible.'

'Maybe they lost you?'

Carly nodded thoughtfully. 'I did grab Cole's hand and we ran away from here; I was afraid you'd catch up with us, so we could have lost them then.'

'They knew you'd return to the flat, so all they had to do was wait for you to come back.'

Her smile had no humour in it. 'God, I feel like such an idiot. Thanks by the way, all of you.'

'Any time for you, doll.'

Carly nodded and dragged her hands through her hair, feeling exhausted. 'Anyway, you were saying?'

'Oh aye. Well, my boys looked after Cole when he was inside because they heard he was your boyfriend. Then things turned bad. Cole shivved another prisoner in Bar-L on Ross's say-so.'

'Oh Christ,' she sighed. 'Did the man survive?' she added as Jane handed her a cup of tea. Carly wrapped her hands around the mug, attempting to drive the cold out of her bones.

'Aye, he did but there was some retaliation. The man in question was from quite a strong firm in Parkhead. My boys protected Cole from that too, until I ordered them to stop.'

'What?' said Carly, surprised.

'I wanted to help Cole but I had to put my sons first. The family from Parkhead are a bunch of mental bastards with quite a few friends on the inside. I didn't want my boys getting shivved too.'

'I suppose I can understand that,' she replied.

'The Alexander family had their own pals in Bar-L who could look out for Cole, so I told my boys to leave it to them. I'm so glad I gave that order because a few days later an Alexander cousin got stabbed in the kidneys. He survived but he only has one kidney now.'

'Jesus.'

'Aye, it's a brutal place. There was a lot of back and forth between the two sides, it really pissed off the governor. Quite a few of them ended up in segregation, including Cole. It really affected him, didn't it?' said Eddie, looking to his sons. 'Dean was inside longer than Harry, so he saw how it affected Cole more.'

Dean nodded. 'Aye, he became angrier and more ruthless. He was all right at first but then he got darker. I'd say that now he's worse than either of his brothers.'

'I find that hard to believe,' said Carly.

'It's true. He got into loads of fights and he usually won too. He kept nagging at me to back him up, even more so when Harry was released. He seemed to think that I needed him now my brother had gone but I told him to sod off. No way was I gonnae risk my release for him. He didn't like that. He tried to set me up for the stabbing of another prisoner but luckily I was in the gym at the time with plenty of witnesses, including a prison guard. They didn't get Cole for it though. He was sneaky you see and always made sure nothing could be pinned on him. He was never overt like a lot of the psychos in there.'

'Jesus,' she sighed. 'I can't believe this. Cole was a Jack the Lad but he was never a serious criminal. He only ended up inside because he put his faith in Ross when he shouldn't have.'

'Prison can take some people like that,' said Eddie sagely. 'It twists them into something they weren't before they went in. Unfortunately, that's what it did to Cole.'

'But he seemed exactly the same to me as before he went in.'

'Did he tonight?'

'He did earlier, when it was just us, but then...' She trailed off as she considered how he'd looked at her. His beautiful eyes had been those of a stranger.

'I find it hard to believe that he'd do anything to hurt you,' Jane told her sister. 'I remember how in love you both were but think about how he spoke to you in prison when he dumped you.'

That was the last thing Carly wanted to be reminded of, but she nodded. 'Aye, he was pretty vicious. I put it down to the trauma of being inside.'

'You were probably right but that trauma has turned him into someone else.'

'You already knew about this, didn't you?'

Jane nodded. 'Uncle Eddie told me all about it.'

'That's why you wanted me out of the way yesterday?'

'Aye, sorry about that. We wanted to do some digging without you asking questions. We hoped to sort it out but it seems we made the whole thing worse.'

'Oh no, what happened? And why are the Alexanders targeting you?' she said, turning to look at her uncle and cousins. 'It can't just be because Dean and Harry refused to help him in prison.'

'You're right, it's not,' said Eddie. 'Cole wants what we have.'

'What's that? Your drug dealing business?' she said, narrowing her eyes.

'So you already know about that?'

'Course I do, I'm no' an idiot. Like I believed you got all that cash from betting on the horses. Does Da' know about it?'

'No, and I don't want him to find out,' Eddie said sternly. 'I've only just got my brother back and I don't want to lose him again.'

'I'd never tell him; I wouldn't hurt him like that.'

'Good,' he said, relaxing a little. 'Our business has become very profitable and the Alexanders want to take it from us. They've been ambitious for a while now and want to break out of Haghill and into other areas.'

'Brian and Jessica would never allow that.'

'You must be joking. Jessica's the ringleader. Brian doesn't seem as bothered about it as his wife. She's the one who's been encouraging her sons to do all this. The Alexanders learnt a lot of useful information about us when Cole was in prison, which was what encouraged them to try and pull off this coup.'

'Jessica?' She frowned. 'That can't be right.'

'There's no doubt. My boys didnae discuss our business dealings with Cole, it was a wee shite called Benton who did some running around for us. He was happy to spill his guts to Cole for a few quid. Dean turned him into paste, didn't you, lad?' said Eddie, looking proudly at his younger son.

Dean nodded, his expression deadpan.

'But I met with Jessica only recently and she said she was trying to keep her boys on the straight and narrow,' said Carly.

'You must be joking,' said Eddie. 'That coo's the worst of the lot. She's got expensive tastes, so she wants more money to satisfy them. She wants the big house, flash cars, the designer gear. None of her family are capable of earning that kind of money legally, so they have to look to illegal methods.'

'She was just trying to get information out of me about you?'

'Aye she was. Sorry, hen.'

'So what happened yesterday that escalated everything?'

'Me, Jane and Harry went to Malcolm Johnson's house. You heard of him?'

'Who hasn't in Haghill? He's a loon that most people around here are afraid of. He'd stab you as soon as look at you.'

'Aye, he is a wee bit stabby but he's recently teamed up with the Alexanders.'

'More fool them; he's a loose cannon.'

'It's no' as daft a move as you'd think. Malcolm has close ties to a family called the Cowans in Barlanark who are up and coming. The Alexanders are trying to join forces with them and were using Malcolm as a go-between. He's no' the ideal choice but he's their only option. We persuaded him to stop working on their behalf.'

'Persuaded him how?'

'You don't need to know about that.'

'Stop treating me like a wean, Uncle Eddie. I can take it.'

'We gave him a good hiding,' Jane told her.

'Why did you have to join in?' Carly demanded of her sister. 'You've been out of that life for a while now.'

'Because Jane still has her contacts,' replied Eddie. 'As well as a lot of influence in Haghill.'

'I wish you hadn't got involved in this,' Carly told her sister.

'I'm sorry but I had no choice.'

Carly sighed and shook her head. 'And did Malcolm agree not to negotiate for the Alexanders?'

'He did, which is why they tried to snatch you tonight,' replied Eddie. 'To make us do what they want.'

'And what's that? Get you to hand everything over to them?'

'Aye. No doubt about it.'

'Why didn't you tell me? If you had, all this could have been avoided.'

'They wanted to tell you,' said Jane, gesturing to her uncle and cousins. 'But I didn't want to get you involved. Looking back on it, that was a bad decision. It almost led to you being kidnapped,' she said, tears welling in her eyes.

Something in Carly relented. She could never bear seeing her sister cry. 'Well, it didn't and that's thanks to you realising I'd gone.'

Jane forced a smile and nodded, blinking away her tears.

'So now you know everything,' Eddie told Carly.

'Why did you get involved in drugs?' she sighed. 'It's a nasty business and it never ends well.'

'Because I was sick of struggling to make ends meet, of working shitey jobs that treated me like crap just to earn a meagre wage. No one cares about the workers any more. We're treated like fucking beasts, forced to work under terrible conditions and if you complain you're sacked and they get someone else in because there's no shortage of people needing jobs. I wanted my boys to have the best and if that was the only way they could get it then so be it. It's no' like I force anyone to take drugs. If someone wants to stuff a load of white powder up their nose that's their business. Why shouldn't I make a few quid off their stupidity?'

'So it's coke you deal in?'

'Aye, and cannabis too. I don't touch heroin, that's really horrible stuff and people lose their minds over the brown. I've seen too many people get killed over it.'

'Aren't you afraid of the bigger gangs getting wind of what you're doing?'

'I'm careful to stay low level. The McVay family are the biggest dealers in this city but they don't mind the small fish like me. They know I'm no' strong enough to tread on their toes. It's greedy bastards like the Alexanders that wind them up, the ones who are never content and always want more.'

'Cole told me you're an armed robber too,' said Carly, eyes slipping to the shotgun on the worktop.

'I used to be, but I packed that in. You can get banged up for years just for carrying a loaded gun, even if you don't do anything with it, so it's no' worth the hassle. Plus, with CCTV it's so much harder to get away with it these days. And don't worry, I never used that gun for robberies, it's far too big and clumsy. I had a sawn off that I got rid of years ago.'

'Then why do you have that gun?'

'For clay pigeon shooting. It's my hobby. I go to this lovely range at Loch Lomond a few times a month. Technically I should keep it locked away but I thought it might come in useful.'

Carly looked to her cousins. 'Do you two deal drugs too?'

'Naw, they're just my muscle,' said Eddie. 'Only I touch all that. I don't want to risk them getting lifted for it.'

'That's something I suppose,' she sighed. 'You've known this was about you from the moment Jane called you in, haven't you?'

'Aye, we have. We thought we could sort it out nice and quietly but we were wrong. I'm sorry, I never wanted you to be dragged into it but we will sort it out, I swear to God.'

'And how do you intend to do that?'

'By isolating the Alexanders from their supporters, which is where Jane comes in.'

'I'm going to take back the Bitches,' said her sister.

'Oh, please no,' said Carly. 'You spent so long trying to get out. You're living a respectable life now.'

'And what has that life got us? Nothing but struggle and hardship, working in a job I absolutely hate, for a pittance. If I take back the Bitches, not only will I keep them in line and stop them from terrorising the local community, but I can make them work for us.'

'What do you mean?'

'Uncle Eddie wants to branch out into Haghill.'

Carly shook her head, appalled. 'You want to become a dealer too.'

'God no. That's the last thing this area needs. Uncle Eddie has a different business venture in mind.'

Carly looked to her uncle, who appeared very pleased with himself. 'What venture?' she asked him.

'We'll be bodyguards for anyone who wants our services,' he replied.

'Like Kevin Costner in that film?' Carly chuckled.

'No, doll, no' like him.' Eddie frowned. 'Since covid, there's been a massive rise in gangs in Glasgow. I don't mean the serious type like the McVays who have an empire and rake in millions every year. I'm talking about the wee ned gangs causing havoc. The cowardly shites that attack someone walking alone and then post videos of it on social media. Real criminals don't paste themselves all over the internet like morons for the polis to see,' he said with disgust. 'The real deal are subtle and stay under the radar.'

'But they're just weans. If you attack them, you'll go to prison.'

'They're committing crimes and hurting people. Anyway, a lot of them aren't weans and we don't intend to tackle them directly, we'll just be a deterrent for those who feel they need it, such as local businesses who are being targeted.'

Carly was unconvinced. 'Are you sure it will work?'

'Aye, course. We did the same thing back in Clydebank. It was very popular.'

'But Cole said...' began Carly before trailing off and sighing.

'What did he say?'

'That you terrorised everyone in Clydebank.'

'He said that to try and turn you against us. We've got a great reputation in that town, ask anyone there.'

'I intended to but Jane stopped me,' she said, glancing at her sister.

'And isn't this idea better than drug dealing?' Eddie asked Carly, ignoring her jibe at Jane.

'Aye, suppose,' she said, wondering if this new venture of his was going to be a front for something even worse than drugs.

'I spotted a gap in the market,' continued Eddie. 'People are being terrorised but the polis are stretched too thin to help them. Those people turn to us. Not only will me and my boys be helping people but the Bitches will as well if Jane gets them back under control.'

'For a price of course?'

'Aye, but we'll only charge what people can afford.'

'You really think this is a good idea?' she asked her sister.

'I do,' said Jane. 'It certainly beats working in that crappy call centre.'

'Will the Bitches agree to it?'

'Some of them already have. I just need to get those who are loyal to Emma on board.'

'And what about Emma herself? She won't just stand aside and let you take back control.'

'Leave her to me.'

'I don't know. What would Da' think of this?'

'Life will be better for him too. We'll be able to pay all the bills without worrying and ensure he has everything he needs.'

'He won't approve.'

'He's not going to find out.'

'We can't keep it from him forever.'

'We can and we will. This is the chance we've been waiting for to improve all our lives. Don't tell me you don't want life to get easier?'

'Course I do but I'm no' sure this is the way, especially as we have to take on the Alexanders and the Bitches to get it. That's a lot of people to fight.'

'Aye, but we can do it. Trust us, Carly.'

When they all stared at her, she sighed and nodded, too exhausted to argue any further. 'All right, I will. How can I help?'

'You can keep your eyes open in the pub,' Eddie told her. 'Listen out for any useful information. People get loose lipped when they're pished.'

'That's it?'

'Aye, that's it. We want to keep you and Rose out of this as much as possible.'

'You mean there's no room for us in your new business model?' she said with a touch of sarcasm.

'We'll have to see,' was all he was willing to reply.

Carly sighed. She felt tired and dazed.

'Why don't you get yourself to bed?' Jane told her. 'You look done in.'

'Aye, I think I will,' she said, hauling herself to her feet and shuffling out of the room without another word.

'Poor Carly,' said Jane. 'She's in shock.'

'I'm no' surprised,' commented Harry.

'She didnae seem very keen on my business idea.' Eddie pouted.

'She's still dealing with what Cole did,' Jane told him. 'We're best talking to her again when she's had the chance to get over it.'

'Perhaps you're right.' He yawned and got to his feet. 'We should all get some rest because we've stirred up a shitstorm tonight.'

16

It took Carly a while to drop off that night. She tossed and turned, tormented by the memory of the way Cole's eyes had narrowed at her, as though all his love for her had gone. If that was true though, how had he so convincingly professed to still being in love with her? She longed to talk to him, to see if it was all true. After all, she'd only had her uncle's version of events and there were two sides to every story.

The next thing she knew it was daylight and Rose was popping her head into her room to say goodbye, and that Uncle Eddie was taking her to school. Judging by how happy and carefree she looked, Rose still knew nothing about the previous night's events. Carly envied her sister her ignorance.

After Rose had left, Carly showered, dressed and headed into her father's room to see him but he wasn't there, his bed left rumpled and unmade.

Panicking, she raced into the kitchen to find him sitting at the table enjoying a cup of tea with his brother and nephews.

'Da'.' Carly beamed, delighted. 'It's great to see you out of your room.' After the depression and lethargy had settled over him when his condition had taken a drastic downturn, he'd never shown any inclination to leave his room.

'Hi sweetheart,' he said, beaming back at her. 'Eddie and the boys helped me in here. I wanted to get out of my room for a bit.' His speech was slow and slurred, his expression mask-like, but his eyes were bright.

'That's really great.' She kissed his cheek. 'How does it feel?'

'Good. I've hidden away in there too long.' He paused and pressed a tissue to his mouth. He cleared his throat before continuing. 'I want to spend more time with my family.'

Carly smiled and hugged him.

'How have things been with the Alexanders?' Alec asked them all.

'Fine, Da',' said Jane. 'It seems to have quietened down.'

'Good.' He looked to Eddie. Because of the mask-like expression, it was sometimes hard to read his moods but Carly could see the worry in his eyes. 'You're not...?'

'No way, pal,' Eddie hastened to reassure him. 'We're going nowhere, especially now I've rented that house for me and the boys.'

'That's wonderful,' said Alec before pressing the tissue back to his mouth.

Carly patted her father's shoulder, knowing he was embarrassed about his symptoms. She had to give Eddie his due, he took everything in his stride and it never seemed like he felt awkward around his brother.

'Are all three of you moving into this house you've rented?' Carly asked her uncle.

'Aye. It'll be a new start. Our family all together, at last.'

'Great,' said Alec. 'Isn't it, girls?'

'Aye, Da'.' Jane smiled.

'Yeah,' said Carly. 'Great.'

She glanced at Dean who was giving her another of his inscrutable looks.

* * *

Carly never found a chance to discuss recent events with her sister in private, even when their father returned to his room, because her uncle and cousins were ever-present. Every time she turned around one of them was there.

'Christ,' she grunted when she exited her bedroom and almost walked smack into Harry. 'Can't I get some space? I'm going demented with so many of us crowded in here together. I'm going out for a walk before I get cabin fever.'

'Not without one of us,' he told her.

'I'm going to get away from you. Everywhere I go you're there and it's doing my head in. This flat is too small for so many people.'

'I can take you out again,' Dean told her.

'That's very kind of you but I couldn't face the city. I need to get away from people.'

'I know a quiet place. I get the same way and I need somewhere to escape to.'

Clearly Dean failed to realise that he was one of the people Carly wanted to escape but at least she would get out of the flat for a while.

'Is it far?' she asked him.

'Not really,' he replied, enigmatic as always.

'Go,' Jane told her. 'Before you end up punching someone.'

'Okay, fine. Let's go,' she told Dean wearily.

* * *

Carly was once again grateful for her cousin's quiet nature. He didn't speak at all during the drive, enabling her to gaze out of the window and lose herself in her thoughts, which were naturally of Cole. She recalled what they'd once shared and wondered how he could have forgotten that so easily. Or had he? Her uncle's word wasn't enough. She didn't know who Eddie was; he'd been a stranger to her for half her life. The problem was, how could she talk to Cole without the rest of his family attacking her, because that had clearly been their purpose the previous night.

It was only when they turned up a narrow country lane that Carly once again became aware of her surroundings.

'Where are we going?' she said.

'This is the road up to Gleniffer Braes Country Park,' replied Dean.

'Aye but... where is it?'

'Paisley.'

'Oh. It seems more remote than that,' she said as he negotiated the tight bends, which were shrouded by trees.

Finally, they reached a small, gravelled car park where they came to a halt.

'Come on then,' said Dean, switching off the engine, flinging open his door and getting out.

Carly climbed out too, her body feeling sluggish and heavy with tiredness after the previous night. 'I don't have the energy for a long trek,' she told him as he locked the car.

'We won't go far, just enough to blow out the cobwebs.'

'Okay,' she mumbled, shoving her hands into her pockets and trailing after him out of the car park.

They wandered along a well-defined trail surrounded by pine trees, once again in silence. Carly breathed in the crisp, fresh air, feeling her mood lift a little. It was quiet, the only people they passed a couple of walkers.

'It doesn't feel like we're in Paisley,' she said.

'I know,' replied Dean. 'It's pretty magical, isn't it?'

'Aye, it is,' she said, eyes bright as she took in the view. 'Is that a river?' she added at the sound of rushing water.

'No, it's the Craigie Linn waterfall.'

Carly had expected a small, piddly trickle of water but on the contrary, the waterfall was quite forceful after the recent rain, pouring down the rocks into the pool below.

After admiring this for a few minutes, they walked a little further until they came to a bench where they decided to rest and look down on the Harelaw Reservoir, the city of Paisley spreading out into the distance behind it.

Carly felt her emotions start to overwhelm her. She was appalled when silent tears began to roll down her face. She was a Savage and Savages rarely cried, especially in front of other people, but she was tired, hurt and scared for her family and she couldn't stop it. From the corner of her eye, she noticed Dean give her a sideways glance but he didn't comment. Instead, he placed his hand over hers and remained a strong, silent presence, which was just what she needed.

'Did Cole mention me when you were in prison together?' she said when she was able to talk without bursting into tears, although her voice sounded choked and husky.

'Yes,' replied Dean. 'Quite a lot actually.'

'What did he say?'

'He said how beautiful, clever and funny you were and how much he loved you.'

Carly's body shuddered as she fought to keep in the tears.

'He also said he couldn't wait to be released so you could be together again.'

'If that was true then why did he dump me and in front of everyone too?' A terrible thought occurred to her and she turned to look at him. 'Were you and Harry in the visits centre when that happened?'

'Aye,' he said a little sheepishly. 'We were.'

'Oh, that's fucking marvellous. More people to witness my humiliation. I never noticed you in the visits centre but then again, I wouldn't have recognised you. Both you and Harry look nothing like the annoying wee shites you used to be.'

'I suppose that can only be a good thing.' He smiled, taking no offence.

'At the risk of sounding needy and pathetic, did Cole still love me after he dumped me in prison?'

'He did, no doubt about it.'

'I'm still struggling to get my head around how much he's changed.'

'You'd understand if you saw what he went through in prison. He was scared when he first arrived and that's understandable. Everyone's scared setting foot in that place for the first time but he had to do dark things inside, mainly at the behest of his own family. It changed him, hardened his heart.'

'It's so tragic because he did have a good heart.'

'Maybe it's still in there, buried deep?'

'Or maybe it never existed and it was an illusion.'

'I couldn't say.'

'I feel like such an idiot for walking into his trap last night.'

'You weren't to know and I think it's more our fault than yours. We should have told you what was going on but Da' said you wouldn't believe us if we'd said Cole, err...'

It was the first time she'd seen Dean lost for words, so she finished the sentence for him. 'Didn't love me any more. Is that what you're trying to say?'

'Aye, but I wanted to phrase it better. Anyway, I'm no' sure he doesn't.'

'He was in on trying to kidnap me. I'd say that's a pretty strong indication.'

'Maybe not.'

'I wish you wouldn't keep saying maybe. I need definite answers right now.'

'If I had them I'd give you them but I don't. I can't read Cole's mind or see into the future.'

'Aye. Sorry.'

'It's okay.'

'Cole told me you were dangerous.'

'I suppose I am.'

'Really? Should I be scared?'

'I don't hit women.'

'That's good to know. If I ask you a question, will you promise not to tell your da' about it?'

Dean considered this before nodding. 'I promise.'

Carly studied him closely and decided he was being truthful. 'Is everything Uncle Eddie said about wanting to be bodyguards for the local community a load of old shite and he's using it as a cover to start dealing in Haghill?'

'No' that I'm aware of.'

'You swear?'

'Aye. He's getting out of the drugs game. It's so brutal. There are people willing to kill over a bit of coke or weed. We've seen other dealers get glassed in the face or have their kneecaps broken over a turf war and that turf can be a single street. It's pathetic and he wants us all out before something bad happens. Me and Harry getting sent down hit him hard too.'

'I thought you were done for assault, no' dealing?'

'We were but those fights were over territory. That was when Da' decided he was gonnae get us out. When we got Jane's call, he spotted the perfect opportunity.'

'Well, I'm glad he's getting you out of drugs. That shite does no one any good. You would all have ended up dead or in prison.'

'I've no doubt you're right.'

'And Uncle Eddie really doesn't have any other plans?'

'If he has he hasnae told me.'

'Is he likely to keep something like that from you?'

He gave another of his shrugs. 'He can be unpredictable but he's usually straight down the line with me and my brother.'

'Okay, that makes me feel a bit better. What do you think about moving to Haghill?'

'Dunno. It's no worse or better than where we are now, so it makes no difference to me.'

'I get the feeling you'd be happy anywhere if you had your books.'

'They're my escape.'

'Is life that bad for you?'

'They're no' an escape from somewhere but to somewhere.'

'I don't understand.'

'I'm fascinated by the past. The modern world doesn't really interest me. It's ugly and shallow. My maw said I was born too late.'

'I see what she means. Do you see much of her?'

His smile flickered. 'No' for ages. She's too wrapped up in her own life.'

'I'm sorry.'

Dean hesitated before continuing, 'She walked out on us years ago, ran off to Blackpool with some prick called Gordon. We didn't hear anything from her, except the odd letter on mine and Harry's birthdays. A couple of months ago, she suddenly turned up on the doorstep. It shocked the hell out of us all. She used to be so pretty but she looked really bad and she stank of booze. Da' was so nice to her; I don't think he ever stopped loving her, despite what she did. She said she wanted to be involved in our lives again.'

'That's a good thing, isn't it?'

'It would be if she hadn't brought along some fucking loser called Wayne the third time she came to visit. She moved to Hartlepool from Blackpool five years ago when she broke up with Gordon and that's where she met Wayne, in the bookies. He's an ugly, rat-faced wee twat. I wouldnae trust him as far as I could throw him. Maw said she's gonnae marry him and he'll be mine and Harry's stepda'. We were both so angry that she thought she could swan back into our lives and start telling us we had to treat him like a da' when our real da' has always been there for us, so we told her to piss off, we're no' interested. She called me when we were in Waterstones yesterday trying to persuade me to come to the wedding but I said no. I want nothing to do with her or that creep. We don't need her; the three of us are fine as we are. She put Wayne on the phone, thinking he could persuade me. He called me an ungrateful little bastard and said he'd drag me to the wedding if he had to. I warned him what would happen if he tried.'

Dean took a long, deep breath. He wasn't used to talking so much all in one go, although it was a relief to get it off his chest.

'What does Uncle Eddie think about this wedding?'

'He's hurt, even though they got divorced years ago. He's been after another relationship himself but he's never been able to find a woman he loves as much as my maw.'

'That's really sweet and, at the same time, so tragic.'

'When us Savage men fall in love, we fall for life.'

'Like my da' with my maw,' she said wistfully. 'He misses her every single day. I'm sorry you're going through so much.'

'It's just the way it is. I have my da' and my brother and now I have my cousins and uncle. That's sort of nice after it just being the three of us for so long.'

'I know how you feel.'

'You didn't seem too happy about us being here.'

'That was because I thought you were up to something. Now I know you're on our side.'

'We'd never do anything to hurt any of you. My da' really regretted the estrangement with Uncle Alec and over money too. He said it was fucking stupid losing his only brother over something so petty and he always swore he'd make it up to him if he got the chance. This is his chance.'

Dean's words were starting to convince Carly that he and his brother and father were working in her own family's best interests after all but she would remain on her guard until she could be absolutely certain. After Cole's betrayal, the mere memory of which was enough to make her heart ache, she certainly wouldn't put it past them.

Carly looked back out at the stunning view. 'I don't know how you can say this world is ugly.'

'I don't mean the world itself; I mean our society and culture. All fast food and celebrities.' He grimaced. 'There's no class or elegance any more.'

The corner of Carly's mouth lifted as she studied this large hulk of a man in his jeans, jumper and puffer jacket. 'You hardly look like an Edwardian gentleman yourself,' she commented.

'I'm talking about people's attitudes to life. Nowadays it's all about speed and greed, people desperate for five minutes of fame or to get rich for doing nothing at all.'

'I'm no' sure a man who beats people up for a living has any room to criticise.'

'Maybe.'

'I have to ask – do things bother you or does everything wash over you, because that's what it looks like.'

'Things do bother me, it's why I need to come to places like this, to get away from it all for a while and clear my head.'

'You sound like you could happily live alone on a deserted island.'

'No, actually. I don't mind people too much, as long as I can get regular breaks from them.' He smiled at her.

'What?' she said.

'I like talking to you. You ask interesting questions and you don't talk about the Kardashians or TikTok or pop singers. All that shite gi'es me the boke.'

'I think I've just been paid a massive compliment.'

'You have. There's no' many people I like talking to. You're also happy to be quiet. It's why I brought you here. If you'd chattered like a budgie, I'd have left you behind.'

'And I wouldn't have blamed you,' she replied, amused. 'You're pretty good company yourself. You let me be alone with my thoughts.'

'I bet they've been a bit turbulent lately,' he said, turning his gaze from her to look out at the view.

'Just a bit. I'm still struggling, not only with what Cole did, but Jessica's role in it all too. She was the only other Alexander I got on with. I thought she liked me but she was only using me to get information about you, Harry and Uncle Eddie.'

'She's another one who's greedy and grasping, willing to put you at risk so she can get the money to buy designer crap.'

'Maybe you're right and the world has gone mad.'

'Course I am. Anyway, I've talked about myself and it's no' often I do that, so now it's your turn.'

'What do you want to know?'

'Is this life all you want or do you want more?'

Carly smiled. It seemed Dean was a philosophical man who was only interested in the deeper conversations. 'I want more. Don't get me wrong, I love working at the pub and living with my sisters and my da' but I do want more out of life. The problem is, I've no idea what that is.'

'You're only young; you've got plenty of time to decide,' he replied, sounding like a man much older than his twenty-two years.

'I remember at school when we filled in that questionnaire online that told you your perfect career, I got office clerk and God that depressed me. I don't want ordinary, mundane, I want...'

'More,' he finished for her.

'Aye, but what is that?' Carly noted how deep in thought he appeared. 'I'm guessing you're the same?'

He nodded. 'I have the same problem. I don't know what I want.'

'How about being a dusty scholar with leather patches on your elbows, smoking a pipe in a library surrounded by books and old manuscripts?'

The corner of his mouth lifted into a smile that she was starting to find rather adorable.

'Sometimes I think that would be pretty nice,' he said. 'Then I think I'd probably get bored after a while.'

'Do you want to be a bodyguard, which is the future Uncle Eddie seems to have mapped out for you?'

He shrugged. 'It'll do for now, until I can figure things out.'

Carly was beginning to hope her Uncle Eddie didn't drag Dean down a dark path because she thought him capable of so much more.

17

'Well, you look better,' Jane told Carly on her return to the house. 'You've got colour back in your cheeks.'

'We went to Gleniffer Braes Country Park,' she replied. 'I'd no idea there was anywhere like it in Paisley. It's beautiful, we even saw some highland coos. Dean said they're used to control the vegetation. You look like you could do with a trip out there yourself, you're really pale.' Anxiety filled Carly. 'Did something happen while we were out?'

'No, it's been quiet. I'm just tired after my late night.'

'Oh, sorry,' mumbled Carly.

'Don't be. I made lasagne, so go and eat before you start your shift.'

Carly smiled. 'My favourite.'

'I know.' Jane smiled back.

She watched her younger sister eagerly bustle into the kitchen. When she'd gone, she looked to Dean.

'Thank you,' she whispered to him. 'You really cheered her up.'

'No problem,' was his casual response.

They entered the kitchen. Jane watched Dean's eyes follow

Carly as she helped herself to the lasagne steaming away in a dish on the worktop.

'Do you want some?' Jane asked him.

'No thanks, I'm not hungry,' he replied, gaze still on Carly.

'If you don't want any then why are you staring at it like that?' she said knowingly.

Dean blushed and looked down at the floor, mumbling something inaudible.

Jane watched him sink onto the couch beside his brother and take out his phone. As he scrolled, his eyes intermittently flicked to Carly, who sat at the table eating her dinner.

'Sure you don't want any lasagne?' Jane asked him with a raised eyebrow.

'Sure,' he said, hastily returning his attention to his phone.

Jane sighed inwardly. The last thing this already complicated situation needed was for Dean to fall for Carly, especially when they were living in such close quarters. She studied her sister, who seemed more concerned with the food than her cousin. Carly had just been badly hurt by Cole, so hopefully another man would be the last thing on her mind. Dean was very good-looking though and her sister was vulnerable, which might lead her to do something she'd regret.

When Carly had almost finished eating, Jane said, 'Harry, why don't you go to the pub with Carly? You've been stuck in all day.'

'Probably not a good idea,' he replied. 'I'll get bored sitting around and end up getting pished. Dean doesn't mind because he has his books.'

Dean's eyes slipped to Jane. He knew exactly why she'd made that suggestion.

'Well,' said Carly, carrying her empty plate over to the sink. 'Whoever's coming with me needs to get moving because my shift starts in fifteen minutes.'

'I'll come,' said Dean. 'I've got some reading to do for my course anyway.'

'Remember what I told you,' Harry said to his younger brother sternly.

'Aye, I do.' He nodded.

'Have a good shift,' Jane told her sister, gently squeezing her arm as she walked past her to the door. Every time her sisters left the flat she worried about them, even though they were now accompanied by their uncle or cousins.

'I will,' she said chirpily before leaving with Dean.

Jane and Harry watched them drive off in Dean's car from the front door.

'My da' should be here in a few minutes,' Harry told her. 'Then we can go.'

'Good,' she replied. 'We might be able to end this situation before it can even start.'

* * *

'So, what did your brother tell you?' Carly asked Dean on their way to the pub.

'Sorry?'

'On your way out, Harry said to remember what he'd told you.'

'Oh, aye. That.'

'Well?' she said when he failed to elaborate. 'What did he mean?'

'To call him if anything even slightly weird happens.'

'Is that it?'

'Aye. Why, isn't that enough?'

'I was expecting something more dramatic.'

'Sorry to disappoint you.'

Carly wondered if he was lying to her, concealing more secrets.

The thought was rather painful after the way they'd confided in each other at Gleniffer Braes.

As soon as Carly arrived at the pub, Derek shot off to use the toilet.

'Does he have a problem?' Dean asked her as he settled himself at the bar.

'Aye, a tiny teabag bladder.'

Dean chuckled.

'Do you think the Alexanders will do anything tonight?' she asked him, lowering her voice.

'Hard to tell. Maybe.'

'Hey, look who it is,' exclaimed a voice.

Jim staggered up to the bar and slung an arm around Dean's shoulders. 'It's the hero of the hour,' he slurred. 'I'll never forget the way you battered that wee fanny in the face with a laptop. Carly, doll, gi'e the lad a whisky. He deserves it.'

'He doesn't drink.'

Jim's eyes bulged. 'Doesn't drink? What shite's this?'

'Dean doesn't drink, he doesn't like it.'

Jim stared at him in amazement. 'How do you live?'

'Very well, thanks,' Dean replied coolly while Carly laughed.

'I'd say you're a big Jessie but I'm too afraid of getting hit in the face. How about orange juice, do you drink that?'

Dean nodded.

'Thank Christ for that. Get the lad an orange juice, Carly and another pint for me,' he added, dumping a ten-pound note on the bar.

'Coming right up,' she said, pouring the drinks.

'The Alexanders are foaming at the mouth to get you back,' he said. 'They're fucking furious.'

'Have you spoken to them, Jim?' said Carly, trying to sound relaxed as she poured his pint.

'Naw, but Brian was in the bookies earlier, fucking fizzing he was. That family's got their sights set on you,' added Jim, nudging Dean with his elbow. 'He was coming out with all this nasty stuff about what he's gonnae do to you.'

'And what is he gonnae do to me?' said Dean with only the merest hint of curiosity in his tone.

'He wants to strap you naked to a chair and go to town on you with a pair of pliers. If you ask me, he sounded a wee bit gay. I've always had my doubts about that bastard. Fancy being married to a looker like Jessica and no' giving her a right good seeing to.'

'What do you mean?' said Carly, quick to pounce on that statement.

'She's had loads of affairs, she's put it about for years. Brian's a fucking mug for letting it slide.'

'Who's she had affairs with?'

Jim's eyes suddenly widened.

'Hello, Jim?' said Carly, waving a hand in front of his face, afraid he was having some sort of fit.

'Oh, sorry, I've just remembered… I left the iron on.'

'What about your change?' she called after him as he ran out of the pub.

'Keep it,' he called back before disappearing out the door.

'What was that about?' Carly frowned.

'No idea,' replied Dean, although he thought he could guess.

'He should lay off the booze; it's sending him doolally.'

'I think that horse has already bolted.'

Derek returned to the bar. 'Was that Jim I saw legging it out of here?'

'Aye,' said Carly. 'He said something about leaving the iron on.'

'Like that bastard has ever used an iron. He probably doesn't even own one.'

'That's just what I was thinking.'

'He's finally lost it. It was inevitable with how many brain cells he's killed off with drink.'

'He said Brian Alexander was telling everyone in the bookies about what he wants to do to Dean after what happened in here.'

'Really? Why should that piss off Brian? Those fannies brought it on themselves and none of them were Alexanders, they were just associates of theirs.'

'Maybe it made them look bad?'

'Naw. Jim must have got it wrong. Maybe Brian was talking about something else?'

Carly and Dean glanced at each other, both wondering if it was the failed abduction of Carly that had got Brian so riled.

The door opened and to everyone's astonishment, Jessica Alexander walked through it alone. She strode straight up to the bar as if she owned the place, ignoring the curious looks she received. Everyone in Haghill had got wind of the bad blood between the Savages and Alexanders and were eager to see what would happen.

'Carly,' she said politely. 'I know you're working but I wondered if I might have a word?'

'I don't think we've anything to say to each other,' Carly replied, still smarting about how this woman had used her.

'I was hoping we could stop things before they get out of hand.' She looked past her to Derek. 'Can I borrow your employee for a wee chat?'

'Only if it's all right by Carly,' he told her sternly. He looked to Carly. 'Do you want to talk to her or shall I throw her out on her arse?'

'I'll talk to her,' she replied. 'She won't leave me alone until I do.'

'Okay, doll.' He turned his scowl back on Jessica. 'But you don't leave this pub,' he told her.

'Fine by me. Can we talk in your back room?'

'You'll talk out here where I can keep an eye on you,' Dean told her.

Jessica's lips curled into an appreciative smile and she stalked right up to him. 'So, you're one of the famous cousins I've heard so much about. Which one are you?'

'Dean,' he replied in his deadpan tone.

'Are you the older or younger brother?'

'Younger.'

'And were you the one who hit Stuart in the face with the laptop and threw his friend across the room?'

'Aye, what of it?'

'Nothing, although I would like to say congratulations. It seems you're a man of many talents,' she said, running her hand down his arm. 'Mmm,' she purred. 'Strong.'

Dean's look said he wasn't in the slightest bit moved.

'We can talk over there,' said Carly, nodding at an empty table in the corner close to the bar.

'See you soon, Dean,' winked Jessica before following Carly over to the table.

'Careful, lad,' Derek told him. 'She's got you in her sights.'

'Naw,' he replied, loud enough for Jessica to hear. 'She's far too old for me.'

Jessica glared at him over her shoulder with her feline green eyes.

Both Dean and Derek kept a close eye on the two women as they settled down to talk.

'I'm surprised you came,' Carly opened. 'Especially after what your sons and their friends tried to do to me last night.'

'I had to come. You might not believe it but that was just business, it was nothing personal. I meant it when I said I like you, Carly.'

'You used me. I thought you were trying to help me with Cole when all the time you only wanted to get information out of me about my cousins and uncle.'

'I wanted to do both.'

'Out of all your family, I thought you were the only one who genuinely liked me, other than Cole. Then I find out that neither of you do.'

'That's not true. I really was very fond of you.'

Carly wasn't sure she believed that any more. 'What would they have done to me last night if they'd got hold of me?'

Jessica's expression was unflinching. 'Whatever it took to get your uncle and cousins to do what we wanted.'

'Would Cole have been a part of that?'

Jessica nodded, her sharp eyes never leaving Carly's face.

Carly forced herself to contain the pain. 'And what do you want my uncle and cousins to do?'

'My family wants to expand, break out of the small time and your family has something that we want.'

'And you were willing to torture me to get it. When did you become so cold, or have you always been that way?'

'It's true that I've always had a ruthless streak and now I'm going to use that to drag my family out of the gutter. I'm sick to death of not having enough money, of living in a crappy, rundown house with a shitty back yard. I want the big dream house with a huge garden and expensive cars on the drive.'

'Have you ever thought of getting a job?' said Carly with a raised eyebrow.

'You mean like you, scrubbing about in this dingy pub for a pittance?' Jessica said, tossing back her mane of hair. 'I'm better than that.'

'You're a cheeky bitch, Jess.'

'No, just ambitious.' She glanced sideways at Dean, who was watching them. 'Good-looking boy.'

'Aye.'

'Is his brother as handsome?'

'Yeah,' replied Carly, although she did think Dean was the better looking of the two.

'I hear they're both staying at your flat.'

'What of it?' No way was Carly going to tell her that they'd found their own place to rent.

'That must make things very cramped. Three attractive girls with two attractive boys.'

'We're no' having orgies every night if that's what you're trying to say.'

'Then you're missing out,' she purred, glancing back over her shoulder at Dean, who stared back at her impassively. Jessica smirked at him before turning back to Carly.

'There's nothing like that going on,' Carly told her. 'I'm still getting over what Cole tried to do to me. What the hell happened to him?'

'Prison happened.' Jessica glowered.

'Blame Ross for that. He's the reason Cole got sent down.'

'Why must you blame him for everything? If World War Three broke out you'd say Ross was responsible.'

'Because he's usually behind any trouble in Haghill.'

'A little unfair. Cole was a grown man when he agreed to help his brother. The responsibility rests on his shoulders alone.'

'Cole could have had a decent life if it hadn't been for his brothers always dragging him into things.'

'He wasn't dragged in, he wanted to join in. He's always been the same, right from being wee, trailing around after his older brothers.'

'So basically you're saying he's never grown up?'

'Yes, until he went to prison. That did it.'

'You actually seem pleased,' said Carly, narrowing her eyes at the older woman.

'I am. There was a time when I thought he would give in to your demands to get on the straight and narrow and my beautiful boy would condemn himself to the life of a drudge, constantly worrying about money, never having enough to drag himself out of the gutter. He came home a man determined to see our family rise.'

'I don't understand,' said Carly, who was genuinely bewildered. 'You told me several times that you wanted to save Cole from going down the same path as his brothers, that you wanted a decent life for him and that you hoped I'd save him.'

'That's true, I did, but not in the way you thought. I want more for Cole than Ross and Dominic have ever achieved because he's far smarter than either of them. He is the one who will raise our family in the world,' she said, zeal shining in her eyes. 'I always knew he was special from the moment he was born and finally he's going to fulfil his destiny.'

Carly rolled her eyes. 'He's not Luke Skywalker.'

'You and I always got on, Carly, and I do like you. You're clever and gutsy but you were trying to tame Cole when he's a wild stallion who should be allowed to live free and I won't let you destroy him. By telling you we both wanted the same thing for him, I was able to keep you onside. You were less of a threat that way and it was clear Cole was smitten, so I knew trying to turn him against you wouldn't work. I told Cole to go out on that job with Ross hoping it would toughen him up and finally bring him over to our way of thinking. We were all ready to move up the ladder but he was holding us back.' Jessica leaned in to whisper, 'Prison was the only way to separate him from you.'

Carly's eyes widened. 'You tipped off the polis that night, didn't you? You're the reason he got lifted.'

Jessica's reply was a sly smile. She watched as Carly shot to her feet and turned her back on her as she struggled to take in this shocking information.

'Carly, hen,' said a concerned Derek. 'Are you all right?'

She didn't reply, staring back at him with hazel eyes that glittered with unshed tears. Suddenly those eyes filled with fire and her upper lip curled back over her teeth.

'Oh no,' said Derek.

'What do you mean, oh no?' Dean asked him.

Before he could respond, Carly had whipped round, grabbed Jessica by her hair and slammed her forward onto the table.

'Get off me,' shrieked Jessica.

'This is all your fault, you fucking witch,' Carly hissed in her ear. 'And I'm gonnae kill you for it.'

She banged Jessica's head off the table before dragging her upright and hurling her to the floor.

'Carly, no,' cried Derek, racing out from the behind the bar when she straddled Jessica and started punching her in the face.

Dean merely turned in his seat to watch and sip his orange juice as Derek wrapped his arms around Carly and dragged her off Jessica.

'Get off me,' she yelled, attempting to free herself.

'Calm down,' Derek told her. 'Do you want to get lifted?'

'Listen to your boss,' said Jessica, hauling herself to her feet and dabbing at her cut lip with her fingers. 'You don't want to go the same way as Cole.'

'I can't believe you did that to him,' Carly cried, her voice full of anguish. 'He was bright and beautiful and you destroyed him.'

'You were the one destroying him, making him soft and weak. I made him strong.'

'I'll tell him what you did,' she yelled, still attempting to free herself from Derek's grip. 'I'll tell everyone.'

'Tell him what you like, he won't believe you. He'll just think it's a sad attempt to divide our family. He doesn't want you back, he never did. He's already sowing his wild oats all over Haghill. You're just a distant memory to him.'

'Piss off out of it, you,' Derek told Jessica when Carly fought harder to attack her. 'Before I set her on you.'

'I'm going, I've said my piece.' Jessica's eyes slipped to Dean. 'Tell your da' that I know all about what he's up to and if he doesn't willingly hand over his nice new deal, his nieces will pay.'

Carly glanced at Dean, who looked puzzled.

'Get out before I throw you out myself,' Derek snarled at her.

Jessica gave him an infuriating smile before stalking out.

'And your whole family's barred,' he bellowed after her.

Jessica left, the door swinging shut behind her.

Carly buried her face in her hands.

Derek looked around him. Naturally all heads were turned their way. 'The show's over,' he barked. 'Get back to your drinks.'

Normal conversation resumed, the awkward silence broken.

'Watch the bar for me, will you, Dean?' Derek called over his shoulder as he escorted a distraught Carly into the office.

'Err, I don't know how,' he replied, never having worked behind a bar in his life.

'It's easy. If someone wants a drink, pour them a drink,' he snapped before disappearing into the office with Carly.

Derek steered her into the chair behind the desk. 'You park yourself there, hen. Do you want a drink? A whisky will make you feel much better; it never fails for me.'

Carly raised her head and forced a smile, a tear sliding down her cheek. 'No thanks.'

'What the hell did she say to make you lose control like that? You've no' done something like that for ages.'

'She told me she tipped off the polis the night Cole was lifted.

That robbery he went out on was a set up. She thought prison was the only way to get him away from me.'

Derek's jaw fell open with astonishment. 'That's insane.'

'I know.'

'But she said you were good for Cole.'

'Apparently not. She said I was turning him soft, taking him away from his real destiny, which according to her is being a criminal. Now he wants nothing to do with me and is shagging everything that moves.'

'You were the best thing that ever happened to that boy. He knows it and the wicked witch of the west knows it too.'

'I can't believe it. All this time I've thought she was a good woman when she's actually an evil bitch.'

'She had a nasty streak when we were at school, bullying younger kids, making up lies but I thought settling down and becoming a mother had softened her.'

'She's got a brick for a heart. How can anyone do that to their own son?'

They were interrupted by a knock at the door.

'What?' snapped Derek.

The door was opened by Dean. 'There's a group of women wanting cocktails and I haven't a bloody clue how to make them.'

'All right, I'm coming.'

'You'd better be quick, they're getting ugly,' said Dean when a chorus of 'Why Are We Waiting?' started up behind him.

'It's not the Bitches, is it?' Carly asked Dean.

'Naw, this lot are far too old.'

One of the women must have heard this comment because a packet of salted peanuts struck him on the back of the head.

'On my way,' said Derek. He looked to Carly. 'Take your time before coming back out. You've had a shock.'

'Thanks,' she said, smiling.

'Right, come on, you,' Derek told Dean, ushering him out and closing the door behind them.

'Is Carly all right?' Dean asked him as they returned to the bar.

'She'll be fine, that lassie's tough. She's had to be.'

'What did Jessica say to her?'

'You're best asking Carly. It's no' my place to tell.'

'Come on Derek, we're gasping here,' said one of the women.

'All right, all right, I'm here. Now, what cocktails does everyone want?'

'Sex on the Beach,' screeched one of the women, making the rest bray with laughter.

'I thought it might be,' he sighed.

18

Carly wasn't sure how she got through the rest of her shift. Derek said she could leave early but the pub was busy and she didn't want to leave him in the lurch.

Dean drove her home. Although he was usually a fan of silence, he was concerned by how quiet she was. Carly gazed out of the window, seeing nothing, her eyes brimming over with sadness.

'I don't know what that bitch said to you back at the pub,' said Dean. 'But don't let it get you down. If you do, she wins.'

Carly shook herself out of her thoughts. 'Sorry, I haven't told you anything that was said, have I?'

'You don't have to.'

'But I want to. She said she was the one who tipped off the polis when Cole was lifted for that robbery.'

His eyebrows shot up. 'What?'

'Apparently I was making him soft and she knew prison was the only way to separate us.'

'Jesus, that's cold. No' even my maw would do something like that.' When she looked at him questioningly, he shook his head. 'That's a story for another time.'

Carly didn't press him; she was far too tired and had enough on her mind. 'She says he's the one that will bring their family everything they want. You should have heard her, she sounded like a proper silly bitch. He's her golden boy and they want what you have.'

'But we don't have the drugs any more, we've already jacked it in.'

'Then there must be something else.'

'I can't think what.'

'Unless there's something your da's not told you?'

'I think we need to ask him.'

Fortunately, when they got back, Eddie was sitting at the kitchen table in conference with Jane and Harry, both of whom looked exhausted. Harry had a small cut to the left side of his head and Jane had a bruise on her right cheek.

'What happened to you two?' said Carly.

'We got into a fight,' began Jane awkwardly.

'With who?'

'Four Bitches who I thought would support me against Emma. It turns out I was wrong. It's a shame because if they had been for me then the rest of them would have followed and I would have control of them again.'

'And by now they'll have run back to Emma and told her all about it.'

'No. We persuaded them not to.'

'Persuaded, how?'

'You don't need to know,' she replied, avoiding her sister's gaze.

'I hope whatever you did tonight didn't cost you a piece of yourself?' demanded Carly.

'It'll be fine,' mumbled Jane, glancing at her cut and bruised hands. 'Anyway,' she said, keen to change the subject. 'You don't look too good yourself, your eyes are all bloodshot.'

Carly sat at the table and told them about her discussion with Jessica.

'Jesus,' said Eddie when she'd finished. 'That's one cold bitch. Grassing on her own son.'

'I never liked her,' said Jane. 'Whenever I saw her, I was always put in mind of Lady Macbeth but I couldn't work out why because, on the surface, she seemed so nice.'

Carly turned her attention to her uncle. 'Jessica said her family wants what you have but I've been reliably informed that you've given up the drugs side of the business.'

'Aye, we have,' he replied.

'So, what do the Alexanders want then?'

'That's what I'd like to know too,' said Dean, turning his gaze on his father.

Carly glanced at Harry, but he looked as curious as his brother.

'I cut a deal with the Tallan family in Springburn,' said Eddie.

'To do what?' pressed Dean.

'How the fuck did they find out?' Eddie growled to himself, hands curling into fists. 'Someone must have talked.'

'Da',' said Dean louder. 'To do what?'

'The Tallans have come up with a winner of an idea. The family owns a couple of brothels and they set up some of their clients, taking videos and photos of them with their girls to blackmail them with. They want me to go to the marks with the footage and make sure they cough up.'

'Jesus,' sighed Dean. 'And you thought it would be a good idea to get involved in that?'

'They're paying me a fucking fortune. It's really easy money and we can rake it in. The Tallans are also involved in cybercrime – ransomware attacks, scam emails, that sort of thing.'

'They can't want you for that,' said Harry. 'You don't even know how to turn off your phone.'

'I've negotiated for us to be the Tallans' main enforcers. This will be the making of us, boys,' he said eagerly. 'I was going to bring Jane in on it too. A woman would put some of the marks off their guard. After what I heard about what happened at the pub tonight, there's a spot for you too, Carly. I'm guessing one of the Tallans leaked the information to the Alexanders.'

'So that's where you've been disappearing off to.'

'When were you going to tell us?' Dean demanded of his father.

'I was going to take you to meet the Tallans in a couple of days. It's all been arranged.'

'You should have checked with us before agreeing to this deal. What if we don't want to do it?'

'Why wouldn't you? This is the chance we've been waiting for and it's better than drugs.'

'You're talking about blackmail.'

'Aye, and your point is?'

'It's sneaky and sly and dirty,' Dean said with disgust.

'We don't have to do it for long, just enough to make our fortune, then we can walk away.'

'And you think the Tallans will just let us do that? I've read about them in the newspapers; they're dangerous, Da. They don't need anyone to intimidate other people for them, they're perfectly capable of doing it themselves. They've got you to do it in case anyone goes to the polis. You'll be the one done for blackmail, no' them.'

'You're no' using that big brain of yours, Dean,' replied Eddie. 'Who the hell's gonnae go to the polis and complain that they're being blackmailed over having sex with a prostitute? First of all, they couldn't stand the humiliation and secondly, although prostitution isn't illegal in this country, brothels are, so there's no way they'd ever admit to going to one.'

'You've got a point there, Da',' said Harry.

'I'm glad one of you gets it,' Eddie told his older son. 'Even if we only do it for a couple of years, we'll be set. And just think, girls,' he told Jane and Carly. 'You'd never have to worry about money again. One of the main reasons I'm doing this is to get you a better home where Alec will have a nice view from his bedroom window, no' a creepy old cemetery. Just imagine, a lovely big bungalow, plenty of space with a real living room. No' having to all crowd into this one room. Peace, privacy.'

Carly glanced at her sister and saw temptation in her eyes. 'I agree with Dean,' she said. 'It's a nasty, dirty business and it could send us all to prison.'

'Or maybe it's about time we enjoyed the good life,' said Jane. 'I'm sick of working my arse off for nothing, to be treated like shite by idiots yelling at me on the phone and useless managers with IQs well below that of bacteria. The morons always get the promotions and I've had enough of it. If I have to take a risk for a couple of years to improve our lives, then I'll do it.'

'And what if you get arrested and sent to prison?'

'Like Uncle Eddie said, the chance of that is minimal. Anyone reporting it would know it would get leaked to the newspapers because I'm guessing all the marks in his scams are rich.'

'Course they are,' said Eddie, who was pleased with her support. 'What's the point in blackmailing someone who doesnae have a pot to piss in? There's no way they'd take the risk; they'd rather pay up. It's perfect.'

'The Tallans are dangerous,' said Carly. 'What if they decide they don't want us taking our cut any more?'

'Why would they? That would mean they were taking all the risk.'

'I thought you said there was no risk?'

'Not for us,' said Eddie. 'But the Tallans have been on the polis's radar for a long time. They're trying to keep a low profile.'

'I don't like it,' said Carly. 'It's too dangerous.'

'What do you think?' Dean asked his brother.

'I think it's a good idea,' replied Harry.

Eddie's eyes lit up. 'So, you're in?'

'Aye.' Harry smiled. 'I am.'

'Christ,' said Dean, dragging a hand through his hair. 'It seems me and Carly are the only sane ones.'

'Why don't you come on a job with me so you can get a feel for it?' Eddie told him. 'You might find you like it and it's easy money. And some of the photos you see, Jesus.' He grinned. 'There was this bloke wearing a giant nappy and a baby's bonnet who liked having a big red—' He recalled his nieces were at the table and cleared his throat. 'Never mind. At least gi'e it a try, Dean.'

Dean looked to Carly, who shrugged.

'All right, Da',' he sighed. 'I'll try.'

'That's my boy.'

'There's a problem though,' said Carly. 'The Alexanders want your new deal.'

'Because they can see what a great opportunity it is.'

'If you're no' careful they'll steal your new opportunity from right under your nose.'

'No, they fucking won't. I'll see them deid first.'

'The Alexanders need to be dealt with,' said Harry. 'The Tallans will be watching.'

'We need to use this situation to our advantage and prove ourselves to them,' said Eddie.

'How?' said Dean.

'By eradicating the fucking Alexanders.'

'What do you mean, eradicate?' demanded Carly.

'Don't panic, I don't mean it like that,' assured her uncle. 'I should have said neutralise. They need to be stopped and we're gonnae have to get proactive and no' just sit around waiting for them to come to us.'

'You mean set a trap?' said Harry, eyes gleaming.

'Aye, son.'

'I like it.'

Eddie looked to Dean. 'Are you in agreement, boy, or will a trap upset your delicate sensibilities?' he said sarcastically.

'No, a trap's a good idea. We need to get this sorted. It's the blackmail bit I don't like.'

'Blackmail,' said Eddie thoughtfully. 'Carly, doll, do you know anything about the Alexanders we can use against them?'

'You mean like crimes they've never been done for?'

'No. I'm talking about weird quirks. Does Cole like to do anything strange in bed?'

'Da',' exclaimed Dean. 'She's your niece; you cannae ask her a question like that.'

'Oh, sorry,' Eddie told Carly. 'My boys will tell you that I open my mouth before I think.'

'It's okay and no, he didn't. And I don't know anything dodgy about any of the others. They were careful to keep anything like that from me, although today in the pub, Jim did mention that Jessica's had a few affairs.'

'Now that's more like it.' Eddie grinned.

'Carly, I don't think—' began Dean.

'Did he say with who?' interrupted Eddie.

'No,' she replied.

'We should have a chat with this Jim.'

'No' Jim Murray?' said Jane.

'Aye,' replied Carly.

'You can't trust a word he says; he's pished most of the time.'

'He did seem pretty unreliable,' said Dean. 'He probably didn't even know what he was talking about.'

'Jim might like a drink but he's no' a liar,' said Carly.

'True,' said Jane. 'But he could have got his facts wrong and if Jessica has had an affair and we make it public knowledge it could get some innocent man into trouble. Brian might go after him.'

'Jim said Brian knows all about it and he's done nothing,' said Carly. 'Jim even hinted that he was gay.'

'Now that I don't believe. When I ran the Bitches, a lot of them complained about how he leered at them.'

'Which makes what Jim had to say even more unreliable,' said Dean.

'Aye, all right,' said Eddie. 'We'll leave him out of it.'

'But if Jessica is shagging about then someone somewhere will know about it, maybe a jealous wife who wants revenge?'

'I've got a better idea,' said Carly. 'When I was with Cole, Ross got into a vendetta with the McLaren family in Port Dundas. He slashed one of the sons across the neck with a knife. The man survived but the family was raging. The McLarens never go to the polis about anything, so they decided to get revenge themselves. Ross struck before they could. He abducted his victim's brother and tortured him with a scalpel and burnt him with cigarettes.' Carly paused as she realised that could have been her fate had her cousins not come to her rescue. She cleared her throat before continuing. 'Ross said if the McLarens didn't back off then he'd take their daughter next, then the grandmother. This was enough to make them drop it. The McLarens have wanted to get their own back ever since.'

'Are you saying we should team up with the McLarens?' said Eddie.

'God no. They're vicious and untrustworthy. They could easily turn on us. I think it would be better if we get the Alexanders thinking they're going to attack.'

'So they stop looking at us?' said Eddie with a gleam in his eyes.

'Exactly. Ross knows that at some point they will come after him, they're just biding their time. Let's make him think that time's now.'

Eddie beamed with pride at his niece. 'You're a smart girl. How do we make them think that then?'

'The McLarens have a calling card. When they're about to attack someone, they carve a devil face into the paintwork of their target's car, usually on the boot.'

'I've heard that story,' said Jane. 'So they really do that then?'

'Aye, they did it to Ross's BMW. He went aff his nut,' she chuckled.

'Why do they warn people they're going to attack?' Harry frowned.

'Because they're stupid,' replied Carly.

'Can you draw us this devil face?' Eddie asked her.

'I can. I saw it myself after it had been carved on Ross's car, which is like his baby. I thought he was gonnae greet like a wean,' she said.

'It's a great plan. While the Alexanders are busy fending off an attack from the McLarens that will never come, we can deal with them.'

'How will we deal with them?'

'Jessica said Cole's her wee golden boy, so we go for him.'

'No,' retorted Carly.

'Don't tell me you still feel something for him after what he tried to do to you?'

'I don't want him hurt.'

'It's the only way. He's the pride and joy, so it'll have the biggest impact on the rest of the family.'

'No Uncle Eddie. You can go for any of the others but not him.'

'That twat wanted to kidnap and torture you. Why the hell are you protecting him?'

'Because I still love him,' she exclaimed. 'And that doesn't just die.'

'It did for him.'

'That's cold, Da',' Dean told him.

'But true and this lassie needs some truth.' Eddie looked back at Carly. 'Cole isn't your boyfriend any more, he isn't even your friend. He's your enemy and the sooner you start thinking of him like that the better.'

'I don't care what you say, I won't let you hurt him.'

'You need to listen to her,' Jane told her uncle as Carly and Eddie stared at each other hard across the table. 'You didn't see how they were when they were together; they were so in love. Don't add to her pain.'

Eddie's eyes flickered at this heartfelt plea. 'All right,' he said gently. 'We'll leave Cole alone, although, if he is everything Jessica says he is, he will be the one who strikes back at us. He won't show you the compassion you've shown him,' he told Carly.

'I know but that's the way it is,' she replied.

'Then we'll go for one of the others.'

'What will we do to them once we have them?' said Jane.

'You don't need to know that. Me and the boys will handle it. Now, this is what we're going to do.'

As Carly listened to her uncle set out his plan, she felt her respect for him grow. He might be greedy and reckless but she had to admit that he was a pretty good strategist. The Alexanders had no idea what was about to hit them.

19

Carly's dreams that night were strange and disturbing. She jumped awake but couldn't recall much, just vague snippets of running through the darkened streets of Haghill, fleeing from Cole who clutched an absurdly enormous knife. No matter how hard she tried, she remained jogging on the spot, unable to run any further while he rapidly gained on her.

She sat up, raked her fingers through her hair and looked at the clock, which told her it was five thirty in the morning.

Carly switched on her light to be confronted by the photos of herself and Cole in happier times. A lump formed in her throat as she took one photo down off the wall. It had been taken at a local nightclub and they had their arms around each other, pulling funny faces at the camera. It was one of her favourite photos, which was why she'd decided to keep it when they'd broken up.

'Where did you go, babe?' she whispered to his image, brushing his face with her fingertips. The man in that picture was not the one who had walked out of Barlinnie Prison. That cheeky, mischievous but good man had died within its walls. The thing that now occupied his body was something else entirely.

Knowing she would be unable to get back to sleep, Carly rose, dressed and crept into the kitchen in an attempt not to wake the brothers. She gasped with shock to see Dean sitting at the kitchen table drinking a cup of tea. Harry was under the duvet on the couch, snoring his head off.

'Jesus, you scared me,' she whispered.

'You don't need to whisper,' Dean told her. 'You won't wake Harry. You'd need a brass band to do that.'

'How come you're awake so early?' she asked him as she prepared a bowl of cereal.

'I always wake up early; I've never been able to sleep in. What about you?'

'Bad dreams.'

Carly carried her bowl to the table and sat down opposite him.

'What do you think about your Da's plan?' she said.

'I think what he came up with to deal with the Alexanders is clever.'

'What about the blackmail thing?'

'I hate it,' he said quietly, looking troubled.

'You don't think some short-term risk is worth a big profit?'

'I'm not afraid of risk but it's just so sordid.'

'I'm with you on that but we were outvoted.'

'You're better keeping out of it and staying at the pub. That's a good place working for a good man.'

'Aye but with crappy pay. We'll never get Da' that bungalow on my wage.'

'Uncle Alec wouldn't want you getting involved in blackmail to get it.'

'True, but it would be so nice to make his last years as comfortable as possible. He's always loved the sea and I know how happy it would make him to see it every day, so I can't deny I'm tempted.'

'I suppose I don't have the pressures that you have.'

'When you have so much weighing you down, you'll do anything to lighten your load. That's why I can understand why Jane wants to go for it.'

'You could let her do it while you stay at the pub.'

'You seem intent on me staying at the pub,' she said wryly.

'Because I don't think you should be anywhere near this black-mail business.'

'I'm just as tough as Jane.'

'I saw that when you went for Jessica. Savage isn't just our family name. It's in our blood.'

'That's what my da' says,' she said, smiling.

'Mine too. They got it from their da'. I was thinking of taking an early morning walk through Gleniffer Braes. Do you want to come?'

'Should we when today's the big day?'

'I think that's even more of a reason to go.'

'Okay, why not? I loved it up there.'

'I'll let Harry know.'

It took Dean a bit of time to rouse his brother enough so he could take in the message.

'All right,' mumbled Harry blearily. 'But be back by eight.'

'We will.'

Harry grunted, turned over and went back to sleep.

It seemed the residents of Haghill were still in their beds as Carly and Dean passed no other vehicles as they left the neighbourhood.

'I don't think I've ever seen the place like this before,' said Carly. 'I like it.'

'It's one reason why I like getting up so early.'

'When will you be moving into the house you've rented?'

'Why, are you getting sick of us?'

'No, but you can't be comfy sleeping on an airbed every night.'

'Me and Harry take turns with the airbed and I'm fine. We'll stay at your place until we've sorted out the Alexanders, if you don't mind?'

'I don't, but can you do me a favour?'

'What?'

'On this outing, please don't mention the Alexanders, the McLarens, my da's illness or any of it. I want to forget about it all for a little while.'

'Fine by me. I'd like a break from it too.'

They lapsed into the silence they both found so soothing, not speaking again until Dean parked the car up at Gleniffer Braes. He led Carly onto a different path to the one they'd taken on their previous visit. There were numerous trails leading off it, going in various directions.

The path led them by an old stone well with a commemorative image of a rather severe-looking gentleman on it. Dean explained this was known as the Bonnie Wee Well and the man was Hugh MacDonald, a historian and poet. Carly just nodded in response to this information, finding it difficult to keep her mind on his words.

'Sorry,' she said when she realised Dean had asked her a question that she'd failed to respond to. 'My head's all over the place.'

'Don't apologise. I was just trying to distract you.'

Carly felt bad when he shoved his hands into his pockets and looked down at the ground, embarrassed. 'I'm crap company at the moment,' she said.

'Because you're thinking about Cole?'

'Aye. I hate it that he's now my enemy.'

'It must be so hard for you. Are you really still in love with him?'

'Like I told Uncle Eddie, you can't just turn it off like a tap but it's not as strong as it used to be. It's not even the fact that he tried to kidnap me that killed some of the love, it was the way he looked at me that night. It was like he hated me but those eyes weren't Cole's, they were a stranger's. I don't understand how prison could do that to someone.'

'Because you've never been inside. If you had, you'd understand. I reckon it was having to hurt other people that did it. He didn't want to do it but his family ordered him to.'

'I assumed Ross gave the order but now I'm beginning to think it was Jessica.'

'Could have been. Each time he had to do it, it cost him a piece of himself.'

'Until there was nothing left,' she murmured. Carly shook herself. 'I don't know why I'm so upset; we broke up ages ago. Do you still have feelings for your ex?'

'No. I don't think I had any in the first place. If I did, they were killed off because she annoyed me so much with her constant gabbing.'

'Why did you go out with her if she got on your nerves?'

'Because she seemed sweet and quiet, at first. I thought I'd found a woman I could enjoy the silence with, but I was wrong.'

'Enjoy the silence? That sounds a wee bit creepy. Not many men would consider that to be a desirable trait in a partner.'

'You're the only woman I've met who can enjoy the silence too,' he said with a shy glance her way.

'I never have before but with you it's really calming. Peace and silence are rare commodities at the moment. They give me the space to...'

'Breathe?'

'That's exactly what I was going to say.' She smiled.

Carly shivered and wrapped her arms around herself.

'You're cold?' Dean asked her.

'Aye, it's a bit nippy. There's a chilly breeze this morning.'

Carly was surprised when Dean wrapped an arm around her and she found herself pressed against his side.

'You're a good windbreak,' she quipped to cover her embarrassment.

'You feel warmer?'

'Aye.'

'Good.'

They remained this way, staring at the well, but Carly was struggling to focus her attention on it, more concerned with Dean pressing against her. She knew she should pull away, he was her cousin after all, but it felt so nice. His presence was solid and comforting. Plus he smelled really good, all clean and fresh. Why shouldn't she enjoy some reassurance with everything that was going on?

Carly allowed herself to sink into him. When Dean felt her relax, he wrapped his other arm around her. Despite the thick padded coat he wore, Carly could feel his heart knocking rapidly against his ribcage.

'Carly?' he said.

She looked up at him. 'Yes?'

But instead of a reply, he pressed his lips to hers.

Her body jumped with surprise and she had a momentary internal struggle, telling herself he was her cousin and she should pull away but it felt too good and the sensible part of her lost the very brief war. She turned in his arms to face him, her hands going into his thick, soft hair. He didn't overwhelm her or attempt to shove his tongue down her throat. His kiss was deep and delicious, and it made her stomach clench with desire. She was disappointed when he pulled away first, leaving her breathless, face flushed.

'I'm sorry,' he said.

'Don't be,' she murmured, feeling as though she were waking from a very pleasant dream.

'I know you're still getting over Cole but I really wanted to do that.'

'I'm glad you did.'

'Really?' he said, eyes lighting up.

'Aye. Truth be told, I've wanted you to do it.' *But I've only just realised it myself*, she thought but didn't add.

'It doesn't freak you out that we're cousins?'

'No, you?'

'No.'

'You're such a long way from the wee boy I used to know, so it doesn't feel strange at all.' In a way, the estrangement of the two families had done her a favour.

Just as they started to kiss again, a group of walkers appeared and loudly began to discuss the fountain, one man in particular pompously reciting facts about it.

'Please tell me I didn't sound like that when I was telling you about the fountain,' Dean asked Carly.

'You didn't at all,' she replied.

When it appeared the newcomers were taking the same trail they were on, they decided to keep walking and stay ahead of the group of cagoules and multi-coloured bobble hats. Dean walked with his arm slung around Carly's shoulders. She couldn't decide whether this was a good thing or not. She didn't want another relationship right now but it felt nice and he was keeping her warm too.

'So,' said Carly after they'd been walking in silence for a couple of minutes. 'Are we going to talk about that kiss?'

'We can if you like,' he replied with a disappointing lack of enthusiasm.

'I mean...' She sighed. 'Actually, I've no idea what I mean.'

'I enjoyed it a lot.'

'Me too.'

'But I know you're getting over Cole and I don't want to be messed about because you're on the rebound.'

Carly knew that was a distinct possibility, so she didn't deny it. 'Still, it was a great kiss. And it really doesn't bother you that we're cousins?'

'It probably would if we'd grown up together but we haven't. I remember this wee girl who always had one sock up and one sock down and a runny nose.'

'I did not have a runny nose,' she exclaimed.

'Maybe it was just that one time but I distinctly remember it running down your upper lip.'

'That must have been Jane,' Carly mumbled, cheeks colouring.

'No, it was definitely you,' he said, smiling. 'Perhaps you had a cold at the time.'

'That was probably it,' she said, cheeks bright pink. 'Anyway, my da' said you had a crush on me when you were younger.'

It was his turn to blush. 'Well, maybe a wee bit. You were always so cute and pretty but the runny nose ruined it.'

Carly chuckled.

'Then, the next time I saw you,' he continued, 'you were this beautiful, strong woman who doesn't constantly gab. In my mind, you're two different people.'

'You think I'm beautiful?' she said.

'Definitely,' he replied, completely unashamed of this confession. 'Especially without the runny nose.'

She playfully slapped his chest. 'Will you stop with that?' she said, making him grin.

'Does it bother you?' he asked her.

'No. I feel the same way. The annoying wee boy is a million miles from this big, handsome and very intelligent man beside me.'

'That's good to know,' he said with a coy smile.

'When I saw you repeatedly bashing yourself on the head with a toy hammer when you were seven, I never thought you'd become so clever. There was something of the window licker about you back then.'

Dean's laugh echoed along the trail. 'Window licker?'

'Aye. You gave off those vibes big time.'

'I'm glad I disappointed your expectations.'

'Me too.'

Annoyance flashed through both their eyes when the same loud, obnoxious voice that had held court at the well echoed behind them. Glancing over their shoulders, they saw the group of walkers on the trail behind them. The rest of the group was admiring the surroundings, ignoring the noisy member of their number, who appeared to be in love with the sound of his own voice.

'No' that prick again,' grumbled Dean. He took Carly's hand. 'Come on.'

He led her off the trail and into the trees.

'Slow down,' she said, rushing to keep up with his long-legged stride.

'I just want to get away from that pack of woolly fannies.'

He came to a halt in the middle of the woodland, out of sight of anyone walking on the trail.

'There,' he said with a smile, backing her up against a tree. 'That's better.'

Carly smiled with anticipation as he pressed his lips to hers. Now they were completely secluded, they let go a little more, Dean unzipping her coat and sliding his hands under her jumper.

'Your hands are freezing,' she gasped.

'I know.' He grinned, sliding them up her back.

'You're a swine,' she said, smiling up at him.

As his lips moved to her neck, whispering her name in what she thought was a very erotic way, his phone started to ring.

'Christ,' he muttered, releasing her and patting his pockets until he located his phone in his coat. 'It's Harry,' he said before answering the call. 'Aye, all right,' he added after listening to the voice on the other end. 'Don't burst a blood vessel, we're on our way back.'

'We are?' said a disappointed Carly when he'd hung up.

'My da's at your flat and he wants to get things moving.'

'Against the Alexanders?'

'Aye, and we both need to be there.'

'I suppose we'd best get back then,' she mumbled. It had been so nice here with Dean. It felt like some wonderful, wild place far removed from the world and all its troubles. Now she would have to return to it all – Cole's betrayal, the mess with the Alexander and Tallan families and her father's illness and all the associated pain.

Dean took her hand as they left the woodland and got back on the trail, heading back to the car. By now there were a few dog walkers about, so they no longer had it all to themselves.

As they returned to Haghill, Dean told her, 'I hope you don't feel awkward about what happened between us back there. If you want to do it again that's more than okay with me but if you don't, I won't pressure you.'

'That's very sweet of you.'

'God knows what we're going to face today and I've no idea how things will turn out. Sometimes it's good to just live in the moment.'

'You're right, it is,' she replied. And he was right. After today, everything could change.

20

Carly and Dean returned to the flat to find the family gathered at the kitchen table, including Alec.

'You're up again, Da',' said Carly, kissing his cheek.

'Aye, sweetheart,' he murmured. 'I enjoyed it before.'

'Da' wants to sit out in the garden this morning,' said Jane, disapproval in her eyes. 'Even though it's cold out.'

'Then we'll have to wrap you up warm.' Carly smiled at her father.

He attempted to smile back but Carly was concerned when she noticed that his face looked even more mask-like than usual and the tremor had returned to his hands. 'Or maybe we should wait for the nurses to arrive and see what they think?'

'That's a good idea,' said Jane.

'That's shite,' said Eddie. 'Alec knows his own mind. If he wants to sit out for a wee bit, then he can. Me and the boys will help settle him in the chair out there.'

'But it is pretty nippy,' said Carly.

'That explains why your face is so red,' Jane told her.

Carly's gaze met her sister's and she saw disapproval there. Did she suspect what had gone on between her and Dean? 'It was really windy up there,' she said.

Jane looked to her father. 'See. You'll make yourself ill.'

'I already am ill,' he replied with some effort.

'At least wait for the nurses.'

'I'll get your coat, Alec,' said Eddie, getting to his feet.

'But—' began Jane.

'He's a grown man,' he told his niece. 'Treating him like a child won't help him.'

Jane sighed with defeat and sank back into her chair. 'Fine, but make sure you dress warm, Da'.'

Eddie and Carly between them put a thick woollen jumper over Alec's pyjamas then his coat. Then they put gloves on his hands and shoes on his feet. Eddie and Harry helped him shuffle outside to the waiting chair and eased him into it before putting a hat on his head and a blanket over his knees.

'There,' said Eddie, tucking the blanket in around him. 'Snug as a bug in a wee rug.'

'Thanks,' said Alec, gurgling in the back of his throat as the saliva had built up there. It was with some difficulty that he swallowed it down and pressed the handkerchief to his lips with shaking hands.

Carly watched from the door and noted the distress that briefly filled Eddie's eyes at the state his once strong and vital brother was now in, and her heart softened towards him. Even though she wasn't sure it was a good idea he was outside, Eddie was only trying to help her father.

'Imagine how happy that sea view would make him,' Eddie quietly told her as he returned to the house with Harry. 'My brother's wanted to live by the sea since he was a wee boy.'

Carly gazed thoughtfully at her father, who looked out at the garden, such as it was. All he had to look at was some raggedy grass, a couple of planters containing dead plants and a grey wall. Perhaps blackmailing rich bastards was worth it to bring him happiness in his final days?

They left the back door ajar so they could keep an eye on Alec.

'Ten minutes then I'm going out there to see if he wants to come in,' Jane told her uncle.

'All right, hen, if you think that's right,' he replied as they all seated themselves at the table.

'Where's Rose?' said Carly.

'In the shower,' replied Jane. 'So we have a bit of time to discuss the plan.'

They went over things again, ensuring everyone understood what they had to do. Just as they'd finished, Rose came into the kitchen, so Jane and Carly went outside to check on their father.

'Are you ready to come back in, Da'?' Jane asked him.

'Five more minutes,' he murmured, his gaze far away.

His daughters looked to where he was staring but there was nothing but the grey wall.

'What are you looking at, Da'?' Carly asked him.

'Nothing. Just thinking about your maw. I miss her.'

It took him even longer than usual to get this sentence out and the sisters glanced at each other uneasily.

'The nurses will be here any minute,' said Jane. 'And they'll tear us a new one if they see you out here in the cold.'

He just nodded and between them his daughters helped him to his feet, holding onto his arms as he shuffled back inside, barely able to lift his feet up off the floor.

'Back inside already, Alec?' boomed Eddie cheerfully.

Carly had noticed that when he was feeling emotional, the volume of her uncle's voice increased by a few decibels.

'Aye,' replied Alec. 'Bit chilly.'

Some saliva escaped from his lips as he spoke and dripped

down his chin. Eddie winced and looked down at the floor while Jane hastened to wipe it away.

'Let's get you back in bed, Da',' said Carly. 'Get you warm again.'

There was silence as the two women assisted him into his bedroom and tucked him in.

'Do you want a hot water bottle?' Jane asked him.

'No, thanks,' he said. 'Better now. I'll have a sleep.'

'Okay,' she replied, planting a kiss on his forehead.

She left with Carly, who gently closed the bedroom door behind her.

'I knew he shouldn't have gone out,' whispered Jane, eyes flashing. 'But Eddie wouldn't listen.'

'He was only doing what he thought was best. Don't be too hard on him. We've made mistakes too.'

'True,' she sighed.

'And we need to be united today. Any falling out among ourselves could be dangerous.' Carly forced a smile when she saw an anxious Eddie hurry out of the kitchen and down the hallway towards them.

'Is Alec okay?' he asked his nieces.

'Aye, fine,' said Carly. 'He's having a wee nap.'

'Oh good,' he replied, looking relieved. He caught the look in Jane's eyes. 'Fine, from now on, you two have the final say over his care.'

'Thank you,' she replied with a grateful nod of the head.

'I'll run Rose to school, then we can put the plan into motion.'

'Excellent.' Her smile reassured him that all was forgiven.

'See you later,' said Rose who hugged her sisters goodbye before leaving with her uncle.

'I worry about her every time she sets foot outside the door,' said Jane.

'Me too,' replied Carly. 'But she's safe at school and she's getting driven there and back.'

As they returned to the kitchen, Jane noted the look that passed between Carly and Dean, both their eyes sparkling as they gazed at each other.

'I take it you enjoyed your walk this morning?' Jane asked them, causing them to break eye contact.

'Aye, it was really nice,' said Carly. 'You should go there one day, it's so beautiful.'

'It's certainly put the spring back in your step.'

'We had a nice time.' Carly shrugged.

Jane decided not to press the issue. They had more important things to think about. She would question Carly about it later.

To avoid her sister's searching gaze, Carly washed up the breakfast things. The nurses arrived and Carly left them to see to Alec just as Eddie returned from dropping Rose off at school.

'Everything okay?' Jane asked him.

'Fine. No problems,' he replied. 'You ready?'

'No' just yet. The nurses are with Da'.'

'Oh, right. Then we'll wait.'

An hour later, Alec was settled back into bed after being bathed by the nurses, and the rest of the family gathered around the table, the five of them regarding each other seriously. Eddie produced a burner phone from his pocket and held it out to Carly.

'Make the call, hen.'

She nodded, took the phone from him and dialled.

'Hi,' she said when the voice on the other end answered, deepening her voice slightly in an attempt to alter it. 'Is Ross Alexander there? No, it's all right. Just tell him that the Savage family are going to attack the garage where his brother works.'

She hung up before the voice at the gym where Ross could be found every morning could ask any more questions.

'That will put the wind up him,' said Eddie. 'Jane, your turn.'

She took the phone from her sister and called the nail bar Jessica frequented. Carly's intimate knowledge of the Alexander family had come in very useful. 'Hi,' she said, lightening her voice, making her sound like an airhead. 'Is Jessica Alexander there? Good. I need you to pass on an urgent message. Tell her the Savages are going to attack her maw's house. Who am I? A friend,' she added before hanging up.

Jane passed the phone to Eddie, who also dialled. 'Aye, all right, pal? Is Brian Alexander there? Tell him to get over to number twenty Montgomery Road pronto. His missus is in bed with the milkman who lives there.' He hung up with a satisfied smile. 'That wee rumour will be all around the bookies in seconds. Don't worry, I already checked out that house and it's empty.'

'Thank God for that,' said Jane. 'Although we can't be sure Brian will even care judging by what Jim told Carly.'

'We can but see. Harry, you're up next.'

He took the phone and dialled. 'Hi, I'm looking for Dominic Alexander. No, don't get him. Aww, ya fanny,' he sighed.

'What?' demanded Eddie.

'The idiot went to get him.'

'It's all right, just stick to the plan.'

Harry nodded and when he next spoke, he made his voice extremely deep and slow. 'Dominic? Aye, this is a friend. I've just seen that pair of Savage cousins hanging around the back of your hoose.' Harry's forehead creased. 'Eh? Naw, I mean those brothers, Jane and Carly's cousins. Yeah, that's right,' he added, rolling his eyes. He hung up. 'What a thick bastard. He thought I meant savage as in brutal. It took him a bit to understand it's our surname.'

'Who's gonnae make the last call?' said Eddie.

'Not me,' replied Carly, knowing that call would be to Cole.

'I may as well do it,' said Harry. 'Seeing how I'm holding the phone.'

'Use the same voice,' his father told him.

Harry nodded as he dialled. 'Hi, can I speak to Cole Alexander? Oh, it is,' he said, surprised to find he was speaking to the man himself. 'You should know, the Savage family are gonnae petrol bomb your hoose.' His eyes narrowed. 'It's no' her, it's those mad bastard cousins of hers. Get over there right now.' He hung up and placed the phone on the table. 'I'm no' sure he believed it. He said Carly would never allow that to happen,' he added, glancing her way.

'It doesn't really matter if he doesnae take the bait,' said Eddie. 'Step one of the plan is in motion. Right now, the other four members of the Alexander family will be tearing about the place, chasing after phantoms.'

'And what if they all talk to each other?' said Jane. 'They'll be suspicious when they hear they all got a warning phone call from different people about different things at the same time.'

'They'll have to check out the warnings; there's no choice. That's all we need.' He got to his feet. 'Jane, Harry, let's go. You two stay here and look after Alec,' he told Carly and Dean.

The three of them departed, leaving Carly and Dean alone. They regarded each other shyly, neither sure what to do.

'Do you want a brew?' said Carly because she didn't know what else to say.

'A coffee would be great, thanks,' he replied.

She got to her feet and walked over to the counter. 'Do you want this fancy stuff your da' bought?'

'That'll do.'

He watched her switch on the kettle and prepare the mugs, fighting the urge to go up to her and wrap her in his arms. He'd already pushed the boundaries today and thought it would be wise to give her a bit of space.

They enjoyed a coffee together, making the most of the quiet before the inevitable mayhem ensued.

When they'd finished their drinks, Carly took the empty mugs to the sink to wash them up and Dean was unable to hold back any longer. He rose, came up behind her and wrapped his arms around her waist. She leaned back against him, reaching around to run her fingers through his hair.

'We shouldn't be distracted right now,' she breathed as he kissed her neck.

'I can't help it. You constantly distract me.'

Carly turned in his arms, wrapped her arms around his neck and they kissed deeply. He pressed her back against the unit, her legs wrapping around his waist. It had been so long since she'd been with a man and her body screamed out for his. He pulled her jumper off over her head, taking a moment to admire her pert breasts in her black bra and her smooth stomach. She was long and lean and her skin was like ivory.

Carly pulled him closer, feeling the most demanding part of him pressing right against her. He slid down her left bra strap while gliding his lips down the curve of her neck to her breasts.

Then the doorbell rang.

'Oh, bloody hell,' sighed Carly.

'We should ignore it.'

She gazed up into his eyes, which had never looked so brilliant before and his face was flushed.

'I wish we could but some of Da's medical supplies are being delivered this morning.'

He sighed and released her. 'You'd better answer it then, but I'll come with you.'

After Carly had pulled on her jumper, they both headed to the door. She pulled it open to reveal Cole standing on the doorstep.

'What are you doing here?' she said in surprise.

He didn't respond, hard eyes flicking from her to Dean and back again.

'Hello?' she said, waving her hand in front of Cole's face.

'I want to know which one of your cousins called my work with some bollocks about someone petrol bombing my hoose.'

'It wasn't us,' replied Carly. Well, it wasn't a lie. It had been Harry.

'That's shite. It was one of you lot and I want to know what you're up to.'

'We're not up to anything. Where do you get off coming around here and making demands after you tried to kidnap me, you total bastard?' She was trying to keep her voice low so her dad didn't overhear but her emotions were starting to get the better of her.

'If this is some shitey plan of yours it won't work,' he said, his voice and eyes dripping with menace. 'We'll still take everything you have.'

'Good luck with that because we've got fuck all,' she retorted.

'You've got your cosy new deal with the Tallan family.'

'No, Carly,' said Dean, wrapping an arm around her waist when she tried to launch herself at Cole.

'You'll leave my family alone,' she spat.

'It's too late for that,' said Cole. 'Things have gone too far.'

'Where has my Cole gone?' she cried. 'When you came to me after you were first released from prison, you were him.'

'It was easy to give you what you wanted.'

'You only wanted me back so you could use me as leverage over my cousins and uncle, didn't you?'

'Yes.'

This single word was a knife in Carly's chest and it took her a moment to catch her breath.

'You were more stubborn than I thought though,' he continued. 'I assumed you'd fall into my arms like you always did. I have to admit it was a hell of a shock when you didn't but I suppose we've both changed. I haven't been the weakling I once was for a long time now. The old Cole was holding me back, so I destroyed him, became stronger, smarter.'

'Why did neither of you tell me you knew each other in prison?' she demanded of them both.

Dean cast his eyes shamefully to the ground. 'Because I didn't want you to know I'd been inside.'

'And I wanted to use it against you both,' said Cole without a hint of shame. 'I knew he wouldn't tell you,' he added with a sneer in Dean's direction. 'He likes to make out he's cultured and sophisticated with his books and classical music but actually he's a fucking animal. I wanted you to mistrust him. It would make it easier to take you if he wasn't hanging around you all the time.'

'So you could use me?' she said, pain once again filling her.

'Aye, and his da' would gi'e us everything we want.'

'This isn't you Cole, it's your maw talking, it's her ambition. I bet she never told you she was the one who tipped off the polis the night you got lifted. It was her fault you were sent down in the first place; she said it was the only way she could think of to split us up.'

'Did he tell you to say that?' Cole snapped, gesturing at Dean.

'No. Jessica told me herself when she came to see me at work. Everything you went through in Barlinnie is down to her.'

'Bollocks.'

'It's true. Ask her.'

'I don't need to because I know she'll say you're lying.'

'I'm not,' exclaimed Carly, tears shining in her eyes. 'You know me Cole, so you know I'm not a liar.'

'This is his influence,' he muttered, gesturing to Dean. 'And his bastard brother too. Have they told you about what they did in Bar-L?'

'What do you mean?' she said, glancing at Dean, whose gaze was locked on Cole.

'I mean they were the fucking terrors of the prison. They even had the mental cases shivering with fright. He's a loon and so is Harry.'

'They did what they had to do to survive inside and they've never tried to kidnap me like you did. You're the real loon, Cole. Maybe you always were and prison brought it out in you.'

'Why don't you ask him about Mick Adams?' countered Cole, turning the full force of his green-eyed glare on Dean.

'Stop changing the subject. This is about you. It's not too late to stop this before someone gets hurt. Jessica said you're the true leader of your family, not Ross, so I know you have the influence.'

Cole's laugh was cold and cruel. 'Like I could stop Ross from doing anything. Besides, we really want your deal with the Tallans. Then I can stop working at that crappy garage.'

'You said that was a good job and you love cars.'

'I love fast, powerful, performance cars, not the shitey motors we get in that place. Do you think I want to spend the rest of my life tinkering with people carriers for a pittance? Naw. I'm gonnae get enough money to open my own smart place in the west end where only the best cars will be welcome.'

'When did you become such a snob? That's your maw's influence again. What the hell did she do to you?'

'Stop dragging my maw into this,' Cole positively snarled, making him look feral.

'Why can't you see that she's damaged you?'

'She was right. You wanted to keep me a wean and now I'm finally my own man you cannae stand it.'

'Don't be ridiculous.'

'It's true. It's like the blinkers have finally been taken off and I'm really seeing you for the first time. Sorry doll, but it's an ugly picture.'

Carly was unable to hold back the hurt gasp.

'Right, you,' said Dean, grabbing him by the front of his coat. 'Fuck off out of it.'

He propelled a grinning Cole backwards into the street. It was then Carly spotted the danger.

21

'Dean, get back inside,' cried Carly.

He turned to see Ross, Dominic and two of their friends emerge from behind a van parked at the kerb and charge towards him. Dean shoved Cole backwards, knocking him into his brothers, all three of them tumbling to the pavement. As he started to grapple with the other two men, Carly snatched up the baseball bat her uncle had left behind the door and ran towards them. She slammed it into the ribs of one of the men, a wicked smile lighting up her face at the sound of the crack. The man screamed and released Dean, who then delivered an upper cut to the second man's jaw that sent him sailing through the air.

Together, Dean and Carly ran back inside the flat and locked the door, pursued by the three brothers.

'Christ, that was close,' she panted.

'Da's plan didn't work,' said Dean.

'It might have done on Jessica and Brian. All we need is for just one of them to fall for it.'

Hammering started up on the other side of the door and Dean

pressed his weight against it. 'Call my da',' he told her. 'And lock the back door.'

Carly nodded, tore her phone from her jeans pocket and frantically dialled while running down the hall into the kitchen.

'Uncle Eddie,' she panted when he answered. 'Cole and his brothers are trying to batter the front door down.' As she reached the back door, she saw two more men clamber over the rear wall and drop down into the garden. 'Shit, there's more of them coming around the back,' she added, slamming the door shut and turning the key in the lock. For good measure, she rammed the bolts home. 'Got to go,' she told her uncle when he said they were on their way.

Carly tossed her phone onto the worktop and jammed one of the chairs from the kitchen table under the handle before returning to the front door carrying a second chair.

Before the chair could be placed under the handle, the door erupted open, knocking Dean backwards. The three Alexander brothers stalked in and hammering started up at the back door.

Carly's heart ached when she heard her dad's bell ring from his room, which they'd given him so he could alert them when he needed something. All the noise had woken him up and he must be terrified. She didn't dare call out to him in case it drew the Alexanders' attention his way.

'Your uncle's gonnae gi'e us his deal with the Tallans,' said Ross, drawing a large knife from inside his jacket. 'Or we'll chop up the pair of you.'

'Maybe the Tallans don't want to do business with you,' retorted Carly. 'Did you ever think of that?'

'They will. My maw can be very persuasive.'

'She's the real leader of your family now, isn't she? It's not you, Brian or even Cole, her golden boy. How does it feel taking orders from your mammy like a good wee wean?'

'What's that ringing sound?' Ross's smile was wicked. 'Is that your da'? Is he so weak he cannae even shout now? That's fucking priceless,' he laughed. 'The great Alec Savage reduced to ringing a wee bell like an old biddy because he's shite himself.'

'Shut it,' spat Carly.

'He cannae even get out of bed to help his own daughter. Pathetic.' A gleam came into Ross's eyes. 'Maybe going for him would have even more of an effect on Eddie?'

'You'll leave him alone,' Carly practically screamed at him. 'You so much as touch him and I swear to God I'll fucking kill you.'

Dean noticed the same rage descend upon Carly as it had in the pub, her lips curling back over her teeth. He recalled Derek's words when she'd reacted the same way to Jessica, and Dean grabbed her and pulled her back when she attempted to spring like a cat at Ross.

'Get off me,' she hissed, struggling in his arms.

'Don't be reckless,' he said, hauling her away from the three men as they advanced on them. The sound of hammering was audible from the direction of the kitchen as the Alexanders' friends attempted to break down the back door.

'Savages never back down,' she snarled at him.

Dean stared into her furious eyes, her words striking him hard. He nodded and released her. Ross and Cole advanced on him, both wary after what he'd done to their friends, leaving Carly to face Dominic.

Before the two sides could clash, the door to Alec's room swung open to reveal the man himself standing there in his pyjamas holding Eddie's shotgun, which shook in his hands. They were all so astonished they stopped to gape at him.

'G-get out,' he mumbled.

His mask-like expression made it appear as though he wasn't in the slightest bit disconcerted about this invasion of his home while inwardly his heart was hammering.

Ross's face split into a malicious grin. 'Put that down, you fucking dick. You cannae even hold it steady.'

'Don't you call my da' a dick ya fucking prick,' Carly spat at him.

'I can still split you apart with this bastard,' Alec told him.

Carly smiled when something of her fierce father returned to his eyes.

Ross advanced on him a couple of steps. 'Don't be stupid, Alec,' he said in a more reasonable tone. 'If you pull that trigger in this confined space you're just as likely to hit your daughter and nephew.'

Carly and Dean stepped back into Jane's bedroom, leaving the three Alexander brothers exposed to the yawning barrel of the shotgun. The corner of Alec's mouth lifted at the unease that flickered through the three men's eyes.

'Get out,' said Alec as loudly as he could.

'All right, we're going,' said Ross, holding up his hands.

He waved at his brothers and the three of them began backing up to the door. They moved so slowly Alec feared he would drop the weapon before they'd gone, his hands shaking uncontrollably.

Dean stepped forward, took the gun from him and advanced on the Alexanders with it, who hastened their exit. When they'd gone, he kicked the door shut. The lock had broken when the door had been busted open, so he jammed the chair Carly had brought from the kitchen under the handle.

'Da',' said Carly, running to him and wrapping her arms around him.

'Are you okay?' he asked her with relief.

'Aye, fine.'

'Jane and Rose?'

'They're both out. There's only me and Dean here.'

'Nice one, Uncle Alec,' Dean told him.

'Help me get him back into bed,' said Carly when Alec's legs went weak.

Dean wrapped a strong arm around his uncle's waist, the shotgun in his other hand.

Once he was settled, Dean left the room to deal with the men still hammering at the back door.

'You were amazing.' Carly smiled down at her father.

He smiled back at her, eyes heavy with exhaustion. 'So were you,' he murmured, eyes already closing. 'My savage wee girl.'

Carly's smile widened. That was what he used to call her when she regularly got into fights. He'd never chastised her; he was just proud she always won. He hadn't had any cause to use that nickname recently. Until now.

The banging at the back door stopped and Dean returned to the room.

'Have they gone?' she whispered.

'Aye,' he whispered back. 'I just waved the shotgun at them through the window and they shite themselves and ran off.'

Outside, there was the roar of an engine followed by the screech of tyres. Carly glanced out of the window to see a car parked at an angle at the kerb and three figures leap out.

'Jane and the others are back,' she told Dean.

He laid the gun on the bedroom floor and reached the door just as banging started up on the other side for the second time that day. He moved the chair and his father practically fell inside.

'Where are the bastards?' he demanded, Jane and Harry behind him.

'They're gone,' Dean calmly replied. 'Uncle Alec saw them off with the shotgun.'

Eddie's face broke into a proud smile. 'Well, well, that's a turn up. He's still got it then. Are you all okay?'

'Aye, we're fine. He got rid of them before they could do anything.'

'Except batter the shite out of the front door. Alec,' he said, bursting into his brother's bedroom.

Alec jumped awake, eyes wide. He sighed with relief when he realised who it was.

'Still kicking arse, eh?' Eddie grinned, looming over him.

'No one threatens my daughter,' his brother replied.

'Good for you, pal,' Eddie said, patting his shoulder. 'It's a good thing I left that in here,' he added, nodding at the shotgun.

'Why was it in here?' Carly asked him.

'Because I wanted to keep it out of Rose's sight. I hid it under the bed.'

'Thank God you did,' said Dean. 'It drove them off.'

'It's okay now, pal, you rest,' Eddie told Alec. 'I'll look after them.'

Alec nodded gratefully before drifting off again.

The five of them retreated into the kitchen to talk.

'I want to know exactly what happened here,' demanded Eddie.

Carly allowed Dean to explain. She felt tired and drained. What Cole had said to her had upset her more than the attempted assault. Although it made her feel shallow and vain, it was the fact that he'd used the word ugly. He used to tell her how beautiful she was. Had that been a lie too?

'Bastards,' hissed Eddie. 'They got wise to our game.'

'Although Jessica and Brian didn't turn up,' said Carly.

'Brian couldn't, seeing how we've got him tied up in a lock-up.'

'That bit of the plan worked then?' She smiled.

'Aye. We found him banging on the door of number twenty Montgomery Road.'

'I can't believe we just kidnapped someone,' said Jane.

Carly glanced at her sister with concern, until she saw the

excitement in her eyes. The old savagery was rearing its head inside them both.

'The Alexanders won't dare attack us again, as long as we have him,' said Dean.

'We can but hope,' said Eddie.

'We also came across Ross's BMW,' said Harry. 'He'd left it near the garage where Cole works, so it now has a lovely wee devil face carved into the boot.'

'That'll make his day,' said Carly, wishing she could see the bastard's face when he saw that bit of vandalism.

'He might suspect we did it,' said Eddie. 'But he'll also worry it's the McLarens. We need to get back to Brian but someone should stay here with Alec. I doubt that shower will come back so soon but I'm no' taking the risk.'

'Me and Jane can stay,' said Harry. 'It's no' fair Carly and Dean go through that again if they do come back.'

'I think that's an excellent idea,' said Jane, noting the way her sister and Dean glanced at each other. She would prefer it if they were out with Eddie rather than here alone.

'Right,' said Eddie, getting to his feet. 'Let's move.'

* * *

Carly felt distinctly nervous as she sat in the back of her uncle's car, Dean sitting up front with his father. Despite her wild younger days, she'd never been involved in something as serious as kidnapping and part of her felt nervous while the rest of her was exhilarated. She had to admit, this was exciting. Thank God her father didn't know what they were up to because he would hit the roof.

She shifted in her seat, attempting to find a comfortable position while her feet sat in a sea of litter.

'When did you last clean out your car, Uncle Eddie?' she said as she accidentally crushed an empty can, the sound accompanied by the rustle of all the crisp packets and chocolate bar wrappers. It was tragically ironic that Eddie, who drank heavily, stuffed himself with crap and clearly didn't exercise, was as fit as a fiddle, whereas her father, who had jogged, played rugby and ate healthily, was so ill. Parkinson's disease couldn't be avoided by a healthy lifestyle but it still felt to be so unfair.

'I cleaned it out, well, it must be three months ago, I think,' Eddie replied. 'I had a hot date with a beautiful redhead and I wanted to make a good impression.'

'Did your date go well?'

'Naw. She got the huff and stormed out of the restaurant. It was a really nice place, so I don't know what offended her.'

'Oh, well. I hope you find someone soon.' Carly thought perhaps his patronising attitudes towards women had upset his date.

'Me too, hen.'

After they came to a halt outside a row of garages on the edge of Haghill, they got out of the car and furtively looked around as Eddie unlocked the garage, making sure no one was watching.

Dean grimaced when he stepped into a large puddle in one of the many potholes riddling the road.

Eddie raised the door halfway. 'Get in, quick,' he told his son and niece.

Dean and Carly ducked inside and Eddie followed, pausing to switch on the light before closing the door all the way.

Carly was shocked at the sight of Brian Alexander tied to a chair, gaffer tape over his mouth, his eyes blazing with a mixture of anger and fear.

'Look at the big man brought so low,' said Eddie with relish, enjoying his enemy's downfall. 'You thought you could get the better of the Savages but you failed.'

When Brian started to frantically mumble into the gag, Eddie tore the tape from his mouth, making the man grimace.

'This is nothing to do with me,' gabbled Brian. 'It's down to Jess and my boys. I wanted nothing to do with it.'

'The first time you speak you throw your wife and kids under the bus, you fucking coward.'

'But it's true,' Brian exclaimed, eyes wide, chest rising and falling rapidly. 'I was happy going to the bookies and the pub, doing a bit of ducking and diving. I like living in my wee house with my family but it's no' enough for them any more. They've all become greedy bastards. It's their maw's influence; she watches those reality TV shows about those berk housewives with all their cash and wants to be like them. She was so sweet when we first met, so gentle and kind, it's why I fell in love with her, but that girl's gone and I don't like what's replaced her.'

They looked at each other when Brian hung his head and started to cry. He was snapped out of it by a sharp backhanded slap to the face from Eddie.

'Pull yourself together,' he said with disgust. 'Greetin' like a fucking wean.'

'Why shouldn't I? I've been kidnapped.'

'You're no' doing your family's reputation much good.'

'So what? Our reputation's hardly helped me today, has it?' Brian looked to Carly. 'You know this is wrong, don't you? I know we havenae always seen eye to eye but you don't want me to get hurt, do you?'

'You've no idea what I want,' Carly replied with a steely glint in her eye, still hurting over Cole's words.

'My son genuinely loved you. It's no' his fault he turned out the way he did. Jess kept pushing him and pushing him until he finally broke and did what she wanted. He did some terrible things in that prison and they erased my sweet boy; it was like he never existed.

He had no choice I suppose. If he hadn't turned into what he's become, it would have killed him.'

'So he really is the monster he seems to be?'

Brian nodded sadly. 'Even though I knew he only wanted to get back with you so he could use you against your uncle and cousins, I hoped you'd bring me back my son but it didnae work out like that.'

Brian's shoulders slumped and he looked so sad Carly experienced a pang of sympathy for him.

'I tried,' she told him gently. 'But he wasn't interested. Whatever was between us has died.'

Carly took a long, deep breath, a weight lifting from her as she realised she really meant what she was saying. And now she would finally be able to fight him.

'Right, you,' barked Eddie, breaking the momentary silence and making Brian jump. 'You're gonnae tell us everything you know about what your sons are up to.'

'No problem.'

'Don't you feel even a wee bit bad that you're gonnae grass on your own family?'

'Why should I? They've been pushing me out for months now, ignoring what I say and obeying every word their bitch queen of a mother says. It's time I looked out for myself.'

'You really are a piece of work.'

'You'd do the same if your boys turned against you.'

Eddie thrust his face into Brian's, making him recoil. 'And that's the difference between us – my boys would never turn against me.'

'Maybe, maybe not,' said Brian, casting a glance towards Dean, who stared back at him impassively.

'Start talking,' barked Eddie, making Brian jump again.

'My boys have started recruiting as many people as they can, not just in Haghill but the surrounding areas too – Dalmarnock, Barlanark, even Laurieston. All lowlifes and petty criminals who'll back them up for a few quid. They're hungry for your deal with the Tallans. My boys and Jess have been wanting to get into the bigger leagues for a while now and, although the Tallans aren't the main crew in Glasgow, they're certainly bigger fish than either of our families and they have good connections. My lot think that if you're out of the picture then they can steal that deal out from under you.'

'There's only five of us,' said Carly. 'Why do they need to recruit so many people? It doesn't say much for them if they can't handle us on their own.'

'They're no' just recruiting to bring you down, they're forming their own crew. In my opinion they've made some bad choices, or rather Ross and Dominic have. Cole's been a bit wiser, cherry-picked from his best allies in Bar-L.'

Brian's words made Carly feel extremely uneasy. They'd thought they were just fighting the Alexanders, but it seemed they were fighting so many more.

'They're determined to impress the Tallans,' continued Brian. 'And they feel that having a solid, reliable crew around them will do that.'

'Some of them don't sound very reliable,' said Carly.

'You're no' wrong there and that could be their downfall.'

'Do you know these people's names?'

Brian rhymed off a list of names which meant nothing to Carly. Some of them however obviously meant something to her uncle and cousin and the way they glanced uneasily at each other did not make her feel better.

'There,' said Brian. 'I've told you everything I know. Can I go now?'

'You seriously think we're gonnae let you walk out of here?' said Eddie.

'Well, aye,' he slowly replied.

'Then you're wrong.'

'If you're hoping to use me as leverage against Jess and my boys it won't work. They'll say keep me and do what you want to me.'

'I believe you,' said Eddie. 'But this is war and in war there are casualties. We need to show everyone what we're capable of when pushed.'

'What do you mean?' said Brian, looking panicked.

Eddie didn't reply. Instead, he nodded at Dean who nodded back and walked over to a toolbox sitting on the floor in the corner of the room.

'What are you doing?' said Brian, sweat popping out on his forehead.

Dean opened the toolbox and produced a pair of pliers.

'What are you gonnae do with them?' exclaimed Brian. 'Will someone answer me?' he shrieked when once again he got no response. He turned imploring eyes on Carly. 'You won't let them hurt me, will you, doll? You've got such a good heart. You won't just stand there and watch me be tortured?'

Carly knelt before him and Brian was shocked by the ice in her eyes.

'Your boys not only tried to kidnap me,' began Carly, 'but they burst into my flat today and tried to attack me and Dean. Worst of all, they threatened my da' and little sister. Did you try to stop them or warn me? No. You just let it happen, which is why I'm gonnae let this happen to you.'

With that, she straightened up and took a few steps back to allow Dean access to their captive.

'Carly, please,' he cried, chest rising and falling rapidly. 'We had some good times together when you came to my house.'

'I don't remember any,' she said coldly.

He tried to appeal to her again but Eddie slapped gaffer tape over his mouth. 'Go on then, son. Then we can get the daft sod out of here.'

Dean looked to Carly, a question in his eyes. Would she think less of him for this? Her encouraging nod reassured him that she wouldn't.

Dean began to pluck out Brian's fingernails with the pliers, his screams muffled by the tape. Life continued on as normal outside, the residents of Haghill blissfully unaware of the torture occurring inside the small, non-descript garage.

Carly looked on, forcing her expression to remain neutral, even though inwardly her emotions were in turmoil. She couldn't deny it was disturbing watching someone be tortured but there was a part of her that was thrilled by this new direction her life was taking. After feeling powerless for so long, struggling to pay the bills, fearing her dad could be taken from her at any time, this control over another person was a potent drug indeed. When her gaze met Dean's, her heart beat even harder.

22

Carly was lost in thoughtful silence as Eddie drove them back to the flat. She'd watched Dean tear out four of Brian's nails on his left hand before giving him a beating. It could have been so much worse for Brian but she got the feeling her uncle had learnt a lesson from what had happened to Cole and didn't want to push his son too far, not just because it might kill everything that was good inside his own beloved son, but because he didn't want Dean attempting to overthrow him either. Nevertheless, the whole sorry scene had been disturbing for Carly to watch. It wasn't the first time she'd witnessed violence but it was the first time she'd seen someone be tortured and she'd forced herself not to flinch from it. As her uncle said, this was war, although admittedly it did unsettle her that she'd so easily been able to watch someone be tortured. She had the feeling she would see a lot worse before this was over and perhaps even be forced to commit similar acts herself. This was about survival and protecting her family, who she would do anything for. She would happily tear out all of Brian Alexander's teeth if it kept them safe, even her cousins and uncle, who were becoming increasingly important to her. Especially Dean.

Twice Dean turned in his seat to glance at her, as though reas-
suring himself she could still bear the sight of him after what she'd
just seen him do. Carly would never forget the look in his eyes after
he'd finished beating Brian. There had been determination there
but undoubtedly sadness too. He hadn't enjoyed what he'd done,
which reassured her that he wasn't a sadist. She met his gaze and
nodded and he breathed a sigh of relief that she was still okay with
what he'd done. Her uncle hadn't noticed; he'd been too busy slapping Brian's face to bring him round. Then they'd loaded him into
the boot of the car and dumped him around the back of a greasy
spoon café, misleadingly called The Dancing Buttercup. They knew
there would be no cameras there because it was a favoured spot for
the local lowlifes to do their dodgy deals.

It was a relief to enter the warmth and familiarity of home.
Carly had never much liked this flat because to her it had always
been a symbol of the moment her father's illness had got worse. But
now it was the place where her family could be together and her
heart lightened to see Jane waiting for her with a smile and a cup of
coffee.

'Ta,' said Carly, accepting it from her and sinking into a chair at
the kitchen table. She didn't take off her coat because she still felt
cold, the morning's events leaving a chill deep in her bones.

'How did it go?' said Jane.

'It went perfectly,' replied Eddie, also accepting a cup of coffee
from her. 'Brian gave us some useful information.'

As he told Jane and Harry what they'd learnt, Dean sat beside
Carly at the table. She felt his hand on her knee and she gave him a
gentle smile.

'Well,' said Jane when Eddie had finished explaining. 'That's a
surprise.'

'This is so much bigger than we initially thought,' said Harry.

'You and Dean seemed to recognise some of the names Brian gave you,' Carly told her uncle.

'Aye, and I wished we didn't,' replied Eddie. 'We know them from prison. They're all nasty bastards with huge chips on their shoulders. The good news is, some of them are a bit thick, but there are a couple who are not to be underestimated. We need to deal with them first.'

'Deal, how?'

'I'm no' sure yet. This requires careful thought because none of them are from Haghill, so confronting them would mean going into their territory and that's never a good idea. I'd rather lure them here.'

'The Alexanders will put them on their guard as soon as they find out what happened to Brian,' said Harry.

'I reckon he'll tell them he didn't talk, despite the torture,' said Carly. 'But they'll know he's lying. He's always been pretty weak.'

'What will they do to him for grassing?' Jane asked her.

Carly's response was a tired shrug.

'If the Alexanders are massing their own army,' said Jane, 'we need to get our own.'

'How are we supposed to do that?' replied Carly.

'I need to get the Bitches back.'

'Will they be enough to take on everyone the Alexanders have on their side?'

'You know how violent some of those girls can be and it'd be a good start.'

'Nae offence, hen,' said Eddie with a patronising smile, 'but I don't think a bunch of lassies will be able to help us.'

Jane arched an eyebrow. 'You've no idea what they can do.'

'Aye I dae – they can vandalise bus shelters and throw stones at windows.'

'They're women, Uncle Eddie, no' ten-year-olds. They can do this.'

'The problem is, not all of them are for you,' said Carly. She gestured to the bruise on her sister's face. 'As you found out earlier.'

'They'll get in line once Emma's out of the way.'

'It's a nice idea,' said Eddie. 'But I've got some people in mind. I think we're better concentrating on getting as many men as we can behind us.'

'Oh, I see.' Jane frowned, folding her arms across her chest. 'You don't think women can fight?'

'Course I do,' he replied patronisingly. 'I just think men are better at it. We're built for it, you see. You women are built for taking care of weans.'

Carly and Jane glanced at each other with raised eyebrows.

'That's a very old-fashioned attitude you've got there,' Jane told him. 'And it's made me even more determined to get back the Bitches.'

'You do that.' He smiled smugly. 'And then we'll see who's better – your girls or my men.'

'Fine by me,' retorted Jane, eyes flashing.

'I'm starting to realise why the redhead stormed out of your date,' Carly told her uncle, making Dean smile.

'I need to make some calls,' said Eddie, producing his phone. 'I'll rally as many people as I can. In the meantime, you four need to keep your eyes open. There's a good chance the Alexanders will come back at us harder when they find out what happened to Brian. Even if it's true that they really don't gi'e a shite about him any more, they'll still have to retaliate to save face.'

He was interrupted by the kitchen phone ringing and Jane rose to answer it. She listened to the voice on the other end. Carly was alarmed when she sighed and said, 'Oh no.' Anxiously she waited for her sister to hang up and explain.

'That was the school,' she said. 'Rose got into a fight. They want me to go in.'

'Not again,' said Carly.

'Again?' said a surprised Eddie. 'You mean she's had fights before?'

'Aye, a lot, but she's been so good since Da' got really ill. She didn't want to stress him out, so this is a surprise.'

'Jeezo, you wouldn't think it to look at her. She's such a sweet wee thing.'

'She can be a little devil when she's angry.'

'Is she hurt?' Dean asked Jane.

'No,' she replied, the prospect seeming to amuse her. 'But she did knock out a boy's front teeth.'

'She battered a lad, did she?' Eddie smiled. 'Good on her.'

'You still think females are only being fit for raising weans?' Jane asked him with a laugh.

'If anyone can change my opinion, doll, I'm sure it's you and your sisters.'

* * *

Dean drove to the school with Jane sitting in the back seat, closely watching Carly and Dean in the front, to see if they cast each other any longing looks but they didn't. Neither did they speak and her sister in particular seemed to be lost in her own world. Jane hoped watching Brian Alexander be tortured hadn't damaged her in any way. Carly was already under so much stress and she feared the mere memory of it would be too much for her. It must have been very unpleasant and personally she was glad she hadn't witnessed it.

At the school, Dean parked as close to the reception as he could and waited in the car while Jane and Carly went inside. They met with Ms Simpson, Rose's head of year, who stared at them dourly. Both sisters were sent hurtling back to the time they'd been students at the school and felt like little children again. Thankfully the victim's parents had decided not to press the issue, despite the fact that their son had lost his front teeth, as there were plenty of witnesses who said he'd initiated the incident by pushing Rose over and mocking her father's condition. Rose had cut her knee and was being patched up by the school nurse and secretly her sisters were proud that she hadn't let her injury stop her from belting the boy in the face.

'Which boy was it?' said Jane.

'Ethan Patterson,' replied Ms Simpson.

The sisters glanced at each other. The Pattersons were closely associated with the Alexanders. Had they orchestrated this attack on Rose or was it a coincidence?

'Doesn't he have a history of bullying?' Carly asked Ms Simpson.

'It's true he does have a history of negative behaviour towards other pupils,' she replied diplomatically. 'Which is another reason why his parents aren't taking things further. I rather got the impression they hope this incident might encourage him to change his ways. I'm very concerned because, it must be said, Rose did respond with a lot of savagery.' The sternness vanished from Ms Simpson's eyes and her expression softened. 'She's a very clever girl and has stayed out of trouble for well over a year now. I'm worried the pressure of the situation at home with your father has caused the stress to build up inside her, and it's exploded today. I want to suggest that Rose sees the school counsellor. Just talking to someone neutral can be an enormous help. There may be things on her mind that she doesn't want to discuss with you for fear of adding to your burden. Her exams are coming up, which are an added strain and she's on track to do very well in them. It would be such a shame if she fell at the last hurdle for the sake of some extra support.'

'I think that sounds like a good idea,' said Carly. 'But it would have to be Rose's choice.'

'Of course. We wouldn't force her into something she wasn't comfortable with, but I do think she would benefit from it. Our counsellor is a lovely, gentle lady. She's usually very busy but an empty slot has opened up, which is Rose's if she wants it.'

'We can certainly discuss it with her,' said Jane.

'Excellent. When the school nurse has finished with her, you can take her home and I'll speak to her tomorrow to see if she wants to proceed with counselling.'

The sisters left and waited in reception for their sister. Both were so relieved that was the end to the incident they looked at each other and laughed.

'Thank God for that,' said Carly quietly, conscious of the receptionist behind the desk close to where they were sitting.

'Aye, that went much better than I thought,' whispered back Jane. 'I was afraid the polis would get involved.'

'It's going to be difficult to do what we need to do with Rose at home today. She'll pick up on what's going on.'

They were forced to stop the conversation when Rose emerged, limping slightly on her left leg. The sisters were surprised when she didn't greet them with her usual radiant smile.

'How's the leg?' Carly asked her.

'Sore,' was her chilly reply.

'Let's get you home so you can rest it. Dean's waiting outside in the car.'

Not even the mention of her handsome cousin was enough to bring a smile to Rose's face.

They returned to the car in silence, Rose limping along behind her sisters. Carly sat up front again while Rose got in the back with Jane.

'All right, sweetheart?' Dean asked her, turning in his seat to face her.

Rose appeared to soften slightly at his charming grin and gave him a small smile in response.

'Ms Simpson said you had a fight with Ethan Patterson,' Jane said.

Rose nodded, still looking miserable.

'And that he started it by pushing you over?'

Another nod while Rose continued to avoid eye contact with her sister.

Both Jane and Carly were becoming increasingly concerned by this display that was so unlike the gregarious girl they knew and loved.

'Do you want to talk about it?'

Tears filled Rose's eyes but she looked angry rather than upset. 'He told me the Alexanders are going to kill you all.'

'What?' said a shocked Jane.

'He overheard Ross and Cole talking with his brother, Billy. They're going to kill you and Carly and my cousins and Uncle Eddie, leaving me and da' all alone,' she cried, the tears spilling down her cheeks now. 'And when da' dies, I'll have no one. Ethan laughed; he thought it was funny.'

Jane enveloped her in her arms and Rose sobbed on her shoulder. The poor girl had clearly been holding her fears in until it was safe to release them all.

'Oh, sweetheart,' said Jane. 'That's not true.'

'But it is,' said Rose, raising her tear-streaked face to regard her. 'The Alexanders threw a brick through our window and have been causing trouble. Even Cole's in on it. I liked him, I thought he was sweet and funny, but he's a prick,' she wailed.

Jane took her sister's face in her hands. 'Now you listen to me – no one is going to kill anyone. Yes, things have got a bit tense between us and the Alexanders but that's all it is. We'll soon sort it out. Ethan was just winding you up.'

'Really?' Rose said suspiciously.

'Aye.'

'You're not just telling me that to make me feel better, like I'm a wee wean?'

'No. We will sort it out, I promise, and we'll all be fine. Uncle Eddie and Dean and Harry have even got a house to rent close to our flat. They've decided to move here so we can be a happy family together. Would you like that?'

'Yes, I would, but I'm still worried about the Alexanders and it really hurts that Cole's turned against us.'

'Cole went through a lot while he was in prison and it changed him. We should feel sorry for him rather than hate him.'

'He used to make me laugh but Ethan said he hates us now.'

'He doesn't hate us. Prison messed him up. Unfortunately, it does that to some people and you shouldn't listen to Ethan Patterson. He's a wee dick.'

This made Rose smile at last. 'Aye, he is.'

'Ms Simpson said you knocked out his front teeth,' Jane said with a raised eyebrow.

'He deserved it. He said horrible things about Da'.'

'In that case, well done.' She smiled, making Rose's eyes sparkle. 'Don't tell Da' about the fight or what Ethan said. We don't want to upset him. We'll say you felt a bit unwell.'

'That might worry him too.'

'We'll say you've got bad period pain. That'll stop him from asking any more questions.'

Rose giggled. 'Periods frighten him.'

'They frighten most men. Just hide in your room when we get home and it'll be fine.'

'Okay. Can I have some of that cookie dough ice cream that Uncle Eddie got? That's really good for period pain.'

'Course you can, he won't mind.'

Rose smiled and settled back in her seat, looking much happier.

When they'd returned to the flat and Rose had vanished into her bedroom with the tub of ice cream after popping in to explain to her embarrassed father why she was home early, the rest of the family once again went into conference in the kitchen.

'I want to go round to the Pattersons and batter the living shite out of that twat, Billy,' hissed Jane. 'I'll also make sure his wee dick brother never bothers Rose again.'

'You can't do anything to Ethan though,' Dean told her. 'He's just a kid.'

'I don't intend to. The example I'll make of his older brother will scare the little bastard rigid.'

'Good idea,' said Carly, who was equally furious. 'Let's do it.'

'Hang on a minute,' said Eddie when the sisters rose and stalked to the door. 'Have you thought through what you're gonnae do? Are the Pattersons a big family? Will they fight to protect this Billy prick?'

'He's got two brothers and a sister,' said Jane. 'One of those brothers is only sixteen, so we don't need to worry about him. The oldest brother moved to Aberdeen two years ago, so we don't need to worry about him either, and the sister's a nasty bitch who we can easily deal with.'

'What about his parents?'

'We'll handle them too.'

'Wait, I...' Eddie sighed when they stormed out of the room, heading towards the front door. 'Boys, go with them,' he told his sons.

They went in Harry's car, Jane sitting up front with him so she could direct him to the Patterson home. Dean kept glancing at Carly during the journey but her gaze remained locked on the window. He knew she wasn't seeing the view; she was lost in her own fury. When they arrived at the Patterson house, he fully expected to see her lips draw back over her teeth as they had when the Alexanders had attacked. He wanted to take her hand but knew his brother's sharp eyes would spot that in the rear-view mirror so he restrained himself. Plus, he wasn't sure she'd appreciate the gesture in that moment.

Dean forced his gaze off Carly. The speed at which his feelings for her were developing was rather startling to him. He'd never met a woman whose mere presence made his stomach flip over with excitement. It was typical that she would have to be his own cousin but he didn't care. He wanted her and he was determined to get her.

23

The Savages pulled up outside a four-storey red brick tenement. The moment the car came to a halt, the two women leapt out, the men hurrying to catch up with them as they stormed inside one of the blocks and jogged upstairs to the second floor. Jane banged on the door, which was pulled open by a tall, thin woman of her own age with wild, curly dark brown hair that seemed to sit up on her head in a frizzy tangle.

'Where's Billy?' demanded Jane.

Sharon Patterson took a drag on her cigarette and blew the smoke in Jane's face. 'How the fuck should I know?'

'So he's no' in?'

'I didn't say that,' replied Sharon with an infuriating smile.

'I'm no' in the mood for your games. Just tell me where he is.'

'Why do you want him? You're no' his type if you're after his cock.'

'The only reason I'd want that thing would be to cut it off. Oh, I've had enough of this,' she said, shoving Sharon roughly aside and stalking into the flat. The living room was airy with a bright bay window. It was clean and warm, a pair of fluffy white cats curled up asleep on the lap of the man sitting on the beige couch watching football on the television. He looked up in surprise when the four of them burst in.

'What the hell's going on?' he demanded.

'Your wee brother attacked Rose today,' said Jane.

'Aye, we know. The school called and said she knocked out his front teeth. My maw's had to take him to the dentist. And you've got the cheek to barge in here all outraged. That wee sister of yours is a demon, everyone knows that.'

'This isn't Rose's fault, it's Ethan's,' interjected Carly. 'He's always been a bully because he's weak and pathetic, like you.'

Billy shot to his feet, sending the cats scattering in opposite directions. 'Who the fuck do you think you are? Get out before I throw you both through the bastarding window.'

Billy was a big man, strong and muscular with dark hair and a matching beard. He would have been handsome had it not been for his eyes, which were small, piggy and set far apart in his head. His thick, blubbery lips gave him the aspect of a particularly vicious toad.

When Dean and Harry tensed, ready to attack, Carly waved at them to stand down before turning her furious glare back on Billy.

'Actually, we're no' just here about our sister beating the shite out of your brother,' Carly told Billy, making him grunt with rage. 'We're here because you've been plotting against us with the Alexanders.' She tilted her head to one side curiously. 'You seem to be under the impression that you're going to kill us.'

'Ethan, you gobby wee shite,' Billy muttered to himself.

'We know what the Alexanders have planned and we're here to tell you that they're going to fail spectacularly and that anyone who sides with them will be punished. We need someone to make an example of and you, Billy, are it. Blame your wee brother for that.'

'Four on one,' he sneered. 'That's hardly fucking fair.'

'Dean and Harry will not lay a finger on you.'

'So, just you two?' he said, looking amused by the prospect. 'Actually, that could be pretty hot. Come on then girls,' he added, opening his arms wide. 'Go for it.'

Harry and Dean watched in astonishment as their cousins simultaneously attacked the large, strapping man. While Jane went in higher, being the tallest, Carly went in low, targeting his knees and groin. It was clear they'd fought together many times because they moved in perfect harmony. As Billy collapsed to the floor, bleeding from his mouth and nose, Sharon charged into the room clutching a rolling pin, screeching at the top of her lungs.

Before the brothers could intervene, Carly turned, grabbed her arm and dragged her to the floor. She stomped on Sharon's arm and tore the rolling pin from her hand.

'Stay down,' Carly yelled at her.

Sharon didn't listen, jumped back to her feet and launched herself at Carly with her arms extended, fingers curled into talons. Carly kicked her in the stomach, knocking her back onto the couch, leapt on her and punched her twice in the face, finally subduing her.

'I said stay the fuck down,' she snarled, lips drawing back over her teeth again.

Sharon groaned and nodded, putting a hand to her burst lower lip.

Satisfied that this time she was going to do the sensible thing, Carly joined her sister in staring down at the fallen Billy.

'What did Ross promise you?' Jane demanded of him.

'A deal with the Tallans,' he muttered back.

'That's not his fucking deal to promise. You will break off your arrangement with the Alexanders,' Jane told him. 'If you don't then we won't take it out on you. We'll come back for her,' she added, pointing to the flailing Sharon. 'And Rose will knock out the rest of your brother's teeth.'

Billy raised his head, lips cut and his right eye badly swollen. He looked like he was about to argue, until he sighed and nodded. 'Aye, all right. I don't want all this shite.'

'Good.' She looked to the others. 'Let's go.'

Dean, who had picked up one of the cats and was stroking it, the animal purring in his arms, gently put it down on the couch and left too.

Billy glared at the cat. 'Traitor.'

The cat gave him a haughty look before settling back down to sleep, using Sharon's splayed hair as a cushion.

* * *

No one spoke until they were back in the car and had set off, leaving the Patterson residence behind.

'I wish our Da' had seen that,' said Harry as he drove. 'Then he might change his mind about women not being able to fight.'

'Savage is certainly the right name for you two,' commented Dean, turning in his seat to face them.

'No one fucks with our wee sister,' said Jane, gazing out of the window with steel in her eyes.

'Did you believe Billy when he said he'd break his deal with the Alexanders?' said Harry.

'I don't know,' she replied. 'He could have just said that to get rid of us, although the threat against his brother and sister might encourage him to keep his word.'

When they returned to the flat, Eddie was sitting talking with his brother in his bedroom.

'Hi Da',' said Carly, concerned by how exhausted he looked. 'How are you feeling?'

'He's all good,' said Eddie. 'We've been discussing old times, haven't we, Alec?'

His brother nodded.

'We were terrors back in the day,' continued Eddie wistfully. 'The scourge of Glesga.'

'I can well believe it,' she said, smiling. 'Can we get you anything, Da'?'

He shook his head. 'No sweetheart. I'll just have a sleep.'

'Oh, sorry,' said Eddie, getting to his feet. 'I've been keeping you awake with my chatter. We'll leave you to it.'

Alec gave his daughters a searching look and Carly knew he was wondering where they'd been but was too tired to ask.

The sound of pop music quietly playing emanated from Rose's room. Carly popped in on her and found Rose lying on her bed reading a magazine. She assured her sister she was okay and Carly left her to it.

'How did it go?' Eddie asked his nieces once they were back in the kitchen.

'Fine,' said Jane. 'Billy and his sister have been put in their place.'

'Nice one,' Eddie told his sons.

'Don't look at us,' replied Harry. 'We didn't do anything. Jane and Carly tore them both apart.'

'Really?' Eddie said, surprised. 'Well, I suppose you caught Billy off guard.'

All four of them rolled their eyes.

'Billy said Ross promised him a piece of the Tallan deal,' Jane told Eddie.

'The cheeky bastard. Who the fuck does he think he is, offering something that isn't his?'

'He's an arrogant sod,' said Carly.

'I wonder if he's noticed the devil face on the back of his car yet?' said Harry.

'I'm sure we'll soon find out.' Carly glanced at the clock on the wall. 'Jesus, I need to be at work in ten minutes.'

'You're better off no' going in,' Eddie told her.

'I have to, I can't leave Derek in the lurch.'

'Doesn't he have anyone else who works for him?'

'Aye, and usually Anita would work this shift but she's off sick. There's no one else and I need the money.'

'I keep telling you no' to worry about money any more.'

'Well, I still have to go in.'

'Fine, Dean, go with her,' he said.

Dean nodded and got to his feet, picking up his brand-new laptop.

'Are you sure it's wise bringing that?' Carly asked him, indicating the computer.

'If anyone does do anything to it, I can use it as a weapon,' he replied with a rare twinkle.

Carly smiled and shook her head. 'Let's go.'

* * *

'Jeezo, lassie, there you are,' rasped Derek when Carly arrived at the pub with Dean. His face was bright red and shiny with sweat and he was hopping from one foot to the other.

'Away you go before you pish yourself,' she told him with a smile.

Derek shot out from behind the bar and dashed across the room, shoving one drunken man aside.

'He should really see a doctor about that,' said Dean. 'Maybe it's a medical problem? He could have cystitis or a urinary tract infection? Does it burn when he pees?'

'I'm very pleased to tell you that I've never asked him,' replied Carly.

Dean settled himself at his usual table while Carly turned to serving the thirsty customers.

Carly felt edgy as she worked and struggled to keep her mind on the job. Twice she gave someone the wrong change and once she knocked a pint of lager over a customer, who was fortunately a regular and took the accident in good part, especially when his new lady friend began wiping his crotch with the cloth Derek handed her.

'What's wrong with you, hen?' Derek asked her, not unkindly. 'This isnae like you.'

'Sorry, I'm just a little tense.'

'Has something else happened?'

'Aye. Ross, Dominic and Cole attacked our flat.'

'What? Cole too?'

Carly nodded. 'He's as bad as his brothers now, if not worse.'

'Are you sure about that?' he said sceptically.

'There's no doubt.' Carly glanced around to make sure no one was listening before continuing. 'He set me up the other night to be kidnapped.'

'What?' Derek exclaimed, loud enough that most of his customers looked his way. He cringed. 'Sorry,' he told Carly.

'His plan would have succeeded too if it hadn't been for Dean and Harry. They saved me.'

'Jeezo, that's crazy. Why would the Alexanders do that?'

'It's a long story and there's some things I can't tell you.'

Derek glanced Dean's way. 'It's something to do with his lot, isn't it? Them coming here was supposed to help you but it's made things worse.'

'No, it's no' like that. Honestly,' Carly added when he appeared unconvinced.

'Does Alec know what's going on?'

'No, thankfully.'

'It must have scared the shite out of him having those Alexander arseholes bursting into your flat.'

'Actually, it didn't,' she told him proudly. 'He managed to get himself out of bed and told them to piss off. He was amazing.' She thought it would be better not to mention the shotgun.

'He always was a strong, brave bugger and no illness will take that from him but Christ, Carly. This is getting out of hand. I mean, kidnapping? That's heavy duty.'

She wondered what he'd say if he knew she was in on kidnapping Brian and torturing him.

'Maybe you should go to the polis about this?'

'No way. Savages do not go to the polis.'

'That's what your da' used to say,' Derek said with a fond smile. 'Does he know you were nearly abducted?'

'Of course not. I'd never put that stress on him.'

'If he did, he'd tell you to go straight to the polis. Be sensible, Carly. What if they try to take you again or what if someone ends up getting killed? The most benign of arguments can quickly escalate and the next thing you know, someone's dying in the gutter with a knife in their chest. I've seen it happen.' Derek felt selfish for even thinking it, but he also worried about his pub getting caught in the crossfire between the two families. He'd already had his window put through, his car had been damaged and a fight had broken out in his establishment. What if next time the whole place got smashed up or set on fire? But Carly was like a daughter to him and he refused to abandon her when she really needed him. 'If you need extra time off, just let me know. You already have so much going on and with this shite on top of it all, I don't want you burning yourself out.'

'But Anita's still off sick.'

'She told me today she's no' coming back. Her back trouble's gonnae be long term, so she's having to give up work. Her niece needs a job though and she's got a lot of experience in the trade, so if you need more time to yourself, you just let me know.'

Carly smiled and patted his arm. 'Thanks Derek, you're such a star.'

'So I've been told.' He beamed back at her.

They looked to the door when it opened and Cole strode in. He moved with his usual sinuous, cat-like grace but his face was set, his expression hard. His green eyes were still beautiful but all the mischief Carly had loved in them had gone. Rather than walk up to the bar he stood in the middle of the room, his presence drawing everyone's attention.

'What do you want?' Derek demanded of him. 'All your family's barred.'

'I've got a message,' he said before his gaze slipped to Carly. 'If you and your cousin don't come out nice and quietly, then we'll burn this fucking place to the ground.'

Shocked gasps ran around the room.

'Cole,' exclaimed Carly.

'You cannae dae that,' exclaimed Derek.

Cole ignored him, his gaze flicking from Carly to Dean and back again.

'You all heard him,' Derek called to the room. 'If anything happens to this place you know who was responsible.'

'And if anyone even dreams of giving evidence against me or my family,' countered Cole, casting that threatening gaze about the room, 'then their own families will suffer.'

This was enough to scare most of the customers, who cast their own eyes to the floor. Some, however, refused to be cowed.

'Where do you get off threatening good people like that?'

demanded Jim, striding up to Cole. 'I'll tan your arse, ya mouthy wee pup.'

Cole's fist slammed into his face so quickly everyone doubted Jim even saw it coming. His eyes rolled back in his head and he toppled backwards to the floor, unconscious.

'Anyone else got something to say?' demanded Cole. He nodded with satisfaction when no one replied. 'Good.' He looked back at Carly. 'You've got five minutes. If you don't come out, then the petrol bombs come in.'

No one spoke as he left the building but the moment he'd gone, the customers all charged for the door, shoving each other out of the way in their eagerness to escape. Carly glanced at Derek and was appalled to see the horror in his eyes. Not only was his pub being threatened but he was losing customers too.

'Derek,' she murmured, blinking back tears.

'Aye, hen?' he murmured back, his jaw hanging open as he watched the last customer leave, the door banging shut behind them.

'I quit.'

This shook Derek out of his stupor. 'What?'

'You've had your pub vandalised and now this. I don't want to ruin your business.'

'You won't.'

Carly shook her head, a tear sliding down her cheek. 'You've been so good to me, you've been like a da' and I really appreciate it, which is why I'm doing this. I don't want you to get hurt and you will be if you keep employing me.'

'Don't let them win,' he told her, gently taking her by the shoulders.

Steel filled her eyes. 'Oh, I can promise you they won't.'

'Good on you, doll.' He winked at her.

She hugged Derek and he hugged her back.

'I hate to lose you,' he said. 'You can always come back when this shite is over.'

Carly nodded, swallowing down a lump in her throat. She hated it that the Alexanders had succeeded in taking her job from her. She only hoped her uncle hadn't been lying when he'd said she and her sister could make some serious money because without her wage they would struggle.

She released Derek and handed him her till key. Then she walked over to Dean, who was still sitting casually at the table as though nothing had happened.

'We'd better go out there before Derek's pub gets attacked.'

He nodded, got to his feet, picked up his laptop and placed it on the bar. 'Can you look after this for me, please?'

'Course,' replied Derek. 'I'll put it in the safe.'

'Thanks.' Dean looked to Carly. 'I've called my da'. He's on his way.'

She nodded, getting the feeling the Alexanders wanted Eddie and Harry to come too. She prayed Jane stayed at home to look after Rose and their father.

'Be careful,' Derek called after them as they left the pub together.

The pair of them came to a halt, a little startled to see how many people had gathered in the street.

The Alexanders were not alone. They stood amid a group of more than a dozen men, some of whom looked terrifying with their cauliflower ears and scars. Clearly these were all brutal, violent people with a long history of mayhem behind them. Also with the Alexanders were the Bitches, all twenty of them, Emma standing at their head looking smug.

When two of the scarred men started to yell obscenities at Dean, Carly asked him under her breath, 'Were you in prison with any of them?'

'Aye.' He nodded, looking perfectly calm.

'They don't look very happy to see you.'

'I suppose I can understand that. I'm responsible for some of their scars.'

The corner of her mouth lifted. 'Nice one.' Carly looked to Cole. 'You need all this lot to stand up to me and Dean, do you? How pathetic.'

'No' just you two,' he replied as a car tore down the street towards them.

The car screeched to a halt between the mob and Dean and Carly. Eddie hopped out of the passenger seat.

'Get in,' he told his son and niece.

'I don't think so,' said Cole.

'Ignore that wee dick,' Eddie told Dean and Carly. 'Get in.'

As the two of them rushed to the car, the gang closed in on it, forcing Eddie to leap back inside.

'Run,' he called to his son and niece.

24

Dean grabbed Carly's hand and they tore down the street. Glancing back over her shoulder, Carly saw Harry's car being rocked by the mob. He revved the engine, and the people standing in front of it leapt out of the way for fear of being run over. Harry took the opportunity to stomp on the accelerator and the car shot down the street, unfortunately in the opposite direction to them. Now those targets had slipped out of their grasp, Carly was alarmed to see the mob tear down the street after herself and Dean.

'Where are we going?' she asked Dean as they ran. 'Because we can't lead that lot back to the flat.'

'I've nae idea. You know this area better than me.' He looked back over his shoulder and if he was alarmed he didn't show it, which rather impressed Carly. Fortunately, they were both fast and in good health, so they were managing to stay ahead of the rabid pack. Already some of the older and unfit members, of whom there were quite a few, were falling back, panting and sweating.

'This way,' she said, pulling him down a darkened back street.

Dean's phone started to ring. He released her hand and pulled it from his pocket and managed to talk as they ran with only a slight breathiness.

'Da', aye. I don't know. Where are we headed?' he asked Carly.

'Tell him no' to worry about us. He needs to get back to my da' and Rose. If that lot don't catch us they might go there.' Carly wondered if Dean would object to help being diverted from them but he didn't and he calmly relayed the message before hanging up.

'He protested but I hung up,' Dean told her. 'You're right, we can lose this lot.'

'Course we can,' said Carly as they took a right onto a better lit street that contained nothing but more rows of red brick tenements.

'This way,' she said, pulling him towards the door leading into one of the tenements. Rather than head to one of the flats, she led him straight through the dank, smelly corridor and out the other side into a communal garden that was all sagging washing lines and paving slabs.

They charged at the grey wall, scrambled over it and dropped down on the other side.

'My friend lives in these flats,' whispered Carly.

Dean nodded in understanding. That was how she knew about this exit.

They looked up and down the street but could see no one, although there was the distant cry of voices.

'This way,' said Carly again.

Dean followed her right, away from the voices and they turned left onto another road full of squat tenements.

'Where are we going?' he asked her.

'Just the next street,' panted Carly, who was rapidly beginning to tire.

They turned another corner onto a road lined with beige new-build houses with dark brown roofs. Dean was grateful when Carly slowed before stopping altogether. She doubled over to catch her breath.

'I haven't run like that since I was on the cross country team at high school,' she gasped.

'I think we lost them,' said Dean, looking around.

'My friend Angela lives on this street. She'll let us borrow her car.'

Dean nodded and followed her to the front door of one of the houses. Clearly someone was in because the glow of lights could be seen from behind the curtains. Carly knocked and while they waited for someone to answer, they constantly looked around, fearing the mob would catch up with them.

The door was pulled open by a pretty, slender woman with a thin, pale face and ash blonde hair pulled back into a messy ponytail.

'Carly,' she said, a little startled to see her friend on her doorstep.

'Hi Angela,' she replied. 'Sorry to disturb you so late but I need a big favour – can I borrow your car?'

'Why?' she asked. She looked to Dean, a question in her eyes.

'Oh, sorry,' said Carly, attempting to sound cool and calm. 'This is my cousin, Dean. We've got a wee bit of trouble and we need to get out of here pronto, which is why we need your car.'

'But you can't drive.'

'Dean can though. I promise we'll look after it and we'll have it back to you in the morning.'

'This is to do with the Alexanders, isn't it?'

'How do you know?'

'Because Cole stopped by earlier and said it would be very bad for me and my family if I helped you. He was scary; I've never seen him like that before.'

'He's changed since he came out of prison,' said Carly bitterly.

'I'm really sorry, you know normally I'd do anything for you, but I believed him when he threatened me.'

Carly's shoulders slumped with sadness but she forced a smile for Angela's sake; she'd been a good friend to her since she was seven years old. 'It's all right. I understand.'

'I'm glad about that,' said a relieved Angela. The sound of a baby crying echoed from inside the house. 'Sorry, I've got to go.'

'Aye, nae problem.'

Angela closed the door and they heard the sound of the key being turned in the lock.

'Some friend she is,' growled Dean, glaring at the door.

'I understand why she refused. She's got a baby and a three-year-old to think of and her man left her two months ago. She's raising the weans alone and life's hard enough for her without getting tangled up in all my shite too.'

'All right, I'll let her off. Maybe if we keep running, they'll get fed up and go home.'

'I doubt it'll be that easy.'

Carly's phone began to ring and she produced it from her pocket.

'It's Jane,' she said.

'We need to keep moving,' Dean said, looking about uneasily.

They set off again at a brisk pace and Carly answered the phone before the ringing alerted anyone to their presence.

'Hi Jane. No, we're fine. We think we've lost them but we're currently wandering about Newmarket Street. We don't want to come back to the flat because we might draw them there. Aye, I know but I don't want to risk it. Have Uncle Eddie and Harry got back safe? That's a relief. No, stay where you are. We're fine, we're not being followed any more. Keep Da' and Rose safe.'

Dean grabbed Carly's arm and pulled her behind a car parked at the kerb. When she looked at him questioningly, he jerked his thumb behind him. Carly looked to see a group of eight men tearing around the corner at the bottom of the road. At least, she thought they were men. It was hard to tell in the darkness. The men stopped to look up and down the road before conferring with each other.

'Got to go,' Carly whispered into the phone before hanging up. She put her phone on silent and slipped it back inside her coat pocket.

They remained crouched, praying that the men went in the opposite direction, but to their dismay the men rushed up the street towards them. When they passed under a streetlight, Carly recognised Ross and Cole.

Carly looked to Dean, who nodded to the left with his head. She followed him as he silently crawled around the far side of the car and the two of them ducked down under the level of the windows, making sure they sat behind the wheels. They held their breath as the posse passed them by, quietly talking amongst themselves.

The men turned right at the top of the street and vanished. Dean and Carly breathed a sigh of relief and got to their feet. At that moment, Cole's head peered around the corner. As he was standing under a streetlight, his diabolical smile was illuminated for them both to see.

'They're here,' he yelled before tearing back down the street after them, closely followed by the other seven men.

Dean and Carly bolted and ran down the road, taking a left turn and then another until they ended up on a busier main road lined with shops, most of which were closed apart from a couple of takeaways.

'He must have known I'd come to Angela's,' said Carly as they ran. That was the problem with having Cole as an enemy – he understood how she thought.

It was fortunate the traffic was light because they dashed across the road without time to think.

'There's the park,' exclaimed Carly. 'It's really big and it's open twenty-four hours, we'll be able to lose them in there.'

'Okay,' said Dean.

Together they raced through the large, ornate, wrought iron gates and down the long dark path. Glancing back over their shoulders, they saw they were still being chased, although a couple of the men were falling behind. Ross and Cole were in the lead, looking worryingly determined.

They took a right turn and raced towards a duck pond. Before their pursuers emerged from around the bend, Dean took Carly's hand and pulled her into the trees. They ducked down and remained still, watching through the shrubbery as Cole and the others jogged up to the duck pond and stopped to look around. There were a couple of lights but they did nothing to illuminate the thick band of trees encircling the pond.

'They could be anywhere,' exclaimed one of the men.

'Then you'd better get looking,' growled Ross.

'How can we see in this? We don't even have torches.'

Ross grabbed him by the front of the jacket and yanked him towards him. 'Use the torch on your phone, you fucking idiot, before I throw you in the duck pond.'

'Oh, that's nice, that is,' retorted the man, tearing himself free of Ross's grip. 'You promise me a great deal with loads of cash and what have I got so far? Nothing but sodding running and threats. Well, I've had enough, I'm off.'

He didn't get very far as Cole punched him in the face, knocking him back several steps. Ross then grabbed him by the back of the coat and shoved him into the pond. The man shrieked and flailed.

'Help, I cannae swim.'

'It's only shallow, ya dick,' said Ross. 'Just put your feet down.'

The man finally found the bottom and stood up, the water barely reaching his waist. 'I was too hot after all the running but I'm fucking freezing now,' he exclaimed.

'Then Ross did you a favour,' said Cole. 'And the next time you think of ducking out on us, it won't be water he throws you into, it'll be a vat of acid.'

The man kept his head down as he hauled himself out of the water, wanting to avoid the angry glares of the Alexander brothers.

When one of the other men sniggered, Ross rounded on him. 'What's so fucking funny?'

'Cole said ducking and it's a duck pond,' he chuckled.

'Shut up and start looking for them,' he roared at the man, who nodded and jumped to it, along with his friends, all of them using the torches on their phones to light their way.

The one who'd been pushed into the pond started to frantically dash about to and fro in an attempt to warm himself back up.

'Even with their phones, they can't find us if we stay quiet and stay down,' Dean whispered in Carly's ear. 'There's too much undergrowth.'

She nodded, gently settling herself into a more comfortable position to wait it out. Carly rather enjoyed the spectacle of that bunch of idiots tripping over things and groaning when they stood in dog shite.

Ten minutes of frustrated searching later, Cole exploded. 'I know you're here Carly and you can hear me. If you don't come out right now, we'll go straight to your flat, drag your da' out of his bed and kick his fucking head in.'

Carly was unable to believe the man she'd once loved could be so callous and cruel. The breath was stolen from her throat and all she could do was gape at Dean stupidly.

'Don't listen to him,' he whispered to her.

'But what if he means it?' she whispered back.

He grabbed her hand when she tried to get to her feet. 'I won't let you do this.'

'I have to.' She touched his face. 'I'll be all right.'

Dean yanked her back down, jumped up and strode out of the hiding place.

'Don't,' she said, attempting to grab hold of his leg but he stepped out of the trees onto the path.

'Here I am,' he said, making all the men except Cole and Ross jump.

'Jeezo, he gave me the fucking fear then,' said the one who'd been thrown into the water.

'Where's Carly?' demanded Cole.

'Nae idea, we split up and you don't really need her. It's me who's in on the Tallan deal. She's nothing to do with it.'

'Grab him,' Ross told his men.

They nodded and lunged at Dean, who calmly allowed them to wrench his arms behind his back.

Cole stood in front of Dean and glared into his face. Then he drew back his fist and punched him, snapping his head to the right. Dean slowly turned back to face him, a smile on his lips. 'The one time you dare to hit me and I can't hit back.'

This enraged Cole and he punched Dean in the stomach, annoyed when he only grunted slightly.

'Take him back to the house.'

As the men marched Dean away, Cole remained where he was, eyes scanning the surroundings. 'I know you're here, Carly,' he called. 'If you know what's good for you, you won't interfere. As long as you and Jane keep out of it, Alec won't be touched.'

Carly didn't respond but she glared at him through the trees, watching as he left, hurrying to catch up with the others.

Quietly she crept through the trees, able to follow them in the darkness thanks to the murmur of the men's voices. Dean walked tall and proud, even though his arms were still pulled behind his back and he was propelled along by two of the men.

As she followed, Carly wondered what she should do. Despite what Cole had said she couldn't just leave her cousin to his fate. She had no doubt they would torture him as he had Brian just for some revenge. Even if they got the Tallan deal, Dean would still suffer. She considered calling her uncle but Cole's threat against her father still rang loudly in her head. He needed protection and Jane alone wouldn't be enough.

Carly realised she would have to handle this situation herself.

When the group of men left the park, Carly hung back, knowing it would be easier for her to be spotted under the streetlights. Cole kept looking back over his shoulder, probably suspecting she wouldn't allow them to simply march her cousin off to his fate. Only when the group had turned off the main road and onto a residential street did she dart out of the shadows to follow, rushing across the road. Carly hesitated to peer around the corner and saw the men were already at the bottom of the street. They went left. Taking a deep breath, she followed. From the direction they were heading in, she guessed they were taking Dean to the Alexander home. What should she do when they got there? She was alone and unarmed. All she'd succeed in doing would be getting herself captured too. What she needed was a distraction that would lure them out of the house so she could help Dean. And what then? They'd come straight for her family. But she had to free her cousin, there was no choice. Whatever happened after that they would deal with.

Carly arrived at the street the Alexanders lived on just in time to see Dean being shoved through the front door by Ross. He and Cole went in and the rest of the men wandered off, chatting, their work clearly done for the night.

Carly's heart thumped in her chest as she walked down the street, keeping low behind the cars parked at the kerb, eyes riveted to the Alexander house.

When the front door opened suddenly, she hastily ducked down behind a small white car and peered around the side of it. It was Cole. He headed down the road, away from her, and she panicked, wondering if he was going to her flat but his walk was casual, apparently in no hurry to get anywhere.

Carly cried out in pain when a hand fisted in her hair and dragged her out from behind the car.

'Got you at last, ya daft bitch,' said a voice.

She was appalled to realise she'd been grabbed by Ross. When she saw Cole heading towards them, a smirk on his face, she realised he'd been the distraction so his brother could sneak up on her.

'You've led us a merry fucking dance tonight,' growled Ross, hauling her towards the house by her hair, making Carly grimace.

'Cole,' she cried. 'Are you going to let him do this?'

He shrugged. 'Why shouldn't I?'

The casualness with which he said this infuriated her. 'I will make you suffer for everything you've done to me,' she yelled. 'I swear to God.'

Her shouts drew the attention of the neighbours. One man opened his front door and peered out to see what was going on.

'Help me, please,' screamed Carly as she was hauled towards the front door, her eyes watering with pain as Ross's grip on her hair tightened and she felt a few strands come away.

'Fuck off back inside unless you want some of the same,' Ross roared at him.

The man's eyes widened and he hastily slammed the door shut.

'No one's coming to help you,' Ross growled in her ear. 'And now you're gonnae find out what happens to interfering wee bitches.'

25

Carly was shoved through the front door of the Alexander home by Ross, and Cole followed, not objecting to the rough treatment. This house had never been the best kept. Jessica hated housework because she claimed it ruined her nails. The furniture was expensive and sophisticated with a cool light grey and green colour scheme but there were rings on the coffee table and the carpet Carly was thrown down onto looked like it hadn't been vacuumed in weeks.

As she hauled herself to her feet, still feeling shocked and a little disorientated, she was appalled to see Dean tied to a chair at the back of the room. She recognised the chair as one that had been taken from the dining table in the kitchen. It was solid dark wood. Dean's forearms lay on the arms, tethered there with rope, and his ankles had been tied to the legs. Dominic stood by his side on guard duty.

'Carly,' Dean exclaimed before glaring at Cole. 'Let her go, you fucking bastards; she's nothing to do with this.'

Ross smiled and looked to Cole. 'I reckon you're right bruv and he does have a thing for her. He must like whining wee shrews.'

'Go fuck yourself, ya dick,' Carly spat at him.

Ross's grin broadened and he shook his head.

Looking round, Carly saw that Jessica and Brian were in the room, Brian still very badly bruised, the left side of his face entirely swollen from the beating Dean had given him.

'This prick says he won't talk,' Ross told Carly. 'But we think he'll open up when we go to work on you with the pliers, like he did to my da'.'

'No,' yelled Dean, attempting to leap to his feet. His bindings held him fast.

'Get another chair,' Ross told Dominic.

He nodded and left the room.

'You should have gone home,' Dean told her, his eyes wide and full of sadness.

'I couldn't just leave you to them,' she replied equally sadly.

'See, bruv, they're at it,' Ross told Cole, clearly enjoying winding him up.

'I don't know anything about my da's deal with the Tallans,' Dean told them. 'I only found out about it recently. You knew about it before me and Harry did.'

'What a load of old bollocks.'

'It's not,' Dean exclaimed with frustration. 'I cannae tell you what I don't know, no matter what you do.'

Carly's stomach lurched when Dominic returned carrying a chair and some rope. She looked to Jessica, who sat on the couch looking calm and unruffled. 'Are you actually going to allow two people to be tortured in your own living room?' Carly asked her.

'It doesn't bother me,' replied Jessica. 'I've got a brand-new carpet coming in a couple of days.'

'If you'd vacuumed this one once in a while you wouldn't need a new one,' Carly snapped back, causing ice to fill Jessica's eyes.

'Don't look at me,' mumbled Brian through his damaged lips

when Carly glanced his way. 'I remember what you told me when I was in your position – I'm gonnae let this happen. Well guess what, sweetheart, that's what I'm gonnae dae too.'

'And what about you, Cole?' she said, deciding to try and appeal to him, even though she doubted it would work. 'After everything we shared together, are you gonnae let this happen?'

'As I've told you before, that Cole is gone,' he replied, no emotion in his eyes.

'You pathetic, vicious wee worm,' she yelled, lunging at him.

Dominic grabbed her shoulders and dragged her backwards towards the chair. Carly couldn't allow herself to be tied down. If she did, she and Dean were done for. She managed to kick the chair over before she could be shoved into it.

'Oh, you daft slag,' muttered Ross.

When he bent over to right it, she kicked out, catching him under the chin and knocking him into Cole.

To everyone's astonishment, Dean leapt to his feet, sliding his arms and legs out of the ropes binding him.

'How the hell did you dae that?' said an astonished Dominic.

Dean didn't reply and instead drove his fist into his face, knocking him back into the fireplace. A vase toppled off and struck Dominic on the head, stunning him.

As Cole and Ross hastily got to their feet, Carly picked up the chair she'd kicked over and ran at Ross with it, knocking him back down again.

'Here, son,' called Brian.

Cole turned and attempted to catch the baseball bat his father threw to him but Brian's aim was off thanks to his cracked ribs and Dean grabbed it instead. Brian's eyes widened and he backed off as Dean brandished it threateningly.

Dean's gaze remained locked on Cole, who squared up to him fearlessly, despite the fact that he had no weapon but the way

Dean expertly brandished the baseball bat encouraged him not to attack.

'Let's go, Carly,' said Dean.

She nodded. 'There's just one thing I need to do first.'

Carly drew back her fist and punched Jessica square in the face, knocking her back into the couch. 'This is all your fault, you bitch,' she spat before rushing to the front door. She spotted something sitting on the console table beside the door with a BMW keyring. With a smile, she snatched it up, Dean rushing after her still clutching the baseball bat.

Once they were outside, Carly pressed the button on the key fob, uncertain whether it would unlock Ross's or Jessica's BMW. She smiled when she saw it was the former's.

'You drive,' she told Dean.

Dean handed her the bat and they both jumped into the front seats. He gunned the engine as Cole rushed out, followed by a limping Ross. Carly turned in her seat to laugh and give them the finger through the window.

'How the hell did you get out of those ropes?' Carly asked Dean as he drove.

'I tensed my muscles when they wrapped them around me, giving me a bit of leeway to shrug myself out of them, which I was able to do thanks to the distraction you caused.'

'I get the feeling it's not the first time you've been tied up.'

Dean didn't reply, although he gave her a knowing glance.

'Jesus,' she sighed.

* * *

The moment they pulled up outside the flat in the BMW, the front door opened and Eddie charged out with his shotgun.

'Stay right there, you bastards,' he yelled, raising the weapon.

'Easy Da', it's just us,' said Dean.

'Thank Christ for that,' he breathed, lowering the gun. 'Are you okay?'

'Aye, we're fine. Let's get inside,' he said, looking up and down the street as though he expected the mob to return.

The three of them rushed back inside, Eddie closing and locking the brand-new metal front door that had been fitted to replace the broken one.

'A pal of mine installed it while you were at the pub,' Eddie told Carly when she frowned at it. 'The back door's been replaced too. If anyone tries to kick either of them in, they'll break their fucking legs.'

'Nice one,' said Carly.

'All right, bruv?' Harry smiled, hugging Dean and patting him manfully on the back.

'Carly,' breathed Jane, rushing down the hall to fling her arms around her, before releasing her and studying her seriously. 'Are you hurt?'

'Not at all. I can't say the same about the Alexanders though.'

'Come on, Da' will want to see you.'

'He knows what's happened?'

'He knew something was wrong and he got so agitated we had to tell him.'

'Oh no.'

Dean and Carly entered the kitchen with Eddie, leaving Harry to keep watch. Rose was sitting at the table, her face etched with worry.

'I'm so glad you're home,' she breathed, leaping up and flinging her arms around Carly.

As she hugged her younger sister, Carly looked over her shoulder at her father, who was sitting at the table looking upset. She released her sister and ran to him, wrapping her arms around his neck. Tears nearly overcame her when he managed to raise his weak arms enough to hug her back, the trembling in his hands violent, his condition agitated by his fear for her.

'I'm sorry for worrying you,' she rasped.

'I'm j-just... glad you're... home safe.' He managed to get the words out, although she could see how difficult it was for him.

She kissed his cheek and released him. 'The Alexanders will be on their way; they're going to be really pissed off that we slipped through their fingers.' Carly didn't want to mention the fact that she and Dean had been abducted in front of her father and Rose.

'And we're ready for them,' growled Eddie.

'But there's only five of us. They have an entire army.'

'They're no' the only ones. My pals are on their way as we speak.'

'Let's hope they get here in time. Why didn't you take the shotgun out with you to the pub? That would have scared them all off.'

'I'm no' wandering around the streets with a loaded gun. If the polis had turned up, I'd have been thrown in Bar-L for years.'

'Someone's coming,' Harry yelled from the front door.

'You three stay here with your da',' Eddie told the sisters, snatching up the shotgun.

He and Dean closed the kitchen door and rushed to the front door which had been flung open. Harry stood on the doorstep, glaring at the assembled crowd of twenty women.

'It's the Bitches,' he told his father and brother.

'Oh, those silly tarts.' Eddie smiled, relaxing and lowering the weapon. 'Go home, lassies,' he called to them condescendingly. 'Pretty wee things like you shouldnae be out in the dark.'

'Piss aff, ya fanny,' Emma yelled back at him, making his grin drop. 'We're going nowhere until we've spoken to Jane.'

'Well, you cannae speak to her, she's busy.'

'Doing what? Wiping the drool from her da's chin?' A few of the Bitches laughed at this statement but many did not.

Fury filled Eddie's eyes. 'Just bugger off you daft cows before you get hurt.'

'It's okay,' said Jane, coming up behind him. 'I'll talk to them.'

'You cannae go out there; they'll tear you apart.'

Jane stepped outside and studied the faces of the women. 'No, they won't.'

'But...'

Harry placed a restraining hand on his father's arm when he moved to intervene. 'She needs to sort this out.'

Eddie nodded, looking worried, although he did stay put.

Jane calmly exited the garden and met Emma in the middle of the road.

'I hear you want to take back leadership of the Bitches,' Emma told her, her lovely face twisted with hate.

'Actually, I didn't want to. Someone was winding you up about that, probably Ross so he'd get you and the girls on his side but now I've changed my mind. Now I do plan to take back control.' Jane glanced at the women as she spoke to gauge their reaction. Some of them looked angry and shouted obscenities, but the majority appeared intrigued.

'You?' Emma laughed. Unlike Jane, she hadn't bothered to assess the women's reactions, so confident was she in her leadership. 'You kept them down, kept them soft.'

'I kept them strong. All you've done is use them to do your boyfriend's bidding.' Jane looked to the rest of the Bitches. 'Is that what you want to be, the Alexander family's obedient little pets? Because that's what Emma's turning you into.'

'Nice try,' Emma told her. 'But that's just shite. Unlike your family, the Alexanders are rising in this world and the smart people will get behind them now.'

'Rising?' Jane laughed. 'Carly and Dean just hammered all five of them.' She smiled with malicious pleasure. 'Your prick of a boyfriend was bowled over by a chair. Hardly *Peaky Blinders*, is it?'

Emma rounded on the women behind her when she heard a laugh but she couldn't spot the culprit.

'Looks like your hold over them is already weakening,' said Jane, drawing Emma's attention back to her.

'You'd like to think so, wouldn't you? But the Bitches have never been stronger and that is down to me.'

'They're overly aggressive and out of control, which makes you a weak leader.'

Emma's eyes glimmered with contained fury. 'What makes you think any of them want you back?'

'I do,' said a voice.

Everyone looked round to one woman in her late teens with long black hair sticking out from under a dark green beanie hat.

'I'm sick of you making us do whatever Ross wants, Emma. We're no' his fucking lapdogs.'

The women around her nodded in agreement.

'Thank you, Jennifer.' Jane smiled with satisfaction.

'What the fuck did you say to me?' screamed Emma, stomping up to Jennifer and thrusting her face into the other woman's. But Jennifer met her furious gaze fearlessly.

'We want Jane back,' countered Jennifer. 'When she was in charge, we were our own people and didn't obey every command of whichever twat you're currently dating, because before Ross it was Danny Hardacre we were battering people for.'

'And you got well paid for it.'

'We got paid even better when Jane was running things and we weren't forced to keep obeying men.'

More of the women nodded firmly and gathered around Jennifer while some still hung back, waiting to see which way this confrontation would go. If Emma did remain in charge of the Bitches, they didn't want to be in her bad books.

'There's only one way to sort this out,' yelled Jane, having to raise her voice to be heard over the din when the women started to argue amongst themselves. She looked to Emma. 'We fight for the leadership.'

Emma looked thoughtful. Although she was aware of Jane's serious reputation, she had a lot of confidence in her own skills. Plus, Jane hadn't been involved in any form of violence for two years, so she would be rusty.

'Just me and you,' added Jane when she saw Emma was seriously considering the offer. 'No one else.'

'All right, let's do it.'

Carly, who had been watching from the front door with her uncle and cousins, rushed over to her sister, ignoring her uncle's call to come back.

'Are you sure about this?' she whispered to Jane as Emma removed her coat and tossed it to Karen, who caught it with one hand and a smirk. 'You know she never plays fair.'

'I can take her,' said Jane determinedly.

'She might have a hidden weapon or her cronies might join in if it looks like you're gonnae win. If that happens, the other Bitches won't step in to help you because they won't want to risk pissing her off.'

'It'll be fine, trust me.' As Jane had rushed outside without her coat, she didn't have one to remove and she was feeling the cold. It would be a relief to start the fight so she could get moving. Jane turned to face Emma. 'No one's to interfere,' she told her loudly enough for everyone to hear. 'This is between me and you. The winner will run the Bitches who will all accept the outcome of this fight, no matter the result.'

The women nodded in response.

A car came down the street, the headlights lighting up the scene. It came to a halt, the surprised driver staring at them through the windscreen. When he beeped his horn, Karen stood in front of the car and yanked up her jumper, revealing her bare breasts.

'Fuck off out of it, you tosser,' she roared, running after the car as it frantically reversed while the rest of the women howled with laughter.

'You go for it, love,' Eddie called to her, grinning broadly.

'That was the vicar,' said Jennifer.

Karen gave her a malicious smile and pulled her top back down. 'Then he got a fucking treat, didn't he?'

Emma looked past Jane to Carly standing on the pavement. 'You can back off,' she told her. 'I don't want you jumping in when I start beating the living shite out of your sister.'

Carly looked to Jane, who nodded, so Carly retreated back to the door of her flat, standing with her uncle and cousins.

'Rose wanted to come out but we wouldn't let her,' Eddie told Carly.

'Good,' she replied. 'I don't want her seeing this and neither will Jane.'

'Can Jane take her?'

'Aye, she can,' replied Carly with a confidence she didn't feel. Jane had been living the peaceful life for so long. Would she even remember how to fight?

Dean placed a hand on Carly's shoulder. 'She's a Savage...'

'And savagery runs in our blood.'

26

The gathered crowd watched anxiously as the fight began.

The two women were both tall, standing at about five foot eight. Whereas Jane was slim and athletic, Emma was more curvaceous. Both were strong and fit.

They circled one another, sizing each other up. Despite their histories of violence, they'd never fought each other before. A couple of warm-up punches were thrown by both women but neither connected.

'Come on, girls,' called Eddie. 'Get a move on. It'll be Christmas soon.' He followed this up with a mocking laugh.

Carly rolled her eyes at his tone, which dripped with condescension. He still didn't understand who these women were.

'Your uncle's a fucking fanny,' Emma told Jane.

She shrugged. 'He has his good qualities.'

Jane ducked to avoid the punch Emma sent her way but it was close as she felt her fist graze the side of her face. Jane retaliated immediately, deciding punching wasn't working, and she kicked out, using her long legs to good effect. She caught Emma under the chin, making her stagger back a few steps, looking astonished.

'Yes,' exclaimed Jennifer, throwing her hands into the air.

Emma didn't hear her as she was too busy fending off Jane, who came at her throwing her fists, striking Emma in the side of the face. She was knocked onto the bonnet of a car that was parked at the kerb but when Jane advanced on her, determined to make the most of her advantage, Emma kicked, catching her in the stomach. Jane retreated a couple of paces, grimacing and rubbing her middle. Emma leapt up and charged at Jane, drawing back her fist. She struck her in the cheek but, to her horror, Jane shook off the blow and punched her right back.

Both women were getting angry now, the cheers of the Bitches filling their ears and fuelling their tempers. Carly was relieved that half their number were now cheering for Jane. As the fight progressed and became more brutal, both women receiving cut lips and bruised cheeks, Eddie's patronising smile turned to shock.

'They fight like men,' he murmured as though the concept were new to him. 'I thought it would be all hair pulling and nail scratching.'

'We tried to tell you,' replied Carly, who was unable to enjoy his surprise because of her fear for her sister. It was clear Jane and Emma were rapidly tiring, both dripping with sweat despite the cold, and they were equally matched. This fight could so easily go either way.

The tide quickly turned when Jane delivered a right hook to Emma's face that threw her sideways onto the same car bonnet, which she hit with a resounding clang. The cheers of Emma's supporters soon died as they watched their fallen leader struggle to get back up, the impact of both the punch and faceplanting into metal almost knocking her out.

As Jane dragged her back up by her hair, eyes full of the hard determination that had driven her to knock out countless oppo-nents over the years, Carly saw Karen pull something from the pocket of her lumberjack shirt, eyes riveted to Jane. A glint of metal told her it was a knife.

'No,' she breathed before tearing across the road before anyone could stop her.

Karen's attention was focused on Jane, so she failed to see Carly running at her. Fay however did and called her friend's name but she was too slow. Carly smacked into Karen, knocking her off her feet and she dropped the knife, which went skittering under a parked car. Carly fell and rolled before jumping back to her feet. Karen had been struck with such force the wind had been knocked out of her and it took her longer to get up.

'You said you wouldn't interfere,' yelled Fay, pointing an accusing finger at Carly.

'I said I wouldn't interfere with the fight between Jane and Emma,' she retorted. 'But she was sneaking up on Jane from behind with a knife.'

'That's a fucking lie,' yelled Karen, who was finally upright, a graze on the side of her face from where she'd skidded across the tarmac.

'No it's not,' said Carly. 'You dropped the knife and it went under that car.'

'It's true,' said a woman called Donna. 'I saw her drop it.'

'This proves that Emma's a cheat and a coward,' cried Jennifer. 'She knew she couldn't beat Jane, so her friend tried to attack her from behind.'

Arguments broke out among the Bitches and Fay and Jennifer began to shove each other while furiously arguing.

'Finish it,' Carly told Jane, who had turned to see what was going on. Her eyes widened. 'Duck.'

Jane obeyed and Emma's fist went sailing over her head. Jane jumped up and the two women started to furiously fight again. Carly saw Karen scrambling for the knife, stretching out to reach for it but Carly grabbed her leg and dragged her backwards across the tarmac. Fay threw herself into the fight and punched Carly in the face, sending her reeling backwards.

'Don't, son,' said Eddie, grabbing Dean's arm when he moved to intervene. 'They have to do this for themselves. If they have help, their reputations will never recover.'

'I'm more concerned about their lives,' Dean exclaimed. 'What if more of them have weapons?'

'The lassies can handle it,' Eddie replied.

Dean looked to Harry, who nodded, and he turned back to watch the fight, looking frantic with worry.

The three men whipped round when they sensed movement behind them to see Alec hauling himself out of the front door with the aid of his walker, wearing only his pyjamas, feet encased in slippers.

'Jesus, what are you doing?' cried Eddie, rushing to his brother's aid. 'You need to get back inside.'

'M-my girls,' Alec stammered, nodding at the fight.

'They're doing just fine, don't you worry. Get inside, Alec, before you catch a cold.'

'No,' he said, eyes flaring with his old determination.

'You stubborn sod,' sighed Eddie. 'Harry, get your uncle's coat and a chair for him to sit in.'

Harry nodded and rushed inside, returning with Alec's thick padded coat and one of the chairs from the kitchen table. Between them, Eddie and Harry managed to get the coat on him and helped ease him into the chair.

'I'll intervene if I have to, Uncle Alec,' Dean told him. 'I won't let them get hurt.'

Alec's gaze was thoughtful as he watched his daughters battle what looked like insurmountable odds. 'They can do it,' he murmured with as much confidence as his brother.

* * *

With a cry, Carly threw herself at Fay who had produced her own knife. She grabbed Fay's arm, shoved it back, wrapped her other hand around her throat and pushed her up against the car Emma had banged her face off. She drove her knee three times up into Fay's stomach, making her gasp and sag to the ground, winded. Carly tore the knife from her and dragged the blade across the tarmac, snapping it before hurling the remains over the cemetery wall.

Meg went for Carly while Jane and Emma still fought savagely. The latter had recovered from having her head banged off a car bonnet and was fighting back with everything she had. Both women were exhausted and injured but neither was for giving in. Carly was the one bearing the brunt as she found herself fighting two of the Bitches at the same time. Even though Jane had her supporters, they were still hanging back.

'She's going to get overwhelmed,' said Dean with anguish when Carly got punched full in the face by Meg. He glanced at his uncle, who didn't seem at all worried.

As he spoke, Carly headbutted Karen and smacked Meg in the eye, making her fall onto her bottom but two more of Emma's supporters rushed to their friends' aid.

'She needs help,' exclaimed Dean.

Just as he'd made up his mind to charge into the fray, there was a chilling screech from the direction of the flat. Rose raced out looking like a wild banshee.

'Rose, don't,' cried Dean, attempting to grab her as she ran by, but she was too fast and he missed.

Dean, Harry and Eddie watched in horror as the girl ran right at the group attacking Carly, who was only just managing to fend them all off. Rose grabbed a handful of one woman's hair, pulled her backwards, and punched her so hard the woman was instantly knocked out. Rose released her and she dropped to the ground. With another wild shriek, Rose leapt onto another woman, shoved her to the ground, straddled her and began repeatedly punching her in the face, all the while continuing her disturbing banshee wail.

'Bloody hell,' cried Harry.

'She's like a wee hurricane,' said Eddie, jaw hanging open in astonishment.

Carly and Rose easily tore through Emma's staunchest supporters, who called to the others for help but they all refused to move. When one woman did look like she was going to answer her friends' cries, one glare from Jennifer was enough to change her mind. Jane in the meantime, eager to end the fight before she was overcome with exhaustion, rugby-tackled Emma to the ground. She rolled her onto her front, rabbit punched her twice in the kidneys, making her scream with pain, before yanking back Emma's head by her hair with such force Emma found it hard to breathe.

'Do you give up your leadership of the Bitches?' panted Jane.

'Fuck you,' Emma muttered, grimacing when Jane pulled back her head even further.

'Don't make me ask again,' she yelled.

'Y-yes, I give it up,' she gasped.

Jennifer and most of the Bitches started to cheer.

Jane shoved Emma away from her in disgust and got to her feet. She ached all over and her hands were cut and bruised but she'd achieved her goal. After looking to her sisters to reassure herself they were fine, which they were, other than a few scrapes, she stood before the Bitches. Carly thought what an intimidating sight Jane was as she regarded all the women sternly, blood smeared across one side of her face. Whether that was her own or Emma's she wasn't sure.

'I now claim leadership of the Bitches,' announced Jane. 'Anyone who doesn't like it can fuck off, but if you do then you don't come near any of us again. If you want to come after me for kicking out Emma then you do it now.' She glared at them, daring them to attack her. None had the courage. 'Good. From now on, we do not do the bidding of the Alexander family. We're our own women.'

This drew more cheers from the Bitches. Jane was swamped with women eager to congratulate her and tell her how glad they were that she was back in charge.

Karen, Fay and the rest of Emma's supporters assisted their fallen leader to her feet, and she stood there swaying and cradling her right hand to her chest. There was a big lump on the bridge of her broken nose and her left eye was completely closed. They got her as far as the kerb before she sank to the ground, needing to rest.

'Hey,' called one of the women. 'Who's that?'

Everyone looked up the street to see a line of more than a dozen men marching towards them, and at their head were the three Alexander brothers.

'What the fuck's going on?' demanded Ross. Finally, he spotted his girlfriend sitting on the pavement looking a bruised and bloodied mess.

Jane turned to face him with a malicious smile, her sisters standing either side of her, the Bitches at her back. 'I've just taken back my leadership.'

'Fuck off. Emma's the leader.'

'Not after I pulverised her.'

Ross looked to Emma and gestured to her impatiently. 'Well don't just sit there, you daft coo, get up and fight.'

Emma shook her head and looked down at the ground.

'I said get up,' he yelled. 'Take back what's yours.'

Emma ignored him, keeping her head bowed.

'Pathetic,' he said with disgust.

Emma didn't respond. Karen sat beside her, gently patting her back and glaring at Ross.

Ross turned back to face the women. 'Fight for us and you'll earn more money than you ever saw in your lives.'

'Fuck off,' retorted Jennifer. 'We're sick of you telling us what to do. From now on, no man gives us orders.'

As this argument rumbled on, Carly looked over to Cole and was surprised to see his gaze was locked on her. Could he have feelings for her after all or did he just feel hatred and loathing?

'You're losing out on a big chance,' said Ross. 'And if you don't do what we want, this lot will gi'e you a big spanking,' he said, gesturing to the men behind him.

'They can try,' said Jane. 'Ladies.'

The men were shocked when the women pulled knuckle dusters, lengths of pipe, knives and hammers out of their coats and brandished them threateningly.

'Get 'em,' yelled Jane.

With a collective roar, the women charged at the men, who were so surprised by this turn of events that their attackers had clashed with them before they'd had the chance to recover. Jennifer smashed one man in the face with a piece of lead piping while Rose sprang at another man like a wildcat and sank her fingers into his eyes, making him scream.

'Now you can join in, boys,' Eddie told his sons.

'Finally,' muttered Dean as he and Harry threw themselves into the fray.

Eddie produced the baseball bat from behind the front door of the flat and stood on guard duty at Alec's side.

Carly found herself confronted by Cole, who stood before her looking threatening, although he made no move to attack. She was unsure what to do. Should she attack him first or should she try and talk him round?

'I don't want to fight you, Cole,' she told him. 'I know you don't feel the same way about me any more but I do still love you, despite everything you've done to me.'

'If you truly love me then you'll persuade your uncle to hand over his deal with the Tallans.'

'Jesus, no' that again. You're obsessed.'

'It's a good deal and whoever closes on it will be set for life.'

'Well, you're too late because my uncle's already closed on it.'

All around them was chaos – men and women frantically grappling, cries of pain echoing along the street. The neighbours who had stood at their windows to watch the fight between Jane and Emma had locked their doors and closed their curtains to distance themselves from the pitched battle occurring on their street. Carly couldn't blame them for that. She wished she wasn't here either although she was rather enjoying finally getting to see her cousins in action. They worked in tandem, tearing through anyone who stood in their way. They were very strong and more than one man found himself spinning through the air before crashing to the ground. The Savage brothers' eyes were lit up with glee.

When a large, hairy man rushed at Carly, raising his fist, Cole yelled, 'No, not her.'

It said a lot about the authority he now wielded that the man lowered his fist, shrugged and went off in search of fresh prey.

'Don't you want me to get hurt, Cole?' she asked him. 'Or do you want to hurt me yourself?'

'I don't want to hurt you,' he replied in that cold way that had once seemed so alien to him but that was now a part of him. 'But I will if I have to.'

An arm wrapped itself around Carly's neck from behind and dragged her backwards. She couldn't see who it was and panic gripped her when she realised she was being pulled towards a waiting car. If she was kidnapped it wouldn't matter that Jane had got back her leadership of the Bitches because the Alexanders would use her to force her uncle to hand over his deal to them.

Carly had no weapons but her determination not to let her family's enemies win was very strong. She made her body go limp and the man holding her shrieked in pain. Why would he do that? She hadn't hit him. Carly smiled inwardly. Now she knew who was holding her.

She drove her elbow into Brian's cracked ribs. He screamed with pain again and released her.

'For fuck's sake, Da',' exclaimed Cole as Carly turned and ran towards the cemetery. She scrambled up the wall and dropped down onto the other side, vanishing from view.

'I told you I wasnae up to it.' Brian grimaced, slumping to the kerb and panting with pain.

With one final glower at his father, Cole ran to the wall and scaled it before vanishing into the darkness too.

27

Dean delivered a powerful uppercut that sent his opponent reeling before the man dropped like a stone. Finally he had the breathing space he needed to look around, desperate to ensure his cousins were all right. He saw Jane and Jennifer working together to take down an enormous man with a huge forehead and thick eyebrows. Rose had grabbed one man's crotch and was viciously twisting it, making him howl in agony, her eyes lit up with glee. Reassured they were safe, he looked around for Carly but couldn't see her anywhere.

'Harry,' he called to his brother, who was fighting a man with a shaved head. 'Have you seen Carly?'

'Naw,' he replied before punching the man in the stomach. As the man bent double, he drove his knee into his face twice before shoving him against a parked car, which he hit hard before slumping to the ground.

'I'll check with Da'. Will you be okay?'

'Nae bother,' replied Harry before tackling another opponent who came at him with a golf club.

'Have you seen Carly?' called Dean as he ran to his father, who was battering a man with his baseball bat.

'I've been a wee bit busy,' replied Eddie before smashing the bat into the man's knee, making him scream.

'I saw her...' began Alec before stopping to cough and wipe his mouth.

Dean forced himself to rein in his impatience when his uncle fought to finish the sentence. When he found he couldn't do it, Alec raised a shaky hand and pointed. Dean turned to where he had indicated.

'The cemetery?' he asked his uncle.

Alec nodded in response.

Dean tore across the road, weaving around the various combatants before he jumped up at the wall, grasped the top, dragged himself over and dropped down out of sight.

Eddie had just finished pummelling the man with the baseball bat when he was approached by Ross, Dominic and their friend Stuart, who still had a large plaster across his broken nose.

'I want my car keys back,' Ross told Eddie while gesturing to his car parked at the kerb.

'Well I havenae got them,' he retorted.

'Who has?'

'How the fuck should I know?'

'I know it was you lot who carved the devil face on the boot, no' the McLarens.'

'I've nae idea what you're talking about. Now,' Eddie continued, drawing back the bat. 'Do you want some of this too?'

Ross nodded at Dominic and Stuart, who raised their own weapons – a crowbar and a hammer.

'Bring it on then, you bastards,' growled Eddie while wondering if he had time to go and fetch his shotgun. He realised he didn't when the two men charged at him.

While the three men fought, Ross turned his attention to Alec, who glared at him from his chair.

'The great Alec Savage,' said Ross with a vicious smile. 'Who cannae even stand up on his own any more. Fucking pathetic.'

Alec didn't bother to reply, knowing his throat would let him down.

Ross knelt in front of him, ignoring the chaos all around him. Alec didn't move or attempt to speak.

'My family's rising,' Ross told him menacingly. 'Going places, and we're gonnae devour yours. Soon, there'll be no fucking Savages around here or anywhere else for that matter. No more whining shrew women.' He glanced round at the sound of a scream and saw Rose twisting another man's baws. She wasn't the one who'd screamed, it was the man. Ross chuckled and turned back to face Alec. 'But the best way to hurt your daughters is by hurting you, their precious da'.' When Ross wrapped a hand around his throat, Alec didn't even move, and continued to regard him with contempt.

'Get off my brother,' roared Eddie. He smashed the baseball bat into Stuart's stomach, doubling him up and he tried to go to Alec's aid but Dominic lashed out at him with the crowbar, leaving Eddie no choice but to defend himself.

As Ross's hand began to squeeze Alec's neck, his jaw fell open as he gasped for air. Grunting with determination, Ross used both hands to throttle him harder. He winced when there was a sharp pain in the top of his left hand, forcing him to relinquish his grip.

'Bastard,' he said when he saw the deep gash there and the small knife in Alec's hand.

Ross drew back his fist to punch him but he was suddenly hauled backwards. His legs were kicked out from under him and he fell onto his back. Ross found himself looking up into the faces of Jane and Rose, whose eyes were lit up with fury. The younger sister looked particularly wild and ferocious. When he tried to get up, Jane kicked him in the face, blood spurting from his nose.

'Sic him Rose,' she said.

Rose leapt on Ross, grabbed his crotch and twisted, his scream ear-piercing.

'Good girl.' Jane smiled with pleasure.

* * *

Carly crept through the graveyard in the darkness. The streetlights failed to reach this area but there was enough moonlight for her to pick her way through the graves. Normally she wouldn't dream of stepping on a grave but she was left with no choice. She inwardly apologised to those who lay beneath her feet. The gravestones were illuminated eerily, their outlines vivid against the silver rays.

She gasped when a figure suddenly appeared before her but it was just a stone angel weeping over a grave.

'Jesus,' she breathed, her heart hammering.

The cemetery was smack bang in the middle of a busy residential area but it felt like she was a million miles from civilisation. Even the sounds of the fight going on over the other side of the wall had faded. She could sense another living presence in here with her, but it was difficult to see. Carly crouched down behind the stone angel, the figure somehow making her feel safe, and she held her breath to listen. There was a rustle off to her left, she was sure of it.

She peered in the direction the noise had come from and tensed when she saw movement flicker from stone to stone, as though someone was purposefully keeping low to avoid being seen.

Carly looked around, wondering where she should go. She was desperate to get back to her sisters. For all she knew they'd been badly injured or worse.

She decided to make her way towards the wall to her left. Hopefully she could get out of here without whoever was pursuing her noticing.

Keeping as low as she could, she crept towards the wall, using each gravestone as cover. She wasn't far from her goal when her foot caught on something and she fell face down, landing directly on top of a grave. Carly raised her head and saw the tombstone looming over her like an evil portent.

The sound had drawn the attention of whoever was following her. She scrambled to her feet and ran at the wall. As she leapt at it, a hand grabbed her foot and she was pulled back down, hitting the ground hard and winding herself. She also cracked her left elbow on a gravestone that had toppled over. Pain shot through her arm and she yelped. As she coughed and fought to recover her breath, she rolled over to see Cole staring down at her, as she cradled her injured arm to her chest.

When he tried to grab her, Carly rolled and he missed. She tried to struggle to her feet but she slipped on a pile of leaves, which had fallen from the yew tree hanging over the cemetery, branches reaching out like clawed hands. When Cole made a second attempt, she kicked out, catching him on the shin and he too yelped in pain.

'You bitch,' he hissed, producing something from his jacket pocket.

Thanks to the moonlight, Carly was able to see that it was a knife.

'Are seriously going to use that on me?' she demanded of him.

'Not if you do as you're fucking told and come with me,' he replied.

'So you can use me as a bargaining chip against my uncle?'

'Aye.'

'You know what? This is getting really old but this isn't just about my uncle's deal with the Tallans, is it? It's about what happened in Bar-L.'

At that moment, a cloud scudded across the moon, blocking the weak light that had illuminated Cole, turning him into a vague black mass. Something about this made the superstitious part of Carly nervous, as though all that darkness represented who he was now. There was no point reasoning with him. He'd got an idea into his head and he would relentlessly pursue it until he either got what he wanted or it killed him.

Carly's hand curled into the ground beside her, closing around a pile of dirt and leaves, the movement concealed from Cole by the darkness.

'I'm going nowhere with you,' she told him. 'I wouldn't put my family in that position.'

'There's no choice,' said the mass of shadows.

The clouds scudded past the moon, its silver light illuminating the cemetery. She didn't hesitate and threw the dirt in his face but he'd already ducked and it missed. However, this gave her the time she needed to get back on her feet and she blindly ran, her injured elbow throbbing with pain. The clouds once more obscured the moon, plunging the cemetery back into blackness. Carly tripped over a gravestone and went sprawling on her front. She turned over and went completely still. If she couldn't see Cole that meant he couldn't see her but she could hear him frantically breathing, as well as the slow tread of his footsteps as he searched for her.

Cautiously she began to shuffle backwards when he sounded to be getting closer, holding her breath so he wouldn't be able to hear her as she could hear him. There was a sudden glow of light and it took Carly a moment to realise Cole had taken out his phone and was unlocking his screen. When she saw the torch on the back of the phone illuminate, she rolled behind a gravestone to shelter her from its light, biting her lip against the pain in her left arm. From this position, she watched him wander about the cemetery, shining the torch up and down the rows of graves.

Carly's hand closed over a stone and she threw it to her right, away from where she wanted to go. Sure enough, Cole raced off in that direction, holding his phone out before him to light his way. Carly waited until he got a good distance from her before getting to her feet and running to the wall on her left. Behind her she heard pursuing footsteps.

She ran smack into someone and was knocked back to the ground, landing on her bottom, steadying herself with her right hand. A torch came on and she found herself once again staring up at Cole.

'What the hell are you doing there?' she demanded.

'Looking for you,' he replied coldly.

'But I was running from you.' She turned to see another figure emerge from the darkness.

Cole shone his torch on the newcomer, lighting them up.

'Dean?' exclaimed Carly with surprise.

'There you are,' he replied, shining his phone torch on her, making her wince. 'Are you injured?'

'Aye, I've hurt my arm.'

She glanced back at Cole who was glaring at Dean with so much hatred it unnerved her, especially in this place in the dark, his face lit up eerily by the light from his phone.

'I was right,' murmured Carly. 'This was never about the Tallan deal, for you anyway, Cole. It's about something that happened in prison.'

He nodded in response, unable to tear his furious glare from Dean.

'Is it to do with Mick Adams?' she said.

Neither man replied.

'Is someone going to answer me?' she demanded, getting to her feet, still cradling her left arm, the elbow throbbing.

'Are you gonnae tell her what you did, Dean?' said Cole, his green eyes seeming to burn in the darkness. 'Or don't you want her to find out what you really are?'

Dean didn't reply, gaze riveted to Cole.

'What happened?' said Carly.

'Mick Adams was serving four years in Bar-L for assault,' began Cole. 'His da' was a close associate of the McLarens. The McLarens paid him three grand to try and shiv me out of revenge for what Ross did to a member of their family. Word got back to me before it could happen and I asked Dean to watch my back. Harry had been released by then. He agreed but when the time came and Mick went for me on the landing, that bastard stood back and did nothing,' he said, nodding in Dean's direction. 'He didnae even shout a warning. I was stabbed four times in the back. Thank Christ each wound missed my kidney, which is what the twat was aiming for, but it still put me in the infirmary.'

'You saw it happen and you did nothing, after promising you'd look out for him?' Carly asked Dean.

'I did,' he replied. 'But I was only obeying orders.'

'That's what the Nazis said,' muttered Cole.

'My da' told me no' to get involved. He didn't want any bad blood with the McLarens.'

'I could have been killed,' yelled Cole. 'And you did nothing because your daddy told you no' to.'

'I don't feel good about it but I was doing what was best for my family, just like you did in that place. You know how it is in there.'

'I'm sorry you got stabbed, Cole,' said Carly gently. 'I didn't know; your family never told me.'

'And I knew he wouldn't tell you either,' he replied, nodding sharply at Dean. 'He wouldnae want you knowing that he's a treacherous, two-faced fucking snake because he wants to get into your knickers.'

'Hold on a minute – you stabbed people while you were in prison.'

'Aye... well... that's beside the point.'

'Err, I think it's exactly the point. You reap what you sow in this life, Cole.'

'Are you saying I deserved it?' he exclaimed.

'No, of course not. But I do think that you're being a wee bit of a hypocrite. It's okay for you to stab people, is it?'

Dean smiled wickedly at the outrage and confusion in Cole's eyes.

'We're no' talking about me. We're talking about how he's a fucking Judas,' he spat, jabbing a finger at Dean.

'So this is why you've been so intent on stealing the Tallan deal,' said Carly. 'For revenge?'

'Aye. It pissed me off that his lot got that sweet deal after what they did to me because it wasnae just Dean, it was his da' too while my family get nothing. It's no' fucking right,' he yelled.

'I'm really sorry for everything you went through, but can't you put it behind you? You're out of prison, free to start your life over again. It's a fresh chance which not everyone gets. Don't throw it away out of the need for revenge. That never ends well for anyone.'

'I knew you'd say that,' Cole sneered with disgust. 'You're into him too, aren't you?'

'He's my cousin,' she retorted, slowly getting to her feet, aching all over.

'So what? Admit it, you fancy him.'

'I will not.'

He thrust his face into hers. 'Admit it,' he yelled.

'All right, fine, I do. I fancy Dean.'

It might have been the darkness and the strange glow of the

torchlight, but Carly could have sworn she saw pain briefly flicker through Cole's eyes. Did he still harbour feelings for her after all?

Before either of them could react, Cole had launched himself at Dean and knocked him back several paces. It was only because of Dean's great strength that he managed to avoid falling over. The men both dropped their phones, which fell so the torches were pointing upwards, lighting up the scene at bizarre angles, making the entire situation seem strange and surreal. All Carly could do was watch them fight, clutching her injured arm to her chest. It was throbbing so much she was starting to fear she'd broken it.

'Dean, he's got a knife,' she cried.

As she spoke, she saw the glint of the blade in Cole's right hand. Dean was being forced to step backwards as he fended off Cole's attack and he tripped over a gravestone and fell. Cole loomed over him with the knife. Carly threw herself down on the ground beside the phones and turned them both over, so the torches were pointing downwards, plunging the cemetery into blackness once more. Carly's heart thudded in her chest and her breath came out in frantic bursts as she could hear muttered oaths and a scuffling sound. She had no idea if the men were fighting or stumbling about in the dark. Deciding it would be a good idea to find out as she wanted neither man to get hurt, she picked up one of the phones and held it aloft. She gasped to see Cole looming over her with the knife, frenzy in his eyes. With a cry, she ducked and scrabbled backwards and the knife went sailing over her head. She managed to keep hold of the phone but the movement sent the torchlight strobing around the cemetery, giving her wild glimpses of crooked gravestones and the weeping stone angel, as well as the clawing branches of the yew tree but she couldn't see Dean. Had he escaped or was he lying on the ground, bleeding out?

When she glimpsed Cole standing right over her, Carly shone the torch directly into his face, making him squint.

'Stop, please,' she cried, scrambling backwards away from him. She could understand why Cole was so angry at Dean but what had she done? Then it struck her – she'd said she fancied Dean, which in Cole's mind made her a traitor.

Carly wasn't sure whether or not to be relieved when she heard the sound of sirens. Was it the police coming to break up the fight? Or was it an ambulance? Had someone been badly injured, maybe one of her sisters? She had to get back over that wall.

Her hand closed around a large stone which she smashed into Cole's hand that held the knife. He roared in pain and dropped the weapon. He threw himself at her, landing on top of her and pushing her to the ground but to her surprise, rather than the expected violence, he stroked her face tenderly.

'I wish I was the man I was before I went inside,' he said sadly before pressing his lips to hers.

Carly kissed him back, sliding her good hand through his hair.

'Dean?' called a voice from the front of the cemetery. 'Carly?'

'It's Harry,' Carly told Cole. 'You need to go.'

Cole kissed her once more before running for the rear cemetery wall, Carly watching him vanish into the darkness.

'Goodbye,' she murmured to his shadow. A cemetery felt like the perfect place to lay their relationship to rest.

28

Carly was exhausted and in pain, so she remained where she was, waiting to be found.

'I'm here,' she called, holding the phone aloft with her good arm, the torchlight highlighting where she sat.

Dean and Harry raced up to her, looking relieved.

'Thank God,' breathed Dean. 'Are you okay?'

'Aye, apart from my left arm.'

'Where's Cole?'

'He ran away when he heard you calling for me. Are the polis here?'

'Aye,' replied Harry. 'And everyone's done one. When they arrived and saw the street was quiet and empty, they left again.'

'Good. I really want to go home and have a hot bath.'

'Let's get you out of here then,' said Dean, helping her to her feet.

'Are you okay? Did he get you with the knife?'

'Naw, he missed. It was too dark for him to see me.'

'Is this your phone?' she said, holding it out to him.

'Aye, cheers,' he replied, taking it from her and slipping it into his jeans pocket.

The brothers helped her limp along and Harry boosted her over the wall while Dean helped her down on the other side. Before his brother could scramble over, Dean pulled Carly to him and kissed the top of her head.

She turned to look at the scene of battle. The street was deserted, the only signs that a fight had just taken place a discarded baseball cap and a bent golf club. The curtains in the windows overlooking the road were all shut, the residents distancing themselves from what had occurred.

As they approached the door to the flat, it was pulled open by Eddie.

'Get in, quick,' he told them, looking up and down the street.

They entered and he closed and locked the door behind them.

'Anyone need a hospital?'

'Carly could do with getting her arm checked out,' said Dean.

'It's just a sprain,' she replied. 'What about Rose and Jane?'

'Oh, they're fine.' Eddie smiled. 'Although, thanks to Rose, the population count around here might drop. No wonder everyone calls her a wee devil. She shocked the shite out of me and the boys.'

Carly just nodded, too exhausted to reply. She limped into the kitchen, still cradling her arm. Her father, Rose and Jane were sitting at the table. Her sisters leapt up to hug her and Carly felt much better when she was able to reassure herself that they were okay, although Jane's face was bruised and her left cheek swollen from her fight with Emma.

Carly released them and hugged her father, kneeling down beside him, smiling into his chest when she felt his hand on the top of her head. Her smile dropped when she looked up and saw the bruises on his neck.

'Who did that?' she demanded.

'It was Ross,' said Eddie.

'Bastard,' she snarled, getting to her feet. 'I'll kill him.'

'There's no need,' said Jane. 'Da' stabbed him in the hand and then Rose twisted his baws so hard she nearly pulled them off. He's been punished.'

'Good, the fucking coward,' she seethed.

'Harry said you went into the cemetery,' Jane said.

Carly nodded and sank down into a chair to explain what had happened, omitting the kiss she and Cole had shared. A lump formed in her throat when her father gurgled with distress as she described Cole lunging at her with a knife.

'It's okay, Da',' she said, patting his hand. 'He didn't hurt me.'

'You've been holding your arm since you came in,' Jane told her.

'That happened when I fell. I wasn't stabbed or anything.'

'You should get that checked out at the hospital.'

'It'll be fine.'

'Let me look.'

Carly sighed and let Jane help her remove her coat. When she attempted to stretch out her elbow she shrieked in pain.

'It's swollen,' said Jane disapprovingly. 'I can see that through your shirt. You need to see a doctor.'

'I just need an ice pack.'

'H-hospital,' mumbled Alec, his expression brooking no argument.

'Okay Da', I'll go in the morning.'

'No.' He paused to swallow the excess saliva. 'Now,' he gurgled.

His hands were shaking badly and he was struggling to talk, the fight having pushed him to his limits. She didn't want to add to his stress.

'All right, I'll go.'

'I can drive you,' said Dean.

'I'll come too,' said Jane.

'I'll be fine with Dean,' Carly told her older sister.

'All right but be careful. No doubt there'll be other people in A & E needing treatment after that fight.'

'They won't be in any condition to attack us, so don't worry. I'll say I fell down some stairs.'

'We live in a flat,' retorted Jane.

'Okay, I slipped in the shower and banged my elbow on the wall.'

'You're dirty after scrabbling about in a graveyard. It's very clear you've no' just got out of a shower.'

'I was walking in the garden and fell over. Is that better?' she snapped bad-temperedly, feeling tired and in pain.

'It'll do I suppose.'

'What happened to your men anyway?' Carly asked her uncle. 'I thought they were supposed to be coming to help?'

'They did turn up but the Bitches had dealt with the Alexanders and their pals, so they weren't needed. I told them to do one when we heard the sirens.'

'So have you changed your mind about women not being able to fight?' she asked with a raised eyebrow.

'Maybe,' he muttered.

Carly smiled knowingly.

'We'd better go,' said Dean when she winced with pain.

Jane helped her shrug her coat back on and slowly she followed Dean outside to his car after he checked to make sure it was all clear. He'd parked it further down the street, so it hadn't been damaged in the fight, unlike Ross's, which was still parked outside the Savage family's flat.

As they drove to the hospital, Dean didn't speak, but Carly got the impression that he was building up to saying something rather than just enjoying the silence.

'What Cole said about what I did in prison...' he began. 'I hope you don't think badly of me because of it?'

'Why didn't you tell me?'

'Because I really like you and I was afraid of putting you off.'

'You must have known it would come out eventually.'

'Aye I did but I hoped I could tell you about it in my own time. I should have known that wouldn't happen,' he sighed.

'It would have been better coming from you but it hasn't changed anything for me.'

'I'm glad,' he said, relieved.

'I've never been inside, so I don't know what it's like, but I can imagine that you do whatever you have to do to get through it. Uncle Eddie didn't want you getting caught up in the Alexander family's vendetta with the McLarens and I can't blame him for that. He was only trying to protect you. Had you defended Cole, it would have put a bullseye on your back and you could have ended up getting stabbed too. But I won't deny that I'm upset about Cole getting hurt. The thought just tears me apart,' she rasped, a tear sliding down her face. 'I suppose his family didn't tell me because they were afraid of me trying to get in touch with him. In his weakened state, he might have taken me back.'

'I hate to say it but he'd already changed by then, although the stabbing did make him even harder, more bitter. It put a massive chip on his shoulder.'

Carly was tempted to ask Dean what the attack on Cole had been like; after all, he had witnessed it. Had Cole been in a lot of pain or had he fallen unconscious? How much did he suffer? But she knew if he explained the incident she'd replay it endlessly in her mind and torture herself with it. Not knowing was infinitely better than that.

'I hope what I did, or rather didn't do in prison, doesn't change things between us?' said Dean.

'Do you mind if we talk about it later? I'm in too much pain.' She groaned, shifting in her seat.

Dean glanced at her and saw there was a fine sheen of sweat on her forehead. He decided to put his foot down and in another ten minutes he was pulling up outside A & E. He found a spot as close to the door as he could and helped her inside. By the time they reached the reception desk, Carly was pale and shaking and she looked so unwell she was seen quickly.

Dean had to wait in reception while she was taken to a cubicle and given some painkillers. Carly breathed a sigh of relief when the pain eased and a soothing warmth overtook her body. She was taken for an X-ray and told she had a fractured elbow but thankfully the fracture was in the radial head, so she didn't need a cast. A sling would do, which she would need to wear for four to six weeks. They seemed to believe her story about falling in the garden, which was good because her tired, foggy brain couldn't have come up with another excuse. Even though she told the staff she lived in Haghill, they were all far too busy to try and press her for more information and didn't connect her to the many injured people – mainly men – who had attended A & E that night. When the doctor left her cubicle, Carly caught a glimpse of Ross writhing in pain on the bed in the cubicle opposite, clutching his genitals and shrieking. He didn't have time to see her as the curtain was whipped around his bed a few seconds later, which did nothing to block out the sound of his agonised cries. Carly smiled. It was nothing less than the bastard deserved.

Carly was discharged a couple of hours later and Dean escorted her out to the car. Before setting off he called his father to let him know they were on their way back.

'I noticed a couple of men in the waiting room at A & E who were on the Alexander family's side,' said Dean as he drove.

'Including one Rose went for. His face was covered in scratches; it looked like a tiger had a go at him.'

Carly's smile was weak and tired. 'Ross was in A & E practically crying with pain.'

'Good. I know now probably isn't the best time,' continued Dean nervously, keeping his gaze firmly on the road. 'But I just want you to know that I would like more with you, Carly. I feel like I've been hit by a train since you came into my life. Jesus, that sounds bad but I mean it in a good way. I'm mad about you and I think we make a great team. Even though we're cousins and people will talk, I think we should give it a go and...' He took a deep breath. 'I'm in love with you. So, what do you think? Carly?' he added when she failed to reply.

Dean glanced at her and sighed when he saw she'd fallen asleep, her head lolling towards him.

'Bugger,' he muttered.

He had the worst timing.

* * *

On arrival back at Haghill, Dean pulled up at the kerb outside the flat and gently roused Carly.

'We're back,' he said softly.

She jumped awake and mumbled something incoherent, her eyes heavy.

'Those painkillers must be strong,' he commented. 'Come on, let's get you inside.'

He got out, walked around the car and opened her door. He reached in to unfasten her seat belt and assisted her out of the car. After closing the door and locking it, he wrapped an arm around her waist and helped her along the pavement. Eddie opened the front door for them.

'Any sign of trouble?' Dean asked him as he and Carly entered the house.

'Naw, all quiet. They'll all be at home with ice packs on their baws, thanks to our wee Rose,' said Eddie with pride in his eyes. 'Jeezo, hen,' he told Carly. 'You look like shite.'

'So would you if you had a fractured elbow,' she muttered.

'Aye, I suppose so. Sit down before you fall down.'

Jane regarded Dean disapprovingly as he helped her sister sink onto the couch in the kitchen. He was handling her as though she were made of glass, which wasn't a problem in itself, but the look in his eyes as he gazed at her was. The man was smitten but Carly was oblivious to the attention.

'Can I get you anything?' he asked her once he'd settled her among the cushions.

'I'm really cold,' she mumbled.

'Here you go,' he said, taking the throw from the back of the couch and tucking it in around her.

'I made you a cup of tea,' said Jane, placing it on the small table at the corner of the couch.

'Thanks,' yawned Carly.

'Dean said on the phone that your elbow's fractured.'

Carly nodded miserably. 'Meaning I won't be able to work for a few weeks, not that I have a job any more after I resigned to protect Derek.'

'I've told you, you don't need to worry about money any more,' said Eddie. 'We'll see you right, especially with this new deal.'

'What if the Tallans hear about all this trouble?' Jane asked him.

'They already have. I called and told them. I also said that we've handled it. They were impressed so the Alexanders did us a favour. It just confirmed for the Tallans that they've gone into business with the right people. There's a place for you and Carly if you want it? If Rose wasnae so young, I'd be hiring her too.'

'Rose is going to university to get a legal career,' retorted Jane.

Eddie held up his hands. 'Fair enough. The point is, you don't need to worry about money.'

'Good to know, Uncle Eddie,' murmured Carly, struggling to keep her eyes open.

'Da' and Rose wanted to wait up for you to get home from the hospital,' Jane told her. 'But they were both so tired I made them go to bed.'

'That's nice,' she replied, fighting the battle to stay awake, her eyes sliding shut.

As she nodded off, she slid sideways onto Dean, who wrapped his arm around her.

'I'm just keeping her warm,' he explained when Jane, Harry and Eddie stared at him, the men only just realising his feelings for Carly.

'She should be in bed,' said Jane. 'She can't stay like that all night, she might roll onto her injured arm. Carly,' she added, gently shaking her awake. 'Let's get you to bed.'

'All right,' her sister yawned and Jane helped her into her bedroom.

'What?' Dean asked his brother and father when they stared at him.

'She's your cousin,' Eddie told him.

'So?'

'If Alec was at full strength, he'd cut off your baws.'

'For what? Caring about his daughter? I think he'd be pleased.'

'The last thing this family needs is a complication like you and Carly getting together. What if it went wrong like it has with every lassie you've ever dated? You couldnae just turn your back on her like you did them because she's family.'

Dean had never thought of it like that and he had to admit, his father made a good point.

'It would cause another rift between our families,' Harry told him. 'Just when we've finally healed the old one.'

'It's different this time. I love her.'

Harry and Eddie raised their eyebrows and glanced at each other in surprise before turning back to him.

'Does Carly know that?' Eddie asked him.

'I told her in the car on the way back from the hospital but she'd fallen asleep, so she didn't hear.'

'Thank Christ for that. Have you shagged her?'

'Da',' he exclaimed, blushing.

'Well, have you?'

'Naw. We've kissed, that's it.'

'Good. Keep it that way. Don't destroy this family, son,' he said more gently.

Dean just nodded. The first woman he'd fallen in love with and now they couldn't be together.

29

Carly felt tired and sore the next morning, although thankfully the pain in her elbow had dulled to a throb. Her sleep had been disturbed a couple of times when she'd turned onto her left side and been woken by the pain.

She wandered into the kitchen in her pyjamas to find, once again, only Dean awake, drinking coffee at the table. Harry was out cold on the airbed, his mouth hanging open.

'Urgh,' she said. 'There's drool all over his pillow.'

'He's a pretty dribbly sleeper,' replied Dean.

Carly chuckled and sank into a chair.

'How's the arm?'

'Aching,' she yawned, running her right hand through her hair.

'Coffee?'

'God, yes.'

Dean nodded, got to his feet and boiled the kettle, keeping his back turned to her as he considered whether he should say what he was desperate to say to her or keep it all in. He wasn't sure he could ignore his feelings for her, they were too strong, but his dad had been right. A relationship between them could damage the family.

'Is it only half six?' said Carly. 'I thought it was later. I wondered why no one else was up.'

Dean didn't reply, too consumed with his thoughts, but Carly didn't think there was anything strange as he was usually so quiet.

He made her coffee, placed the mug on the table in front of her and retook his seat.

'Thanks,' she said, wrapping her right hand around it. 'This sling is going to really piss me off.'

'At least it's not a cast. They're even worse. I fractured my wrist when I was thirteen after falling off my bike and it made my skin itch really badly.'

'There is that I suppose.' Carly frowned. He was shuffling in his seat and he appeared preoccupied. 'Are you okay?'

'Aye, I'm fine.' Dean sighed heavily. 'Actually no, I'm not. There's something I really want to say to you but my da' and brother think it's a bad idea. I actually told you it last night on the way back from the hospital but you'd fallen asleep, so you didn't hear.'

'Say what?'

He sighed again, raked both hands through his hair and nervously tapped his right foot on the floor. 'That I'm in love with you.'

'Oh,' she said, staring at him in surprise.

She looked so disconcerted he immediately regretted his rashness. 'Sorry, I shouldn't have said that. I'll leave.'

'No,' she replied when he got to his feet. 'Please, sit down.'

Dean nodded and reluctantly retook his seat. He sat there staring down at his hands, unable to meet her eye, terrified of rejection.

'I do know that I really like you, Dean,' she began slowly, picking over her words. 'And that I care about you a lot, but I don't know if it's love.'

'I see,' he mumbled to his hands.

'I'm no' saying that it's not,' she hastily added. 'But my head's all over the place. You have to understand that I thought Cole was the love of my life, then he went to prison, dumped me, came out of prison, said he wanted me back and then I found out it was all a lie so he could use me. If all that hadn't happened, then things would have been different but I'm not in the right place for another relationship right now. I need to deal with what Cole did to me before I can even consider another man. He pulled a knife on me last night,' she rasped. 'Something I never thought he'd do and you deserve a woman who isn't haunted by her ex. You're strong, kind, clever and absolutely gorgeous, everything a woman could ever want in a man and I won't risk hurting you.'

Dean nodded grimly. 'I see.'

'There's also a great chemistry between us and you've no idea how much I would love to explore that but right now I need to concentrate on getting over recent events, as well as how my life has changed. I really hope you understand.'

Dean took a deep breath and raised his head to look at her. 'Course I do,' he said gently.

'Thank you.' She smiled back at him.

'So, there is hope for us one day?'

'Aye, definitely. You said Uncle Eddie and Harry know about this?'

'Yeah but I didn't tell them. They guessed my feelings for you last night when we came back from the hospital. They think us getting together would be a bad idea. They're worried about things going wrong between us and another rift developing.'

'That is a good point. What if you got fed up of me talking?' she teased.

'I could never get fed up of listening to you,' he replied, placing his hand over hers and running his thumb up and down it.

Despite how rotten she was feeling, tingles started up inside her. 'That's so sweet. Let's just concentrate on getting this new business up and running. Who knows what the future holds?'

Dean patted her hand before releasing it. She'd given him hope, which was enough, for now anyway.

EPILOGUE

THREE WEEKS LATER

Eddie and Jane led the way, the former as the head of the Savage family, the latter as the leader of the Bitches. Behind them followed Dean, Harry and Carly, minus her sling. She'd decided to leave it off just for this meeting. Their family needed to look strong.

They entered The Waddling Duck pub in Springburn, a Tallan family stronghold. To their surprise, it was a very pleasant place, the sort of pub you'd come to for Sunday lunch with the family. A log fire roared at the head of the room, while the punters were talking quietly and behaving themselves.

A man in a black tracksuit with white stripes up the arms and a dark blue baseball cap on his head was waiting for them and led them through the pub into a back room. He might have looked like a ned but he was serious and polite. The man opened the door to reveal a large conference table around which sat eight chairs. Two of those chairs were already occupied by men sporting smart suits and neat haircuts who appeared to be in their early to mid-forties. At the head of the room behind them were two more men in tracksuits and baseball caps. The bodyguards' thuggish appearance failed to conceal the fact that they were very intelligent and capable. Carly glanced at Dean, who she could tell was as surprised as she was, but both were doing their best to conceal it.

The two men in suits didn't rise but they smiled at their guests and indicated for them to sit down.

Harry and Jane took the chairs closest to the men while Dean and Carly sat opposite each other, and Eddie took the chair at the end of the table.

'It's good to finally meet you all,' opened one of the men with steel grey hair and designer stubble. He was handsome with a strong jaw and aquiline nose. He looked fit and athletic. 'For those of you who don't know, my name is Roderick Tallan. Aye, I know it's a terrible name but as the eldest son, I inherited it from my grandfather and his father. Everyone calls me Roddy, which is only slightly preferable. This is my brother, Neil.'

Although just as smartly dressed as his older brother, Neil was a little podgier and his cheeks were jowly. They both had piercing dark grey eyes that said they saw everything. Carly could imagine that it would be impossible to pull the wool over the eyes of these two.

Eddie made the introductions for his own family, the men nodding politely at each of them in turn. Carly was so surprised by how quiet and thoughtful these two men were. The Tallans had a reputation for being almost feral but she was starting to see that there was so much more to them.

'You look surprised.' Roderick smiled at Carly.

'Me?' she said, shocked to be addressed directly. 'No.'

'We've carefully cultured a certain reputation for being, well, let's face it, violent animals but that means the polis are kept busy looking at the lesser activities of other family members so our real work goes unnoticed.'

'Clever,' she replied.

'We think so,' he said without an ounce of arrogance. 'We watched your uncle and cousins for a while before approaching them. They're people we think we can do business with. What happened recently at Haghill has convinced us that you and your sister would be assets to our organisation. Your family impressed us.'

'What about the Alexander family?'

Roderick shrugged. 'What about them? They're morons. They were responsible for all the trouble in Haghill. They've no subtlety about them and subtlety is key to our operation. Your family however are different. You all have qualities that are ideally suited to this business.'

Roderick leaned back in his chair and Neil rested his arms on the table, ready to speak.

'I take it Eddie has already explained the nature of the business you'll be involved in?' said Neil.

The Savage family nodded.

'And you're all on board?'

They nodded again.

'Excellent. Welcome to the firm.' He smiled, revealing neat, even white teeth. 'We have two rules here – number one, you keep your heads down and do your work quietly and without a fuss. David, who showed you into this room, will be your go-to. We won't meet again, not unless something major happens. Rule number two, you don't discuss your work with anyone outside the organisation and that of course includes the polis. Grasses are dealt with very harshly and there are no second chances. If you do get lifted, you say nothing and we'll send our own solicitor to the station to deal with the matter. Getting lifted in itself isn't a problem; after all, it happens to the best of us. Even me and Roderick have been there. What's important is how you handle it. The polis are sneaky bastards and will use tricks and threats to get you to talk. They'll even threaten those you love the most, but you don't say a word because what we can do to you if you do talk will be a lot worse than anything that lot can think of. Understood?'

They all nodded again.

'Excellent. Well, feel free to go through to the bar and have a meal on us. Order whatever you want – desserts, wine, enjoy yourselves. Think of it as a welcome to the firm present. We'll be in touch soon.'

'Thank you,' said Eddie before getting to his feet.

The rest of the family followed suit and quietly filed out. Carly couldn't help glancing back at the Tallan brothers, who were watching them carefully. Roderick winked at her as she left the room.

David showed them to a spacious table at the back of the room. He didn't speak and left them to it.

'You all did very well in there,' was all Eddie said before picking up one of the menus to peruse it.

None of them replied, not wanting to discuss it in a public place. Carly wondered if someone was listening and this was a test.

'It's a good menu,' commented Harry, studying his own.

'Aye,' said Eddie. 'Well, since it's on the house, I'll go the whole hog and have a steak.'

'I thought you might.' Harry smiled. 'I think I'll join you.'

'Good lad.' Eddie put down his menu and smiled at his nieces and sons benevolently. 'Our family's on the rise,' he told them. 'And it's about bloody time. Life's gonnae get a hell of a lot easier for us all.' His expression turned serious. 'But let's no dae anything to bugger it up, okay?'

They all nodded in understanding.

He grinned and clapped his hands together. 'Good. Now, what's everyone having? I'll go and order.'

After they told him what they wanted to eat and drink, Eddie went to the bar. Harry and Jane, who had become very good friends, began chatting, which left Carly and Dean, who were seated beside each other, to talk.

'How's the elbow holding up?' he asked her. 'Shall I get your sling from the car?'

'No thanks, it's okay. To be honest, it's a relief to finally have it off.' She coloured when she realised what she'd said. 'I meant the sling.'

Dean smiled. 'Aye, I got that. Well, it looks like we're gonnae be working together closely.'

'And that's the only thing we can do closely, for now anyway,' she told him quietly.

'I know. It's such a shame though.'

Carly smiled when she felt his hand on her knee under the table. 'It's the sensible thing to do. And be careful; we don't know who's watching us.'

Dean nodded and removed his hand.

Carly thought it strange how she'd barely thought about Cole since that terrible night when their families had fought each other. He was part of her past. She'd been a child when she'd loved him but Dean brought out in her all the emotions of a woman. The Alexander family had been very quiet since their spectacular failure and had given them no trouble since. Carly had taken great pleasure in the fact that Ross had had to walk around with the aid of a walking stick for a couple of weeks after an operation to fix his torn scrotum, a well-deserved punishment after he'd attacked a helpless man. Emma had gone around saying she'd dumped him because he'd been unable to perform in bed while he told everyone he'd dumped her for losing the Bitches. Emma too had been lying low, the four women who had been her closest allies leaving the group with her to start their own gang but with Jane running the Bitches they were no threat. Jane had already replaced them with much smarter and more reliable women, making the loyal Jennifer one of her lieutenants. It had been a sobering lesson to Jane that any leader could be toppled but Carly had absolutely no doubt that she would keep the Bitches in order. Jane had already handed in her notice at work but Carly had agreed to go back to working at the pub part-time when her elbow had healed.

'There was something you didn't tell me,' Carly said to Dean.

'And what was that?'

'The reason your da' gave you for the rift between him and my da'.'

'I already told you it was over money.'

'That was definitely part of it but I know that you're keeping something back from me.'

'No, I'm not,' he replied.

'If there's something I should know...'

'Carly, I promise you there isn't anything you should know.' He pressed a hand to his chest. 'Hand on heart.'

'All right, I believe you.'

'Finally,' he said, smiling.

Despite her words, Carly got the sense that more was going on than she knew but she decided to let it drop. Whatever had happened was between her father and uncle; it really was none of her business. Her family was finally reunited and she loved it. The last thing she wanted to do was prod at old wounds and cause another rift. One thing she'd learnt lately was that it was best to leave the past in the past.

Dean was relieved when Carly didn't press him for any more details. He was afraid the answer to her question would indeed cause another rift in the family, one they would never be able to recover from. Although he hated lying to her, he would do anything to stop that from happening. He would not lose Carly now he'd just found her.

* * *

Roderick and Neil watched the Savages leave from the window.

'What do you think?' Neil asked his brother.

'They're perfect,' replied Roderick. 'I particularly liked the younger sister, Carly.'

'I might have known, you perv. She's half your age.'

'That's how I like them.'

'They're more intelligent than I thought. They won't be so easy to manipulate.'

'There are ways around that. They're obviously a close family and will do anything to protect each other.'

'We can't know that for sure. They might surprise us and throw each other under the bus. Especially Eddie. He has a ruthless streak.'

'He's greedy too and that can always be exploited. We'll see how they get on in their new roles before deciding what to do with them next.' Roderick's eyes glimmered with pleasure. 'No matter what happens, we can't lose. Either they'll make us a big pile of money or they'll become convenient scapegoats.'

Neil nodded and took a sip of extremely expensive Scotch. 'Our spies in Haghill tell me the Alexander family are still desperate to raise themselves in the world.'

'Good. The Savages will need that tension to keep them on their toes and if they don't work out as we hope, we know we have a back-up plan in the Alexanders.'

'Who aren't as capable as the Savages.'

'No, but they're desperate and desperate people are even easier to manipulate than greedy ones.' Roderick's chuckle was deep and dark. 'So many puppets to play with.'

'You're a sadist, Rod,' replied Neil.

'I know and I love it,' he said, lips curling into a wicked smile as he thought of all the things he'd like to do to Carly Savage.

MORE FROM HEATHER ATKINSON

We hope you enjoyed reading *Savage Sisters*. If you did, please leave a review.

If you'd like to gift a copy, this book is also available as an ebook, large print, hardback, digital audio download and audiobook CD.

Sign up to Heather Atkinson's mailing list for news, competitions and updates on future books.

http://bit.ly/HeatherAtkinsonNewsletter

Why not explore the bestselling Gallowburn Series...

ABOUT THE AUTHOR

Heather Atkinson is the author of over fifty books - predominantly in the crime fiction genre. Although Lancashire born and bred she now lives with her family, including twin teenage daughters, on the beautiful west coast of Scotland.

Visit Heather's website: https://www.heatheratkinsonbooks.com/

Follow Heather on social media:

twitter.com/HeatherAtkinsoɪ

instagram.com/heathercrimeauthor

bookbub.com/authors/heather-atkinson

facebook.com/booksofheatheratkinson

PEAKY READERS

GANG LOYALTIES. DARK SECRETS.
BLOODY REVENGE.

A READER COMMUNITY FOR
GANGLAND CRIME THRILLER FANS!

DISCOVER PAGE-TURNING NOVELS
FROM YOUR FAVOURITE AUTHORS
AND MEET NEW FRIENDS.

JOIN OUR BOOK CLUB
FACEBOOK GROUP

BIT.LY/PEAKYREADERSFB

SIGN UP TO OUR
NEWSLETTER

BIT.LY/PEAKYREADERSNEWS

Boldwood

Boldwood Books is an award-winning fiction publishing company seeking out the best stories from around the world.

Find out more at www.boldwoodbooks.com

Join our reader community for brilliant books, competitions and offers!

Follow us
@BoldwoodBooks
@BookandTonic

Sign up to our weekly deals newsletter

https://bit.ly/BoldwoodBNewsletter

Printed in Great Britain
by Amazon